Elizabeth Villars is a full-time writer whose novels include *Wars of the Heart* and *Lipstick on his Collar*. The late Helen Van Slyke called her 'a spellbinding storyteller'. She lives in New York City.

Katherine

Elizabeth Villars

HEADLINE

First published in Great Britain in 1993
by HEADLINE BOOK PUBLISHING PLC

First published in paperback in 1993
by HEADLINE BOOK PUBLISHING PLC

10 9 8 7 6 5 4 3 2 1

ISBN 0 7472 4030 2

Printed and bound in Great Britain by
HarperCollins Manufacturing, Glasgow
Typeset by CBS, Felixstowe, Suffolk

HEADLINE BOOK PUBLISHING PLC
Headline House
79 Great Titchfield Street
London W1P 7FN

Lest we forget.
— Captain Nathan Brittles

I

Katherine Walden was not unaware of the alienation of modern life in general or the impersonal indifference of New York City in particular. When she read of the stabbing of a woman while neighbors watched from behind locked windows, Katherine was as horrified as her own neighbors reading their morning papers behind their respective closed doors. When a recently mugged friend said she hadn't expected the two doormen who stood watching to come to her aid because, after all, they weren't her doormen, Katherine admired the friend's resiliency and black humor. When she read in the *Times* that in case of rape she should shout 'fire' rather than 'help' in order not to scare off potential rescuers, Katherine smiled in grim irony. Katherine Walden was not unaware of alienation and indifference. She simply hadn't had any firsthand experience of them. The tradesmen in her neighborhood often gave her hearts and kidneys for her two cats and were genuinely distressed when they lost her dry cleaning. The doormen and superintendent of the prewar building where she lived showed their appreciation for the little trouble she caused and the respectable Christmas gifts she gave by almost never routing her mail and packages to neighbors. The two psychologists whose books she ghosted were

1

appreciative and, in their own words, supportive. One had even offered to discuss her problems without fee, though she had mentioned no particular problem to him. Her mother, who lived in Florida with her second husband, was interested in her only child, but she was, mercifully, also interested in her own tennis score, her husband's well-being, and the health of the stock market. The man Katherine was in love with was married, but no so intensely married that he couldn't spare Monday and Thursday nights, Wednesday lunches, and an occasional weekend thrown in for good behavior. But her friends were the best of all. Her friends had never heard the word 'indifference,' didn't know the meaning of 'alienation'. Katherine Walden was fortunate in her friends and knew it.

On the day she turned thirty-six the four closest called to wish her a happy birthday, and two of them even repeated invitations she'd refused the previous week. Katherine was of two minds about birthdays. Though she prized her own and looked up the day on which it would fall each year as soon as she bought a new calendar, she thought it was foolish to ask friends, even friends like hers, to take similar notice. But they did. They all called that September afternoon.

Paige Richmond rang in at a little after three. 'I hope I'm not interrupting you, but you shouldn't be working today anyway. Happy birthday. Change your mind and come for dinner. Proverbial potluck, but we'd love to have you.'

Paige's potluck, Katherine knew, would be three full courses with homemade pasta, compliments of Dr Stanley Richmond, Paige's own home-baked bread, and a friendly, unpretentious little wine. Paige's potluck was not something to turn down

2

out of hand, but Katherine turned it down for the second time in a week.

'Thanks, but Nick's coming up.'

'Well, why didn't you tell me that when I asked you last Thursday?'

'I didn't know last Thursday. He just called.'

Paige was silent for a moment, but Katherine could imagine her calculations. Nick's turning up for her birthday was good. Nick's calling at the last minute to say he was turning up was bad. Paige, however, prided herself on her tact. She merely asked what he was giving Katherine for her birthday.

'How do I know? Probably nothing. I don't think he remembers it's my birthday.'

'He must if he arranged to get away tonight. Haven't you dropped any hints? About what you'd like, I mean.'

'There's nothing I particularly want,' Katherine said, but she knew she wasn't being entirely honest. What she wanted was for Nick to remember her birthday. It didn't matter how or with what. It mattered only that he remembered it on his own, and for that reason she'd been scrupulously careful not to mention it for the past two months.

'I always give Stanley a list,' Paige said. 'It eliminates all that agony about whether to return something I don't like and hurt his feelings or resign myself to living with it.'

Paige wasn't exaggerating. Katherine remembered a birthday several years ago. Paige hadn't been able to decide whether to return the wrong Gucci handbag for the right one or to carry the wrong one and flatter Stanley. Fashion had triumphed over sentiment, Paige had returned the handbag, and Stanley had learned his lesson. The following year he'd given her a check with his signature inked in and the amount left out. Paige had pronounced it a very thoughtful gift. Katherine had had the feeling she'd gotten the suffix wrong but let it go.

Katherine said she had work to finish before Nick arrived and got off the phone with a promise to call tomorrow to report what, if anything, Nick had given her, but she managed to type only three lines before the phone rang again.

'Listen, luv,' Erica Kenyon said, 'I know you and birthdays and all that humility, but I'm not going to let you spend this one alone.'

'I'm not going to. Nick's coming over.'

There was a moment's silence, which was significant because when Erica was in her office she didn't waste telephone time. Katherine knew what was coming. She wished it weren't because she hated the way Erica talked about Nick and, for that matter, the way Nick talked about Erica. Each of them made her feel she was betraying the other by merely listening.

'So the single girl's Clarence Darrow has come through. You get an extra evening in honor of your birthday.'

Katherine laughed and ran her fingers through her hair. It was straight to her shoulder and the color of polished copper. Strawberry blond her mother christened it when Katherine was a child and never wavered from the description.

'You won't give him credit for anything.'

'Let's just say I'm not taken in by a pretty face and the fact that his wife doesn't understand him.'

Katherine ran her fingers through her hair again. 'He never said his wife didn't understand him. He says she understands him perfectly. She just doesn't like him.'

'Then why'd she marry him?'

4

'God, Erica, why did I marry Stephen? Why did you marry Michael?'

'Don't mention that bastard's name to me. Did I tell you he's going to marry her? That is, if she's old enough to sign her name on the marriage license. Otherwise, he's going to adopt her.'

'I'm sorry.'

'Hell, I'm not. It's better than divine retribution. I can't wait to see him with a new batch of babies. If Lisa had been in diapers for another month, I would have had to commit Michael. But he's forgotten all that. I imagine it'll come back to him soon enough. Listen, Kat, I've got another call. Happy birthday again. I hope Clarence makes it memorable. In case you can't tell, that's not sarcasm. I mean it.'

'I know you do,' Katherine said, but found she was talking to a dead phone. In her office Erica never hung up; she merely pressed buttons to switch lines.

Katherine turned her chair so she was facing the window behind her desk. The rain was coming down in sheets, and the gusts of wind battered the spindly trees and blew the slippery masses of yellow and brown leaves around their fenced-in bases. Across the street a doorman was blowing his whistle for a cab as if he were doing urban birdcalls. A big yellow Checker sped by, sending up a cascade of water. The wave went only as far as the doorman's knees, and Katherine could imagine the cabdriver's disappointment – just as she could sense Erica's.

She and Erica went back a long way. They'd met their first afternoon at Smith, roomed together for three years, and gone to Europe together the summer after they'd been graduated. They'd come back to New York together and gotten jobs together and even married around the same time. Katherine's marriage had lasted only three years. Erica's another eight, and their friendship had outlasted both. Katherine was probably Erica's closest friend. She was also her literary client. And she often had the feeling that she disappointed Erica in both capacities. It was as if Erica were a cheerleader working the crowd up to a splendid pitch, and Katherine a team that refused to come out of the locker room to play.

The doorman across the street had managed to secure a taxi, and a girl of about ten ran out of the building under the protection of his umbrella and hopped into the cab the way some kids hop onto a bicycle. Katherine turned back to her desk and clicked on her electric typewriter; but her mind was not so easily charged, and she was grateful when the phone rang again. Before she could say hello, Beth Sarmie Rosenthal Sullivan Sarmie sang a full chorus of 'Happy Birthday'.

'I just got in from a ten-city tour, and I'm absolutely dead and soaked through – it's pouring and there was no limo and it took me forever to get a cab – but I had to wish you a happy birthday before I even took off my coat. Did you catch me on *The Mike Douglas Show*?'

'Oh, Jesus!' Katherine's hand clawed at her hair. 'I forgot. I'm sorry.'

'They thought I was so terrific they want me back. Listen, Kitty, I've got to dash because I haven't even talked to the kids yet, but I had to say happy birthday. Call me next week and we'll do lunch.'

'What will we do to it?' Katherine asked, but she was talking to a dead phone. Beth, like Erica, had no time to waste on long good-byes, and Katherine was glad because she hadn't meant to be bitchy. Erica would say she was jealous of Beth's success, and Erica was probably right. Mike Douglas didn't want Katherine to appear on his show to discuss whether there was too much sex in her books. Beth always answered no and illustrated the point with an appropriate anecdote about her thirteen-year-old daughter. Doubleday and Brentano's did not want Katherine to autograph her latest book, which was not, strictly speaking, hers but Dr Ego's or Dr Altruist's, as she'd named the two psychologists five years ago when she'd begun writing their books. The names were strictly arbitrary since Altruist was no less megalomaniacal than Ego, and Ego was no less of a self-styled do-gooder than Altruist. Erica was right. Katherine was jealous of Beth's success, and her talent, and, most of all, her guts. Beth hadn't chosen to skulk in the locker room. One day after her first husband had gone off to his Park Avenue office, where he put a few dollars' worth of wire on adolescents' teeth in exchange for a considerable portion of their parents' yearly income, and her two children had gone off to their progressive school, where they learned to film documentaries before they learned to read, Beth had sat down to write a novel. Six months later she'd finished it. The rest, as they say, was history. But the worst part of it was that success hadn't spoiled Beth. She still had time for her old friends. Witness the telephone call. Katherine could picture her standing in the enormous bedroom overlooking Central Park, her Burberry raincoat dripping on the Persian rug, her kids demanding attention, while she took time to wish her childhood friend a happy birthday. Beth was not only a more successful person than Katherine, but a better person. She'd never let Erica denigrate the man she loved or Nick make sly comments about her best friend.

Katherine had just gotten out of the shower when

the phone rang again. 'I'm in a phone booth,' Cynthia Greer said, 'and I can't get the door closed and it's raining all over me, but I wanted to say happy birthday.'

Katherine looked at the puddle spreading around her own feet. She hated her feet. They were long and thin and raw-looking. Even Nick admitted her feet were no good. 'How can legs like that,' he'd asked once, running his hand down her thigh and over her calf, 'end in feet like that?'

'I'm on my way to dinner with a vendor but I just remembered your birthday and had to say happy.' Cynthia sounded rushed, but then Katherine couldn't remember a time when she hadn't. Years ago, when she'd been home with three small kids, she'd sounded harassed. After she'd gone back to work in a department store, she'd sounded frenzied. Since she'd been made a buyer a month ago, she sounded frantic.

'How's the new job?'

'Terrific. Maddening. I'm working like a dog, and Doug's being a perfect prick about it.'

'I'm sorry.'

'Sorry's not productive, Kay, not even operative. I keep telling you, there's no time to be sorry when you're fighting for your life. God, what am I doing standing here in the rain, lecturing you about this? I ought to know better by now.' Katherine started to say something, but Cynthia cut her off. 'I know, I know. You believe in the cause, but not the movement or the methods. Well, no one ever won a revolution by seeing both sides of an issue. I really do have to run. Call me tomorrow and we'll set up a lunch for next week.'

'Right on,' Katherine said to the cats when she'd hung up the phone, but she knew she was more annoyed at herself than at Cynthia. With Cynthia she occasionally came out of the locker room to play – only to be put on the defensive. And when it came to offensive teams, Cynthia's was strong, if somewhat lacking in finesse.

Katherine went into the kitchen for some paper towels to mop up the puddle she'd made beside the bed. There was no Persian rug, but the old hardwood floor was handsome. She wondered if Beth had wiped up her puddle or if she'd had the housekeeper do it. Probably the cleaning woman.

She returned to the bathroom and examined herself in the mirror above the sink. Her eyes were green all right. She'd never figured out why the trait was associated with jealousy. The face was thin with fine-boned features and a high forehead. It wasn't a great face, but it was good enough. The chief problem was a long upper lip that gave people, quite unjustly, the impression they were being judged and found wanting. She'd always hated the lip until Nick told her that it was aristocratic, a Bourbon lip, he'd called it.

By six-thirty she'd put on a fresh pair of jeans and a sweater that did not have tea stains on it, arranged Ego's notes and the manuscript in neat piles on the desk that stood at one end of the long living room, and placed a small pitcher of martinis in the refrigerator. Then she looked around the apartment again. It wasn't much unless you judged it by New York standards, and then it was a great deal. The living room had, in addition to the usual furniture and the desk, a dining table at the far end of the room, what the ad had called a wood-burning fireplace and what Katherine had discovered burned nothing more than a matchbook, and two windows facing south that flooded the room with light on good days. There was a tiny entrance hall, just big enough for a closet and table, a small kitchen, a bedroom that also faced south, and a bathroom which was so old the tiles were slightly discolored, although the sink and tub were built to a roomy scale. The apartment was in the low Nineties between Fifth and Madison, too far uptown to be fashionable, but Katherine preferred being close to the park to being fashionable. She had not been able to afford the apartment when she'd rented it six years ago, but if she hadn't taken it then, she never could have afforded it today.

When the buzzer rang, the two cats – Franklin, an orange marmalade, and Eleanor, a big gray with white paws – dove under the bed. The doorman had not called up from the lobby with a name, but then he'd stopped calling to announce Nick more than a year ago. 'Good evening, Mr Larries,' was all he said now, and the elevator man said the same and took him to the eighth floor without asking.

Nick Larries, the single girl's Clarence Darrow as Erica called him, looked very wet and very happy. His dark hair was plastered to his forehead, and there were beads of water on those eyelashes that would have been unfair even on a girl; but he was smiling a wide smile that accentuated the squareness of the jaw. It was one of those sincere smiles that could only be described as infectious. Like legionnaire's disease, Erica had agreed once.

Despite the briefcase and umbrella in one hand, the flowers in the other, and the drenched raincoat, he kissed her at the door, which was something he never did.

'You *are* in a good mood,' she said.

'Celebrating. Is it safe to leave this stuff out here or should I make a mess inside?'

'I resent that. This is the fashionable Upper East Side. Of course it's safe. For the umbrella. Bring everything else inside.' She put his briefcase and shoes in the bathroom in front of the radiator and hung his coat on the shower curtain rod over the tub. When she came back into the living room, he handed her the flowers which she'd taken from him once but put down again while she hung up his things. 'Roses,' she said when she'd torn off the paper. 'I can't imagine what I'd get if it were a significant round-numbered birthday like thirty or forty.'

He'd been sitting on the couch taking off his socks, and when he looked up at her, she had the feeling she'd said something wrong. Maybe it was the reference to forty. No reason to assume he'd be around in four years.

'My God, I really am a bastard.'

It was exactly what Erica always said, but there was no point in mentioning that now.

'I forgot. I mean, I didn't forget completely – I put your present in my briefcase when I got to the office this morning – but by the time I called this afternoon I'd forgotten. What a selfish bastard I am.'

She wished he'd stop quoting Erica. It was very disconcerting.

'Then what are we celebrating?'

'You know that little electronics company that was fighting a take-over. We won. They even get to buy back the stock the conglomerate had bought. It will cost them something, but they're still independent.'

'Well, I'd say that's more important than a birthday. You've been working on that for months.'

He was holding his wet socks in one hand, and

Franklin was wrestling with them furiously while Eleanor eyed them jealously from across the room. Franklin loved Nick even more than he did Katherine. Eleanor and Nick detested each other. 'I'm sorry,' Nick said, and when he looked up at her, his eyes were even more unfair than his lashes. They were that dark and that sincere and registered pain the way a seismograph records movement in the San Andreas Fault. There was no doubt in her mind that he was sorry.

'We ought to celebrate.' She went into the kitchen and came back with a pitcher of martinis and two glasses. By that time he'd returned from the bathroom where she'd put his briefcase. He was carrying a package wrapped in blue and white striped paper.

'You see, I didn't forget entirely. I just forgot momentarily because of that electronics thing.'

'It's not a secondhand book,' he went on as she unwrapped it. 'Genuine first edition of *The Great Gatsby*. You'll notice the erratum on page two hundred five. Everyone knows about the erratum on page two hundred five.'

Not only had he remembered, but he'd remembered ingeniously, and she thanked him, and kissed him, and thanked him again, and turned the pages with reverent fingers. The heavy paper had begun to yellow and flake at the edges.

'I'm sorry I couldn't find one with a dust jacket. It's a lot more valuable with the dust jacket. Oh, hell, Katie, what I'm really sorry about is the way I came in here. I was so high on me and that damn electronics thing I had even forgotten your birthday. Sometimes, like now, I don't understand why you put up with it.'

'It?'

'Me. Our so-called arrangement. How come you haven't told me to go to hell and linked up with some divorced editor or shrink or someone?'

'If you knew what was out there, you wouldn't ask me that.'

'I'm serious.'

'So am I,' she said, but she knew he was being serious in a different way. Those twin seismographs were registering a major shift toward guilt.

'Then why?'

'Because of your eyes.'

'I'm serious,' he repeated.

'Okay.' She took a sip of her drink. 'Because you're passionate and I'm not.' He started to say something, but she went on quickly. 'I'm not talking about sex. I'm talking about things. Like getting so excited about that electronics business. You can be a pain in the ass that way – you're extremely opinionated – but at least you aren't dull. And you really do believe. You should have been a politician. The old-fashioned kind. Then I could have named Franklin after you.'

He sipped his drink and rubbed the fur on Franklin's back. She could tell he was embarrassed, but also pleased.

'Also because you call yourself a lawyer rather than an attorney. And you never want to share your feelings with me, and you see things rather than experience them, and you read books instead of look at them. In publishing no one ever reads books anymore; they look at them. And you don't jog, though sometimes you're a little nutsy about fencing. In other words, you are definitely not "with it."'

She was sitting cross-legged on the couch, and he put a hand on her thigh. 'If you don't mind my saying so, I think your reasons stink.'

'There's one more. Because you're shy.'

'You just said I was an opinionated pain in the ass.'

'About some things you are. About others you're shy.'

He leaned forward to pick up his glass from the coffee table but didn't take his other hand from her thigh. 'Okay, what am I shy about?'

She took another swallow of her drink. 'I've lived alone for ten years. During that time men who barely knew my first name and probably had no intention of learning my last have asked me if I wanted to fuck, screw, ball, make it, and, in one case, make it with him and his wife. It's obvious, to me at least, that I want to do all those things with you – with the exception of the part about the wife – and yet after more than two years, you still think you have to court me to get me from here to' – she nodded toward the bedroom – 'there. That's how you're shy.'

He smiled, but it was not his usual easy smile. 'I didn't think you knew.'

'Am I the village idiot? Tonight, because you were excited about that electronics thing, you kissed me at the door. But usually you look as if you're going to shake my hand. Correction, you act as if you're going to shake my hand. Your face always looks as if you've been thinking lascivious thoughts all the way uptown in the cab, and I'm not supposed to know about them.'

'That's because I generally have been.'

She took the book from her lap and put it on the table. 'Then what are we doing sitting here?'

She supposed everyone made the same jokes about sex and used the same clichés because there just weren't that many ways to describe pleasure, and probably one of the oldest and silliest phrases that lovers had been exchanging for centuries was that they fitted, but the amazing thing, Katherine always thought, was that she and Nick really did. He was only a few inches taller than she was, and wiry, and she always thought that their bodies measured and matched perfectly. Her husband, Stephen, had been six feet four with massive shoulders and a terrifying chest. He'd also been relentlessly athletic in bed, though something of a rookie. It wasn't his fault. They'd both been young. Nick was no less enthusiastic, only less frantic. And he wasn't afraid of time-outs. He could spend endless amounts of time exploring one part of her body, though never, she had to admit, did any other part of her feel neglected. Nick was an intelligent man. He could do several things at once. He could also do several things both simultaneously and in sequence that had the ability to turn Katherine into the single-minded zealot all her friends wanted her to be.

'And that,' Katherine said when they were lying on the big double bed later – the quilt had slid to the floor, and Franklin was sitting at the foot with his back to them, elaborately ignoring their sweaty bodies – 'is one more reason I don't tell you to go to hell.'

The phone rang three more times that night. The first time Katherine did not bother to answer it, and they lay in bed listening to the voice on the answering machine.

Hi, Wraith, it's Barry.

'Is that Ego or Altruist?' Nick asked.

'Altruist.'

'He calls you Wraith?'

'He thinks it's cuter than Ghost.'

I just had a terrific idea for the book, the voice on the machine continued. *I don't think we've hit the sex*

15

angle hard enough, and it seems to me if we could follow the scene where the husband's impotent with her going into the bathroom and masturbating, it would be dynamite.

'Christ,' Nick said. 'Doesn't he know he can be arrested for leaving a message like that on tape?'

'That's one of the tamer ones.'

I made some notes about what she ought to be doing and thinking while she's masturbating ...

'Presumably,' Nick said, 'you need instruction.'

... and maybe even how she doesn't need him anymore ...

'I don't like that part,' Nick said.

... and I'll send them over tomorrow. I don't think we've probed her feelings about her genitalia enough and—

The tape machine clicked off.

'Will he call again?' Nick asked. 'I can't stand the suspense.'

'Not until tomorrow morning.'

'He sounds like a dirty old man.'

'He's younger than you are.'

'But hot for your body.'

She moved closer to Nick beneath the quilt, measuring her body against his. Sometimes she made fun of his enthusiasm for fencing, but never of its results. It was difficult to keep from touching him. 'Nope, only my mind. He likes the way I turn the prime meat of his thought into hamburger for the masses.'

'The meat of his thought is right. He sounds as if he's beating it while he talks to you on the phone.'

'Don't talk dirty,' she said, pushing Franklin off Nick's stomach and taking his place. 'You know it drives me wild with desire when you talk dirty.'

The second phone call came just after Nick had left.

His coat and shoes were still wet, and it was still raining out, and when Katherine got back under the covers after walking him to the door, she felt almost guilty about her comfort.

'I didn't wake you, did I?' her mother asked. 'I would have called earlier, but we just got back from the club. Martha Miller's birthday.' Her mother was sixty, her husband sixty-three, and in addition to playing tennis every day, they both kept up with a wide circle of friends.

They went through the usual questions about everyone's health and the usual birthday wishes, and then her mother asked about Nick.

'Why don't you sound more disapproving?' Katherine laughed. 'What kind of a mother are you anyway?'

'Oh, I'm disapproving enough. Don't forget, I'm part of another generation. To me you're a scarlet woman. On the other hand, you sound a lot happier as a scarlet woman than you ever did as the good little wife.'

'I was never a good little wife, that was the problem.'

'Maybe. At least you're not still running around with that psychiatrist.'

'I never knew you didn't like Matthew.'

'You never asked whether I liked him or not.'

'I take it you didn't.'

'He was the most pompous man I ever met. At the time your father said it was an occupational hazard – like miners and black lung disease – but Matthew was extreme even for a psychiatrist.'

'I can't believe it. I thought you liked him; he thought you were crazy about him.'

'Because I let him kiss me hello and good-bye?'

'I can't believe it,' Katherine said again, and she

was still amazed after they'd hung up and the phone rang for the third time. It was a little before midnight.

'Sorry to call so late,' Erica said, 'but I didn't want to intrude on you and Clarence. Did he make the eleven-oh-five to Westport?'

'He doesn't live in Westport.'

'All married men live in Westport. Some of them just call it by another name. I trust your birthday was blissful. Champagne, roses, and promises of undying love.'

'Martinis, roses, and a first edition of *The Great Gatsby*.'

There was a missed beat in the conversation. Katherine could imagine Erica rubbing the long chin that gave her a combative air. 'Clarence has good taste,' Erica said finally, 'but I didn't call in the middle of the night to talk about his taste. I forgot to ask you this afternoon. When do you think you'll have the finished manuscript of *Winner*?'

'Today's Tuesday. Maybe Friday. No, the typist will need more time. Next Tuesday. I'll drop it off next Tuesday. How's that?'

'Make it around eleven. I have a lunch date, but I want some time to talk to you.'

'About what?' Katherine asked, but her words merely clashed against Erica's good-bye and she was again left holding the dead receiver to her ear.

The wonderful thing about working at home, Katherine always said, was that you could live in New York and visit it, too. Katherine hadn't fought a rush hour for five years, and when she surfaced on Fifth Avenue or Fifty-seventh Street like a groundhog coming up for a look around, she was always full of expectation. The view down Park Avenue to Grand Central framed by the Pan Am

Building always made her hold up her head and walk a little faster. The limousines lined up in front of the RCA Building behind Rockefeller Center always made her slow down for a glimpse inside. The Chrysler building made her wish she'd lived in the thirties, the Plaza in the twenties, and the old Villard houses, dwarfed now by the new hotel, in the nineties. Parts of New York made her long for other times, but never for other places. She loved the men in gray suits and clipped hair who walked quickly on Park Avenue and looked at you surreptitiously. She admired the women with expensive briefcases and driven faces on Fifth. She marveled at the girls in four-inch heels and green hair around Bloomingdale's. She tried not to smile when the construction workers in front of the Modern Museum discussed her anatomy as if she were an abstract painting. She was fascinated by the big, silly, and to her incomprehensible sculpture in front of Erica's building.

Erica worked in the literary division of a large agency that handled actors, opera singers, and assorted 'talents' whose faces were instantly recognizable around the world. Whenever Katherine went there, she kept her eyes open for such faces, but the only celebrity she'd ever seen was former Mayor Lindsay, and that was after he'd left office and reached the nadir of his career. He gave Katherine a vote-winning smile nonetheless.

The offices were impressive, with as little furniture and as much gray industrial carpeting as possible. The carpet ran up the walls and over the ceiling. Erica said it was like working inside an elephant's stomach. Katherine found it less whimsical. The decor reminded her of a mental hospital, and she always had the feeling that if she raised her voice or made a fuss about anything, attendants would appear from nowhere, pin her against the gray-carpeted wall with swift efficiency, and truss her in a starched white jacket.

The receptionist looked up from the book she was reading and yawned. Katherine's face was not instantly recognizable.

Katherine gave her name and said that Ms Kenyon was expecting her, but when the receptionist got Erica on the phone, she asked the name again. Apparently it was no more instantly recognizable than her face.

Five minutes later Katherine hesitated in the door to the office when she saw Erica was on the phone, but Erica smiled, mimed a kiss, and motioned her to the chintz-covered sofa without missing a beat in the conversation. The flowery sofa and the white lacquer parson's table that served as a desk were out of keeping with the stark gray landscape of the rest of the agency. They were also, Katherine knew, a sign of Erica's importance. Erica went on talking for some time, and Katherine went through the motions of feigning deafness. Her eyes moved from Erica's long, perfectly shaped nails that were beating a tattoo on her blotter to her own. Hers were jagged, but she decided she liked the color better. Erica's looked like dried blood. Her own were milky pink, like seashells worn and polished by the tide. She turned from her nails to the spines of the books on the shelves. Finally she picked up one of the volumes that stood upright on the small white table beside the sofa and began to leaf through it.

'Hollywood,' Erica said as she put down the phone, 'is crazy.' Katherine agreed that it probably was, though she had no firsthand experience of it. 'I just got forty thousand dollars for a two-word title.

That's twenty thousand dollars a word. I can't deal with that world.'

'You give a good imitation.' Katherine dug into her briefcase and came up with a slender manuscript. '*Voilà!* The final draft of *How to Be a Winner*, asterisk, asterisk, *When Everyone Around You Is Losing at the Game of Life.*'

'Poor baby. If only we'd known back in General Lit-tri-ture Two-ninety-one that we were preparing ourselves for this. Is it as bad as the others?'

'It *is* the others. Only the case histories are new.'

'Don't tell me he gave you case histories this time.'

'Of course not. I had to make them up again. You'll find yourself on page one hundred eighty-four.'

Erica had been leaning back in her swivel chair, and now she sat up abruptly. 'You're kidding.'

'Of course, I'm kidding.'

Erica leaned back again and adjusted the glasses on top of her head. They sat gingerly on the thick dark hair cut in a mannish, high-powered style that reminded Katherine of a fifties crew cut. 'But you'll find the most unpleasant case history is named Gwen. I always name the real sickies after Nick's wife.'

'Do you think Ego will want any changes?'

'Changes! He won't even read the manuscript. He never does. Only checks the subtitles. Seventeen Potholes on the Road to Self-Realization. Eight Exercises for Flexing Your Happiness Muscles. Five Ways to Be Your Own Best Lover.'

'It sounds like a masturbation manual.'

'No, that's Altruist. I should be finished with his manuscript by the end of next month. Mid-life crisis will never be the same. By that time the new batch of notes, or rather the same old notes with the new title, should be on the way from Ego.'

'That's what I wanted to talk to you about. I don't think you ought to do his next book.'

There was a moment's silence as Katherine ran her fingers through her hair. 'The editor's unhappy? Or Ego's agent found someone who's cheaper? I know Ego is satisfied.'

Erica leaned across the desk. Her features, though bold, were not unattractive. It was only the haircut that made them appear that way and accentuated the long chin, and overly wide nose and mouth. 'Don't panic, Kat. They all love you. You're everybody's favorite ghost. I'm the one who doesn't think you ought to do the next book. Look, you've done four for Ego and three for Altruist. You've made a lot of money. Not as much as Beth Sarmie, of course, but a lot. Now it's time to see what you can really do. It's time for your novel.'

'What novel?'

'Don't try to kid me, luv. I remember that locked drawer full of manuscripts at school.'

'That was school. Everybody had a drawer full of manuscripts.'

'I know you want to write a novel.'

'I've written three for Altruist.'

'I do not call fictional dramatizations of agoraphobia, infertility, and mid-life crisis serious novels.'

'I have nothing to write about.'

Erica took a thin black cigar from a box on her desk. 'Life. The human condition.' She held a match to it and blew out a small cloud of smoke. 'The female condition.'

'I thought I covered that in agoraphobia, infertility, and mid-life crisis.'

'I'm serious, Kat. I want you to write about being

a woman. About the anger of being a woman.'

Katherine looked out the window to the view behind Erica's head. The sun turned the black glass of the skyscraper across the street into patent leather and reminded Katherine of the Mary Janes she'd worn as a child. 'I'm not angry.'

'You damn well ought to be. You're being exploited by three men.'

'I'm not exploited, Erica. You know that better than anyone. I get thirty percent of Ego and forty of Altruist.'

'And what percent do you get of Nick?'

'Nick hasn't forced me into anything.'

'No, you just drifted, the way you do into everything. But Nick is beside the point now. I want you to do a book about a woman and her anger. It's not only serious, it's commercial. That's what everyone wants these days. It's all I hear from editors. "I want a book about real women." "I want a book about the changes women have gone through." "Give me a book with a strong, sympathetic heroine women can identify with." And the movie people will go for it, too. Do you realize how many female stars are looking for meaty parts? But keep it small. Just the woman, the husband who did her in, maybe a lover and a kid. Hollywood's big on small casts these days. And no exotic settings. They're too expensive. And no crip flicks.'

'No what?'

'Nothing about terminal diseases or fighting back from a crippling injury. We've saturated that market.'

'And I was thinking of a feminist *The Sun Also Rises*. She comes back from Vietnam with a botched tubal ligation—'

'You can joke, but I'm giving you a great idea, Kat. It's a real issue, and it's salable. Women's books are making money like crazy. If you have any sense, you'll get on the bandwagon. Do you want to spend the rest of your life pulling the strings that move those two psychologist dummies' mouths? It's time you stood up and said something yourself. I get excited just thinking about it. I'll sell the hell out of it.' Erica stood.

It was always a shock when you saw all of Erica Kenyon. Her hair was mannish, and her face plain, but her body was entirely feminine and quite extraordinary. She had high, rounded breasts, a tiny waist, and a behind that invited trouble on crowded subways. Nick had said once that the fact that a mind like Erica's inhabited a body like Erica's went farther to prove there was no God than all the Turkish soldiers bouncing all the Armenian babies on their swords.

'I have to run. I'm late now. Lunch with Carella. Would you believe it? I just got him a hundred thousand for his next book and he can't even write his name. Write me a novel about the anger of being a woman and I'll get you two.'

'And lunch at the Four Seasons?' Katherine asked.

'And lunch at the Four Seasons,' Erica agreed, easing her toward the door. 'I know you can do it, Kat. I believe in you even if you don't.'

II

During her freshman year in college Erica had considered going to medical school. She might, Katherine thought as she emerged from the shadowy lobby into the sharp September sunshine, have missed her calling. What a superb diagnostician. Tell me where it hurts, she'd asked, and gone right to the spot.

There was no reason Katherine shouldn't think about writing her own book. For that matter, she'd been thinking about it for five years. Longer than that, she supposed. Well, now she'd begin to think about it seriously, but she wasn't going to talk about it. She knew too many people who talked about their books endlessly and never put a word on paper.

'Erica wants me to write a novel,' she said that afternoon as she and Paige were walking down Madison Avenue to pick up Paige's son from school. Though she was only an inch shorter, Katherine always had to work to keep pace with Paige, who had an athletic, dependable body with broad shoulders, an enviably flat stomach, and long legs that were a little too muscular. Paige joked that no matter what she wore she always looked as if she'd left her hockey stick at the door. Her face was thin and angular, but in its way as healthy-looking as her body, and the smooth brown hair that turned

25

under neatly at the ends swung from side to side as she walked. Paige was the kind of woman other women called handsome.

'What does Nick say?'

Katherine told herself it was her own fault for bringing up the matter and swore she wouldn't mention it again, but that night when Beth called to tell her to be sure to get this week's issue of *People* because she was in it – again – it was too good a chance to pass up. Beth's opinion would at least be professional.

'I think it's a great idea,' she said. 'I'll give you a quote. "A tremendous read. Unputdownable" – Beth Sarmie.'

Cynthia Greer was even more enthusiastic. 'I've been telling you that for years. When I think of the way those two men have used you.' Cynthia had a way of pronouncing the word 'men' that made it seem like one of the dirtiest in the language. Children and animals pricked up their ears at the sound. 'You do the work and they get the recognition – and the money. You don't see that happening to men. How many male ghostwriters do you know?'

'I don't know any other ghosts, male or female.'

'Well, I'm willing to bet it's a pink-collar profession. We're bred to invisibility, just as they're bred to the limelight. We're bred to fear success; they're bred to go after it tooth and nail.'

'Erica thinks I ought to write about women's anger.'

'Alllll rrrrright,' Cynthia said. It was a very contemporary sound, and Katherine was always fascinated by it, though she'd never been able to imitate it. 'Alllll rrrrright,' Cynthia repeated.

'Erica thinks I ought to write something on my own,' Katherine said to Nick that night. 'A novel.'

They were sitting in bed, eating enormous roast beef sandwiches, courtesy of the Eighty-sixth Street Delicatessen delivery service.

Franklin rubbed his head against Nick's bare shoulder in an attempt to leave his scent and establish proprietorship, and Nick cuffed him away. 'What about?'

Katherine took a bite and debated whether to tell him. 'Women's anger,' she said finally.

'I should have known.'

'Well, you have to admit we have something to be angry about.'

'Everybody's got something to be angry about. I'm angry I had to work my way through school. You and Erica never had to do that. There's a guy at the office who's damn angry because he's got an autistic kid.' He cuffed Franklin again. 'Franklin's angry that you cut off his balls. And just to be equitable, Eleanor doesn't much like not going into heat anymore.'

'I knew I shouldn't have brought it up.'

Nick took the last bite of his sandwich and moved the plate so Franklin could eat the scraps. 'Look, feminism isn't the issue, Katie. Whether you want to write a novel about women's anger is. I just don't think you're that angry. But then I could be wrong. Maybe you're angry as hell and hide it. Maybe every time I walk out of here you throw things and terrorize the cats and call Erica to complain about what a bastard I am.'

'If I'm angry, why does it have to be at you?'

He gave her a strange look. 'Okay,' he said finally. 'What are you angry about?'

'Economic inequality.'

Nick looked around the bedroom. The king-sized bed and dresser were from her marriage; but the

Harper's and *Scribner's* magazine posters on the wall were the results of the auctions she'd gone to with Paige, and the federal armoire commemorated, splendidly, the paperback sale of Ego's last book.

'You aren't exactly one of the ten neediest cases.'

'I'm talking about women in general.'

'You know, of course, that women control most of the money – I forget the exact figure – in the country. All over the United States men are dropping dead of coronaries and their widows are sitting in vaults clipping coupons.'

'Like my mother, you mean.'

'I've never even met your mother. But if you want to get personal, let's go back to me. If you're really angry, you ought to be angry at me. I never take you anywhere anymore except when you come downtown for lunch. I turn up two nights a week and put you on hold for the rest of the time. I expect you to drop everything whenever I can get away. I am, as I'm sure Erica has told you, a real bastard. So I'll ask again. What do you do when I leave here? Throw things at the cats? Swear you'll never see me again?'

'Usually I read for a while and go to sleep. Sometimes, like last week when it was raining, I feel guilty that I can get back into bed and you have that long trek home.'

Nick took a long swallow of beer and smiled. 'Write what you want, sweetheart,' he said in his tough-guy voice, 'but don't ever get into a fight ring.'

Katherine and her friends saw each other often, spoke on the phone regularly, and still felt the need to communicate by mail. They were continually stuffing newspaper clippings, magazine articles, and *New Yorker* cartoons into envelopes and sending them off to each other. The fact that they tended to read the same papers and magazines did not stop them from snipping and sending. You never knew when someone was going to miss something. The week after she went to Erica's office, Katherine received a clipping in an envelope with the agency's logo. A short paragraph from the *Times*'s 'Metropolitan Diary' told of a young man who boarded a commuter train somewhere in Connecticut and read his paper quietly until reaching town. As the train entered Grand Central, the young man slipped off his wedding band, dropped it in his pocket, folded his paper, and went off to work.

'Did you get my clipping?' Erica asked the next time they spoke.

'Nick wears a wedding band, but thanks anyway.'

'I wasn't thinking of Nick. I just thought you'd get a kick out of it.'

When Katherine considered it months later, she still couldn't make up her mind whether Erica had decided to straighten out all aspects of Katherine's life at once and enlisted Beth and Cynthia in the attempt or it had been coincidence. Katherine didn't have much faith in the coincidence theory because beginning with that day in her office, Erica had gone at her as if she were Jerusalem and Erica were Richard I.

The second stage of the siege began on a Sunday when Katherine arrived at Erica's apartment a little after noon. Erica had called Friday night and asked Katherine to brunch. 'The kids will be with Michael and his child fiancée.' Katherine beat a lively tattoo with the heavy brass knocker on Erica's front door. The apartment had been a doctor's office until Michael had turned it into what the real estate brokers called a maisonette and the *Times*'s magazine had called a statement. 'An Architect Turns Thirteen Examining Rooms into a Laboratory for His Own Ideas,' the subhead in the design section had read.

Michael had departed more than two years ago, though his imprint lingered, and Katherine was surprised when a strange man opened the door Michael had designed and had specially constructed. The man had a soft, round face and a stomach that matched. He was not wearing shoes, and after Erica introduced him, he excused himself and went off to finish getting dressed.

'For God's sake,' Katherine said, 'why didn't you call me and tell me not to come.'

'Because Josh is here? Do I have to drop everything just because a man turns up?'

'Of course not, but I could have come anytime. Incidentally, where and when did he make his appearance?'

'He's a client. I sold his first book – nonfiction – Friday night, but I couldn't reach him to give him the good news until yesterday.'

'And last night was the celebration?'

Erica smiled and the long chin grew a little longer. 'He was very grateful. Come into the kitchen with me. I was just making a pitcher of bloody marys.'

'Thanks, but I think I'll do a disappearing act. Tell Josh it was nice meeting him. And congratulations on his book.'

'Don't go. More people are coming. Josh called a friend. I met him once. You'll like him.'

Katherine stopped in the door to the kitchen. 'I doubt it, but I'm not going to stay around to find out. Thanks anyway. I'll call you tomorrow.'

Erica caught her arm. 'Don't be ridiculous. You

can't leave now. Besides, it's only brunch with a few people. I'm not asking you to go to bed with him.'

'Saving that for after the eggs?'

'You have to admit it would be a novel experience. Sleeping with someone who doesn't have to get up and run home to his wife afterward.'

'Look, I'm sure he's Mr Nice. Supports an invalid mother—'

'Ex-wife.'

'You're kidding.'

'Just a little squirrely. He pays her Payne Whitney bills.'

'All right, he is Mr Nice, but—'

But just then Mr Nice rang the bell, and Josh padded toward it in his running sneakers.

Mr Nice was nice enough. He arrived wearing a cowboy hat with a magnificent band of feathers around the crown and a pair of tooled leather boots that had never seen terrain rougher than the Lexington Avenue IRT, but when he took off his hat, the boots didn't look quite so silly. There was nothing really wrong with him except that Katherine could tell from the way he held his head that he was accustomed to being admired. That and the fact that he wasn't Nick.

After two rounds of bloody marys Erica said she was going to start the omelets, and Katherine offered to help.

'No, you two stay here and drink. Josh will help me.' Josh trotted after her in his sneakers with the bright stripe.

'So you're a writer,' Mr Nice said.

'A ghost.'

'Still creative. I'm a producer. Commercials. I couldn't stand being in something uncreative.' He stretched his long body out in one of the two Knoll chairs Erica had won in the custody settlement and contemplated his boots. The toes looked lethal. 'Erica said you're involved with someone.'

'Did she tell you how much I weigh and what my ex-husband does for a living, too?'

He smiled. She could tell from the way the corners of his mouth crept up slowly that he thought the smile was a weapon. 'No, but she said the guy you're involved with is a lawyer.'

'Not very creative.'

'Don't be angry with her. She just thought we ought to start off honestly. And I like the fact that you're involved . . .'

'You make me sound like a puzzle.'

He ignored her and flashed the weapon again. 'Or rather, I don't like the idea that you're involved with someone else, but I like the fact that you can be involved. This town is full of women who are so busy making it they don't care about relationships. I always tell Josh, my sex life is great, but my love life stinks.' Josh jogged into the living room, carrying a bread basket filled with croissants and bagels. 'Right, Josh?' Josh admitted it was right and returned to the kitchen.

'You have any kids?' Mr Nice asked. Katherine said she didn't. 'Me neither. I'd love to have a kid. I love the idea of fathering.'

'Not parenting?' Katherine asked.

'I'm sorry.' He shot her another couple of calibers from the weapon. 'I guess that was sexist. I love the idea of parenting.'

When Katherine offered to help clean up, Erica did not refuse. She was too curious. 'How do you like him?' she whispered as she scraped leftover eggs into the trash.

'He's very creative.'

'Don't be a smart ass. Just because Clarence walked out of an old Wall Street firm and started his own with a couple of other lawyers doesn't exactly qualify him for the Nobel Prize.' Erica was scraping more angrily now, and the sound of silver against china was loud and abrasive over their whispers.

'He says his sex life is great but his love life is terrible.'

'Terrific. He's ripe.'

'Do you mean you've been divorced for two years and haven't heard that one before?'

Erica had been bending over the trash can, and now she straightened and put the last plate down on the counter noisily. 'Do you think Nick is as faithful to you as you are to him? Do I have to remind you about that pregnancy scare with his wife?'

Erica did not have to remind her and knew it.

'I'm sorry, Kat. I don't want to hurt you. I just wish you'd wake up to what's going on.'

'What's going on?'

'You're being used.'

'And you think that cowboy out there wouldn't use me? What about Josh last night? Or was he just paying his ten percent agent's fee?'

'Maybe that's what he was doing. And maybe I was just collecting it. Christ, I wouldn't care if you were only having an affair with Nick.'

'You're always telling me that's all it is.'

'You know what I mean. If you were just screwing him and didn't give a damn about him, I'd say, "Great. Terrific. Who cares if he's married? Kat's getting hers."'

'Doesn't that strike you as a little twisted? It's

okay if I don't care for him, but there's something wrong if I do?'

'What's wrong is that you let him call the shots. Monday and Thursday nights and Wednesday lunches.' Erica turned off the water she'd been running over the stacked dishes and faced Katherine. 'Look, it's one thing if you use someone like Nick for pure pleasure. It's something else if you get mixed up with them.' She gestured with her head toward the living room. 'At least there's a chance something will come of it. But there's no chance with Nick. He'll never leave his wife. So for the rest of your life or as long as he sticks around, you're left with Monday and Thursday nights and Wednesday lunches. Like steak and eggs to a man on a low-cholesterol diet.'

Beth Sarmie had lived in a penthouse apartment with a terrace on four sides and an oak-paneled living room that had been imported from some English country house in the old robber baron tradition even before she'd sold a single book. Her first husband paid no alimony, but one night, when she was a little drunk, Beth had admitted to a $150,000 a year in child support. 'He can afford it,' Beth had said, and Katherine guessed from what she'd heard about Dr James Rosenthal, the orthodontist, that he could. Beth had lived in the apartment with the two children after the divorce, and when she'd married Ted Sullivan, a *Time* magazine writer, they hadn't bothered to move because there was plenty of room for all of them and a study for Ted, and now Sullivan, too, was gone, and Beth and Jessica and Jonathan rattled around in the ten-room, four-bath, three-wood-burning-fireplace apartment.

When the elevator door opened on the private foyer, Katherine found a young man waiting for her. At first she thought she'd seen him before; then she realized it was only the resemblance. She couldn't name the picture, but somewhere in the Metropolitan Museum she'd seen a Renaissance page with the same mass of dark curls and the same full, sensuous cheeks. He looked about twenty, too old for Jessica, too young for Beth, but Katherine had a feeling he belonged to Beth. She didn't think he was the baby-sitter.

'You must be Kitty. I'm Topper.'

'Like Leo G. Carroll?'

'What?'

'Nothing. I'm sorry. Hello. *Topper* was an old television series with Leo G. Carroll. And a movie with Cary Grant.'

'It's short for Christopher.' He handed her the glass he was carrying. 'Beth said you'd want a martini. She said you can wait with me in the living room or you can go into her room while she finishes changing.'

Katherine had no desire to wait in the living room with Topper, but she told him she would.

Though it wasn't cold out, there was a fire going, as Katherine had known there would be, and from one wall, where the draperies had been left open, she could see the lights of Central Park West glittering above the blackness of the park. She sat on the sofa facing the fireplace, and Topper sprawled on the floor across from her.

'Beth said you two have known each other for a long time.'

'We were walked together in our carriages.'

'No kidding.' He was propped up on one elbow, and his eyes were level and calm, almost glazed.

'We were born within two weeks of each other.'

'No kidding.'

'I'm Jessica's godmother.'

The glazed eyes blinked. 'No kidding.'

Katherine rummaged around for other bits and pieces of the past she'd shared with Beth that might continue to astonish Topper. The first day of kindergarten I cried and she held my hand. In eighth grade we were both in love with Eddie Leahy. Freshman year at Smith after she lost her virginity, she cried and I held her hand. No kidding, he'd say. No kidding. But Katherine offered none of that history, and they sat in awkward silence. At least it was awkward for her. Topper seemed content to lie there looking at her and blinking occasionally.

She took a sip of her drink and realized he didn't have one. 'Aren't you drinking?' He had to be old enough to drink.

'Don't like the stuff. It's shit on the body.'

'And Topper's body is a temple.' Beth stood framed in the double doorway. She was wearing a black velvet robe tied at the waist with a gold cord. Her hair made a curly halo around her small, heart-shaped face, though the hair was neither so dark nor so thick as Topper's.

'You're looking very Medici tonight.' Katherine stood, and they touched cheeks and kissed the air. Then they both sat on the sofa, and Beth handed Topper her empty glass. For all his hatred of foul pollutants he was a wizard at the bar. Katherine wondered if Beth or his parents had trained him. He handed Beth a fresh drink and sprawled on the floor across from them again.

'Topper doesn't drink. He smokes and snorts.' Beth might have been reporting that he went to Yale and was studying to be a brain surgeon.

36

'No kidding,' Katherine said, but neither of them seemed to notice.

'I'm trying to switch, too. These things' – Beth held up her glass – 'are fattening as hell.' When they were teenagers, Katherine's mother had always insisted that Beth was dangerously underweight, and a few months ago Erica had diagnosed her as an anorectic. 'Coke gives me a nonfattening high.'

'Like Tab, you mean?' Katherine said.

'And it's much better for sex.' Beth's and Topper's gazes met and mated like animals in heat, and Katherine sipped her drink and looked at the fire and sipped her drink again and waited for the coupling to end. It did when Jessica entered the room. She was a pretty girl with long black hair and a full lower lip on which precociousness and vulnerability seemed to be doing battle. She crossed to where Topper lay and stretched out behind him on the rug, her body a comma punctuating his own. She wound her arms around his waist, nuzzled the back of his neck, and clamped both legs around one of his. 'Hi, Kitty,' she said over his shoulder, 'Hi, Stepdaddy,' and nuzzled his neck again.

Topper rolled over on his back, Jessica climbed on top of him, and they pretended to wrestle. His hands were like a master baker's kneading the small blue denim mound that was her behind.

'Have you started your homework?' Beth asked her daughter. At least Katherine assumed the question was directed at Jessica rather than Topper. Consistency and loving discipline, Beth had always told Katherine, were the secrets of raising kids.

'Go watch television with Jessie and Jon for a while,' Beth said to Topper after dinner. 'I want to talk to Kitty.'

'Isn't he adorable?' she went on when he was out of the room but clearly not out of hearing.

'Cute as a button.'

'And absolutely indefatigable.' Beth lifted her eyebrows into twin steeples intended to convey the religious experience of sleeping with Topper, but Katherine was more impressed by Beth's prowess than the boy's. She always had trouble pronouncing 'indefatigable'.

'Look, Beth, I know it's none of my business, and I don't know a damn thing about kids, but do you really think all that is healthy for Jessica?'

Beth crossed her legs lotus fashion on the couch and smoothed her caftan over them. 'All what?'

Katherine ran a hand through her hair. 'All that ... well ... repressed sexuality.'

Beth laughed. Her old laugh had resembled a hyena's but in a nice lighthearted way. This new one had been polished for television talk shows. It rose and fell smoothly, like an electronically controlled fountain. 'It's not repressed. It's right out there in the open. Not like us when we were kids. That's what's so wonderful about it.'

'You think it's wonderful to have your thirteen-year-old daughter rolling all over the floor with your twenty-year-old lover?'

'He's twenty-one, and I think it's wonderful that Jessica's proud of her own body and curious about his.'

'What if the curiosity gets out of hand?'

'I've already thought of that. I had to when I left him here while I was on tour.'

'You left him with the kids while you were on tour!'

'The housekeeper was here, and nothing happened; but even if it had, what would be so

38

terrible? I'd rather have Jessie lose her virginity in her own home with someone older and accomplished than fumbling around in some back seat with an awkward kid who's so hot to get laid he doesn't even care about pleasing her.'

'At thirteen? With someone twenty-one? Who's sleeping with her mother?'

'You don't have kids, Kitty. Times have changed. Thank God. Girls aren't repressed the way we were. They aren't ashamed of their bodies, and they don't think sex is dirty.'

'I didn't say sex was dirty. I'm just not sure it's a thing of beauty between a thirteen-year-old kid and her mother's lover.'

'Nabokov didn't agree with you.'

Beth seemed to have missed the point, but Katherine didn't want to go into that now. 'We weren't discussing books; we were discussing your daughter.'

Beth got up from the couch, walked over to the hearth, and began poking around in the embers with an andiron. 'Exactly. *My* daughter. I know what I'm doing, and I don't want to talk about it.' She came back to the couch and sat cross-legged again. There was no trace of anger on the small, heart-shaped face that she posed like a valentine. 'But I do want to talk about you. I had lunch with Erica this week. Are you going to write the book?'

'Maybe.'

'Maybe! For Christ sake, Kitty. For once in your life say yes. A definite, unequivocal yes. It'll be great. Now what about Nick?'

'What about him?'

'Erica says it's still the same. Everything on his terms.'

'The terms are okay with me.'

Beth put a hand on each knee and leaned forward as if she were going to say something significant. She'd become quite a good actress. 'Listen, Kitty, I'm going to tell you something it took me thirty-six years and two marriages and a lot of tears and misery to learn. You've got to stop letting yourself be stepped on. Jimmy walked all over me. After the divorce I swore I was never going to let that happen again and then walked into the same trap the second time. But I finally learned my lesson. I've got money and I've got fame and, more important, I've got power because that's what money and fame buy. I've got a twenty-one-year-old kid with a twenty-one-year-old body. I can wake him up in the middle of the night because he always has a hard-on and he never heard of impotence and he won't call me a ball-cutting bitch. Do I have to remind you what life was like with Ted, the Don Juan of Time Inc.? The Don Juan of Time Inc. until we got married, that is.'

'I know, Beth. I'm sorry.'

'Don't be sorry. It was okay until we got married. Besides, he did a lot for my prose style. Anyway, that's one of the things wrong with women today. They spend too much time being sorry about old marriages. That's not where it's at. Men know where it's at. Money, power, and young bodies. Men have always known that. It took me thirty-six goddamn years to learn it.'

'Nick,' Katherine said. He was standing in front of the full-length mirror in her bedroom, knotting his tie, and she was sitting up in bed with Eleanor on her lap. 'Do you think about money and power much?' If he thought about young bodies, she didn't want to know it, at least not right now.

'I think about power all the time. That's what

corporate take-overs are all about.'

'Before I met you, I never knew there were law firms that specialized in corporate take-overs.'

'Before you met me' – he turned back to her – 'you thought deer ate meat.'

She pushed Eleanor off her lap and walked to the closet for her robe. 'I didn't grow up in the country.'

'Neither did I, but I still knew deer weren't carnivorous. Why are you worried about money and power?'

'Beth says men are born knowing about them, but women have to learn the lesson. And most of them haven't.'

'Listen, sweetheart, I'd love to talk about money and power—'

'You do a lousy Bogart.'

'That was supposed to be Cary Grant. Anyway, I'd love to stay here and discuss money and power with you, but I've got a two-thirty appointment and it's going to take me at least half an hour to get downtown and I'd like to grab a hot dog on the way so my stomach doesn't rumble all through the meeting.' He put an arm around her as they walked to the door. 'All the same, thanks for lunch.'

On days when she was not expecting Nick in the evening, Katherine usually took long walks in the late afternoon. Sometimes she walked on Madison Avenue and stopped to look in the windows of galleries and stores that sold fabulous paintings and prints or exquisite antiques or foolish articles of a more recent vintage or luxurious clothing or Scotch salmon and Russian caviar for unconscionable prices. Sometimes she walked on Park, where the women were invariably better dressed than she, and the architecture bland, but in the fall you could get sun on the east side of the street and in the spring the islands in the middle of the avenue were riots of color. On most days, however, she walked on Fifth. Fifth Avenue above Fifty-seventh Street was the best. On one side was the park, on the other, the long expanse of gray and white stone with somber colored canopies and brass that was aged but never tarnished. There were more good buildings on Fifth than on Park, and there were remnants of another age, too, the old mansions of millionaires' row serving now as consulates and embassies and museums. And on Fifth there was always someone important dashing from building to limousine or limousine to building. Once she'd seen a row of long black cars with an important politician in one and a small army of mean-faced men in the others. The men were looking at the gathered crowd suspiciously, and Katherine could see their rifles, though they held them below window level. She told Nick about it the next night. 'One of them had a submachine gun. Can you imagine? A submachine gun on Fifth Avenue.'

'Would you know a submachine gun if you saw one?' he'd asked her.

'I knew you'd say that. The man next to me said it was a submachine gun.'

It was on Fifth that she'd planned to stroll one afternoon late in September, but Paige Richmond called and asked if she wanted to keep her company. 'I have to take Tim to Brooks.' He'd been Timmy for the first six years of his life, but now on the eve of entering first grade he'd turned Tim overnight.

'He outgrew his kindergarten blazer, and he needs some trousers, too, and some ties.'

'And a dinner jacket?'

'Do you want to come or not?'

Katherine said she did.

On the fourth floor of Brooks Brothers Katherine

admitted that the tiny blue blazers and miniature rep ties were, as Paige said, adorable, though she didn't think Tim looked quite as adorable in them as Paige thought he did. He was a cute kid, but then most kids were cute at that age.

The tailor got on his knees to measure the gray flannel pants, and Tim put one small brown shoe on his shoulder.

'Stop it, Tim,' Paige said, but her face gave her away. The sharp angles softened and said Tim could do whatever he pleased whenever he pleased.

The man tried to smile. It was the kind of smile a baby gives when it has gas.

Tim raised his foot and brought it down on the man's shoulder with more force. Paige took Tim's foot and placed it on the pedestal where the man had stood him. Then she gave his knee what could only be called a love pat. Unlike Beth, Paige did not worship the twin gods of consistency and discipline.

'Taking Tim out,' Paige said, 'is a public service. He's done more for birth control than the entire Margaret Sanger clinic.' But at that moment the tailor told Tim to turn toward his mother. 'God, doesn't he look precious? Like a miniature Stanley.' Katherine admitted that he did, in fact, look like a miniature Dr Stanley Richmond.

The tailor sent Tim into the dressing room to try on another pair of pants, and Paige wandered over to the tie rack.

'How's Nick?'

Katherine said he was fine and braced herself for what she knew was coming.

'Has he said anything about divorce?'

'We're not married.'

'Cute, Katie, very cute.'

'I've told you before. Nick has no intention of

leaving his wife or, rather, his children—'

'God, not that old line: "I'd leave if it weren't for the kids."'

'Well, wife or kids, it's the same thing. He told me that when I first met him.'

'That was more than two years ago. People change their minds, you know.' Paige moved on to the shirts, and Katherine followed her. 'Last week I bought Tim half a dozen oxford shirts – pink, blue, yellow, striped – and when we got home, he spread them out on the bed for Stanley. It was just like the scene with Gatsby and Daisy. Has he mentioned it since?'

'I haven't heard from Gatsby in months.'

The handsome face turned to Katherine and gave her a disapproving look. 'Has Nick mentioned leaving his wife since that first time when he said he wouldn't? I mean, you must talk about it.'

'We don't.'

Paige was silent for a moment, seemingly absorbed in the difference between two striped shirts. 'That's probably better,' she said finally. 'Men hate to be nagged. You've got to be subtle. Still, you must have some idea whether he's thinking about it.'

'I know you don't believe me, but I don't have any idea. I rarely think about it unless you or someone else brings it up.'

'I don't believe you.'

Katherine shrugged. 'It's true.'

'Then you're abnormal.'

The idea was not new to Katherine, but she said nothing and followed Paige back to the fitting area. Tim was on the pedestal again, and every time the tailor reached for a leg the boy withdrew it. 'Either that,' Paige said, 'or afraid. Stephen scared you off marriage.'

'Stephen didn't scare me off marriage. I'm only

44

amazed I didn't scare him off. As he told me repeatedly during the divorce, marriage to me was no damn fun.'

'We saw him and Jill last weekend.'

Tim turned to his mother for final approval. Paige gave him a beatific smile and told him to get dressed. She seemed suddenly interested in the two ties she was carrying.

'Okay,' Katherine said. 'You know I'm curious. How is Stephen?'

'He looks wonderful.'

'He looked wonderful in that picture in the business section of the *Times* last year. He looked wonderful when I married him.'

'They bought a new house. The swimming pool is such a perfect kidney Stanley said he had the itch to perform surgery.'

'And how's the lovely Jill?'

'Don't be bitchy, Kate. If you didn't want him, why shouldn't someone else have him?'

'You're right. I'm sorry.'

'She's fine, but your name is still not mentioned in her presence.'

'They've been married nine years.'

'She's extreme, but I can understand her feelings. If Stanley had been married before, I'd have a hard time dealing with it. That's why I don't believe that Nick's wife doesn't bother you.'

'I never said she didn't bother me. I said I didn't think about his leaving her.'

'You sound as if you're satisfied with your life.'

'I'm not dissatisfied.'

'You ought to be. I don't mean to sound cruel, Kate, but I'm only thinking of you. Why else do you think I keep asking whether he's going to leave her? I'm not exactly prodivorce, and I'm definitely anti-other woman. If I were Nick's wife's friend, I'd hate you and tell her she ought to give him some kind of ultimatum. But I'm your friend, not hers, and you're the one I want to see happy. And I don't think you are happy with bits and pieces of Nick Larries. You really ought to have someone. It's natural law.'

'Like gravity, you mean?'

'Joke, if you want, but you know I'm right. Even your cats have each other.'

'Yes, but they've been neutered, and I'll thank you to keep your hands off Nick.'

If Paige thought she'd had the final word, she wasn't taking Cynthia Greer into account. Katherine arrived at Cynthia's office at twelve-thirty as arranged, but Cynthia was on the phone and stayed there for fifteen minutes while Katherine read *Women's Wear Daily*. When she finished that, she went through the rack of nightgowns and robes that hung in front of the grimy window of the small office.

'So this is what a buyer's office looks like,' she said when Cynthia got off the phone.

Cynthia pushed the helmet of yellow hair back from her eyes and gave the dirty green walls a distracted look. Their ugliness didn't register on her face. It was a chubby girl's face, but a pretty one, all smooth lines and easy curves. The cheeks were full and the chin was soft and the eyes were big pale blue saucers. The mouth was full, too, but it didn't seem as soft and the smile was ready but canny. Cynthia, Erica had said back in school, knew exactly what she wanted and exactly how to go about getting it. Erica had been right, it turned out, only about the second part.

'It isn't much, but I'm practically never here. I'm either on the floor or in the market.'

'Well, congratulations on it – despite the decor – and on the promotion. I'll treat for lunch.'

Cynthia stood. Although she was short and her body, like her face, was round, she gave an impression of tremendous energy. 'I only have time for a quickie. I'll let you buy me overpriced alfalfa sprouts at the health bar.

'Doug isn't exactly happy about the job,' she said when they'd found a table in the restaurant. It was barely big enough to accommodate both their trays. 'In fact, he's being a perfect prick about it.'

'So you said on the phone.'

'And it's going to get worse after Thanksgiving. Six days a week and late every night.'

'I can see why he's upset. He isn't going to see much of you.'

'He's upset because he doesn't have a full-time maid and housekeeper anymore. Or rather, he does, but it isn't me. He's upset because I've got money of my own and friends of my own and a life of my own. He's scared shitless.'

'Maybe you should try to reassure him.'

'The way he reassured me all those years? For ten years – until I went to work – Doug told me how important I was to him and then went off and left me with three kids, a dirty apartment, and all those grubby little tasks he was too important to take care of. Shit and string beans.'

Katherine looked up from the tuna surprise that held no wonder. 'What?'

'Marilyn French. *The Women's Room*. Shit and string beans. It's the housewife's lot. Doug consigned me to a life of shit and string beans. I should have known better. I did know better. I wanted to have an abortion, but he insisted we get married.'

'Cynthia . . .'

Cynthia's head snapped up. Her eyes beneath the silky blond helmet were wide with anger, and her mouth was a stubborn line that cut across the round face. 'What?'

'Nothing,' Katherine said quickly.

'Well, we got married. And Doug had all the fun while I had all the drudgery. Now it's my turn. Do you see anything wrong with that?'

'Not if it's what you want.'

'It's what I'm entitled to. You don't know, Kay. You never had the shit and string beans.'

'That's what I hate about "the movement". Not the substance, but the rhetoric. Your life was not all shit and string beans. All men are not pigs and oppressors. And I don't believe in sisterhood. Or rather, I believe in it, the same way I believe in brotherhood. I just don't think it exists.'

'Apparently.'

'What's that supposed to mean?'

'By having an affair with a married man, you're betraying your own kind.'

'My own kind?'

'Another woman.'

'What if she doesn't care?'

'Is that what he tells you?'

'It could be true.'

Cynthia's chubby fingers ripped open the small package of diet sweetener as if she were tearing off the yoke of male oppression. 'It could be, but I wouldn't believe it unless I heard it from her.' She liberated a second package. 'If neither of them cares, why are they still together? Erica says he'll never leave his wife.'

'*He* says he'll never leave his wife.'

'They usually lie about that. If he says it, it must be true. He'll never leave his wife.'

48

On the first Wednesday in October Nick Larries left his wife.

III

'How would you like a roommate?' Nick asked. 'Temporarily.'

He and Katherine were having lunch in a small French restaurant that had moderately good food, moderately high prices, and moderately bad murals of Paris on the walls. It was exactly like a couple of hundred other French restaurants in midtown Manhattan, but they lunched there regularly because of the maître d', who, in keeping with the restaurant, was only moderately good at his job but something of an old friend.

For the first year and a half that Katherine had known Nick he'd taken her to lunch at a place on Forty-ninth Street that was slightly more elegant and considerably more expensive. At first Katherine had thought Nick had chosen the restaurant because it was not frequented by lawyers, at least not by lawyers he knew. Then she discovered they went there because it was owned by two elderly French brothers who had, half a century ago, raced sports cars professionally. In one of his fantasy lives Nick had raced the Bugattis and Ferraris pictured on the walls of the bar, and in real life he'd actually gone around the track at Lime Rock in an Austin Healy once.

Six months ago the brothers had sold the

51

restaurant, and Nick and Katherine had followed Georges, the maître d', to this new one; but there was more missing here than the two brothers who gossiped about the old days with Nick, the pictures of the vintage sports cars on the walls, and the old-fashioned rich food that had no pretenses to being *nouvelle* anything. A part of Katherine's past was missing too.

The first time Nick had taken her to lunch, they'd gone to that other restaurant. They'd met at a party Nick had attended alone, for business reasons, and Katherine had been taken to by Matthew, the psychiatrist her mother had secretly detested. The first things she noticed about Nick were that he had a way of standing in a three-piece gray flannel suit that made her wonder what he looked like out of it; that he was funny, though that might have been the result of all the time she'd spent with Matthew; and that he wore a gold band on the third finger of his left hand. He called her the following day and asked her to lunch. Katherine always told Nick that she wished she could say she'd struggled with the moral implications of having lunch with a married man, but she hadn't struggled at all. She'd just said yes.

Nick raised no moral issues at that first lunch or the one after it. He called a third time, and she said yes again; but she was beginning to wonder if perhaps he was in the market for a ghost. 'Maybe he's a lunch fetishist,' Erica suggested. 'He gets his jollies having lunch with other women.'

'He's too thin.'

At the third lunch Nick told her about going around the track at Lime Rock. They also talked about a movie they'd both seen, a book she'd just read, and music, about which they knew little and still managed to disagree completely. They did not

touch on anything sexual, romantic, or even personal.
In fact, they did not even touch.

'Do you mind if I ask you something?' Katherine
said when the coffee arrived. He turned toward her
on the banquette, and she could tell by the guarded
look in his eyes that he knew it wasn't something
about books, movies, or the track at Lime Rock. He
also moved his left hand on the table as if he were
hoping the gold band would catch her eye. He was
expecting a personal question all right, but not the
personal question Katherine asked. 'Why do you
keep taking me to lunch?'

He smiled, not exactly a snake oil salesman's smile,
but not a Dutch uncle's either. 'Why do you think I
keep taking you to lunch?'

'I know what it seems like, I mean, what I thought
originally' – she wasn't doing this very well – 'but
now I'm not so sure.'

'What did you think originally?' He was still
smiling, and for the first time she didn't like him.

'Forget it.' She turned away from him and leaned
forward over her coffee. As she did, a strand of hair
fell forward over her cheek. He pushed it back from
her face.

'You were right,' he said. 'Would you like to have
dinner tonight?'

'I don't think I can do this twice in one day.'

'I wasn't planning to. Dinner was a euphemism.'

They never did have dinner that night, though
they had drinks in the bar of the same restaurant
before they took a taxi up to Katherine's apartment.

'There's something I ought to tell you,' he said.
His timing was, if not impeccable, scrupulous. Their
martinis had reached the point where the lemon peels
in the bottom of the glasses were only half-covered

with liquid. 'I have no intention of getting a divorce.'

She finished her drink, and as she put the glass down, she caught a glimpse of their reflections in the tinted mirror behind the bar. Rose-colored mirrors, she decided, were as good as rose-colored glasses. 'Do you mind if I ask you another question? Have you ever done this before?'

He looked at her very steadily. 'Occasionally.'

She looked back at him very steadily. 'You could have fooled me.'

They surprised each other that night. There was no reason, given the circumstances, that each should have thought of the other as overly proper, but they had. It was very pleasant to discover they'd been wrong.

The next morning Katherine called Matthew and told him she didn't think they ought to see each other anymore. He put her on hold for a moment before he answered because his man from Sherry-Lehmann was on the other line with some news about a shipment of Bordeaux. Katherine waited for a few minutes, but when she began to feel that she too was aging and not as well as the wine, she hung up. She never heard from Matthew again.

Nick called that morning, and they had lunch again at the restaurant on Forty-ninth Street, where they agreed they couldn't possibly go on seeing each other daily. They hadn't, but they had continued to see each other three times a week, frequently at the French restaurant. They went there when he won the case against the pharmaceutical company, and when she turned thirty-five, and when he turned thirty-seven, and when her second novel, which was really Altruist's second novel, was sold to the movies, and the day they had that enormous fight about politics which wasn't about politics at all but about the fact that he was going away on vacation, and the day a few months later when he told her about Gwen.

Katherine had *sole meunière* that day, and he had some kind of veal. At the end of lunch the uneaten mess on her plate was white with gold flecks, and his was beige. They were sitting across from each other, but he looked at her less than he did when they sat on a banquette. His eyes were slippery like the mushrooms that lay in a pool of sauce on his plate.

'My wife thinks she's pregnant.'

How I spent my summer vacation by Nicholas Larries, Four B. For bastard. 'Congratulations.'

'I'm sorry,' he said. She didn't say anything, and he still wasn't looking at her. 'I don't suppose you'll want to see me anymore.'

She almost slammed her wineglass down then. 'Stop feeling sorry for yourself.' It was the closest she'd come to recriminations: he had never made any promises, and she had never asked for any. She was willing to assume responsibility for herself but not for anyone else.

The lovely Gwen hadn't been pregnant and things had gone back to normal and they'd gone back to the restaurant, but in New York only buildings with landmark status remain unchanged and landmark status is hard to achieve. Occasionally Katherine missed the old restaurant but never more so than now, on the day Nick asked her if she wanted a roommate, temporarily.

'How temporarily?' Katherine asked.

Georges approached with the menus; but Nick shook his head, and the long, morose face receded into the haze of other diners.

'How would you like a roommate? I threw in the

temporary part because I didn't want to frighten you.'

'I'll have to think about it.' Katherine took a sip of her drink. 'I've thought about it. When can you move in?'

'I suppose we ought to do something. To commemorate the occasion.'

'Strike a coin?'

'Tell Georges?'

'That you're leaving your wife? He thinks I am your wife.'

In fact, they didn't even order another round of drinks because Nick had a meeting that afternoon. Nonetheless, something about the lunch was different, or at least something about Katherine. 'You really are frightened,' Nick said when the waiter brought the check.

'Just surprised.'

He kept his head down as he added the tip onto the credit card slip and signed his name, but she knew from experience that the calculations didn't take all his attention. 'Look,' he said without looking up, 'you can throw me out anytime you want.' He tore off one of the carbons, stuffed it in his jacket pocket, and smiled at her. She thought it was a damn phony smile. 'No, you'd never be able to do that. We'll have to figure out a sign. Something you can do to tell me to pack up and get the hell out.'

'A little strychnine in your martinis?'

'Make codfish cakes. On Saturday night. Every Saturday night my mother used to make codfish cakes. I hated them. The only time my father ever hit me was one Saturday night when I refused to eat them.'

'I don't know how to make codfish cakes.'

He stood and pulled the table away from the

banquette for her. 'That's what I'm counting on.'

Katherine always found it difficult to get back to work after lunching out. Today she knew it would be impossible. Despite her news, or maybe because of it, she did not want to talk to Erica or see Beth or use Cynthia's discount to buy herself something or meet Paige, who'd said she'd be at Sotheby's all afternoon.

Katherine left Nick on the corner of Fifth and Fifty-fourth and headed toward Doubleday. She could waste an hour without even trying, more if she got as far as the record department. She didn't. The racks for new paperback releases in front of the store stopped her. Ego's face stared out from row after row. The effect was alarming, as if a mad scientist had gotten carried away in a grotesque cloning experiment. She stood staring at smug, suntanned face after smug, suntanned face, at narrow forehead after narrow forehead. On more than one occasion that meager strip of brow had caused Katherine concern for the future of evolution. He was smiling his big, cap-toothed smile, the one he worked so hard on, harder certainly than on any of his books. When his first book had come out, he'd explained the philosophy of that smile to her. 'I'm a psychologist,' he'd said, wrinkling the narrow brow until it almost disappeared under the dark, crinkly hair. 'But I'm also a salesman. Look at that smile.' He'd tapped the book with one of his thick fingers. 'It's sincere. It also spells success. S-U-C-C-E-S-S,' he added in case she didn't know how to. 'No one's going to plunk down ten bucks to take advice from a loser. It's macho enough for the men. Right?' She'd looked from the enormous white teeth on the jacket to the real, if not natural, thing and gave what she hoped was a noncommittal nod. 'But sexy enough for the women.' She hadn't even been able to nod that time.

Macho. Sexy. Katherine looked at row after row of those big, synthetic teeth smiling that predatory smile. Just when you thought it was safe to go back in the water . . .

A woman brushed past her and picked up one of the books. She was a nice-looking woman, a sensible-looking woman, and she was carrying the badge of achievement – a briefcase. Did she really believe there were eleven blue-chip investments in herself that would double the value of her emotional portfolio or six self-tests to reveal her secret sensual side?

The woman must have felt Katherine staring because she looked up from the smiling Ego on the cover. 'I've been waiting for this to come out in paper for months. His first two books changed my life.'

Katherine knew she was making a mistake. Nick would say she was certifiable. Erica would tell her to shut up and let the woman buy the book because Katherine's thirty percent of Ego's six percent royalty was four and a half cents, and if you let a million or two women like this one buy the book, those pennies added up. But she took the bait. 'How?'

The woman looked up from her handbag where she'd been fishing around for her wallet. 'What?'

'How did the first two books change your life?'

'Well, you know, they *changed* it.'

Just be glad she liked them, Katherine told herself, and climbed to the second floor to look at the other paperbacks, but she had a hard time going through the racks because every cover had her name on it. From *Emma* by Katherine Walden at the beginning of the fiction wall to *Nana* by Katherine Walden, in translation, of course, at the end, she was well represented. When she walked to the front of the store again and saw one of those cardboard boxes Erica called dumps filled with Egos, she narrowed her eyes until it was her photograph on the cover. There was no smile, sexy or otherwise, on her face. She looked serious and intense but not pretentious. Must avoid pretension at all costs. She was sitting at her desk in a turtleneck sweater with her hair hanging straight and unstudied around her face and Eleanor on her lap. The likeness was so good that people kept coming up to her in bookstores and telling her how much they'd loved her book. 'It changed my life.'

She was standing in front of the display when a man in a business suit reached around her and picked up a copy of Ego. Katherine went downstairs to the record department without waiting to see whether he was buying or merely browsing.

When she got home a little after four-thirty, she hung up her coat so the cats wouldn't nest on it, kicked off her shoes, and checked the answering machine. It was an old ritual in a new order. Usually she'd check the tape first to see if Nick had called.

There were three messages on the tape, or rather three calls and two messages. Katherine had decided long ago that there ought to be a cruel and inhuman punishment for people who hung up immediately or hung on breathing ominously into the phone. But then again she supposed there ought to be a cruel and inhuman punishment for people who let machines answer their phones.

The second message was from Altruist. Now there was a man made for answering machines. He reminded her of an actor who's never worked before a live audience but takes to a camera instinctively.

I just read Chapter Eight, and it's dynamite! What a team we make!

'Not since Colette and Willy,' Katherine said to Eleanor, who'd jumped up on the desk to rub against her.

Altruist gave a self-satisfied chuckle that made Katherine remember Ego's smile. *And you don't change as much of my stuff as you think. That masturbation scene I gave you is dynamite.*

'Gave me!' Katherine scratched Eleanor's head. 'He talks dirty to me on the phone for ten minutes between patients one morning and thinks he's written a scene.' Eleanor purred. There was nothing she liked better than a good, hard head scratching.

We really got inside her head – as well as her body. A salacious laugh. Nick was right. They ought to lock up Altruist for making obscene phone calls. *I may not know as much about writing as you do, Wraith, but I sure understand the female psyche. Now when you get to her next appointment with her therapist . . .* The tape clicked off, and Katherine felt a surge of gratitude for the limitations of modern technology.

The next voice was Erica's, asking Katherine to call her back. She would have, anyway, to break the news. So much for the low-cholesterol view of love.

'Out playing again, eh?' Erica asked when the secretary had connected them. Erica always insisted she understood writers in general and Katherine in particular and appreciated how hard they worked even if they didn't hold a job or report to an office. Not for her the long, aimless phone calls that assumed just because Katherine was home, she had nothing better to do. But even Erica couldn't resist the occasional jibe.

'Actually I was home, but I couldn't tear myself

away from the television. And the bonbons.' There was a moment's silence as if Erica suspected Katherine really had spent the afternoon watching soap operas and eating candy. 'I was downtown having lunch with Nick. He's off his diet.'

'I didn't know he was on one.'

'The low-cholesterol one. From now on it's steak and eggs all the time. He's moving in.'

The silence was longer this time. It probably set the record for Erica's office silences. 'Sorry for the pause,' she said finally, 'but it's hard to congratulate you with a mouthful of crow.'

'I don't want you to eat crow. Hell, I never thought he'd leave either.'

'But he isn't just leaving his wife. He's leaving her and moving in with you. Did you ever ask him to?'

'Of course, I never asked him to. I told you, we never talked about it.'

'So he just assumed he could.'

'He didn't just assume. He asked if he could at lunch.'

'Boy, does he know his patsy.'

'I could have said no.'

'*One* could have, Kat, but you wouldn't. You took in Eleanor, too, when you found her wandering the streets.'

Katherine stopped scratching Eleanor's head and started on her own. 'But I want Nick to move in.'

'I thought you liked living alone. That's what you said every time I predicted – incorrectly as it turned out – that he'd never leave his wife.'

'I do like living alone. But I like living with Nick more. At least, I think I'm going to.'

'You're not frightened?'

Katherine didn't answer immediately, but Erica

seemed to have plenty of time this afternoon. 'Maybe a little nervous.'

'Well, at least you admit it,' Erica said, and Katherine recognized the tone. It was the one Erica used when she'd closed what she thought was a good deal. 'Anyway, congratulations or good luck or whatever I'm supposed to say. Times being what they are, with girls getting younger, us getting older, and New York getting gayer, you could have done worse. Now that we've got your personal life in order, at least for the moment, what about the book? Ego's agent called this morning. I don't mind letting him stew for a day or two. Maybe it will head off what we laughingly call the negotiations. What is it now – four books? – and with each one he tries to nip a few percentage points off your take. I'm going to love telling him we're not interested in *Son of How to Be a Winner*.'

'I'm not sure I'm not interested.'

'What is wrong with you, Kat? I've given you the idea. I promise you I can sell it. Do I have to write it for you, too?'

'You could probably do a better job.'

'You know I was joking. I can't write my way out of a paper bag.'

'And I don't think I can write the kind of book you're talking about. After I left Nick this afternoon, I went to Doubleday. The last Ego is out in paper, and they had about a thousand copies in the new releases racks. While I was standing there, entranced by his sexy, macho smile, this woman came over and picked up a copy. She looked perfectly normal with none of the outward signs that put you off, like a wad of gum in her mouth or more signatures on her than the Declaration of Independence. And she was carrying a briefcase. I'm beginning to wonder about those briefcases. All over the city women are running around with expensive leather cases, and you know what I think is inside? A makeup kit, maybe an extra pair of panty hose, a grocery list, and a book by Dr Leo Robbins, a.k.a. Ego. The woman bought the book. She told me she'd been waiting for it to come out for months because the first two changed her life.'

'You mean you think you owe it to your public to do another book with Ego?'

'I mean, if I did a book alone, I don't think I'd have a public. I write those books for Ego, but they're his ideas – or lack thereof. I couldn't come up with that stuff if I tried. We laugh at it, Erica, but this woman thought it had changed her life.'

'I still don't get your point.'

'You said you wanted a book that women could identify with. I don't think I can write a book that women will identify with. At least not the women who keep buying Ego's books, and apparently there are millions of them. Is everyone really that unhappy or that stupid? Do they really believe that they're going to save their marriages or find decent jobs or keep their kids off drugs by standing in front of the mirror and saying, "I like you. You're nice"? That's Exercise Seven in case you didn't recognize it.'

'You know what your problem is?' Katherine could tell from the exasperation in Erica's voice that she was about to find out. 'You're afraid to come out of the closet. It's okay to keep churning out books so long as you don't have to risk putting your own name on them. Remember that celebrity autobiography you ghosted a few years ago?'

'*When the Cameras Rolled*, better known to the three people who bought it – including my mother – as *When the Names Dropped*.'

'That's the one. Along comes this aging movie star, aging illiterate movie star, who wants to write his autobiography. So his agent suggests an "as told to" and rounds up a reputable journalist, which these days means anyone who's ever sent a letter to the Op-Ed page. But the reputable journalist discovers it's more work than he expected. I think it was all the foreign names. Even Lupe Velez threw him. By this time the publisher is nervous because they already have too much money out on the book, so they turn to me. Enter Katherine Walden. The only woman who ever ghosted an "as told to". It lends a new dimension to the word "self-effacement".

'Look, Kat, I've got to go. A drink with an agent from the Coast. California to you. Do me one favor. Stop thinking about it. Stop talking about it. Stop asking strange women in Doubleday about it. Just sit down and give it a try. Write me five thousand words. Five thousand lousy words – you do that in your sleep for Ego and Altruist – and I'll take it from there. Now I really do have to run, but this Hollywood thing won't take long. Want to meet me after for a movie – or dinner – or both?'

'Thanks, but I can't. Nick's going home to get his stuff, then driving back into town.'

There was no pause this time. 'Sorry. I forgot your altered status. I guess I'll have to find myself a new movie and dinner date.'

'I didn't say that.'

'You didn't have to.'

'He'll be with his kids Saturday. Why don't we do something then?'

'Sure,' Erica said. 'We'll work around Nick.'

Nick returned a little after nine that night. The elevator man helped him carry one suitcase, one hanging bag, a briefcase, and a long carrying case with his fencing foils, the few feet to the apartment door. Did he really travel that lightly, or had he meant it after all when he'd said 'temporarily'?

'You don't exactly give hostages to fortune,' she said.

'What do you mean?'

'I mean your possessions. There aren't many.'

'That's wife and children, Katie. Hostages to fortune are supposed to be wife and children. Possessions are just something I figured you didn't have room for.'

IV

Katherine didn't hear Nick get out of bed on
Saturday morning, which was strange because in
three days she hadn't grown accustomed to his all-
night presence in the bed, but then he'd been very
quiet. And it was very early. The squeak of the
bathroom door awakened her. As he came back into
the bedroom, she saw the cloud of steam behind
him. He'd already showered.

'What time is it?' she asked.

'Go back to sleep.'

'That's not an answer.' She moved the clock radio
until she could see the digits. 'Seven-thirty. It is
Saturday, isn't it?'

'I couldn't sleep, so I thought I might as well get
started.'

'You told them you'd pick them up at ten.' She
stopped abruptly. When he'd called home –
correction, former home, current children – last
evening, he'd used the phone in the bedroom, and
she'd made a point of going into the kitchen. She
had also made a point, once in the kitchen, of not
turning on the radio or running the water or even
using the electric can opener.

He was sitting on the end of the bed, putting on
his socks, not the long black ones he wore to the
office but shorter gray wool ones.

'Then I'll be early.'

She turned over and pushed another pillow under her head. 'Will they be ready?'

'If they're not, I'll wait.'

Over coffee with Gwen. In the kitchen where he'd spent a weekend putting up ceramic tiles a year and a half ago and cut the tips of his fingers to shreds. She'd said that was bound to ruin their usual Monday night, but Nick had only proved his resourcefulness.

'I'll make you some breakfast.'

'Don't bother.' He was already into a pair of corduroys and a sweater. 'I'm not hungry. I'll get some coffee on the road.'

The road to reconciliation. 'I have to make coffee for myself anyway.'

He put on an old herringbone jacket that was as new to her as the gray socks. 'Go back to sleep, Katie. I'll see you tonight.'

He patted her head on the way out of the bedroom, then made the mistake of doing the same thing to Franklin, who was curled at the foot of the bed.

She did not go back to sleep. She made herself a cup of instant coffee because she didn't care enough about coffee to make a pot for herself. She bet the lovely Gwen ground her own beans. She read the *Times* from cover to cover, but there was never much in the *Times* on Saturday. She took a shower and washed and dried her hair and made the bed and cleaned up the two glasses they'd left in the bedroom the night before. She opened one of the drawers she'd cleaned out for Nick. His socks were rolled into neat little married pairs. There were lots of long black dress rolls, two gray wool, three navy wool, and several white wool showing red and blue tennis stripes. There were no argyles. When she'd married Stephen, he'd had half a dozen pairs of argyles, all knitted by a Vassar French major. At ten o'clock she called Erica. 'Are we on for today?'

'We and everyone else. Beth called last night and asked if I wanted to have lunch. It must be Daddy's weekend all over America.'

'What about Topper?'

'Maybe he's with his daddy, too. Then Cynthia called and asked if we'd come downtown and lunch somewhere around her because she has to work today but she feels a need for moral support. The only one we're missing is Paige, but she's still a member of that exclusive club called the first-marrieds. It's a little like still being a Mouseketeer.'

Katherine often thought that if she were dropped out of a time warp into Manhattan on a Saturday, she could tell the day and the hour without calendar or clock. Saturdays walked differently from weekdays, not necessarily slower or faster, but differently, and dressed in a special way, and felt better than any other day of the week. It might have been a legacy from school, but if it was, it hadn't diminished over the years.

On Saturday mornings respectable-looking men paraded their dirty linen through the streets – four shirts wrapped in a fifth whose arms had been tied in a gordian knot of propriety. Women pushed and dragged metal carts full of shopping bags holding the mundane staples of their culinary lives or the exotic raw materials of special occasions, the kinds of things that couldn't be picked up on the way home from the office. Kids, out of their private school uniforms but still in uniform, careened through the streets on skateboards and roller skates. As the day progressed, the galleries filled up and the lines began to form outside the big shows at the Whitney or the Modern, and on Lexington Avenue in the low Sixties street vendors and shoppers bargained and baited each other and fought for their territorial rights. And everyone lunched. All over town, in the glassed-in sidewalk cafés, in dark hamburger bars, in noisy coffee shops, at the blond-wood counters of health food stores, at down-at-the-heel restaurants where big wooden sidewalk stands advertised brunch with free bloody marys, at places which didn't have to advertise because they had suddenly and inexplicably caught on, people lunched. Couples in love holding hands on top of the table, bored couples aware of everyone but each other, couples who discussed the relative merits of television sets and sofas, and couples who looked ill at ease and eager to impress each other because they'd just waked up together for the first time. Men lunched with children, awkwardly with a single six-year-old, raucously with a group of two or three, sullenly with a lone and angry-looking adolescent. Grown women lunched with their mothers, discussing fabric swatches and winter coats, husbands and fathers, and you could tell that some loved each other and some hated each other and some were too bound to each other to know what they felt. Men lunched with other men, talking seriously or gossiping shrilly, oblivious to the women around them. And women like Katherine and her friends lunched. Amid the food and drinks they laid out their lives and picked and probed until someone touched something soft, and the emotions spilled out like the yolks of their eggs benedict.

Katherine and her friends met on the ground floor of the CBS Building in a restaurant that had gone through several incarnations and was likely to go through several more. It had little to recommend it except proximity to Cynthia, who had to get back to work, and the fact that it wouldn't be too crowded on Saturday. The food was only mediocre, but the room was impressive, built to a grand scale with high ceilings and a southern wall of windows. Long beams of sunshine slanted through them, lifting the smoke and dust particles of the room and holding them in delicate suspension.

'I really can't afford this place,' Cynthia said as she joined the others, who had already ordered drinks. The restaurant wasn't expensive, only overpriced. 'I'm trying to save my salary in case I leave Doug.' She pushed her blond hair behind her ears and smiled at each of them in turn. The smile invited approval, though she must have known in that circle approval of marital separation needed no invitation.

'I'll treat,' Beth said. 'Write it off as research. My next novel will be about a successful buyer.'

'Thanks, but I think I'll save your generosity for when I do leave him.'

'That was quick,' Katherine said. 'A minute ago it was if you leave him.'

The waiter appeared, and Cynthia ordered a Perrier with a twist. 'I'm determined to take off ten more pounds. I've already shed four.'

They all told her she looked terrific. She didn't look terrific, but she did look good.

'I vacillate,' Cynthia went on. 'About Doug, I mean.'

'Didn't we all?' Erica removed a package of little black cigars from her handbag and passed them around. Cynthia took one. 'Divorce may be a pain in the ass, but predivorce is worse. First there's the trial separation. That's when the kids mope a lot and you talk to each other on the phone every other night. After a couple of weeks you begin to "date". The only advantage is that the sex is better on the dates than it was when you were married. Then you decide on a trial reconciliation. He gives up the popsies he's been sleeping with, and you give up eating chocolate chips in bed. Then the sex deteriorates, and you stop talking and start screaming again, and just about the time you figure you've finally got the courage to tell him to leave after all, he comes home and says he's decided a divorce is the only answer. Get ready for pure hell, Cyn.'

'Oh, come on, don't romanticize it for her,' Katherine said, but she knew that in fact Erica had airbrushed the picture. She'd failed to mention her crying jags and the bouts of panic and the stomach ailment a series of specialists had failed to diagnose. Or maybe she'd just forgotten them.

Erica exhaled a long trail of smoke and squinted through it at Katherine. 'Look who's talking. Maybe you can't remember back to your divorce, luv, but I still can. Either you'd throw Stephen out and he'd check into a hotel for two hours until you went down there and brought him back, or you'd walk out and come to my place, where the picture of another blissful marriage would send you right back to Stephen. The worst thing about divorce is the indecision leading up to it. And let's face it, Kat, decisiveness is not your long suit.'

Beth signaled the waiter, and they ordered. 'The second divorce is a lot easier.' She spoke as if she were part of a panel discussion. 'Jimmy and I went through all that trial garbage; only I can't say it was the worst part because things were pretty ugly during the divorce, too. If you want to find out how cheap a man can be, try divorcing him. But with Ted, it was over in record time. Of course, there had been ugly times before the breakup because of the sex – or lack thereof – and I had one scare during the divorce when my lawyer said I might have to make some kind of settlement because by that time I was making a lot more than Ted. But all in all, the second time was a lot easier.'

'Keep that in mind, Kat,' Erica said.

'You can't get a divorce if you're not married.'

Cynthia swirled the lime around with her swizzle stick. 'You can still get screwed, though. And I'm not talking about sex. I hope you drew up a contract, Kay. Everything ought to be in writing. What belongs to whom. How you divide the rent, bills, food, all that stuff. Who cooks, who cleans up.'

'You mean who makes the string beans and who takes care of the shit.'

'You won't think it's so funny when you find yourself supporting him. Everyone talks about the strides women have made financially. You know what they mean? Now women can support men who are supporting first wives and kids.'

Katherine tied another knot in her tortured swizzle stick. 'According to you, they can't win. If they don't pay lots of alimony and child support, they're bastards, and if they do, they're freeloaders.'

'What does Nick's wife do?' Erica asked.

'Take courses. She's trying to find herself.'

'You're in for a lot of trouble, Kat.'

Beth, who'd been leaning back in her chair, sat up straight. Her long dark eyes stopped combing the room and came to rest on Katherine. 'There's only one thing I want to know. Is he a good lover?'

Katherine would have given a great deal to be back with potential divorce and written contracts. They all looked at her expectantly while the waiter put down their plates. 'Well?' Beth asked after he was gone.

Katherine lifted a half piece of rye bread from her sandwich and began to spread mustard on it. 'Only when he ties me to the bed.'

Beth's long, narrow eyes grew wide for a second; then she saw Katherine's slightly one-sided smile. 'I mean it, Kitty. Is he a good lover? Topper's the best lover I've ever had, except for an Arab I met at a party in London last year. There's a lot to be said for Eastern thought. To say nothing of practice.'

'Michael spent the last two years of our marriage memorizing the *Kama Sutra*,' Erica said. 'It didn't help.' She took a big bite of her sandwich.

Cynthia squeezed lemon juice over her salad, and her mouth puckered as if she were already tasting it. 'I wouldn't care if he were good, bad, or indifferent. So long as he wasn't Doug. After sixteen years it isn't sex, it's reflex. And damn unfair. I'm the only one of us – probably the only thirty-six-year-old woman in America – who's slept with one man in her entire life. One goddamn man in thirty-six years. They ought to put me in Ripley's or the Smithsonian or something.'

'You can't say you haven't had the opportunity,' Katherine said. 'I remember those parties you and Doug used to give. I have the dubious honor of having been propositioned in one night by two of the best minds of our generation. At least, Doug said they were two of the best minds of our generation. They didn't want to discuss Kant or Hegel with me.'

Cynthia laughed. 'I remember that party. The chairman of the department, that venerable white-haired gentleman whose book we all swore by in Intro to Philosophy, cornered you in the bedroom.'

'Was I disillusioned.'

'Were you flattered,' Erica corrected. 'Those parties were crazy. I wonder if all academicians are like that, or only philosophers.'

'It must be an occupational hazard for philosophers. They spend so much time contemplating their navels, their minds just naturally wander down to' – Beth dropped her voice – 'their cocks.'

Katherine laughed and shifted in her chair, which no longer felt like a hot seat, but Beth had not got where she was in life by a lack of perseverance. 'You still haven't answered us, Kitty.'

'She's not going to,' Erica said.

'I don't know what you mean. A good lover. A great lover. The best lover since some Arab in London. You make it sound like the Olympics. So many points for good technique in foreplay. A few tricks imported from the mysterious East win you a bronze medal. Coupling in strange and difficult places takes a silver.' She stopped abruptly.

Erica started to laugh, and her glasses slid down from her short hair to her wide nose. 'Look at her face! Beet-colored. Okay, Kat, where did Nick put it to you? The IRT at rush hour? The fountain at Lincoln Center? Bloomie's makeup department on a Saturday morning? No, not Bloomingdale's. Nobody would notice.'

'All I meant was that I think feelings are more important than expertise.'

'Quaint,' Beth said.

'Endearing,' Erica added.

'What makes you think men have feelings?' Cynthia asked.

The conversation turned sober and professional over coffee. Erica mentioned a trip to the Coast. Cynthia said in her first month as a buyer she'd made every day. 'That means matched or beaten last year's figures for that day,' she explained. Beth said now that she'd just about finished promoting her current novel, she could get started on her next one. They all agreed Katherine ought to write her own book. Katherine admitted she was thinking about it.

Cynthia looked at her watch and said she had to get back to the store. When she took her wallet from her handbag, Beth told her to forget it, but Cynthia shoved a handful of bills toward Beth and hurried out of the restaurant.

Erica signaled the waiter for more coffee. 'Do you think she'll leave Doug? Or rather, throw him out. Leaving a husband is one thing, but leaving a three-bedroom rent-controlled apartment that's bound to go co-op any day is something else.'

'It's only a matter of time,' Beth said. 'First the job, then the divorce.'

Erica lit another little cigar. 'She really is funny about that job. You'd think no one had ever worked before. You know the old game of having your secretary get the other person on the phone before you get on? Only Cynthia doesn't have a secretary, so every time she calls me, she says hello and then puts me on hold. Still, you have to give her credit. She made buyer awfully quickly. But that's Cynthia. She's always gone after what she wanted. It was the same with Doug.'

'It was worse with Doug,' Katherine said. 'She launched a full-scale attack on him.'

Beth took out a credit card and put it on top of the check. 'Didn't we all in those days?' She took the money Erica and Katherine handed her and put it in her wallet. 'I remember Christmas vacation of my senior year. My mother had a thing about romantic settings. So every night when Jimmy brought me home, there was a fire going. And you know how my mother was about dirtying the living room with ashes in the grate. He proposed the next to the last night of vacation, and from the way my mother looked at those ashes the next morning, you would have thought they were Joan of Arc.' Beth signed the slip, took the receipt from the waiter, and they all stood. 'The funny thing is that Ted and I decided to get married in front of a fire, too.'

'You need a new scene,' Katherine said.

'I've got a new plot. No more marriages.'

Katherine and Erica walked with Beth to the salon where she was having her facial, then continued up Madison Avenue. The air was so fresh that not even the exhausts of Manhattan could soil it, but the weather that encouraged brisk walking had also brought out every self-respecting New Yorker and brought in half the population of the surrounding suburbs. Erica and Katherine walked slowly, separating to get around groups, stopping to look in windows.

'Beth will get married again,' Erica said. 'She said she wouldn't after Jimmy, too, and in less than a year she and Ted were lying in front of that fire making plans. I give her another year and she'll be ready.'

'You don't think she'll marry Topper?'

'I think there's a good chance she'll marry someone just like him. Though I wouldn't put it past her to grab some fat, balding fifty-year-old so long as he had clout. First the solid professional man, then the boozy would-be poet, now the mover and shaker.'

'I just don't think of Beth as that callous.'

They stopped for a traffic light, and Erica turned to Katherine. 'Beth isn't callous. She'll convince herself she's in love with him. Just the way she was with Ted and before that with Jimmy, no matter how she makes fun of that attack she and her mother waged.'

'I remember that Christmas. And Cynthia's campaign for Doug, too. I bet there isn't a girl from our dorm who doesn't remember that.'

Erica stopped in front of a window to look at a blouse. It was lace with a frilly collar and looked very unlike her.

'What I can't figure out,' Katherine said, 'is why we didn't. Wage concerted campaigns. I don't mean that in a superior way. I just don't understand why we didn't.'

They started walking again. 'Stephen asked you to marry him so damn fast you didn't have time to launch a campaign.'

'What about you and Michael? You went home for the weekend to tell your parents you were going to break the engagement and came back with the wedding date moved up.'

'My parents didn't exactly pressure me.' They stopped on the corner of Madison and Erica's cross street. 'Just pointed out that I'd never do any better. That was the way they put it. Do you want to come in for a while?'

Katherine said she'd better not because she had some stops to make on the way home, but Erica could tell from Katherine's face that she was still thinking about their conversation. 'It doesn't make any difference, Kat. The fact that Cynthia and Beth waged campaigns to get married and you and I didn't, I mean. We may have thought we wanted more than a nice safe marriage to a nice safe young man with a nice safe future, but we wanted that, too, and we were good little girls and went ahead and got it.' Erica laughed and pushed the dark glasses up on her hair. 'And you know what? It doesn't make a damn bit of difference in the long run. We all ended up the same.'

They touched cheeks, and Erica turned and started down the side street. Katherine stood for a moment watching her move through the shadows and narrow streaks of sunlight that filtered over the shorter buildings. A delivery boy glided by, riding his grocery wagon like a hot rod, and turned to watch Erica walk. He said something in Spanish, but Erica just kept walking, her beautiful body a cutting edge against the world's indifference, and Katherine turned and started up Madison Avenue again.

The patches of sunlight were slight and far between now, and she turned up the collar of her jacket and put her hands in her pockets. The air was chill and electric, charged by the people spilling out of the shops and galleries, by the cars swerving and jockeying their way up the street, by the late afternoon's promise, and the evening's potential, and the fierce ambition to make one more purchase or tour one more gallery or cross one more street before the light turned.

Katherine moved with the same determination, though she had no stops to make and nothing to buy. She'd lied to Erica about that partly because she didn't want to admit she was eager to get home to Nick and partly because she'd had enough of the conversation at lunch and the analyses that had followed. After all these years the postmortems were intimate, and inevitable. Katherine wondered how many times they'd met for lunch or dinner or some occasion and then, as each of them peeled off, the others had rehashed what she'd said and speculated on what she'd meant, as they had today. When Cynthia had returned to work, the three of them had given her marriage and job and life a once-over. Then Beth had disappeared behind the overdecorated doors of Georgette Klinger, and Erica and Katherine had calculated her marital odds. Katherine decided there were advantages to living the farthest uptown, to being the last to leave the cab or the one to walk the final few blocks alone. Advantages, but no guarantees, she reminded herself. She knew her friends. Their interest in each other was not casual. If the opportunity for analysis did not present itself, they would, in the vernacular of the day, make it happen.

Katherine stopped in front of an antique store. A long mahogany-framed mirror in the center of the window reflected her image. She hadn't put on any lipstick after lunch, which only made the long upper lip – judgmental or aristocratic, take your choice – look longer. Her lashes were as dense as Nick's, but to less effect because hers were pale. The Lord giveth with one hand and taketh away with the other.

'Didn't Kitty look awful at lunch last week?'

'Kat really ought to do something about herself.'

'I love her, but she's getting a little old for that long-haired, no-makeup look.'

Katherine turned from the window and began walking uptown again. Her friends were not that petty. But they were that concerned.

'Kay was crazy to let him move in.'

'You know Kat. He snaps his fingers and she jumps.'

'I don't understand it. Kitty was never like that when she was married.'

'She told me once, when they'd had a fight, that Nick was her divine retribution for the way she'd treated Stephen.'

'That sounds like Kitty.'

'She really ought to have some kind of contract for her own protection.'

Talk about grass-roots movements. Katherine could picture the scrawled signs as they picketed her apartment house. FREE KITTY WALDEN. SAVE THE KATS. NO MORE NICKS. The only trouble was that she was perfectly free and felt no need to be saved.

The lights were on in the living room, which meant Nick was home, but there was no sign of him. She called his name. No answer. She walked into the bedroom and switched on the overhead light. He was stretched out on the bed with his face in the pillow.

'I'm sorry. I didn't realize you were asleep.'

He mumbled something.

'What?'

'I wasn't sleeping,' he said without taking his face from the pillow.

'How were your kids?'

A muffled sound came from the pillow. It sounded like 'fine', but she couldn't be sure.

'What did you do?'

There was another muffled noise, this time unintelligible.

She was still wearing her jacket, and she put her hands in her pockets and shifted her weight from one foot to the other. 'I can't understand you.'

He picked his head up from the pillow. 'I brought them back to town. We went to a museum, a restaurant, a movie, and FAO Schwartz.' He reeled the words off as if they'd been running through his head for a long time and put his face in the pillow again.

She sat on the edge of the bed and put her hand on his back. He didn't move away, but she had the feeling from the way he stiffened that he wanted to. 'It sounds as if you had a rough day. I'm sorry.' There was no noise from the pillow this time. 'Do you want a drink?' The answer sounded like 'sure'.

She filled the ice bucket in the kitchen, carried it into the living room and poured scotch and club soda into two glasses. It looked as if it were going to be too long a night for martinis.

When she put the glass on the table beside the bed, he didn't look up. 'Do you want something with it?' There was no answer. 'Some cheese or something?' He confided his answer to the pillow, but she thought it was no. 'Do you want more soda?'

He lifted his head but still didn't look at her. 'Just leave me alone.'

It was not the kind of answer she'd wait around to hear twice. She went into the living room and slammed her glass down on the coffee table. When she realized she was still wearing her jacket, she hung it in the front closet; then she went into the kitchen and filled the ice trays. The cat dish was empty, so she opened another can and refilled their water bowl, but neither Franklin nor Eleanor came at the sound of the electric opener. They were no fools. They knew what heavy steps, rattling hangers, and slamming cabinet doors meant. They were hiding under the bed just as Nick was hiding on top of it. And she'd been looking forward to coming home to Nick. They were right. He was a selfish bastard. Other men had kids. She remembered Matthew. He'd seen his children every weekend, but on Saturday nights, when he'd arrived at her apartment, he'd been exactly the same as when he'd come straight from seeing patients.

Katherine went back into the living room, sat down with her drink, and longed for the good old days, three days ago. She took a long swallow of the scotch. That's probably what Nick was thinking. Then let him go back to them. He'd never talked about the kids much before. Half a week out of the house and he was suddenly in the running for father of the year.

Maybe Erica had a point. She'd been crazy to let him move in. She'd had a perfectly nice life. Nick. Freedom. An apartment where she could type at midnight or get drunk alone and sing Cole Porter songs to the cats or simply sit in the living room without listening for sounds from the bedroom. Was he rattling ice cubes, turning pages, walking, snoring, breathing?

She went back into the bedroom. He'd made a dent in the drink, but he was still lying with his face in the pillow. Franklin had come out from under the bed and was curled up in the small of his back, the little Quisling. After taking a robe from the armoire and an old flannel granny nightgown from a drawer, she marched into the bathroom. She couldn't slam the door because of all those decades of paint. Bastard, she thought. Now I have to huddle in my own bathroom to get undressed.

When she came out, clutching her clothes in a pile, she noticed he'd progressed from his stomach to his back, if you could call that progress. He was staring at the ceiling, and his glass was empty.

'I'm sorry,' he said, but he didn't take his eyes from the overhead light, and his voice sounded exactly as it had when he'd told her to leave him alone.

She dropped her clothes on a chair and walked around to his side of the bed. 'Want me to freshen this?'

'Thanks,' he said without looking at her. When she returned to the bedroom, the television was on and he was propped up on his trusty pillows, pretending to watch a rerun of a sitcom. Or maybe he wasn't pretending. Who knew what went on in the mind of a catatonic father?

She sat on top of the quilt on her side of the bed. There was a considerable expanse of no-man's-land between them. She remembered the decisions of her adolescence before bucket seats became standard equipment. If you sat too close on the first date, you were fast. If you hugged the door, you were frigid. Listen, Nick, she wanted to say, I'm not that kind of girl. I can't sit here in bed with you all night in silence. But Nick was watching a commercial for toupees as if he expected a scalping before the night was out, and she found, as hairpieces gave way to mechanical exercising machines, which he needed about as much as he did a toupee, that she could sit there all night in silence. And she did.

Katherine's friends always said they envied her her mother. Nina Walden never nagged, rarely interfered, had always been understanding. 'The only problem,' Erica had joked more than once, 'is that your mother never gave you anything to rebel against.' Still, Nina Walden was human. She had her philosophical precepts and kernels of wisdom garnered over the years or handed down from her own mother that she occasionally felt obliged to share. One of them was that a husband and wife, or these days any facsimile thereof, should never go to bed, or at least to sleep, angry. On the first Sunday morning after Nick moved in, Katherine learned that her mother was wrong. How you went to sleep didn't matter, only how you woke up.

She'd gone to sleep a little after one with her back to Nick. He was watching John Wayne go back to Bataan, and she swore she wasn't going to forgive him. When she woke up a little before five, Nick was sleeping with his back to her. She wasn't going to forgive him, and as soon as he got up, she'd reclaim the bed, the apartment, and her freedom. She was still thinking that later in the morning when she felt his hand on her hip. At least she thought she felt it. It was hard to tell through the flannel nightgown and woolen robe. Katherine didn't move.

'I'm sorry.' Unlike last night, he sounded as if he were. She turned over so she was facing him. Those seismographic eyes were indecent. Couldn't he hide anything?

'You look awful.' It was true. His face was a charcoal sketch of itself with black smudges under the eyes and heavy shading around the jaw and upper lip. His skin looked paper white in the light filtering through the windows. Neither of them had closed the curtains the night before.

'You don't look so hot yourself.' His hand moved up to the tie of her robe. 'Were you expecting a fire during the night?'

'I thought disaster had already struck.'

He didn't say anything, but it wasn't because he was concentrating on finding his way through the layers of clothing. As she knew from experience, Nick could do more than one thing at a time.

'You're a bastard.'

He murmured something. It might have been confirmation. It might have been disagreement. Or it might have been commemoration of the fact that he'd managed to find his way through the layers of wool and flannel.

She could have kept arguing. And it wasn't those hands that were so devilishly clever with woolen robes and granny nightgowns or that damn hard fencer's body or even that mind that could do two things simultaneously that stopped her. At least it wasn't those things entirely. She didn't want to argue with Nick. She hadn't wanted to last night, and the fact that she had, or he had with her, or that they'd both sunk into silence didn't seem a valid reason for continuing to fight this morning.

'That isn't a solution,' Katherine said later that morning, when they were sitting in bed with the *Times* and coffee.

Nick looked up from the magazine section. 'I'm not doing the puzzle.'

'You know what I mean. You can't just say you're sorry and forget it.'

'I haven't forgotten it.'

'Neither have I.'

'Do you want to fight about it?'

'I'd like to discuss it.'

He was still holding the magazine section as if it were the last line of defense. 'Listen, Katie, something happened to me. I'm sorry I took it out on you, but that doesn't mean we have to spend the day analyzing it. Communicating. Sharing our feelings. Letting it all hang out.' He ran the litany in the same voice she used when she quoted Ego and Altruist.

'Clever son of a bitch, aren't you?'

He put down the magazine section and reached for her. 'Anyway, I think we communicate just fine. I think we're terrific communicators.'

When Katherine went away to college, her parents had instructed her to call collect every Sunday. She no longer called collect, and her timing was more erratic; but two weeks rarely went by without a phone conversation with her mother. When Nina called that Sunday afternoon, Nick answered because they'd finally roused themselves from bed and Katherine was in the shower. She turned off the water, and while she toweled herself, she listened to Nick going through the amenities of meeting the girl's family, circa 1980.

'Well, it's nice to meet you, too, "if only over the phone."'

'You sound as if you're at a goddamn cocktail party,' Katherine said as she wound the towel around her and came out of the bathroom. Nick ignored her.

'No, she's not busy. She was just . . . reading the paper.'

'For God's sake, Nick, if we live together, she knows you're here when I shower.'

He gave her a black look. 'I'm looking forward to meeting you in person, too, Mrs Sales.' He'd even remembered her mother's married name. If Katherine's father had been alive and telephoned, Nick probably would have called him sir. Katherine took the phone from him.

'I take it that the fact that Nick answers the phone on a Sunday afternoon means that he's there on a more permanent basis,' her mother said.

Katherine thought of last night and looked at Nick, who was pretending not to listen. 'For the moment.'

'I guess no one thinks in terms of permanency anymore. At least no one in your generation. Lillian Small was over for dinner last night. All she did was complain about her son's divorce.'

'Everyone always cries on your shoulder.'

'You don't.'

'I haven't got anything to cry about.' She saw Nick's lashes flutter at that, but he didn't raise his eyes from the paper.

'They why don't you sound happy? Did I call at a bad moment?'

Katherine said no and changed the subject, but her mother returned to it before they hung up. 'These things take awhile, Kate.' Katherine didn't ask what things, and her mother didn't say. 'And that's all the advice you're going to get from me today.'

Katherine's mother had implied that it took time for two people to adjust to each other. She hadn't said anything about others' adjusting to two people, though that, too, Katherine suspected, took time.

One morning the following week, as she was sorting the bills, flyers, and magazines that made up her mail, she found an envelope with the name of Cynthia's store in the upper left-hand corner and 'Greer' scrawled above it. Inside was a newspaper article with 'FYI' scribbled across the top margin. *A Workshop for Mixing Love and Money* the headline read. Katherine skimmed the article about 200 people, mostly couples, who had met to learn about prenuptial contracts, relationship planning, and the two-paycheck marriage, and put it on the side of her desk with the catalogues of things she'd never buy and the bills she'd put off paying. That was where Nick found it when he came home that night.

'Is this a hint?'

'Not from me. Cynthia sent it.'

'I should have known.' He stood beside the desk reading it. 'Listen to this. "According to a noted New York attorney" – your friend Cynthia underlined "noted New York attorney" – "finances and property rights are like sex. Refuse to discuss them, turn them into taboos, and they're sure to sabotage your relationship. Explore your own and your partner's feelings about them, and you'll experience new levels of understanding, trust, and pleasure."'

Katherine steeled herself for the diatribe against Cynthia, but when Nick looked up from the article, he was smiling. 'Hey, baby, want to go into the bedroom and discuss finances and property rights?'

She took the article from him and threw it in the wastebasket.

'Couldn't we just stay here? I mean, I know it sounds kinky, but well, I've always wanted to discuss finances and property rights on a desk.'

'Just remember, sweetheart, nothing's kinky between two consenting adults. Three if you count Cynthia.'

Of all Katherine's friends only Paige seemed to understand her reluctance to indulge in long evening telephone conversations now that Nick had moved in, or rather they all understood it, but only Paige approved of it. What she didn't approve of was the hour at which Nick returned home.

'He's the only attorney I know,' Paige said when she called one night at seven-thirty and Katherine did not settle down for a long talk, 'who gets home by seven every night.'

'Maybe he's a quick study.'

'Maybe, but I hope his partners recognize the fact.'

Katherine had picked up the phone in the kitchen, but she knew from experience that voices carried from there to the bedroom, where Nick was reading and watching the news simultaneously. Katherine told Paige something was burning, though there was nothing cooking, and got off the phone. She swore she wouldn't repeat the conversation to Nick. She didn't repeat it, only used it as a starting point.

'Do most people in your office work late every night?' she asked Nick during dinner.

'Who's asking, you or Paige?'

'I was just curious. She said most attorneys work very late.'

'Most do. That's one of the reasons I got out of that blue-chip firm that was about as big and as straight as the Republican party. It didn't matter how hard you worked, only how hard people thought you were working. Guys stayed till nine or ten to make sure other guys saw they were staying. When I found myself carrying an empty briefcase home at night, I knew I had to get out. Now I work late when I have to, and I carry a briefcase when there's something to put in it. And you can tell Paige that the firm is in no immediate danger of going under.'

'I wish you wouldn't make me sound so stupid.'

'Only suggestible, sweetheart.'

V

'Let me tell you about publishing parties,' Katherine said when she picked Nick up at his office. 'They're different from other parties. In fact, they aren't parties at all. More like primitive rites – mating dances for the powerful, tests by fire and alcohol for everyone else. Agents will talk to editors, subsidiary rights people will talk to reprinters, and the author will talk to his friends. At the end of the evening he'll feel his book is the event of the season – he'll be wrong; if it were, the party would be someplace swankier than his editor's apartment – and a couple of deals probably will have been made by people who never met the author and have no intention of reading his book.'

'And you'll be in a lousy mood.'

'We won't stay long enough for that.'

The door to the apartment where the party was launching both author and book was open, and guests were milling around it, spilling out into the hall and down toward the elevator. They might have been arriving or departing, but judging from the number of glasses clutched in hand, Katherine suspected they were merely trying to appear to be doing one or the other. For an industry that thrived on social contact, publishing was peopled by an inordinate number of men and women who swore they went out infrequently and then only under duress.

Katherine introduced Nick to a few people, but when the question of his profession came up, as it did almost immediately, and they discovered that he was a lawyer rather than one of that new breed of lawyer-agents, their eyes glazed over or began to roam the room for more fertile conversational soil.

'I can't win,' Nick said when he returned from his first trip to the bar with drinks for both of them. 'A girl at the bar asked me what I did, and I was so tired of boring people that I told her I was a writer. "Who isn't?" she said.'

'Next time say you make movies. Have you ever seen so many people working a room so hard?' But not everyone was working the room, at least not working it professionally, and on his way to the bar a second time Nick got waylaid by a girl who, Katherine thought, looked much too young to be out alone. It was then that Frank Reidy found his way to her side.

The worst thing you could say about Reidy was that he was dishonest; the best was that he was incompetent in his dishonesty. He had a habit of claiming to represent clients whom he did not represent. According to Erica, he'd once been on the verge of selling the memoirs of a notorious mass murderer until the editor, who was about to fork over what is called in the trade a six-figure advance, made a few inquiries and discovered that Reidy had no more access to the mass murderer than did the average tabloid reader. He did, however, have access to both Ego and Altruist and had been their agent ever since they'd burst upon the literary scene. Looking up at Reidy now, Katherine could only think they made a fitting, if unholy, triumvirate.

92

Over the years she'd come to divide the faces of drunks – and Erica and everyone else said Reidy was a drunk – into three categories. There were the soft ones that went suddenly slack, the beefy ones that grew florid and expanded like balloons, and the lean ones that turned mean. Reidy's face belonged to the last category.

'How's the sexiest ghost in town?' Everyone, including Reidy's wife, said he was a womanizer as well as a drunk, but Katherine didn't believe he was the former precisely because she knew he was the latter. Once she'd run into him on a midtown corner a little after three o'clock in the afternoon – that sobering moment when editors and agents are returning from the lunchtime romance of planning future deals to the office reality of evading phone calls about present deals – and Reidy had been so drunk he hadn't known who she was. They'd stood talking for a few minutes before he put the blurry face – at least she assumed it was blurry to him – together with the name on the contracts and the woman he'd seen in a meeting the previous week. Surely a serious womanizer would have to be more in command of his mind as well as his body.

'If you mean me, Frank, I'm fine.'

'Erica tells me you'll have Barry's novel finished soon, but she won't tell me when you'll be ready to start Leo's next book.'

Dr Leo Robbins, alias Ego, was not about to let his agent and his ghost convene without him, and he drifted over just in time to hear the last words. 'How's my little ghost doing?' He put an arm around her waist and gave her the sexy, macho smile. 'Rarin' to go?'

Katherine made a noncommittal sound. No point in burning the bridge until she'd decided that she really was going to try to swim the river.

'*Going the Distance.* How do you like that for a title? Frank thinks it's great.'

'Super,' Reidy corrected.

'What's the subtitle?' Katherine asked. There was always a subtitle.

'*How to Stay in the Race for Self-fulfillment When Everyone Around You Is Dropping by the Roadside.*'

'Super title,' Reidy repeated. 'Plays off the whole running thing. Echoes of the marathon.'

Katherine looked at Reidy. The face was no longer mean. He might try to get more than his 10 percent in commission, but she had to admit he gave 100 percent in support.

'This is going to be the biggest one yet,' Ego said. 'Wait till you hear the stuff on realizing your potential. It's sensational. I'm counting on you, Kate, to get it down right. Now that you've got your writing skills together.'

'I didn't know they'd been apart.'

'So when do we start work?' Ego asked, as if she hadn't spoken. Katherine had learned some time ago that he and Altruist rarely listened to her. She supposed that was their prerogative. Unlike their patients, she didn't pay.

Reidy was contemplating his glass. 'Kate isn't sure when she can start work.' He lifted his face to her and bared his teeth in a small, feral smile. 'At least that's what her agent says.' Reidy's eyes moved to Ego, and they exchanged a look of perfect understanding. It contained percentage points and dollar signs and a determination not to be taken by these two broads.

'Obviously this isn't something we can discuss here.' Ego wrinkled his forehead until his hairline and eyebrows came dangerously close to meeting.

Then his face relaxed, and he gave Katherine's waist another squeeze. 'Don't wait too long, Kate. The material for this one is so hot I don't want to give it a chance to cool off.' Ego drifted off, leaving his agent to deal with the distasteful matter of ghosts who were beginning to think they were authors and demanding to be paid as such. As an artist he would not stoop to bargain.

'You heard what Leo said,' Reidy told her. 'I wouldn't wait too long to get started.'

'You mean now that I've got my writing skills together?'

Reidy's eyes were opaque. Ego was his client. 'Leo's name is worth millions. Ghosts are a dime a dozen.'

'And you're working on getting the price down to eight cents.'

He leaned over until the long, mean face was next to her ear. 'That's why, as an agent, I'm so fuckin' good, babe. And so good fucking.'

Katherine drew away from him. 'Dorothy Parker said it first. And better.'

Reidy looked down at her with a corrupt smile. 'Who's Dorothy Parker?'

It was impossible to tell whether or not he was kidding.

Guests were crowding the living room now like angels determined to get the answer about the head of that pin, and it took Katherine a little time to find Nick. He was sitting on a bench in the entrance hall with the girl, who looked every bit as young close up as she did from a distance. Nick interrupted his lecture on the connection between certain law firms and the editors of certain law reviews to introduce them. The girl explained she'd been working as an editorial assistant for the last year – secretary,

Katherine translated – and had decided to go back to school.

'Publishing isn't anything like what I thought it would be. Nobody talks about the books, only about how much money they paid for them,' the girl was saying as Altruist descended upon them.

Katherine always found the first sight of Dr Barry Greene shocking. When she spoke to him on the phone, as she did constantly when they were working on a book, she pictured him as he'd been when she'd first met him. On the infrequent occasions when she came face-to-face with him, she realized how much he'd changed. The old Altruist had been an oversized teddy bear of a man with a big, soft stomach that pulled against his print nylon shirts and spilled over the waistband of his baggy trousers. His head had been a bald globe circled by a corona of yellow hair that covered his ears demurely, his face florid and fleshy, and his smile ready. There had been something almost endearing in the way he seemed to wallow in his own physical awkwardness. But that had been the old Barry Greene, a man with a modest suburban practice, a doctorate in psychology from what sounded very much like an agricultural college, and a single article in an obscure journal to his writing credit. The new Barry Greene was the author of three novels that had met with, as the jackets said, critical and popular acclaim. He'd moved his office to Park Avenue, taken the framed diploma off the wall, and traded the wife to whom he'd dedicated the first book for the girl he'd hired as a free-lance publicist to promote the second. He'd also shed forty pounds, replaced the old baggy clothes with narrow shirts worn open to reveal three gold chains where once creases of flesh had nestled, and shaved the corona of hair. His second wife had confided to him, Altruist had confided to Katherine, that bald men really were more virile.

Altruist's eyes flickered from the girl to Nick before coming to rest on Katherine. 'I was hoping you'd be here, Kate. I had a dynamite idea for the end of the book during my last hour.'

Katherine pictured some poor patient pouring out her heart on Altruist's couch – and emptying her purse into Altruist's coffers – while he did diabolical plot twists in his head. She also pictured the manuscript of *Crisis* she'd delivered to the typist two days ago.

'It came to me just like that,' Altruist said, turning his back on Nick and the girl in order to pursue the problems of plot and character, form and content in privacy. 'I think it would be relevant if we made her pregnant at the end. Then she'd have to choose between having another baby in mid-life or pursuing her new career.' Over Altruist's shoulder Katherine saw Nick and the girl move off in the direction of the bar. 'Or maybe she could decide to do both and the husband could show how far his consciousness had been raised by offering to stay home with the baby while she went out to work. Now that's a dynamite idea! I know it's been done with younger men, but think of having a guy in his forties, a successful guy in his forties, decide to give up his career and opt for full-time fathering. The more I think about it, the more I like it.'

Katherine could mount several arguments against this dynamite idea, but experience had taught her that with Altruist the most concrete were the most successful. 'We performed a vasectomy on the husband in Chapter Two. The operation was successful and, according to you, entirely painless.'

'Well, what about the lover?'

'She said good-bye to him two hundred and seventy-five pages ago.'

'Oh.' Plot intricacies were not Altruist's long suit. 'There's always a sperm bank. I'm really into mid-life childbearing. Women are experiencing pregnancy later in life, and it's the only base we haven't touched in the book.'

Katherine started to say that they hadn't covered rape or euthanasia either but realized the joke was too dangerous. Dynamite, he'd say. We could have her raped and then pregnant. We could put the husband on life-support systems. 'Look, Barry, why don't you read what we have? If you're unhappy with the ending, we can talk about it then.'

'Fair enough,' Altruist said, and took a shrimp from a tray held by one of those undergraduates-turned-waiter who, it seemed to Katherine, worked every party these days, dispensing hors d'oeuvres and arrogant disapproval in equal measure. 'Anyway' – he mopped a drop of cocktail sauce from the curly yellow hair on his chest – 'I'm hot to get going on the next one. You're not going to believe the idea.' Katherine assured him she'd believe it. 'I figure I've covered women's emotional problems pretty thoroughly. I understand women – I'm probably more liberated than you are – and I've done a lot of good. And that's where it's at. Doing good. Big advances and best-seller lists are okay, but what counts is that my books help people. I got a letter from a girl the other day—'

'You were going to tell me about the next book.' It was important to intercept Altruist immediately because if there were two conversational balls he could run with, they were the therapeutic value of his books and letters from his fans.

'A behind-the-scenes look at a therapist's life.' He

stopped as if waiting for a reaction, but when she gave none, he seemed to understand. She was rendered speechless by the brilliance of the idea. 'The American public is dying to know what really goes on in a therapist's private life. You know, his marriage, his children—'

'His remarriage.'

'That, too,' he said solemnly, and stopped another waiter for a second shrimp. 'I don't want to hurt anyone, but I have to write the truth. This will be an important book for me as well as my public, Kate. I want to see how I've grown as a writer.'

About the way Charlie McCarthy grew as a comedian.

'I plan to give you a lot more input in this one. I can't expect you to understand the motivations and human behaviors . . .'

What was this, Katherine wondered, the cocktail party version of Chinese water torture? *Ghosts are a dime a dozen.* Drip. *Now that you've got your writing skills together.* Drip. *I want to see how I've grown as a writer.* Drip.

'The expression is human behavior. Singular.' She took the last swallow of her drink, and as she did, she noticed that Nick and the fledgling law student had returned to the bench in the foyer. 'Or collective or something like that. "Human behaviors" is psychologists' jargon.'

He looked at her as if he didn't quite recognize her. 'Well, sure, Kate. That's what I keep you around for. You're the writer.'

'I thought you wanted to see how you'd grown as one.'

This time he didn't just look at her. He established what she was sure he called eye contact. When he spoke, his voice was like Noxzema on sunburnt skin.

'You seem to be feeling a lot of anger tonight, Kate. You wouldn't by any chance be pre-menstrual?'

This time it was Katherine who established eye contact. 'You underestimate yourself, Barry. It isn't just the female mind you understand. You've got the body down pat, too.'

She moved off quickly before he could begin to explain – she knew he'd have an explanation – and found Nick at the bar. 'Are you having another or are you ready to leave?'

'Whenever you are.'

'What happened to Little Bo Peep?'

'Went home to get started on her law school applications.'

'Didn't she want help?'

Nick smiled, and for a moment she wasn't sure if he was going to speak or crow. 'She suggested it.'

When Katherine had left the party, she'd been sure she'd made her decision, or rather Ego and Altruist had made it for her, but by the following evening, when her desk was covered with notes scribbled on yellow legal pads and the wastebasket was filled with more of the same, she'd begun to wonder. Maybe Ego wasn't so impossible, or Altruist so absurd. Then Nick arrived home and dropped a large manila envelope on her desk.

'Arrived by messenger this afternoon, but the elevator man said he didn't have time to bring it up. Do you want a drink?'

Katherine said she did and opened the envelope. The covering letter began 'Dear Kate' and ended 'Best, Dr Robbins'. Katherine remembered 'The Name Game and How to Win It' from Ego's first book. In between the salutation and the closing Ego explained that he knew they hadn't settled anything yet, but he was so excited about the new book and was so sure she'd be when she saw the outline that he'd decided to shoot it right up to her.

'What is it?' Nick asked as he put her drink down on the desk. She handed him the folder, and he began to leaf through it. 'He must be kidding.'

'I wish he were. That's what he calls the philosophical germ of the book. I'm supposed to turn it into an epidemic.'

'Listen to this. "Freedom. Tell reader must make own." He underlines "make" three times. "Give example of ways. (One) Go to office barefoot. (Two) Dance in streets. (Three)—" Oh, come on, Katie, he can't be serious.'

'"Wear a prophylactic on your nose,"' she finished for him. 'Every one of Ego's books has a section on freedom, and that seems to be his idea of it. I guess he keeps hoping I'll use it.'

Nick picked up his drink and, still carrying the folder, moved to the couch. 'What's all this stuff? Little Francie Frigid and Little Izzy Insecure?'

'He seems to think his allegorical characters are cuter than case histories. They go the way of the prophylactics. I take the point and make up a case history. There's a Nick in the last book and a Gwen in the last two.'

'What was wrong with Gwen?'

'Once she was a closet eater; the other time she was pathologically shy.'

'Struck out both times. What was wrong with Nick?'

'A rigid personality who couldn't express his feelings.'

He put the folder on the coffee table. 'What are you going to do about it?'

'You mean about this so-called book?'

He squinted across the room at her, though he was not nearsighted. 'I didn't mean about my so-called rigid personality.'

She ran her hand through her hair. 'I thought I knew this morning, but now I'm not so sure.'

'If you're doing it just for the money, you don't have to. I can cover the rent for a while and maybe even throw in a takeout Chinese dinner.'

'Is that a complaint about my cooking?'

'Are you kidding? Nobody can open a can of soup the way you do. Stop changing the subject.'

Katherine looked at the mess on her desk. 'The money's only part of it. What if I can't do it?'

'Then you go back to ghosting.'

'Thanks a lot.'

'You want me to say I know you can do it?' He stood, walked around the desk to the back of her chair, and put his hands on her shoulders. 'She may look like a dumb strawberry blonde to you, friends, but here is one of the all-time greats of the writing biz. The scope of Tolstoy. The psychological insight of Dostoevsky. The sensitivity of Proust. And the power of Hemingway.'

'Do you realize you didn't mention a single woman?'

'My apologies.' He slid his hands down her sweater. 'And the tits of Jane Austen.'

'If you're so damn funny, you write . . .'

'Try it, Katherine. Just try it.'

VI

Katherine got down to work. As the parks department workers raked up the last vestiges of autumn color and the city turned the unrelenting gray it would remain all winter, as Paige stepped up her auction schedule, Erica increased her business lunches to four a week, Beth autographed books in shopping centers across the metropolitan area, and Cynthia girded herself for the Christmas rush, Katherine worked. She worked all week, and sometimes she worked on Saturdays when Nick saw his kids, and she might as well have worked on Saturday nights because he still didn't require or even want her company when he returned from seeing them. She worked even when she didn't seem to be working. Ideas, words, and phrases came to her at odd times. One afternoon at the butcher's where she was treated with more deference now that she no longer bought that badge of the single life, one lamb chop, four lines came to her that were destined, she was sure, to win the American Book Award. Two days later, as she was cutting through a maze of double-parked cars, she came face-to-face with the impossibility of the first paragraph as it now stood.

Wherever she went, her index cards went along. She made notes of people she saw on the street, conversations she overheard on the bus, the way the traffic lights looked one night when she and Nick were coming home from the movies in the rain. There were blank cards all over the apartment, in the kitchen, the bedroom, even the bathroom in case of an emergency. 'It's like Freud and his dreams,' she told Nick. 'If you don't write something down immediately, you're likely to lose it.' It never occurred to her that it might be disconcerting to have someone break off a conversation in mid-sentence to make a note or reach for the cards on her night table first thing in the morning the way some people do for a cigarette. Erica gave her a flashlight pen for making notes in the middle of the night, but that disappeared mysteriously after a few days. Then Nick began making his own contributions. 'Boy meets girl, boy loses girl, boy gets girl' was printed on a card in the medicine cabinet. 'Happy families are all alike' met her one morning in the refrigerator. 'The butler did it' was tucked into her sweater drawer. In among the cans of cat food she found 'Let me tell you about the rich. They are different from you and me.' One night when she went to make drinks, she found 'Yes, she was a true blonde' propped up against the gin bottle.

She carried the card into the bedroom, where Nick was sprawled out in his proper Brooks Brothers oxford shirt and proper Brooks Brothers striped boxer shorts. Franklin was on his stomach, and they were watching the evening news. She handed him the card. 'I don't get this one.'

'Didn't you read Mickey Spillane when you were a kid?'

'I never got further than *The Amboy Dukes*.'

'That was *haute* literature compared to Spillane.'

'It was the only book my mother ever took away from me.'

'And you call yourself an educated woman. I knew that finishing school didn't teach you anything. We used to pass Mickey Spillane around. Until the pages got stuck together.'

'And you say Altruist's sick.'

'I said Altruist ought to be locked up for making obscene phone calls.'

'He made another one yesterday. Only it wasn't very obscene. First we discussed, or rather he told me at length, who he wants to star in the movie of his latest opus. Forget the fact that it hasn't been sold to the movies and that if it is, he'll have nothing to say about anything. When the second book was bought by the movies, he actually put a director's chair in his office. Then he got to what he'd really called about. Now that I was working on my own book, I wasn't going to mention to anyone that I'd ghosted his, was I?'

'What'd you say?'

'I told him ghosts are like gentlemen. We never kiss and tell.'

By the first week in December Katherine had finished two chapters and an outline. She showed Nick the neatly typed manuscript but didn't ask him to read it.

'Is that all there is?'

'Erica doesn't want any more. Apparently it's *déclassé*, to say nothing of foolhardy, to write the book before you sell it. She said half the editors don't read anyway, and if you give them too much to look at, it just puts them off. According to her, in Hollywood you don't even give them anything on paper. You just talk the idea.'

'Are you going to let me read it?'

'Not yet. I've just about screwed up my courage for Erica's professional opinion. I'm not ready for your personal one.'

'You mean you don't think I can give it an unbiased reading?'

'I mean, I don't think I can give you an unbiased hearing. If you don't like it, I'll cry. If you say you do, I won't believe you.'

Erica couldn't wait to see the outline and pages. She told Katherine, who called the morning after she'd shown them to Nick, to bring them down that afternoon. Katherine was on her way out the door when Nick called.

He began to explain something about a client he had to see that evening, then stopped. 'Listen, Katie, I'll call you right back. David's on the phone.' David was his older son.

Katherine sat at her desk, opened her coat, and waited. She could hear as well as feel the heat from the radiator behind her. She debated taking off her coat. She considered calling Nick from the lobby of Erica's building. The phone finally rang.

'I'm sorry.' He sounded inconsolable, but she had a feeling it had nothing to do with keeping her waiting.

'How's David?'

'He's in a piano recital tonight.'

'I thought he played the flute.'

'That's Mark. David plays the piano.' He sounded like a teacher with a slow and not particularly winning child.

'Sorry.'

'I don't know what to do.'

'About what?'

'I told you. The recital tonight.'

'I thought you had to see a client tonight.'

106

'That's why I feel so lousy.'

She ran a sweaty hand through her hair. 'You never took piano recitals that seriously when you were living at home.' A semantic error. This was supposed to be home.

'That's the point. I was living with them then.' He hadn't said 'home', but Nick could think on his feet. Only he probably wasn't on his feet now. She could picture him sitting behind the big desk with all the Mark Cross leather accessories that Gwen had bought him over the years. At least she assumed Gwen had bought them. She hadn't asked that first time he'd taken her to his office. It wasn't a very large office, but all those impressive legal tomes on the shelves made it look substantial. Much too substantial, she'd said, for what he had in mind. Not that he'd taken her to his office for immoral purposes. They'd planned to go back to her apartment for that. But they'd gone out to dinner and stopped at his office afterward, and while Katherine had been examining all those leather accoutrements on his desk, he'd been examining her, and when she'd looked up and seen those eyes that were no good at hiding anything she'd known exactly what he was thinking. She'd said they could go back to her apartment; but he'd just smiled, and they'd managed to work up a considerable passion on that brown leather couch that reeked of cigarette smoke and big deals where businesses were saved and corporations thwarted. It had been that night on the couch she'd been thinking of at lunch when Erica had teased her, but she knew from Nick's voice that he wasn't thinking of it now.

'It's only a piano recital, Nick. No one was ever marred for life by a piano recital.'

'You don't understand.' It was an accusation that

left no room for explanations.

'I understand how you feel. I'm just trying to be rational.'

'Try being rational with an eight-year-old kid.'

I can't manage it with a thirty-eight-year-old man, she thought, but Nick went on as if she'd taken up enough of his precious time. 'I'll be late tonight. About ten or eleven.' He didn't say if he'd be late because of the client or because of the recital, and she wasn't going to ask.

Katherine buttoned her coat again and looked at her watch. She'd planned to go by bus as part of her new frugality program, but now she had to take a cab.

In the lobby of Erica's building an early Christmas tree decorated entirely in red bows projected a businesslike image of festivity.

'I can't wait to read it,' Erica said when Katherine handed over the slim sheaf of papers.

'I bet you say that to all your clients.'

'I do, but I mean it with you. I have a screening tonight, but I'll get to it as soon as I get home. You aren't by any chance widowed, are you?'

'As a matter of fact, that's exactly what I am tonight.'

'Is D'Artagnan down in the Village, fencing again? Why can't he go to the Harvard Club and play squash like everyone else?'

'Because he isn't like everyone else.'

'You're as bad as my benighted ex-husband. He has a penchant for juveniles, and you talk like one. Go kill half an hour shopping, or lock yourself in the library and read our other clients' books until I'm ready to leave.'

Invitations to screenings were always for two, and

over the years Erica had taken Katherine to a good many of them. She'd come to enjoy the ritual as much as the movie, sometimes more than the movie.

The screening rooms were small but comfortable oases in slightly down-at-the-heel office buildings on the West Side. They were always filled with people and gossip it was Erica's business to know. One editor had been fired, a second had just got his own imprint, and one house was about to take over another. The lights went down to a whispered chorus of 'Let's have lunch'. Once or twice people had mistaken Katherine at Erica's side for someone who mattered and whispered 'lunch' to her.

During the movie there were few comments, fewer even than in a regular theater because they were guests, and there was almost no aroma of marijuana. Katherine enjoyed the twin absences, but the time she looked forward to most was the aftermath of the screening of a bad movie. The crowds standing in the small upstairs lobbies waiting for elevators were like classrooms full of kids waiting to be let out for recess; only instead of energy, they were bursting with one-liners. As they spilled out of the elevators and onto the street, the quips crackled in the night air like softballs off a bat.

Erica matched puns with an editor and gags with another agent, and then she and Katherine walked a few blocks south to an inexpensive French restaurant in the theater district that had changed less since their first days in New York than they had. 'Hearty bourgeois fare,' one magazine had written years ago. 'For hearty bourgeois girls,' they used to joke because at that time they'd been secretly sure they were anything but.

'If we're going to have dinner in silence,' Erica said when they were halfway through a first drink,

'I'll get my briefcase from the checkroom and start on your manuscript.'

Katherine had been thinking about Nick, as she had through a good part of the movie. Unlike Erica, the movie had not required her full attention. If he'd seen the client, he'd come home feeling guilty about David. Either face in the pillow or eyes fixed catatonically on the television screen. She was beginning to think that instead of getting him a drink, she ought to hook up an IV to the scotch bottle. If he'd gone to the recital, he'd come home worried about the client, in which case there'd be limited life signs in the form of a passionate interest in the eleven o'clock news.

Katherine looked across the table at Erica. She'd pushed her glasses up on her hair, and there were faint shadows beneath her eyes where the cover-up makeup had worn away. 'When you and Michael split up, was he very guilty about the kids?'

'That bastard? The only guilt he's ever heard of is spelled g-i-l-t, and having been trained in the Bauhaus tradition, he doesn't believe in it.' Erica leaned forward, her elbows on the table. Her eyes were paler than the shadows unfortunately, but they were very sympathetic. 'I take it Nick is feeling guilty about his kids.'

'He stops just this side of self-flagellation.'

'Does he talk about it?'

'He talks about the kids all the time. David – that's the older one – plays the piano. Mark plays the flute. I thought I was going to be charged with a felony when I got their instruments mixed up this afternoon. David's the analytic one. Mark's the intuitive one. They're both brilliant, of course. David's Olympic material. Mark isn't as good at sports, but he's a born leader.'

'Was he always like that?'

'Until two months ago all I knew was that Nick had two kids he took to the beach on weekends. He also had a Sunfish he took to the beach on weekends.' She must have spoken louder than she'd meant to because a man at the bar who'd stared when they'd come in, and stared harder when Erica had taken off her coat, turned to look at them again. 'I know I'm making too much of it. He's bound to calm down after he gets used to things, but in the meantime, it's driving me crazy. I dread Saturday nights. The apartment's like a wake when he gets home – with Nick as the corpse. And I never know when it's going to strike during the week. It's like living with a reformed alcoholic and waiting for him to fall off the wagon. Only Nick doesn't stagger in drunk. He stalks in angry.'

Erica signaled the waitress for another round of drinks, though Katherine had been ready to order. 'Why's he angry at you?'

'I didn't mean he was angry at me. He's obviously angry at himself. I just happen to be the only other human in the apartment.'

'So he takes it out on you.'

The waitress brought fresh drinks and took away their empty glasses. It was after nine. Katherine hadn't eaten much during the day, and she was feeling the gin. She was also regretting that she'd started to talk about Nick. 'He doesn't take it out on me. Forget it, Erica. I had to bitch to someone, and now that I have, I feel better.'

'At least until Saturday.'

Katherine thought of her typewriter with longing. There you simply painted over the words with a white liquid, and they disappeared.

'Listen, Kat. No, wait a minute. I can't hold these

111

things the way I used to.' Erica pointed to the empty glass, got up, and walked to the ladies' room, and the man at the bar followed her with his eyes. 'Listen, Kat,' she said again when she returned, and Katherine knew Erica had been thinking of what she was going to say the entire time she was gone. 'I know you thought I was hard on Nick at first. All right, not just at first. And I admit I was wrong about his not leaving his wife and not caring about you. He's left his wife. And he seems to care about you. But that's no excuse for using you. Or rather men seem to think it's the best excuse for using you.'

'He's not using me.'

'You're the one who talked about Saturday night wakes and living with an alcoholic. A mixed metaphor – unless you're Irish. I'm not telling you to leave Nick. Or rather throw him out. I couldn't live with him, but that doesn't mean you can't. All I'm saying is that you seem more depressed tonight than you ever did when you were seeing him a couple of times a week. And if you aren't happy living with someone, what's the point?'

What was the point? Katherine wondered when she got home a little before midnight and found Nick already asleep. She was quiet getting ready for bed because she didn't want to wake him, though she had the feeling that if she did, he'd pretend she hadn't.

In the faint light from the bathroom she looked at the keys and pens and coins that he always left on top of the dresser. There was no indication of whether he'd seen the client or gone to the recital. She got into bed with her back to Nick. Whichever he'd done, he could still find a way of taking it out on her. His absence was ruining the kids' lives. His guilt about his absence was ruining his work. And she'd caused his absence. At least that was the way he made it seem when he withdrew from her like some goddamn photosensitive plant closing up for the night. Erica was right. What was the point of living with someone if you were happier living without him?

The next morning Katherine awakened before the alarm went off. Her anxiety about Nick's moods was as finely tuned as any digital clock. Eleanor must have sensed that she was up because she jumped on the bed and began cleaning Katherine's hair as if it were her own coat. That isn't affection, Katherine thought, only hunger. You want breakfast. She'd been sleeping with her back to Nick, but he must have sensed the cat's movement because Katherine felt him stir behind her, then reach one arm around her. She didn't move, but her mind was clicking off probabilities. The arm might mean everything was all right. I've returned to the land of the living. It might mean, though this was unlikely, I'm sorry I took it out on you yesterday afternoon. Or it might mean that Eleanor had disturbed his sleep and his arm had moved in reflex. Perhaps Eleanor had triggered a dream as well as a reflex and Nick thought he was lying there with an arm around the lovely Gwen. She'd know the answer in a moment when the alarm went off. If he got up and went straight into the bathroom without looking at her, she was in for another day of ostracism.

The alarm went off, and she silenced it quickly. He groaned. No clue there. He groaned every morning when the alarm went off.

Several seconds passed, and Katherine felt the muscles in her arms and legs growing tense. 'Did

113

you sleep well?' he asked finally. A clue – he was speaking to her – but not much of a clue since it was what he said every morning. And he always sounded like Cary Grant when he said it, though he wasn't doing imitations, only assuming his public persona. His habits were infuriating, but his manners were decent. She made an ambivalent sound and waited for the next clue. This one was unmistakable. She felt one of his legs between her own. Katherine stopped figuring probabilities. Nick could do two things simultaneously, but he couldn't wear two faces. When he retreated, he did it wholeheartedly. He didn't talk to her, didn't touch her, didn't even look at her. When he returned, he returned with a vengeance. Nick, Katherine had learned in the last two months, was a great one for homecomings.

'How did you sleep?' she asked. If he could do Cary Grant at this hour, she could muster a little Myrna Loy.

He reached his other leg around hers and caught her knee so she was forced to turn to him. 'Like a proverbial baby.'

'I'm going to be late again tonight,' he said an hour later. He was rushing because he was late now, and the red and yellow paisley tie he was knotting over the blue striped shirt made Katherine think he might be color-blind.

'That doesn't go,' she said.

He shrugged and buttoned the vest over the tie. 'I have to see that client.'

'How was the recital?' she asked as she followed him from the bedroom to the front door.

'Off-key. Ten eight-year-olds mangling Chopin and Rodgers and Hammerstein. You couldn't tell which was which.'

114

'Sounds like fun.'

'It was awful,' he said blissfully. 'I'll call you this afternoon.'

After Nick left for the office, Katherine showered and dressed and drank a cup of coffee while staring at the phone. Then she made the bed, cleaned up the bathroom, and concentrated on not looking at the phone. Erica had said she'd call as soon as she'd finished the pages.

Katherine had read more than she wanted to in the *Times* about the decline of reading levels among college freshmen, the increase of theft in the suburbs, and the high rate of suicide during the holiday season, when the phone finally rang. It was Paige.

'Hi, my name is Paige Richmond. You probably don't remember me, but we went to school together. So did our husbands. Or rather my husband and your ex-husband.'

'Okay, I'm sorry. I know I haven't called, but I haven't called anyone.'

'Is living in sin that time-consuming?'

'I've been working. In fact, I delivered fifty-five miraculous pages and an outline to Erica yesterday. I'm waiting to hear from her now.'

'I'll get right off. I just wanted to know if you felt like shopping today. I plan to get a running start on Christmas.'

It was better, Katherine thought, than sitting in the apartment staring at the phone, but the phone rang again almost as soon as she'd put it down.

'It's good,' Erica said. 'It's fine.'

'You really liked it?'

'There are a couple of things I might suggest changing, but they're so minor we can worry about them later.'

'Does that mean you're going to send it out the way it is?'

'I already have. The messenger is winging his way downtown even as we speak.' Erica mentioned the name of a small publisher.

'Why them? I mean, I'm not complaining. Just curious.'

Erica laughed. 'Did you want an auction like Beth's?' Beth's publisher, she and Erica had decided a year and a half ago, did not properly appreciate her talents, so on her last book they'd refused the offer of a perfectly respectable $85,000, submitted the partial manuscript to several other houses, and come out with a $150,000 advance.

'I may have wanted an auction, but I didn't expect one. After all, Beth Sarmie's a household word. Katherine Walden's like one of those emerging third world nations, only easier to pronounce.'

'I sent it there because it's a small house, so you don't get lost in the shuffle, but it's part of a bigger publishing group, so you get the distribution and the clout.' Katherine liked the way that sounded. She'd never had clout. 'And because it's perfect for Sydney Hellerman.'

'I thought you wanted a woman editor.'

'Sydney is a woman. Did you see the ad in this morning's paper for the book on the old girls' network and how to use it? That's Sydney's book.'

'I don't think I'm aggressive enough for her.'

'As long as your book is. And speaking of aggression, how's Nick this morning?'

'Nick's not aggressive.'

'Withdrawal is the thinking man's aggression, Kat. That's one thing I learned from eleven years of marriage to Michael. When I bought red towels for

116

his black-and-white bathroom, he didn't speak to me for three days.'

'Erica liked it,' Katherine said to Paige when they met later that morning on the second floor of Tiffany's. Paige was wearing a camel's hair polo coat and low-heeled brown boots with brass hardware that stopped just short of spurs, and she did in fact look as if she'd left her hockey, or rather her polo, stick at the door. 'She's already sent it out.'

Paige looked up from the cuff links the salesman had spread over the little velvet tray on the counter. 'Sent it out?'

'Submitted it to a publisher.'

'Congratulations.'

'There's nothing to con—'

'Do you think these are too flashy? Stanley doesn't wear French cuffs often, and I don't want him to look as if he hangs around gambling casinos.'

Katherine looked at the pair of cuff links Paige was holding and the three other pairs on the tray. 'I like the plain silver with the kind of stripe better. My father had a pair like that.'

'The gold and silver barbells look more expensive.'

'The gold and silver barbells are more expensive.'

'I'll take these.' Paige handed the barbells to the salesman, took a Mark Cross card case from her bag, and leafed through it until she found the right charge card. 'Do you want to look for anything while we're here?' When Katherine said she didn't, Paige decided they'd head downtown and stop in at Cynthia's office. 'I found a magnificent velvet smoking jacket for Stanley. It's five hundred dollars, but Cynthia offered to let me use her discount. Now that I've got the house exactly the way I want it, Stanley really ought to have a smoking jacket. Can't you see him in front of the fire?' Katherine said she could, but she knew from the look on Paige's face that her image wasn't nearly as vivid as Paige's.

Cynthia rarely closed the door to her office and when she saw Katherine and Paige in the hall, she motioned them in and went on screaming into the phone. 'I don't care if your whole goddamn company is home with the flu, Harry. You promised me that merchandise Tuesday. This is Wednesday. Do I have to tell you how many days till Christmas, too? If those robes aren't here by tomorrow afternoon, that's it, Harry. Don't count on another order from me. Ever.' Cynthia slammed the receiver down, but when she looked up, she was smiling. It was the old knowing smile etched a little deeper with pride. She leaned back in her swivel chair and stretched out sturdy legs that, like Cynthia, had been under wraps for ten years. No more pants, she'd announced, now that she had to project a professional image. 'That ought to show the bastard.'

'Which bastard?' Katherine pushed one of the nightgowns hanging on a rack over her chair out of the way.

'My boss. He called me in the other day. "Listen, doll," he said. "You wanna be a housewife or you wanna be a buyer? You wanna be a housewife? Go home and play nice with your professor husband. You wanna be a buyer? Then cut the crap and stop making nice with the vendors. You gotta be an animal, doll. A fuckin' animal." Eloquent prick, isn't he? Well, I'll show him I can be as much an animal as he can.'

'Why would you want to?' Paige asked.

Cynthia gave her an impatient look from under the long yellow bangs.

'Maybe there's something wrong with me,' Paige

said after they'd left Cynthia and gone across the street to a coffee shop for sandwiches. Paige had appropriated Cynthia's discount, but she was having more difficulty with her philosophy.

'Because you don't want to be a fuckin' animal?' Katherine asked after they'd ordered.

'We went to a dinner party last night. A proctologist who refers a lot of patients to Stanley. There were three other couples. One of the women was in law school, another was getting her master's in family counseling, and the third ran a nostalgia boutique. You should have seen their eyes roll back in their heads when they heard Timmy was in school and I did, as the nostalgia lady succinctly put it, nothing. "But how do you fill up your day?" she asked. "Not by selling Mickey Mouse watches for a hundred dollars a pop," I told her.'

'Good for you.'

'Well, I didn't exactly say it. She's the proctologist's wife, and Stanley would have killed me.'

Katherine patted Paige's hand. 'That's okay. It's like sinning. Intention counts, too.'

'You know, Kate, sometimes I think you're the only one of the group I still feel comfortable with. Cynthia thinks I'm a feminist Benedict Arnold. Erica's just waiting for Stanley to leave me for some succulent young med student so she can say, "I told you so". And to Beth I'm just part of the great unwashed public.' Paige sipped her coffee, and her face turned bitter. 'I have no *power*.'

Katherine remembered Erica's words that morning. She wouldn't mind having clout if she didn't have to become a fuckin' animal to get it. 'Maybe you make them uncomfortable because you're content with your life.' There was at least a kernel of truth to the statement, and Paige must have found more than that because the wide mouth relaxed until the small lines around the corners disappeared.

'How are things with Nick?'

'Fine,' Katherine said. She wasn't going to make the same mistake she had with Erica.

'Have you met his kids yet?'

'No, thank God.'

'You're going to have to meet them eventually.'

'Eventually is soon enough. Kids don't like me.'

'Don't be ridiculous. Tim's crazy about you.'

There wasn't even a kernel of truth in Paige's reassurance, and Katherine wondered if friends lied to make each other feel better or simply to avoid being embarrassed by the truth themselves.

'I don't understand what Nick's waiting for.'

'I think he wants them to get used to his leaving.'

'Doesn't he realize the position he's putting you in? It's degrading for him to pretend you don't exist.'

'He doesn't pretend I don't exist. He just doesn't discuss me with two little boys. Anyway, I'd rather spend my Saturdays with friends or working than at Little League games.'

'Baseball season's over, Kate.'

'See, I told you I'm no good with kids.'

'I still don't think it's fair to you.'

'Maybe not, but it sure is easier on me.'

Nick's Saturday arrangements may have been easier for Katherine, but though she realized the lack of logic behind her feelings, they were also annoying to her. They made her feel like an X-rated movie. Katherine Walden is not fit for minors, even when accompanied by parents. She was brooding on the problem and telling herself she was foolish to brood on it the Saturday after she'd had lunch with Paige. She'd spent the day shopping alone because that was the only way she could accomplish anything, and she'd ended up accomplishing a great deal, including tennis sweaters for her mother and stepfather, movie posters and records by peculiar-sounding groups for Beth's and Erica's kids, and some antique maps of New York that she'd been all over town to find for Nick. She was pleased with her progress, to say nothing of her expertise when she snatched a cab from a couple dressed entirely in leather and fur, but that peculiar blend of guilt and triumph every New Yorker feels at having beaten his fellowman to a taxi disappeared as soon as she was inside it. Her watch said six-thirty, and Nick was bound to be home. If she were lucky, he'd be watching an old movie rather than lying facedown in the pillow.

For an intelligent man Nick had an astonishing penchant for mindless activity. At first she'd thought nights spent watching westerns and war epics, transmitted from Boston and Atlanta by the miracle of modern cable television and accompanied by strange commercials and incorrect weather forecasts, were Nick's idea of atonement for the sin of leaving his sons. Gradually she'd come to realize that he actually enjoyed watching John Wayne save America from its native inhabitants and potential invaders. He reminded her of a religious fanatic who enjoyed the penance more than the sin. But she was prepared for him this week. She'd bought herself two new paperbacks.

Only she wasn't prepared for Nick because he was not lying on the bed with his eyes glued to the television screen but standing vertical in the kitchen, opening a can of cat food. He'd never done that before. Franklin must have taken him by the hand and led him to the cabinet.

'I thought I'd start dinner.' He dumped the contents of the can into the dish. Katherine noticed that it was encrusted with the remains of the food she'd given the cats that morning, but she wasn't about to quibble with his housekeeping.

'Did you have a good day?' She asked the question she had learned not to ask on Saturdays.

'Awful.' He practically sang the word. 'Five hours of the *Star Wars* saga back to back.' He started out of the kitchen.

'I thought you were going to start dinner.'

He put his arm around her waist. 'Don't push your luck, sweetheart. I fed the cats. I'll make drinks. I'll even dial the Chinese restaurant later. But unless you want cornflakes don't push your luck.'

When he brought in the drinks, she was in the bedroom stacking her purchases, all except Nick's maps, in a visible corner, where they'd keep nagging her until she wrapped them. He walked past the television without turning it on, put her drink on the dresser, and sat on the end of the bed with his own. 'What are you doing next Saturday?'

'Nothing so far.'

'How would you like to see the tree at the Met, check out the windows at Altman's and Lord and Taylor's, swing past the tree at Rockefeller Center, and end up in a blaze of glory at FAO Schwartz?'

'No ice skating at Rockefeller Center?'

'You can do that while the boys and I have lunch. What do you say?'

She said sure.

VII

That week Katherine met Nick's children and Nick
met Erica, or rather Nick met Erica on new terms.
Katherine had introduced them once in the past, but
it had been like trying to put the poles of two
magnets together. The resisting force was too strong.

She invited Erica to dinner on Wednesday. 'If
you can stand my cooking.'

'What's wrong with your cooking? You used to
make great tuna and melted cheddar sandwiches.'

'That's what's wrong with my cooking. Tuna melts
aren't exactly *haute cuisine*. They aren't even *nouvelle
cuisine*. In fact, Nick says they're stomach-turning.'

'Then why doesn't Nick cook?'

Katherine told herself it was her own fault for
serving Nick up that way. Erica never could resist
carving. 'Do you want to bring someone?'

'No one to bring.'

'Whatever happened to Josh?'

'He went to Colorado to finish his book.
Apparently the creative juices don't flow on Bleecker
Street. He needs the inspiration of snow-covered
mountains – and uncovered snow bunnies, if you
ask me. I'm thinking of taking up abstinence. Not
very rewarding, but it's becoming terribly chic if the
media's to be believed.'

There was no reason to be nervous about making

dinner for Erica and Nick. She'd cooked for each of them dozens of times. But she'd never cooked for both of them together.

Nick came into the kitchen when he heard a noise that was less than a crash but more than a cabinet closing. Romaine and escarole littered the floor. Katherine held up the salad spinner. 'Nothing broke. It's plastic.' She bent over to pick up the lettuce and dropped the spinner again. Nick caught the container and began putting the lettuce in it.

'I have to wash it again.'

'I won't tell if you don't. Calm down, Katie. Everything will be all right. We'll have a few drinks, Erica will eat her veal and go home, and we'll go to bed. Saint-Simon wouldn't give the evening a footnote.'

'You'll be nice to her, won't you?'

'As nice as she is to me.'

'Nick.'

'I'll be fuckin' charming,' he said and the shade of Marlon Brando-Stanley Kowalski flickered through the kitchen.

He wasn't exactly charming, but he was nice.

He took Erica's coat and was surreptitious about taking in her body, though Katherine knew he'd done a thorough job of it. Of course, he had some help from Erica, who was wearing a wraparound skirt that opened when she moved and a silk blouse that was pretty far open even when she didn't. Katherine owned the same blouse but knew she didn't look the same in it. He brought Erica a drink. He even lit her little black cigar for her. And they talked. They talked about publishing and corporate take-overs or publishing houses, about movies, and about children. Nick said that he supposed raising boys was somewhat different from raising girls. In the kitchen

Katherine stood with a pot of pasta she was about to drain poised in midair. 'What he means . . .' she called, but they ignored her.

'There are some differences,' Katherine heard Erica saying, 'but not as many as you might think.' Nick said that was probably true. Katherine carried in the veal and pasta.

After dinner they settled in the living room with coffee and brandy. Erica was on the sofa, showing a considerable expanse of leg. Nick was sitting across from her, enjoying a considerable expanse of leg.

'What do you think of Kat's book?' Erica asked. After she'd given her stamp of approval and sent it out on submission, Katherine had let Nick read it.

'It's not really his kind of . . .' Katherine began.

'I liked it,' Nick said.

'I have great expectations. Especially for paper later on, which is where the real money is. How are you going to like living with a best-selling author?'

Katherine opened her mouth to explain to Erica that Nick's ego was not so fragile and to Nick that Erica hadn't meant to bait him and to both of them that the chances of her becoming a best-selling author were slim, but Nick was too quick for her. He said he'd like it fine.

Erica left before midnight. It seemed much later to Katherine. She felt like a ballboy who'd spent the evening running around the court after conversational misses and outs. The fact that neither Nick nor Erica had faulted hadn't made the evening any less exhausting.

'See, that wasn't so terrible,' Katherine said as she and Nick were carrying the cups and saucers and glasses into the kitchen. She'd been aiming her voice at exhilaration but had hit shrillness.

Nick emptied an ashtray into the trash and headed

back into the living room.

She followed him. 'Well, was it?'

'It was fine.'

'Do you like her?'

'I'm in love with her.'

Katherine picked up the last two glasses and followed him back to the kitchen. 'I mean it. What do you think of her?'

'She has a great body.'

'Sexist pig.'

'Not as great as yours.'

'Lying sexist pig. But it was a nice evening, wasn't it?'

'Let's just say we all stayed awake.'

Nick was standing at the circular information desk inside the museum with two little boys. Katherine saw them before they saw her, and she couldn't decide which one hurt her more, the older boy who had dark hair and big dark eyes and looked exactly like Nick or the younger one who looked nothing like him and therefore, Katherine reasoned, must resemble his mother. If he did, the lovely Gwen was lovely indeed. The boy had shaggy blond hair that covered his ears and his eyebrows and a sweet impish face. Oh, God, Katherine thought, please don't let him be one of those precocious kids who know how cute they are.

When Nick introduced them, the boys looked up at her as if they knew they were supposed to but would rather not, said hello, then went back to staring at the floor.

Nick led the way into the museum, each boy holding one of his hands and Katherine trailing a step behind. The huge tree, tinged with soft blue and bearing elaborate carved angels like rare gifts, dominated the center court, and the crowd that pressed around it whispered their admiration in deference to the religious significance of the occasion and the piped-in Gregorian chants. Now and then children's voices rang out above the hushed tones, but they were not Nick's children's voices. The boys were very quiet as Nick pointed out the details of the small figures around the crèche, and Katherine tried to think of something to say.

They went upstairs to the children's gift shop and bought reproductions of old ornaments and a model of a medieval village, and while they were waiting in line at the cash register, a woman turned abruptly and hit Mark in the face with her shopping bag. Mark looked surprised. Katherine looked panic-stricken. 'Are you all right?' No Gregorian chants were piped in here, and her voice rang out above the noise of the shoppers. Mark looked from her to Nick as if debating his options.

'You're okay,' Nick said quickly. 'Relax, Katie,' he muttered as he turned back to the cash register, but his mouth was a thin line that looked as tense as she felt.

Everywhere they went that day, there were crowds of adults dragging hordes of children. While Nick and the boys looked at windows where toy dogs wagged mechanical tails and automated children skated on glass ice, Katherine examined the crowd, trying to separate the families from the divorced daddies, the mothers from the mistresses. The only giveaway was the occasional woman screaming at or shaking an occasional child.

Nick and Katherine talked incessantly, though never to each other. In front of Altman's windows they discussed Beatrix Potter; in front of Lord and Taylor's, turn-of-the-century New York. At lunch they talked about Katherine's cats, the boys' beagle, and animals in general. The boys were polite, but it was obvious they didn't think Eleanor and Franklin were appropriate names for cats, even after Katherine explained about their namesakes. On the second floor of Schwartz's she got a brief respite while all three of them fell upon the model trains and cars and planes. Katherine stood in front of the elevator, watching mothers carrying parkas and fathers carrying kids, siblings fighting with siblings and husbands arguing with wives. Kids cried and screamed and begged for things. Parents promised and bargained and threatened. Mechanical toys went up and down, back and forth, and around in circles. Katherine thought longingly of the proximity of the Plaza's Oak Bar.

The day had been exhausting but not definitive. The boys, Katherine realized, did not see her as the good fairy, but neither did they view her as the wicked witch of the North. She was, like five-hour *Star Wars* orgies, strange sandwiches called souvlaki, and museums, one more thing that happened on Saturdays since Daddy had left home. They might hope that she, like those other strange things, would go away and life would go back to normal, but they didn't seem to be ready to do anything to make her go away.

Katherine didn't think much about the children after that Saturday perhaps because she was feeling so much like a child herself, or at least like an adolescent. Waiting to hear about her manuscript was like waiting to hear about college admissions. Would the envelope be fat or thin? Would Erica's phone call be long and full of details about contracts and options or short and consoling? Katherine felt

128

as if she were about seventeen. According to Nick, she was acting that way, too.

'What do you want to bet that damn radical feminist rejects me the day before Christmas?'

'Which damn radical feminist?' Nick asked.

'The editor Erica sent my manuscript to.'

'First of all, nobody does anything the day before Christmas. Secondly, if she does, she won't be rejecting you, she'll be rejecting the book.'

'Easy for you to say.'

'What's taking her so long?' Katherine asked Erica.

'Ten days is not long, Kat. Ten days is overnight. You're lucky I'm a friend. Any other agent would have stopped taking your calls a week ago.'

'Erica says you're nervous,' Beth said when she called one morning.

'Nothing that a couple of Valium wouldn't control. Only I don't take Valium.'

'Do you want some?'

'Thanks, but I think I'll stick to my fingernails for a while.'

'I'm getting out of town for a couple of hours. Why don't you come along? I ordered a limo.'

'How out of town?' Katherine was tempted but hesitant. She'd never in her life driven in a limousine, but she didn't relish the idea of sharing the front seat with the driver while Topper and Beth cavorted behind the smoked glass in the back.

'Just to the cemetery. I always visit my mother on her birthday. Come on, Grace would love to see you.'

Half an hour later the doorman called upstairs to tell Katherine there was a limo waiting for her. When she reached the lobby, he pronounced 'Miss Walden' as if it were an expensive brand name and opened the front door for her with a flourish. The driver who was holding the door to the car was less impressed. Even without looking at her – his eyes were somewhere on the third floor of the building – he seemed to know she didn't measure up.

In a corner of the back seat, which was like a soft gray womb with deeply upholstered cushions and thick carpeting that ran up the walls, Katherine found what looked like a couple of miles of sable. All that was visible of Beth was the small dark face smiling over the top of the deep collar and the twin points of snakeskin cowboy boots that peeked out from the hem.

'Talk about drop-dead chic,' Katherine said as she sank into one of the seats. She thought her knees were going to hit her chin. She knew she'd never be able to get out. 'Where did you get that?'

'Don't disgrace me in front of the driver, Kitty. He thinks this is a class act.' She held an arm swathed – that was the only word for it – in sable out toward Katherine. 'Do you like it?'

'Does anyone not like sable? It is sable, isn't it? I can barely tell cashmere from camel's hair.'

'It's sable. A Christmas present from me to me.'

'And who deserves it more? Except perhaps me.'

'I thought your moral scruples, to say nothing of those two mangy strays you live with – no offense to Nick intended – wouldn't permit you to buy a fur coat. What I don't understand is how you can eat meat but refuse to wear fur.'

'What I don't understand is how you can be opposed to child abuse and still do terrible things to Topper's body.'

'Who says they're terrible? You know, last week I was walking past a construction site in this coat and one of the hard hats made that tongue-clicking sound they all think is so irresistible and asked me what

I'd done to get a coat like this. I told him I'd written a couple of best sellers.'

'Good for you,' Katherine said, but she must have sounded as if she didn't mean it.

'Sorry, Kitty, I wasn't thinking. But you've got to stop worrying. Erica says she's very optimistic.'

Katherine looked past Beth out the window. The sun had been achingly bright when she'd come out of the building, but the smoky glass turned the East River, the Triborough Bridge, and the entire landscape dirty gray. 'Erica can afford to be optimistic. It isn't her manuscript they're rejecting.'

'Even if they do reject it – and I'm not saying they're going to – there are other houses in town. You know how many rejections I got on my first novel?'

'How many?'

'I forget. But it took Erica awhile to sell it. And none of my books has been made into a movie yet. One of yours is going to be a made-for-telly.'

'One of Altruist's. A ghost is lowlife in publishing but nonexistent in movies. Either you get a screen credit or you don't. And I don't.'

'You will, Kitty. It takes time. I sold my first book for peanuts.' Beth leaned back against the deep upholstery, and with her dark skin and small, pointed chin she looked like a sleek little mink in sable's clothing.

'And now look at you. Going to visit Grace in a sable coat and a limousine.' Katherine looked at the telephone that dangled from the rear window like a ripe fruit and the console in front of them with a television, a couple of hundred buttons, and probably a hidden bar. 'Are they all like this? Phones and televisions and God knows what sybaritic goodies?'

'Not all, but I figure if I'm going to do something,

I might as well do it right. Besides, I've been waiting for them to show that midday interview I taped last month – they keep postponing it – and I wanted to catch it on the way home from the cemetery.'

'Just as I said, Grace would be proud. A sable, a limousine, and a television to watch yourself on.'

'I wonder about that a lot. Or at least sometimes. She'd be proud of the books, but I think she'd have a hard time with the rest of my life. Kitty, when your father died, did you feel free? I mean, besides feeling terrible, did you feel free after a while?'

Katherine looked at the rows of buttons on the console and tried to remember what she'd felt. 'I was frightened. For myself and for my mother. I was lonely. I remember wishing I had a sister or brother.'

'I guess I ought to feel guilty about it, but for the first time in my life I feel free. If my mother had been alive, I don't think I'd have had the courage to leave Jimmy. She would have told me I was crazy to even think of it, and I probably would have listened to her. I remember when my aunt wanted to divorce my uncle. He'd been screwing his secretary forever, and everyone in town knew it. My aunt said she couldn't take it anymore, but my mother and her sisters talked her out of divorce. At least you have security, they kept saying.'

'You have security.'

'Which I've worked damn hard for.'

Katherine agreed that she had and didn't mention the $150,000 a year in child support.

'No wonder we're all so screwed up when you think about how we were raised.'

Katherine looked through the gray window at the gray scenery along the Long Island Expressway. 'It was a bitch, wasn't it? Cashmere sweaters and braces on our teeth. Mothers who made us do our homework and drink our milk and fathers who sent us to college. Talk about hardship and oppression.'

'They straightened our teeth and bought us nice clothes and sent us to college so we could find husbands – the right husbands.'

'Maybe, but there was nothing stopping you from looking around once you got there.'

'All I know,' Beth said, and started to tie the belt of her coat because the car had turned off the main highway onto a narrow two-lane road, 'is that I'm not going to make the same mistake with Jessica.'

When they reached the cemetery, Katherine stayed in the car and let Beth visit Grace alone. There had been no snow in town; but there was a thin film out here, and the tombstones were gray rectangles in the white ground. The graveyard looked like an exceptionally well-kept Lilliputian village, and Beth, standing with her head down and her hands thrust into the pockets of her sable coat, was the Swiftian giant who towered over it all. Katherine wondered what she was thinking. Was she apologizing to her mother because she felt finally free? Was she berating her mother for hindering her emancipation with straight teeth and expensive clothes? Or was she simply showing Grace her new coat and telling her that the latest book was in its third printing? Why not? Katherine thought. If she ever sold her book, she knew she'd wish her father were alive to take pride in it and her.

Katherine was surprised when before turning away from the grave, Beth took a handkerchief from her coat pocket and slid it under her dark glasses. 'For a woman who swears by money and power,' Katherine said as Beth got back into the car, 'you sure are an old softie.' She'd purposely omitted the part about young bodies. She didn't want to talk about young bodies in a cemetery.

When they got back to town, Beth insisted Katherine come home with her. 'You know you're not going to get any work done. And we can call Erica from my place to see if she has news.'

Erica had no news, which was all the more reason, Beth said, for Katherine to stay. 'If you go home, you'll just pace the apartment and kick the cats. Besides, the kids will be here soon and you haven't seen them in ages.'

Jonathan arrived first and disappeared into what used to be Ted Sullivan's study with two friends.

'Want to know how to keep kids off the streets?' Beth asked. 'Buy a home computer. We've become the hangout for the entire upper school. Did you notice the tall kid? According to Jon, he's a genius. They're working on some perfectly terrifying scam to break into the Pentagon's computer.'

'Can they do that?'

'As Jon tells it, that kid can do anything. I wouldn't doubt it. Succulent little devil – isn't he? – with those tight jeans and that blond hair that's always in his eyes.'

'Beth, he's fourteen.'

'Fifteen. He's a year ahead of Jon. The perfect age for indoctrination. "When you talk about this in years to come – and you will – please be kind."' Beth flashed a wicked elfin grin. 'Don't look so horrified, Kitty. I'm only teasing.'

When Katherine got home later that afternoon, she made herself a cup of tea and sat down with the morning paper. She hadn't gotten any farther than the front page that morning, and the more frivolous parts were still waiting for her. She read one article about what rich people were giving for Christmas and another about what rich people wanted to receive for Christmas and told herself that the only thing worse than articles like these were the people who read them, but she kept turning pages. Toward the end of the third section she found a piece about a noted psychiatrist – Katherine wondered if, for journalistic purposes, there was any other kind – who had just completed a study of daughters' responses to their mothers' deaths. Many, he said, experience a profound and almost exhilarating sense of freedom. Either Beth was a faster reader or she didn't bother with the news sections.

A week before Christmas, when Katherine had decided there would be no news until after the holidays, Erica called. 'Ho, ho, ho, what does little Kat Walden want for Christmas?'

'World peace.'

'Not a book contract?'

Nick came running at the sound of Katherine's scream. 'You sold it?'

'Twenty-five thousand American dollar bills,' Erica said. 'Not bad for a first novel. In fact, damn good. You must have a terrific agent.'

'I don't believe it,' Katherine said to Erica. 'Where are you going?' she asked Nick, who'd just taken his coat from the hall closet, but he merely smiled and waved on his way out the door.

'Maybe he's going for a pack of cigarettes.'

'He doesn't smoke.'

'Maybe he's leaving you because he can't take your newfound success.'

'Erica!'

'I was just kidding, luv. Don't get testy. You're supposed to be overjoyed.'

'I am overjoyed. Tell me more.'

'What more do you want to know? Sydney loves it twenty-five thousand dollars' worth. In three installments.'

'Three? Isn't that unusual? With Ego and Altruist we always got half on signing and half on completion.'

'I don't believe it. Five minutes ago this woman would have given her book away just so long as someone would publish it. Now she's complaining because she's getting a third rather than a half up front. You know, Kat, you're my oldest and dearest friend, but sometimes you sound like a goddamn author.'

'You say that as if it were a dirty word.'

'In our business it is. Ask any agent or editor. Money's tight. A lot of houses are paying in thirds these days.'

'They're hedging their bets. In case they don't like what I turn in.'

'Goddammit, Kat, twenty-five thousand for a first novel is not exactly hedging bets. You know what Joyce got for *Ulysses*? Twelve hundred dollars.'

'If I wrote like Joyce, I wouldn't need the money to shore up my confidence.'

'That's a new one. I've heard authors say they need money because the bank is foreclosing a mortgage or a kid needs an operation or divorce is imminent, but you're the only one who needs more money to shore up her confidence. Now would you like to discuss the book, or is the money all you care about? Sydney says she wants to talk to you after the holidays. There are a couple of changes—'

'You see.'

'Just a couple, Kat. What do you think editors are for?'

'Lunching. That's what you always say.'

'Sydney's different. She edits as well as lunches.'

Erica was still telling Katherine about the proposed changes when Nick returned. He was carrying a long florist's box and was out of breath. 'You think it's easy to find a flower shop open at this hour?' It was seven-fifteen.

At seven-thirty, after Katherine had finally gotten off the phone and arranged the dozen red roses in a vase, a delivery boy arrived with another florist's box. 'I can't believe Erica did this, but no one else knows.' Katherine opened the box. Inside were a dozen white roses and a card in Nick's handwriting: 'Just as I said. Tolstoy, Dostoevsky, Proust, and Hemingway.' 'You're crazy,' Katherine said. At seven forty-five the same delivery boy returned. This time he was carrying a round bouquet wrapped in paper rather than a box. Katherine tore off the paper. Inside were anemones and carnations and another card in Nick's handwriting: 'And Jane Austen.' 'You are absolutely nuts,' she said. At eight o'clock the boy turned up again. He was smiling as he gave Katherine another bouquet wrapped in paper and took another dollar from Nick: 'And Katherine Walden.' 'You're not only crazy, you're sinfully extravagant.'

'Why not? Now that I've got a woman who can keep me in the manner to which I plan to become accustomed.'

Katherine put the latest bouquet, which had a lot of sweet peas and snapdragons, on the dining table and moved the red roses to the bedroom. 'Where should we lay out the body?'

He stopped her in the bedroom door. 'I have some ideas about that.'

'I thought you were going to take me out to dinner.' Even standing up, they fitted perfectly.

'I am. Eventually.'

They never did go out to dinner that night. They lay in bed for a long time talking. She told him about the first story she'd ever written, an illustrated saga of a raindrop in a cloud that drifted to London, Paris, and Rome.

'Don't tell me any more,' Nick said, 'until I get my insulin injection.'

'I'll have you know I won a prize and the story was on display in City Hall.'

'That's what you get for growing up in a small town.' He got up and made them more drinks and came back to bed and told her about the time he'd made a laughingstock of himself on the high school radio station and the time he'd almost been thrown out of school for showing an explicit, for that time, Bergman movie at the film society and the time he'd fenced against one of the Hungarians who'd come over after the 1956 revolution and almost won. And she told him about the freshman mixer where no one had asked her to dance and she'd hidden in the ladies' room all night, which he pointed out may have been one of the reasons no one asked her to dance, and the time her apartment had been broken into while she was at a peace rally and the time she and Erica had taken the wrong channel boat in France and ended up at the wrong town in England and had to spend the night in a train station.

Around eleven they decided they really ought to eat something, so she made sandwiches and brought them back to bed, and they talked some more. She said now that she had the contract, she was afraid she wouldn't be able to do a decent job on the book. 'It must be wonderful to have some nice secure job where you're not constantly worried about failing.'

Nick laughed and fed Franklin a scrap of ham.

138

'Show me the job and I'll fill out an application.'

'You don't worry.'

'I worry about every case I handle.'

'You never say anything.'

'What good would it do? You'd either worry along with me or tell me everything was going to be all right, and with all due respect, sweetheart, you know very little about legal precedents.'

'You're a strong, silent, patronizing son of a bitch.'

'Flattery will get you nowhere.'

She moved the tray that was between them to the foot of the bed. 'Wanna bet?'

VIII

Not since she was five and her parents had come home from a business trip to Chicago with a Madame Alexander doll that drank from a bottle, wet her diaper, and had washable lamb's wool hair had Katherine had such a Christmas. In stores the hostile crowds always seemed to be scratching and clawing at another counter, and salespeople actually asked if they could help her. One night she came out of FAO Schwartz laden with shopping bags and two oversized models for David and Mark, and a man who was getting out of a big Checker cab waited and held the door for her. At an intermission of *The Nutcracker* with Paige and Timmy, a glass of white wine and the sight of so many scrubbed little faces, some as white as the lace collars, others as flushed with excitement as all that burgundy velvet, conspired for one heady moment to make Katherine contemplate adding her own tiny bang to the population explosion. Like a missionary sniffing a convert, Paige stroked Timmy's hair and told Katherine she wasn't too old to have children. 'Stanley says you've still got several good childbearing years ahead of you.' Katherine thanked Stanley.

She took Jessica for lunch at the Plaza because the girl was still at the age where Topper could be topped by *fin-de-siècle* marble and mirrors and cheesecake covered with whipped cream and strawberries. She took Erica's daughters to *Annie*, where they sat so close to the stage that the girls went home with the smell of greasepaint in their noses and a burning ambition for a life in the theater in their hearts, and Katherine went home with a headache that lingered through three aspirin and faded only after a second martini.

One night when it was raining, she stood on the corner of Park Avenue and Fifty-third Street in the middle of the rush-hour frenzy because the reflection of the colored lights in the wet pavement seemed like a reflection of everything going on inside her. She spent, drank, and ate too much, slept too little, and felt absolutely indestructible – except in moments of panic when she was sure she was going to be run over by a bus or killed in a taxi accident before she had a chance to finish her book. Even when Nick came home from his office party slurring his words and tripping over Franklin, she couldn't summon much indignation.

He sat on the side of the bed in his coat and smiled the innocent, smug smile of the drunk. 'You're beautiful.'

'You're drunk.'

'I love you.'

She was trying to take off his coat and jacket simultaneously because she didn't think she could go through the ordeal twice. 'I bet you tell that to all the secretaries. Or at least to the one who got lipstick or blusher or whatever the hell it is all over your shirt.'

'Aha! Sexist piglet! Not a secretary. She's a lawyer. Only she calls it attorney.'

'Watch yourself, ace. I may be open-minded, but

I'm not long-suffering.' She had managed to get his shoes off and open his belt and was tugging at the legs of his trousers. He was lying back on his elbows, but he wasn't being co-operative.

'I can take off my own pants.'

'I'll just bet you can. Every chance you get.' In his condition that was pure provocation. His long fingers made a swipe at her, but she sidestepped it and went on tugging at his pants. 'I don't give a damn about you; but I'm crazy about this suit, and it just came back from the cleaners.'

The smug smile was back, and this time it wasn't innocent. 'You lie. You're crazy about me.'

She gave a final tug and pulled his trousers free. 'Just crazy, as any one of my friends will tell you. Go to sleep.'

She turned out the lights and closed the door so her records wouldn't bother him, but from the sound of his snoring, which started almost immediately, the Second World War wouldn't have bothered him.

'Just how charming was I last night?' he asked the next morning.

She turned over and looked at him. Nobody ever died from a hangover, but Nick looked as if he might be the first exception to that rule. His eyes were two black hollows in the death mask of his face. 'You want my opinion or the lawyer's with the indelible lipstick?'

The death mask seemed to shrivel a little, and Katherine knew he'd forgotten that part of the evening until now. She wondered how much there had been to forget, but she didn't wonder very seriously. 'Don't worry about it, ace. These are the 1980s. You can't be jealous when a man comes home with lipstick on his shirt and not on his fly.'

Katherine wasn't jealous, and for once she had

the sense not to mention the incident to any of her friends. Besides, she preferred the happy drunk to the hostile father of the year. Katherine hadn't seen that man in several weeks, but that didn't mean he wasn't still lurking around the apartment just waiting for his cue. She was sure Gwen had given him the perfect excuse on the Sunday after Christmas. Speculating on how long the lines at the various movies would be, they were still in bed with the paper when the phone rang. A woman asked for Nick. She didn't identify herself, but then she didn't have to. Katherine handed him the receiver. 'I believe it's your wife.' Katherine studied the recipes for New Year's buffets in the magazine section while she debated the etiquette of the situation. She could go into the kitchen and let Nick talk to his wife in private, but she didn't want him to talk to his wife in private.

'Yes, Gwen, I know how your father still feels about Roosevelt. I've always admired his constancy.'

Katherine turned the pages. She never did the puzzle, but Nick inked it in boldly.

'I didn't put the kids up to anything, Gwen. We were talking about cats.' Nick swung his legs over the side of the bed so he was sitting with his back to Katherine.

'Don't call her my girl friend.'

Katherine stared at the words scrawled horizontally and vertically and wondered what she was supposed to be called.

'Besides, the kids ought to learn that everyone doesn't think the way your father does. Your father ought to learn that. Maybe you ought to tell him.' Nick hunched forward so his elbows were resting on his knees. 'Yes, Gwen, I know that unlike me, you're not still trying to prove something. It's just a shame you got married while you were.'

Katherine thought she could hear Gwen's words of agreement, then some more she couldn't understand.

'Okay, then what the hell did you call to talk about?'

There was a longer silence, and Katherine continued to stare at the crossword puzzle. How did he know so much about rivers in Indochina and arcane words for inedible foods?

'I wasn't trying to sabotage you, Gwen. How did I know what you were going to buy them. For that matter, why didn't you think of asking me what I was going to get them?'

The answer to that went on for some time.

'All right, Gwen. Next Christmas I'll check with you first. And all birthdays from now on. I'll have my lawyer contact your attorney . . . I'm not being sarcastic, Gwen. Well, maybe just a little. And Merry Christmas to you, too.'

He handed the receiver to Katherine without turning around, and she replaced it on the phone. He was still leaning forward with his elbows on his knees, and now he dropped his head into his hands. Katherine waited for the sentence. What is it this time, Judge? Thirty years' hard labor? Ten in a minimum-security prison? Or just another night in solitary?

'As you may have guessed from the conversation, we both listened a little too carefully to what the kids wanted for Christmas. Only I got there with the goods first because I got the kids for Christmas Eve.'

'Were they very disappointed?'

'She didn't say.' He sat up abruptly, then threw himself back against the pillows like a man coming in for a crash dive. 'Oh, the hell with it, Katie. Nobody was ever scarred for life by getting two ten-speed bicycles for Christmas.' He was staring at the ceiling, which had on similar occasions in the past held such fascination for him. 'Did you hear that about her father? The kids mentioned the cats or FDR or something Christmas Day, and the old man nearly had a heart attack. Forty years later and you're still not allowed to mention the name Roosevelt – unless it's Teddy, and he's not too crazy about him either – in his house.'

'You two must have gotten along famously.'

'Politics were the least of it. He's a pious old bastard, too. He's sure he owes his millions to God's direct intervention. One Christmas I got a little tight and said something about the immaculate misconception. He didn't talk to me for six months.'

Suddenly he started to laugh. 'The more I think about it, the more I like it. You know how David gets that serious, pompous look when he's trying to explain something?' She didn't, but this was not the time to tell him that. 'I can just picture him explaining the New Deal to the old man in that high, condescending voice. Jesus, that must have been a sight.'

The terrain looked safe, and she pushed aside the papers and moved next to him. 'Are you sorry you missed it?'

He reached an arm around her. 'Nope, but I love picturing it.'

Beth Sarmie gave a party on New Year's Eve. She and Topper had planned to go away for an idyll in the Vermont snow, but he sprained his ankle skiing the day after Christmas.

'I thought he was such a good skier,' Katherine

said. According to Beth, Topper excelled in all physical endeavors.

'He is, but he was stoned. So we've decided to stay in town and have some people over. Nothing vulgar and New Year's Eve-like. Just a few hundred intimate friends. You and Nick are first on the list.'

'Thanks, but we always stay home on New Year's Eve.'

'What do you mean, you always stay home? This is your first one together.'

'Exactly. We're starting a tradition.'

'You ought to come, Kitty. It's going to be an A-minus, B-plus party. It would have been an A party if I'd started earlier, but who knew Topper was going to hurt his ankle? Anyway, those people can do you a lot of good. You can stay home and screw anytime. For all I care, you can go home and fuck your brains out afterward; but you're going to have a book coming out soon, and it won't hurt to know the right people.'

'Sorry. Nick and I never go to anything less than an A party.'

'You aren't important enough to be that discriminating.' There was a moment's pause while Katherine debated whether she ought to be annoyed. 'Yet,' Beth added.

There was, however, no excuse for not going to Stanley and Paige Richmond's open house on New Year's Day, especially since Paige assured Katherine they hadn't invited her former husband, Stephen. 'He and Jill took the kids south for the holidays. Just think, you could be lying around in the tropical sun right now.'

'I burn in the tropical sun.'

There was no reason not to go to the Richmonds, though Nick tried to find one.

'If you go to the party,' Katherine said, 'you'll get all my friends over with at once.'

'Like running the gauntlet.'

Meeting Katherine's friends was not in the least like running the gauntlet for Nick. They could not have been nicer to him, more eager to draw him out, discover his opinions, ascertain his character – in short to take Nick Larries's measure. And like a child having his height gauged against a wall, Nick could not resist a little horsing around.

The Richmonds were standing just inside the door of the brownstone they'd bought three years ago. They'd restored the moldings, taken down walls to open up the high-ceilinged rooms, and installed an enormous kitchen on the basement level where everything wheeled, swiveled, or traveled. 'Built-in,' Paige had announced, 'is out.' The house was a gem, but with the exception of the kitchen it was not entirely suited to Stanley and Paige. Despite the high ceilings and newly opened rooms, the house had been built to the smaller urban scale of another century, and the Richmonds were made to the larger human scale of this one. Like his wife with her imaginary hockey stick, Stanley, who was big and fair with pale eyes behind heavy horn-rimmed glasses, always gave the impression of having just come in from the great outdoors. And his appearance, like Paige's, was not accidental. He courted it as carefully as he did the referring doctors who were invited this afternoon.

Stanley reached out a hand that looked too big to perform surgery and gave Nick's a hearty shake. 'Glad you could come. I'm Dr Richmond, and this is my wife, Paige.'

Nick pumped Stanley's hand with equal heartiness. 'An unusual first name.'

'Paige?' Stanley asked.

'No, Doctor.'

Stanley's big fist gave Nick's shoulder a playful punch. 'Excellent, Counselor, excellent. Call me Stan. Stan and Paige.'

'Do you want to leave now,' Katherine whispered when they'd moved to the living room, 'or should we wait till they throw us out?'

'What should I have said? I'm Lawyer Larries?'

The party was just beginning, and the room and the small crowd gathered in it were like an engine that might or might not turn over. Conversations started, then stalled. People greeted each other as if they were gears trying to mesh. The loudest voice in the room and the only one that didn't sound strained belonged to Doug Greer. His words boomed off the elegant moldings. His laugh roared to the high ceilings. Doug was the fuel that could start any stalled party. He was, people often said, the one person you could always count on to be up at a party. According to Cynthia, that was because he was always so down at home. 'He spends all his time brooding about the meaning of existence. And who's going to be elected chairman of the philosophy department.' But Doug was definitely up now, and Cynthia was nowhere in sight.

'She'll be here later,' Doug explained in answer to Katherine's question. He stroked the thick beard that was supposed to soften the angles of his long, thin face. Doug was tall and gaunt with thin lips, a long, thin nose, and hollows in his cheeks. The body looked dry, and the face ascetic, but the beard, the wavy brown hair that flowed back from the receding hairline, and the voice, especially the voice, were luxuriant. 'One of her vendors' – the word slid off his tongue now as familiarly as *'formalists'* and *'pluralists'* – 'is giving a party today, too. I told her I'd stop there with her, but she thought I'd be bored.' Doug didn't sound as if he could be bored at a party.

Katherine left Nick with Doug and went off to smooth Paige's ruffled feathers. 'Is he always so sarcastic?' Paige asked.

'Nervous. He knows he's being looked over by everyone.'

'At least he dresses decently. Did you see the jacket on Stanley's associate? I told Stanley he was making a mistake when he took him into the practice. If God had wanted men to wear polyester, he never would have made sheep.'

The room was growing more crowded now, and the aura of awkwardness was melting at the same rate as the ice in the second drinks. Beth arrived with Topper limping behind her.

'How's your ankle?' Katherine asked.

'Mending,' Beth said, and Topper smiled beatifically.

Beth told Topper that she wanted a bloody mary and Katherine that she wanted to meet Nick, and Topper hobbled off to the bar while Katherine led her across the room to where Nick and Doug were still talking.

As Katherine had told Topper the first night she'd met him, she and Beth went back a long way together. Katherine knew instinctively how Beth would react to Nick. She raised the dark little heart-shaped face and gave him the provocative smile that had been perfected for double entendres on talk shows. 'We missed you last night, but Kitty said you wanted to celebrate alone. Did you bring in the new year with a bang?'

'Actually we spent the night reading a good book.'

Nick mentioned the title of Beth's latest novel.

'I like him,' Beth said to Katherine as if Nick weren't there. 'He's all right.'

He might have been all right, but he was neither young enough to be interesting nor powerful enough to be useful, and Beth drifted off to case the rest of the party.

Erica arrived late and angry. Her face looked red and blotchy, and Katherine wondered if she'd walked over or if there was another explanation for her complexion. 'I'll talk to you after I get a drink.' She was back in minutes with a tall glass filled with a dangerously dark-colored liquid. 'Do you know what that bastard did today?' she asked, pulling Katherine away from the others. 'He came to pick up the kids. He and the little woman – and I mean little; she doesn't look much older than the kids – are taking them to brunch. He asked if he could bring her in to see the apartment. According to him, it's still the best design job he's ever done, and he wanted her to see it.'

'What did you do?'

'What in hell could I do? Tell him to show her the pictures that ran in the *Times* a few years ago? There I was in my ratty old flannel bathrobe and no makeup, looking about a hundred years old, and there's the second Mrs Kenyon skipping through the apartment, ohhing and ahhing as if she were going to have an orgasm any minute.' Erica took a long swallow from her glass.

'Is that straight scotch?'

'There's ice in it. I got back at him though. It wasn't much, but it was something. He damn near died when he saw I'd rearranged the furniture in the living room. "You moved the Knoll chairs," he said as if I'd defaced the "Mona Lisa".' Erica took another swallow of her drink. 'Okay, I got it off my chest. Now I'm not going to talk about it anymore.'

'How was the party last night?'

'You should have been there. Beth's right when she says it doesn't hurt to know the people who can review your book or make a movie of it.' Erica turned to Nick and Doug, who seemed to have latched onto each other. 'You're a bad influence on her, Nick. She should have been at Beth's party.'

'Why does everyone assume I was the one who didn't want to go?'

'Because Kat always went before you came along. Where's Cynthia?' she asked Doug.

'Taking care of business.' Doug picked up his students' slang the way an animal adopts protective coloration.

Cynthia did not arrive until after seven. By that time a good many of the guests had left. A good many more were still hanging on, unable to go out to dinner because of the buffet Paige had laid out on the dining-room table a few hours earlier, unwilling to go home and confront the fact that the holidays were over. The party had divided along professional lines, with doctors at the end of the room that had been, before renovation, the back parlor and laymen scattered around the rest of the room, with backgammon players at the table in front of the windows and self-styled foreign policy experts in the dining-room. The doctors didn't all look alike; they just gave that impression because of the carefully trimmed hair that was combed elaborately forward and over the ears, the smooth, closed faces, and their manner of studying their toes and nodding at regular intervals while they listened to each other. They were like a small army – four of them even wore the same uniform – but they'd divided up into three companies, and Katherine wondered if the divisions were according to specialty. Surgeons by the fireplace, internists on the sofa, gyn-obs by the window please.

Stanley was at the bar mixing Irish coffee with scientific precision, Erica was a one-woman FDA determined to test his product before it was mass-marketed, and Paige was smiling bravely and telling a woman that the Lalique ashtray she'd broken was just something they'd picked up last time they were in France and not in the least valuable.

'You're a game girl,' Katherine whispered as she passed her. Cynthia had just come in the front door.

'And where have you been?' It was a rhetorical question, but Cynthia seemed eager to answer it.

'Have lunch with me this week, and I'll tell you all about it.'

Katherine watched as she took off her coat. Cynthia had been losing weight for the past two months, but the new body hadn't been visible beneath the old clothes. Now the butterfly had emerged from its cocoon, and the effect was startling. Cynthia's figure would never be as good as Erica's, but it could probably get her into as much trouble on a crowded subway, maybe more in the white silk knit dress that would have shown every line of her underwear if she'd been wearing any.

'Let me guess,' Katherine said. 'You've been at a meeting of your consciousness-raising group.'

'Is Doug angry?'

'I'd be,' Katherine said, and followed Cynthia into the living room.

If Doug was angry, he did a good job of hiding the fact. He seemed less upset about Cynthia's later arrival than pleased that she'd finally turned up. And Cynthia seemed downright overjoyed to be

153

there. From the way she kissed Doug and asked him if he'd been having a good time and hung onto his arm she might have been wandering the streets of New York all afternoon in search of her husband. In fact, Cynthia was so busy asking Doug questions and explaining to him at length and in detail why she'd been held up at the other party that she didn't say any of the things to Nick that Katherine had expected her to say. In fact, she said nothing to Nick except 'hello' and 'good-bye'.

'So much for the gauntlet,' Katherine said in the taxi on the way home. 'You seemed to like Doug.'

'We talked sailing all afternoon. He must be pretty good. Or was pretty good at one time. He said he used to crew on some of the big ocean races. Could change a spinnaker in thirty-two seconds. Until he learned to change a diaper in the same amount of time.'

'That sounds like Cynthia speaking.'

'A lovely woman, your friend Cynthia.'

'You didn't even speak to her.'

'Did anyone at the party? The poor guy kept looking at his watch. At first I thought I was boring him. Then I realized he was waiting for her. Where was she anyway?'

Katherine debated her loyalties for a moment. 'Supposedly at a party for business, but I suspect hanky-panky.

'What did you think of Paige?'

'Why do I get the feeling that she and the good doctor just stepped out of a *New Yorker* short story? Or rather an ad.'

Katherine remembered an evening two weeks ago when she'd stopped at Paige's to drop off a book she'd borrowed. The cleaning woman had opened the door for her, and Katherine had found Paige sitting in front of the fire with Timmy on her lap. There were candles flickering all over the room, and Paige was wearing a long plaid skirt. She was reading *A Child's Christmas in Wales* to Timmy, and when she looked up and saw Katherine, she was genuinely surprised. The tableau had been arranged for Stanley's benefit.

Katherine stepped out of the cab and waited while Nick got his change and tipped the driver. 'She really is kindhearted underneath it all.'

'If you say so.'

They suspended the postmortem in order to agree with the doorman that it was cold and reassure the elevator man that appearances did not lie and they had in fact been out.

'What about Beth?' Katherine asked when they were in the apartment.

'These are supposed to be your friends, sweetheart.'

'I'm just curious about your reactions. Besides, it isn't as if I were talking about them with anyone else.' She followed him into the bedroom. He was already out of his jacket and tie, and she kicked off her shoes. She wasn't accustomed to high heels, and her feet were numb.

'Beth's a nice small-town girl who can't get over the fact she's making it in the big town. But I like her boyfriend better. Does the kid have vocal cords?'

'Only his doctor knows for sure. And speaking of doctors, that comment about first names wasn't exactly tactful.'

Nick took off his trousers and dropped them over the back of a chair. 'Dr Stan said it was excellent, if you remember. He also said you were an excellent woman. But don't get a swelled head because he urged me to try the baked ham, which was excellent, and the wine which was excellent, and told me what he claimed was an excellent dirty joke he'd just heard from a patient who is a noted star of stage and screen. Those are his words, not mine.'

'He and Paige always have been impressed by names.'

Nick dangled his shirt in front of Franklin, who pawed at it deliriously. 'Impressed by names. Sweetheart, you number among your friends some of the biggest celebrity fuckers in this city. But lest I take Dr Stanley for a lightweight, he got down to some serious talk as well. He wanted to know what I thought – as an attorney, of course – of all those restrictions hampering doctors from doing their appointed duty. He was especially incensed at the idea of having lay members – can you imagine, lay members – on boards of inquiry into medical practices.'

'Oh, God, I hope you didn't tell him.'

'I changed the subject to tax shelters. Then he really warmed up. Do you want a drink?'

'A light one.' She went into the bathroom to take off the makeup that was as unusual as the high heels. When she came out, Nick was already sitting up in bed. Even in winter his skin was about three shades darker than hers, and his chest and arms looked very hard. 'You still like Erica, though. Or at least you don't mind her.'

He shrugged. The gesture was uncharacteristic and too elaborate.

'Does that mean you don't like Erica either?'

'She's all right.'

'She didn't say anything to you, did she?'

'Why, did you tell her something I'm not supposed to know?'

'I didn't mean that. She was angry this afternoon – and drunk – and I thought she might have taken it out on you. Like that comment about your being a bad influence on me.' It was cold in the room, and Katherine put on a robe and crossed to his side of the bed. He moved his legs so she could sit. 'She doesn't really mean anything by it, you know. She thinks she has to take care of me.'

'If you say so.' He picked up the magazine she'd left on the bed and started to leaf through it. It was *Vogue*. Nick did not read *Vogue*.

'All right. What did Erica say to you?'

He didn't take his eyes from the magazine. 'Nothing.'

'Tell me.'

'Wanna fuck?'

Katherine started to laugh. 'I'm serious, Nick. What did she say?'

'She said a lot – most of it slurred and totally incoherent – but what it boiled down to was "Wanna fuck?"'

Katherine stood and walked around to her side of the bed where Nick had left her drink. She took a sip. 'When did all this happen?'

'I went upstairs to look for a bathroom. There was one off a bedroom, and when I came out, she was sitting on the bed.'

'And she just said, "Hi, Nick, wanna fuck?"'

'I told you, she wasn't very coherent. She said her ex-husband was a prick, and I was probably one, too; but I was a nice prick, and we were all such good friends, and you weren't possessive, and I imagine you get the gist of it.'

Katherine leaned back against the pillows. She didn't feel exactly relieved, but she did feel better. 'The gist of it is that she was drunk and depressed, and she's lonely; but that isn't exactly an outright proposition. You're imagining that.'

Nick closed the magazine. 'Look, sweetheart, I've imagined a lot of things in my life. That someday I'd be chief justice of the Supreme Court. That I'd be an Olympic fencer or crew for the America's Cup. Even that I could go on seeing you and stay married. But I do not imagine drunken women putting their hands on my cock. Your friend Erica has a grip like Dr Stanley's. Is that graphic enough for you?'

He went into the living room and came back with a LeCarré novel she knew he'd already read. She picked up *Vogue*. An hour later she said good night in a tone that lowered the temperature in the room a good ten degrees and turned on her side with her back to him.

'Why take it out on me, Katie? I didn't do anything.'

'I know. You can't help it if you're irresistible to women.' It was dumb to cry, and she knew she never would have if she hadn't been drinking slowly but steadily since three o'clock that afternoon. Behind her she felt the mattress shift under Nick's weight as he moved.

'That's right,' he said. His chin was in the hollow between her neck and shoulder, and he seemed to be giving off a lot of heat. 'I'm irresistible. Now go to sleep.'

She could tell from his breathing that he took his own advice almost immediately. She couldn't. Erica had been drunk, and the worst part of it all was how embarrassed she'd be when she remembered. If she remembered. Erica had been drunk, and Nick hadn't been interested, and Katherine had a book of her own, and Nick was snoring softly into the hollow

158

of her neck. And she'd be damned if she'd let anything spoil that.

IX

Erica telephoned Katherine at the end of the first week in January to say that her contracts had arrived and Sydney Hellerman was going to call her for lunch. She sounded perfectly normal and perfectly friendly, and only at the end of the conversation did she stray from business. 'God, I'm glad the hols are over. The older I get, the better I understand all those yuletide suicides. Thank God we can get back to normal.'

Lunch with an editor was not normal for Katherine. Editors took Ego and Altruist to lunch and invited her to their offices to discuss manuscript changes, which over the years had become almost nonexistent. With solid gold names like Ego's and Altruist's on the jacket, Erica said, editors didn't much care about the dross inside. Sydney Hellerman, however, was willing to take Katherine to lunch, not to one of the high-powered, low-calorie restaurants where big deals were made, but to a perfectly nice French restaurant, a $25,000 advance restaurant. Katherine was glad they hadn't paid five. It would have been awful to discuss her first book over a bauernwurst at Zum Zum.

People rarely looked the way you expected them to, but Sydney Hellerman looked so much the way Katherine had imagined her that for a moment she was sure they'd met somewhere. Sydney was short – even sitting down, she looked short – and stocky with an enormous shelf of bosom that jutted out over the table. Her hair was cut close to the head like Erica's; but there was less of it, and her nose and mouth were thin. But the eyes were Sydney's salient feature. Like an alert bird's, they didn't so much look into your soul as calculate your next move.

Sydney told her she was excited about the book. Katherine said she was excited about it, too. They ordered drinks. Sydney asked about her background. They talked about the Ego and Altruist books. They looked at the menu. Sydney said the fish here was excellent and the veal was good, too. Lunch arrived, and Sydney told Katherine about the advantages of publishing with her house, which, as Erica had pointed out, combined the individual attention of a small imprint with the clout of a major publishing house. Katherine savored the scallops and the sound of the word 'clout' again. They ordered coffee, and Sydney went to work.

'My chief criticism is that we don't like the woman enough.'

Katherine was shocked. 'I'm crazy about her.'

Sydney was not amused. 'It's important that we have a sympathetic heroine.'

'Some of the things she does aren't very sympathetic. In fact, they're downright nasty.'

'But she ought to do them in a nice way.'

Katherine said nothing.

'I think she'd be more sympathetic if we understood the oppressive forces that shaped her. We need to get a grip on her early conditioning. Sexual stereotyping in childhood. The way she was forced to play with dolls. You know the kind of thing I mean.' Sydney smiled briefly.

'I don't want to turn her into a caricature.'

'Of course not, but you want to strike a chord of recognition. Now the only other major fault I can find is with the husband.'

'Only? They're the two main characters in a four-character book.'

'We ought to get more of a feeling of male hostility.' Sydney leaned forward as if she were going to say something confidential. 'Most women would be shocked if they realized how deeply men hated them.'

'Most men would be pretty surprised if they knew what a lot of women thought of them, too.'

'The reader has to understand how completely the husband despises her.'

'But he doesn't despise her completely. He still has affection for her. That's one of the problems.'

The calculating eyes focused on Katherine, and she thought she knew what was coming. *Are you now or have you ever been a member of a marriage?* But unlike certain investigating committees, Sydney didn't ask you to name names from the past, only swear allegiance in the present. 'I thought you were a feminist.'

The long upper lip grew longer as Katherine considered the question. 'Actually I consider myself more of a postfeminist.' She saw the way Sydney's eyes snapped up from the check she'd been signing. Perhaps it had been unfair to take advantage of her while she was figuring the tip, but Katherine wasn't sorry. She regretted only that she didn't have an answer for the next question. What was postfeminism?

But Sydney was too smart for her. 'Of course,' she said as she stood. The solid cannonball body teetered absurdly on short, birdlike legs. 'Still, it will be a stronger book if the husband really despises her.'

Outside the restaurant they shook hands, and Katherine thanked her for the lunch. 'Now go home and get to work,' Sydney said. 'I can't wait to see the rest.'

Katherine didn't go home and get to work. You could go back to an office at three o'clock and get some work done, but by the time she got uptown and settled down to her typewriter, it would be almost time to turn it off. She wandered through the January sales and bought sheets, and a shirt for Nick, and a satin nightgown that she knew she'd never sleep in but would be nice to wear making drinks at night or coffee in the morning, and three paperbacks, and all the time she kept thinking of what Sydney had said. Maybe she was right. Maybe it would be a stronger book if she followed Sydney's advice. Everyone needed an editor, and Erica said Sydney was a good one.

At a quarter to six she met Nick in front of a movie. He was already in the ticket holders' line, and his nose was red from the cold. 'I'm sorry I wasn't earlier,' she said.

'No point in both of us freezing. How was lunch?'

'I'm not sure.' The line started to move. 'She wants to get more of a feeling of sexual oppression and misogyny.'

Nick didn't answer her until they'd found seats. 'You writing a novel or the party platform?'

Katherine had some ambivalence about the answer. 'How was your meeting this morning?' she asked, but the lights had already dimmed, and the *Cahiers du Cinéma* subscribers behind them made ominous hushing noises. Somewhere to her right she smelled the combined aroma of marijuana, which she didn't like, and popcorn, which she did, and realized she was hungry. She was constitutionally unsuited to business lunches, couldn't hold her own and a knife and fork at the same time. 'I think she wants to make it the party platform,' Katherine whispered. The group behind them grew uglier in their disapproval, and Nick reached beneath the coat on her lap and took her hand.

That January Katherine worked from the time Nick left in the morning till he returned home at night. Then she turned off her typewriter but not necessarily her mind. Notes still littered the apartment, though Nick no longer made his own contribution to them.

She saw little of her friends; but she continued to speak to them on the phone regularly, and the grapevine grew more heartily than ever. Cynthia's affair made for a vintage harvest.

'Cynthia has discovered infidelity,' Erica said. 'Only being Cynthia, she thinks she invented it.'

'Does anyone know who he is?' Beth asked. 'Or more to the point, is he anyone?'

'What about the kids?' Paige wondered.

'What about Doug?' Katherine said.

On the last Saturday night in January, when she and Nick went across the park for dinner at the Greers', Doug was still the essential Doug, or at least the public one. As Katherine and Nick got off the elevator, he was standing in the doorway of the apartment, filling the space with his tall, gaunt frame, his big smile, and his booming voice. He was the old reliable Doug, almost. It took Katherine a minute to realize what the difference was.

'Your beard! You're naked!'

'I thought it was time for a change,' he announced to Katherine and Nick and anyone else on the fourteenth floor who might be interested.

'How do you like it?' Cynthia appeared beneath Doug's long arm that was propped against the doorjamb. She looked even better than she had on New Year's Day. Her pale skin had a gloss to it that might or might not have to do with makeup.

'I do,' Katherine lied. She usually distrusted beards because she was convinced that most men grew them for instant character or easy individuality. Doug's beard, however, had had the opposite effect. Now that it was gone, the contrast between the nervous martyr's face and the traveling salesman's manner was even more disconcerting.

'It's as if he's someone else,' Cynthia said. 'I keep thinking I'm having an affair.' She smiled at Katherine, and Doug opened his thin mouth to let the laughter out, and they all went into the apartment.

'I am, you know. Having an affair,' Cynthia said later when she and Katherine were in the kitchen.

'So I've heard. You were practically wearing a sign New Year's Day.'

'What an afternoon! We sneaked away from that other party. He says . . .' Cynthia dropped her eyes; but the smile playing around her mouth was proud, and Katherine knew what was coming. She wished it weren't. Repeating intimacies to a third person was like taking an atheist to church. The experience might be impressive, even moving, but it would not be convincing. 'He says,' Cynthia went on, 'that I'm the most passionate woman he's ever known.'

Katherine made a noncommittal noise. It sounded as if she were gagging, but Cynthia didn't notice.

'He's very sensitive. But powerful, too. Do you know what it's like to find a strong man who's not afraid to be weak?' Katherine made another cryptic sound. It, too, came out as a sign of imminent nausea. She didn't like listening to Cynthia's breathless account of sex and passion in the garment industry while Doug and Nick sat two rooms away, swapping sailing stories. Katherine gave thanks for prewar apartment buildings. Maybe if fewer people lived in L-shaped rooms with posterboard walls, there'd be fewer divorces.

'Marty is in touch with his feelings. Not like a goddamn philosophy professor.'

'Do you want to save these potatoes?'

Cynthia opened a cabinet, and plastic containers of every size swiveled out on shelves attached to the door. Years ago, before Cynthia had become a lingerie buyer, she'd been a first-rate kitchen buyer, though of an amateur standing. Since she'd given up her cooking classes, she'd put most of her acquisitions away, but Katherine knew that behind the early American doors of the cabinets lay the history of the last twenty years of American cooking. What an archaeological dig! The first layer would reveal the terra-cotta quiche dishes from Italy and the special bread pans from France, the copper au gratin dishes and the oversized wok. That was the *haute cuisine* stratum. The next layer traced the growth of the family in culinary life. Here were the remnants, some still in working order, of machines that made ice cream and ground peanut butter, popped corn and grilled hot dogs, mixed milk shakes and extracted juice. Finally came the earliest level, the artifacts attendant to a rite of passage, commonly known as wedding presents. Here lay electric coffeepots, frying pans, and hot trays. For the historian rather than the archaeologist the bookshelf provided a wealth of written source material, beginning with *The Joy of Cooking* and *The Good Housekeeping Cookbook*, progressing through various *New York Times* volumes, and ending with the complete works of Julia Child, Marcella Hazan, *et al*. Since Cynthia had gone to work, she rarely used the books or the artifacts – the phone numbers of a Chinese kitchen and the local pizza stand were stuck to the refrigerator door – but she still knew her way around them. Cynthia had the kind of easy confidence in the kitchen that was born of years of experience. She breezed through the small area now, putting leftovers away, making coffee – not in the old electric pot but in the Chemex on which the Modern Museum had put its stamp of approval – and whipping cream laced with brandy without missing a beat in her actions or her conversation. She whipped the cream and her enthusiasm for the powerful, sensitive vendor simultaneously. 'Marty looks macho, but he doesn't act macho,' she said. 'He says the women's movement has done a lot for him, too.'

'Don't tell me. Let me guess. It's allowed him to cry.'

'Something that sailing machine in there would be ashamed to do.'

Katherine didn't know if Cynthia was referring to Nick or Doug. 'Where does Doug fit into all this?'

Cynthia turned off the electric beater and began to spread the cream over a chocolate torte. 'The philosophy department is electing a new chairman again. I could screw the entire faculty on his desk, and all he'd want to know was how each of them was going to vote. Besides, Doug has no complaints.

This is the best thing that's happened to our marriage since his parents took the kids and sent us to Europe. I'm happier. Sex is better. Even the kids have noticed the change.'

'In you, I hope, not in sex.'

'If anything, Marty's going to save this marriage.' She finished spreading the whipped cream and held the spatula out to Katherine, who ran a finger over it.

'Wow.'

'It's good, isn't it?'

'It's good, but that isn't what I meant. I don't want to disillusion you, Cyn, and I'm glad you're happy; but the last person who told me an affair was going to save her marriage ended up in a very nasty custody battle. Just be careful.'

Cynthia dropped the spatula in the sink and put the cake and coffeepot on a tray. 'Whoever it was couldn't handle it. I can. Super juggler. Good wife. Great mother. Successful buyer. And, according to Marty, dynamite lover.'

'You've got to do something about that inferiority complex, Cyn.'

They'd teased her the same way in school. When she'd come back from class with reports of brilliant insights that had astonished professors and students alike, when she'd returned from weekends at New Haven and later Cambridge with innuendos about Doug's friends who would have preferred to be her friends, when they'd swapped vacation stories and Cynthia's holidays had always turned out to be the most exciting or unusual or rewarding, they'd teased her about her flair for self-aggrandizement. And when the subject had arisen in Cynthia's absence, they'd exchanged smiles of one part guilt to one part superiority and excused her because everyone knew that Cynthia was sensitive about being the only one of the group on full scholarship and touchy about her weight and insecure about a mind that might have been overrated by New Brunswick, New Jersey.

Cynthia picked up the tray and started out of the kitchen.

'Just one more thing,' Katherine said. 'What about Mrs Marty? Weren't you the one who said I was betraying my own kind with Nick?'

Cynthia stopped and turned to Katherine. She was smiling the old knowing smile. 'There is no Mrs Marty. He's already divorced.'

Cynthia may have been fraternizing with the enemy – with more than one of the enemy it seemed from the way she stood with her arm around Doug's waist as they were all saying good night – but she hadn't forgotten they were the enemy. Doug and Katherine kissed good-bye. Cynthia and Nick did not.

'I hope you've got cab fare,' Nick said as he pulled on his gloves. 'Otherwise, it's the crosstown bus.'

Katherine saw a light go on in Cynthia's eyes. 'Pretty casual,' Cynthia said as if she were joking, but they all knew it was a deadly serious matter to her. 'Don't you two have a financial agreement about who pays what?'

'Sure we do,' Nick said. 'Whoever has money spends it.' Nick clapped his gloved hands together, though it wasn't cold in the apartment. 'The only problem is that Katie's more practical. She's always the one who remembers to go to the bank, so she's always the one who has the cash.'

'You said that just to annoy her,' Katherine said when they were inside the taxi. She did have cab fare.

Nick laughed, but when they'd crossed the park and she hadn't spoken again, he asked if she was angry.

'I just don't think it's necessary to be rude to people when they've had you over for dinner.'

'Listen, sweetheart,' he said, and in the shadowy light from the oncoming cars his mouth looked tense, 'you remember that dumb article she sent. Finances are like sex. Well, a little bordelaise sauce doesn't entitle her to intimacies.'

All through February and March Katherine worked at making the book stronger. It was harder work than ghosting, and lonelier. She no longer stopped automatically at three or four every afternoon because if it was going well, she didn't want to and if it wasn't going well, she was afraid to. She no longer picked up the phone to read another of Ego's outrageous ideas to Paige or complain to Beth about Altruist's impossible plot twists. She couldn't even justify an afternoon spent curled up on the sofa in the reading room of the New York Society Library because she didn't have to do any research. She found herself talking so much to Eleanor and Franklin that she actually welcomed Altruist's call one afternoon. Until he began talking.

His fan mail was getting out of hand. 'I really ought to get you to answer it.' He gave a childish giggle. Katherine said nothing. He was debating going out to Hollywood when they started shooting the television movie of his second book. 'I know all the stories about what it does to writers, but I'm not easily corrupted.' There was no giggle this time. Katherine ran a hand through her hair and clenched her teeth. He was thinking of cutting his office hours back to three days a week in order to have more time to write. Katherine said nothing. He didn't notice.

'The galleys for *Crisis* came up by messenger today.'

'How do they look?'

'I haven't had a chance to glance at them yet.' There was a low, gurgling sound as if he were clearing his throat. 'That's why I called. How would you like to read them? I mean, as the official wraith you know the book better than I do. You'd be more likely to spot a missing paragraph or something like that.'

Katherine scribbled idly on the yellow legal pad. The lines formed a head with an arrow going through it, and there was nothing hidden or Freudian about it.

She enjoyed reading galleys. The words she'd struggled over always took on a pleasant substantiality in print, and the long sheets gave her a nice feeling of professionalism. But if she didn't mind reading galleys, she did mind doing a job Altruist was too lazy to do, another job Altruist was too lazy to do. It still amazed her that people who hated to read books wanted to write them.

'I think you'd better go over them, Barry.' Maybe if she didn't say 'read', he wouldn't find the task so daunting. 'After all, your name is going to be on the jacket, and I wouldn't want to be responsible for letting something slip by that might embarrass you.'

She heard him sigh as he took up the burden of fame again. 'I suppose you're right. Look, Kate, if you change your mind – not about the galleys but about the ghosting . . .'

She told him work on her own book was going so well and her publisher was so pleased with it that she couldn't even think of anything else. Eleanor, who'd been sitting on the desk watching the moving pencil, rubbed her head against Katherine's hand. That was the nice thing about cats. You could lie – even cheat and steal – and they went on loving you as long as you opened that can of tuna and liver every morning.

Still, it was not a bad time to be locked in a house with a typewriter and two cats. Beyond the window behind her desk the days were bleak and abbreviated. In the afternoon the sky turned a murky gray with long yellow streaks of pollution that were New York's skywriting. Sometimes the wind rattled the window, though after Nick put up weather stripping – an ingenious invention Katherine had heard of but never bothered to do anything about – it no longer blew through the cracks. She made pots rather than cups of tea and watched the world go about its business on the street below, oblivious to sympathetic characters and stronger plots. The trees that partially obstructed her view from the eighth floor during the rest of the year were bare now, and she could see that the roller skates and skateboards had all but disappeared as children in down jackets and women in furs hurled themselves against the wind from the east. Men left in the gray morning looking gray themselves and returned home with faces made invisible by the dark. Doormen stayed behind closed doors, going out only to fight for taxis. On the harshest days the battle for cabs intensified, and the porters didn't polish the brass because the cleaning solvent would freeze. Every Friday afternoon women supervised while doormen loaded skis on top of cars and suitcases and children into them. And Katherine drank more tea and wiggled her ugly toes in her childish furry slippers and forced herself to turn away from the window to her typewriter. When it rained or snowed, she telephoned the butcher and the small grocer at the corner and the liquor store around the block and had them deliver, but she always felt guilty when she did and ended up ordering more than she needed.

Everyone went away. Paige and Stanley left Timmy with the woman they called their girl and for two weeks went to Little Dix where Stanley could jog on the beach rather than along the East River Drive. They'd never been able to get reservations at Little Dix before, and Paige said it was more exciting than the day she'd gotten into Smith. Beth went to Barbados to invite her muse. She also invited Topper and Jonathan and Jessica with one friend each during their winter break. Cynthia went to Chicago, Dearborn, St. Louis, Dallas, and Houston to visit branch stores and to her powerful, sensitive vendor's apartment for lunch twice a week. Erica went to the Coast and came back with a mangled vocabulary and more horror stories.

'I never took so many meetings in my life,' she said.

'Where did you take them?' Katherine asked.

Erica apologized and said she had to watch her language. 'And just when I finally got lunch down pat, they threw breakfast meetings at me. Where everyone drinks Tab.'

'I think I'm going to be sick.'

'But the real stomach turner was a lunch I had with a VPP. Very Powerful Producer. Everyone kept coming over to say hello to him.' Erica dropped several names, but Katherine caught only half of them. 'One director stood there for about fifteen minutes talking about some actress he was considering for a part. The producer had used her in his last picture. I may have been invisible, but she was a piece of meat. "Can she act?" the director asked. "Are you kidding?" the VPP said. "Can she remember her lines?" "If you have enough cue cards." "Can she walk out of her trailer by herself?" "If she's got her makeup on. Pores like the Grand Canyon and she's self-conscious." I thought they'd just about covered it, but the director had one more critical question. "Does she put out?" Can you imagine? In this day and age?'

'What did the producer say?'

'He said, "That kind of talent she's got." And meanwhile, I'm munching away on my bean sprouts and sipping my Perrier. You have to undereat those bastards. Can you imagine his saying that while I was sitting right there?'

'You wanted equality,' Katherine said. What she didn't say was that the question didn't seem such a far cry from queries about Nick's talents and comments about Arab lovers.

Katherine could have gone away that winter. Her mother asked her to come down to Florida for a week or two every time she called. She even offered to pay her fare.

'I'm too old for you to pay my way,' Katherine said.

'Don't be disrespectful,' her mother answered.

'Do you want to go?' Nick asked when she got off the phone.

Katherine was thinking it would be nice to get away from the cold and be taken care of for a while. She was also thinking that the irises of Nick's eyes had turned black the way they did when he was worried. 'I wouldn't get any work done down there.'

'You're ahead of schedule on the book. A week or two won't kill you.'

She thought of telling him not to push his luck. Instead, she told him she didn't want to go without him.

She did not, however, hibernate entirely. They went to every decent movie and some that were not so decent, though none was X-rated. They went to a few plays. They went to the ballet once while Paige and Stanley were away and couldn't use their tickets, and the Carlyle once to hear Bobby Short sing Katherine's kind of music, and to a country and western bar once to hear Nick's. When the rodeo came to Madison Square Garden, he wanted to take her, but she refused to cross the ASPCA picket lines. Every several days Katherine said she needed airing, and Nick took her out to dinner. And they attended three parties given by friends or business associates of Nick's. At the first, a small dinner, the hosts were old friends whom Nick had known since his first job. They went out of their way to be nice to Katherine, and the wife looked as if she'd like to turn her steak knife on herself when she called Katherine Gwen. There was a terrible silence while someone coughed and someone else scraped a fork against his plate, but Nick just laughed. 'Katherine,' he said. 'Her name is Katherine.'

The second party was given by a client of Nick's, and they knew no one except the host. Like Katherine's friends, most of the guests had been born outside New York, but they'd been born farther outside New York than its suburbs. The women called themselves and each other gals, and the men drank bourbon or beer; but they all did it consciously. They'd been in New York for some time. Around eleven they gathered in the living room and sang a rousing ditty called 'Up Against the Wall, You Red-necked Mothers'. Katherine and Nick got a little drunk and sang along and left the party with promises to see several people in the near future. When she got up the next morning, Katherine was amazed to hear the song running through her head. Nick came out of the shower singing it.

Another lawyer gave the third party in a sprawling old Park Avenue apartment that had elevated the idea of clutter to a philosophical principle. With the exception of two young men and a few odd bachelors, all the men were on their second wives, some on their third. They'd kicked over the traces with a vengeance. The wives weren't merely younger; they were as different from their husbands – and by definition their first wives – as possible. One dry husk of a man, with a thin puritan mouth and the kind of bad teeth that, in New York at least, signified good breeding, was disconcertingly demonstrative with a tiny Japanese girl. A bantam man with a belligerent manner and grating accent, both vintage New York, arrived with a tall, thin woman who had one of those double southern names and cheekbones that looked as if you could shave wood with them. The host, a handsome, urbane man who wore an ascot and looked as if he were in a revival of a Noel Coward play, probably didn't even notice the determined lines around his wife's pretty mouth. She didn't so much smile as bare her teeth.

There were a great many lawyers at the party. One of them, the bantam, was asking Nick if he'd noticed that only the most successful attorneys went back to their Harvard reunions. 'I don't know,' Nick said. 'I've never gone back.'

There were several young women who wore no-nonsense suits with silk blouses open one button too far and talked about tax law and sexual discrimination. One of them introduced herself to Katherine.

'Is that the one who left the lipstick on your shirt?' Katherine asked Nick. 'Or was it blusher?' They were still at the party, and Nick just smiled his public smile.

'I hate goddamn attorneys,' he screamed as they hit Park Avenue.

They started to walk north. 'I thought you were having a good time.'

'Boring,' he said. 'Pompous,' he screamed so that the doorman gave him one of those looks Park Avenue doormen reserve for people who live in other buildings. Nick rammed his hands into the pockets of his trench coat, looked up at the dark stone slabs that made a canyon of the avenue, and began to sing, 'Up against the wall, you red-necked mothers . . .'

They were becoming a couple. They were becoming so much a couple that the woman down the hall who had barely smiled at Katherine in the elevator for the past six years invited them to dinner.

'It's my ineffable charm,' Nick said.

'It's the fact that she's married to a younger man,' Katherine explained, 'and she didn't feel safe until you appeared on the scene.'

They didn't go. 'I don't believe in friendship by proximity,' Nick said. 'That's why I left the suburbs.'

'And I thought it had something to do with me.'

He continued to see his children every Saturday. Gradually they began to come on Friday night and stay for the entire weekend. Katherine wasn't sure which was worse, two perfectly pleasant but perfectly strange little boys on the couch that opened up in the living room or Nick on a Saturday night when he felt he wasn't seeing enough of them.

Katherine learned to make such culinary delights as SpaghettiOs, which involved opening a can and plopping a glutinous orange mass into a pot. She learned to do jigsaw puzzles again, though she was not very good at them and the boys became impatient with her. She learned not to say anything when small hands trailed cookie crumbs around the apartment and left black smudges on the wall. When she was a child, her mother had always scolded her for putting her hands on the walls; but though the walls were hers, the boys were not, and she said nothing. At least she thought she said nothing.

'For Christ's sake,' Nick screamed one Sunday afternoon when Mark dropped a piece of apple pie, and Katherine leaped toward it as if to catch it in midair. Katherine went into the kitchen with the piece of pie, and Nick followed. 'Keep it up, and they'll be afraid to set foot in the apartment.'

'I'm sorry. I'm not accustomed to kids.'

'I never would have guessed it.'

She hadn't noticed before how his mouth shriveled when he became sarcastic.

'I'm sorry I jumped at you about the pie,' he said when he came back from driving the boys home that evening. 'It's just that you've got them scared to do anything in this place.'

She thought of the scratches on the hall floor from the fencing matches and the raisins she'd found in her typewriter last week and the howling of cats being pursued through the apartment. 'Not exactly anything.'

'What is that supposed to mean?'

'Nothing. Forget it.'

'No, I want to know what you mean.'

'I just don't think they feel all that restricted. I

179

mean, all that wrestling and pillow throwing and screaming . . .'

'What the fuck do you want us to do? Sit and read?'

'I don't want you to sit and read, and I think all that physical stuff is terrific. You can see they love it. All I was saying was that I don't think they feel so terribly restricted here.'

She could tell from the hard look in his eyes that he wasn't listening. 'Okay, I'll go back to seeing them alone on Saturdays.'

'You see them alone now.'

'What's that supposed to mean?'

He didn't have to ask again this time. 'It means you never talk to me when they're around, and if I ask you a question, you answer in that stop-bothering-me tone, and most of the time I feel like the maid who opens the couch at night and closes it in the morning and serves the SpaghettiOs. Correction. The maid-cum-hooker because something about two little boys in the next room works like a goddamn aphrodisiac on you.'

'We know it doesn't on you, don't we, sweetheart?'

He was on the mark there. As far as Katherine was concerned, two kids on the other side of a thin door were a new form of contraception, 100 percent effective and almost, if not entirely, free of side effects.

'Don't call me sweetheart. You aren't Humphrey Bogart.'

'I was being sarcastic.'

'I never would have guessed.'

He went into the kitchen and came back with a glass of milk and a piece of that damn pie on a napkin. No wonder David and Mark trailed crumbs

180

around the place as if they were auditioning for *Hansel and Gretel*. 'Look, Katherine, it's hard enough entertaining them all weekend. I can't entertain you, too.'

'I don't want to be entertained. I just don't want to feel like some stranger who wandered into the group by mistake.'

'I can't stand feeling pulled apart.'

Now there was a news flash.

X

Nick decided to take the kids to his parents the following Saturday. Paige wanted to know why Katherine wasn't going. 'Because his parents are a nice old couple who would probably faint if Nick turned up with another woman. They still think a weekend away will save Nick's marriage. A weekend away with Gwen, not with me.'

'They don't sound so nice to me,' Paige said.

'All the more reason not to meet them.'

Erica congratulated Katherine on having demanded a day to herself. 'It's about time he stopped treating you like an *au pair*. Now you can come shopping with me. Independence Day shopping.'

'Aren't you a little early?'

'I'm late, luv. About two years too late. That's how long ago Michael moved out, and do you realize I'm still living in his bedroom, with his black leather Eames chair, his dressers without knobs, and his bedspread that looks as if he stole it off a monk's back? I'm going shopping, Kat. I'm going to buy ruffled curtains and flower-printed sheets. I'm going to get one of those little round tables instead of that wooden box for a night table, and I'm going to put a long print skirt on it. Michael would die. I'd buy a canopied bed if they weren't so expensive. Pick me up on Saturday around eleven. I'll be waiting with my magic plastic cards clutched in my hand.'

Katherine followed directions again, and again a man opened the door of Erica's apartment; but this time he was not strange. Mr Nice was not wearing his cowboy hat, but the boots with their pointy toes were still in fighting shape. He said it was terrific to see Katherine. He said he'd hung around until she got there just to catch her. He asked how her book was coming. He said he had to get going and patted Erica's beautiful ass on his way out the door.

'How long has he been waiting around to catch me?'

'Since last night. He just got back from Colorado and brought Josh's manuscript with him.'

'I'm getting a sense of *déja vu*.'

'Don't be judgmental. The kids don't spend that many weekends with Michael.'

'I'm not. I'm delighted. I'm just sorry I keep horning in this way.'

'You're not horning in. First of all, he really did have to leave. And besides, was I horning in when I had dinner with you and Nick?'

'That's different.'

Erica had been carrying coffee cups from the living room to the kitchen, and she stopped and looked at Katherine. 'Because you're an established couple and I'm still desperate enough for one-night stands?'

'You know I didn't mean that.'

Erica turned and went into the kitchen, and Katherine followed her. 'I'm sorry, Kat. It's not you, just my goddamn life. I'm too old to be sitting around wondering if someone will call again.'

'I thought we didn't have to wait for the man to call anymore.'

Erica closed the dishwasher and straightened. 'You

know what that gets you. You call, buy the groceries, make dinner, and if you're lucky, you get laid condescendingly. God, I hate men. I hate married men who pretend they're not and married men who tell you they are with their hands on your thigh. I hate gay men who don't look it and gay men who do and are prettier than I am. I hate old men like my father who think I'm a failure because Michael left and young men like Topper who think all I need is one magic roll in the hay with them. I hate Hollywood producers who never make a pass because I'm thirty-six and have pores as big as the Grand Canyon and on-the-make writers who always make a pass because they think I'll work harder to sell their books. I hate goddamn men. I just wish my hormones did.'

'You know it's more than that.'

'I know.' Erica rubbed her eyebrows with her thumb and forefinger, and for a moment Katherine thought she was going to cry. 'I'm like some idiotic eighteen-year-old who still walks around expecting things.'

Katherine put her hand on Erica's shoulder. 'Why shouldn't you? You've been divorced only a couple of years. Think how long I lived alone before I met Nick.'

'That's what I am thinking of. Geriatric romance.'

They took a cab downtown, and Erica bought everything she'd threatened to and a few things more. She seemed to grow more cheerful with each purchase. 'Michael ought to bring the little woman around now. She'd get a culture shock.'

They came out of the store into the darkness, and the cold air was like a stinging slap against their faces.

'Do you think spring will ever come?'

'Probably not. You should have gone away. You still can.' Erica wrenched open the door of a taxi a fraction of a second before another woman reached it. The woman muttered something, but Erica smiled sweetly and got into the back seat. 'Why don't you go to Florida to visit your mother? You have for the last couple of years.'

'I wouldn't have got any work done.'

'You could have stayed with Beth in Barbados. The kids weren't there for long, and she has an extra room.'

'Can you picture the two of us sitting in our respective rooms, listening for the sound of each other's typewriters? Besides, Topper was there most of the time.'

'Besides,' Erica corrected, 'you didn't want to leave Nick.' She took a small black cigar from her handbag, and Katherine pointed to the no-smoking sign. 'If he can blast that music, I can smoke. Why didn't you and Nick go away?'

'He's saving his vacation for the kids this summer.'

Erica exhaled a long ribbon of smoke. 'I haven't even met those kids, and I'm sick to death of them. I don't know how you stand it.'

'That's the way Nick comes packaged.'

'You ought to get away, you know. People need vacations from each other. You need a vacation from Nick. And those kids. To reestablish your independence, your sense of self-worth.' The years had taught Erica which verbal buttons to push.

'If I go away now, I'll lose time on the book.'

'How's it coming?'

'I'd be the last one to know. Some days I hate it. Some I love it. All I know is that if Sydney's wrong, I've gone off on one hell of a tangent.'

'Sydney's not wrong. Talk about having a finger

186

on the pulse of the American reading public. She has a scanner on its brain. In the last two weeks three different editors have mentioned postfeminism to me, but Sydney's the only one who already has a book on it under contract.' Erica flicked her ashes into the pristine ashtray. 'Sydney can spot a trend a month before it hits *New York* magazine and two weeks before *People*.'

'What do you want to do next weekend?' Nick asked that night.

Katherine thought of her conversation with Erica. 'Do I have a choice?'

'Anything you want.'

'So long as it's the Museum of Natural History or a G-rated movie.'

'I thought we could go away.'

'Disneyland?'

'Don't tell me. Let me guess. You had lunch with the *girls* today.'

'Only Erica.'

'Erica is enough. I meant maybe the two of us could go away. Alone.'

'What about the kids?'

'Gwen is taking them to Washington to see her sister.'

It didn't matter how the game was played, Katherine told herself, so long as you won.

'We might as well take the weekend now because I'm not going to have much time for the next couple of months. Grant is leaving, which means more work for everyone until we replace her.'

'Who's Grant?'

'Diane Grant. You met her at that party. You reminisced about Smith.'

'She reminisced. I listened. She intimidated the

hell out of me. Did she get a better job?'

'Just decided to leave. She said she's proven she can do the success trip – I'm quoting her – and it isn't worth it. Apparently she's always wanted to paint, so her husband got her a loft in Soho. You know, I've always wanted to win the Admiral's Cup. You wouldn't like to get me an ocean racer, would you?'

'You made your point. Where do you want to go for the weekend?'

Nick's weekend plans were not as aimless as he'd made them sound. It didn't matter where they went so long as they went to New London. There was a submarine base there and a submarine museum and – 'get this, Katie' – a genuine World War II sub you could tour.

Katherine had grown accustomed to Nick's enjoyment of his penance, but she hadn't expected to have to share it. 'Why don't we just stay home and watch John Wayne movies?'

'You'll love it. We'll drive up Friday night and go on to Boston Saturday. We'll stay at the Ritz-Carlton.'

'Aren't you afraid you'll get the bends going from a sub base to the Ritz?'

On Friday Katherine arranged to have the doorman come in to feed and water the cats, called the news delivery service and asked it to hold the Saturday and Sunday papers, and packed her and Nick's clothes in one suitcase. 'How do you like them connubial apples?' she said, grabbing her black cashmere sweater from the bed before Franklin could nest on it. Most of her working shetlands looked as if they needed a shave, but she was still protective of her good clothes. Katherine packed with the precision of someone who did it rarely. Rolled socks and underwear nestled inside shoes; tissue paper protected clothes and fought off wrinkles. The suitcase was full but not overflowing, and she closed it with ease and a sense of pride. Then Nick came home and started taking things out of drawers and closets. He flung his camera, telephoto lens, and Swiss army knife on the bed.

'We're not camping out, Nick.'

'You never know when it's going to come in handy.'

He went into the living room and came back with a quart of scotch.

'I think they sell liquor in Boston,' she said.

'But they don't in New London at eleven o'clock at night, and when you get a load of the Mystic Motor Inn, you're going to want a drink.'

'I thought we were going to Howard Johnson's.'

'I couldn't get into there. You see, everyone's hot to visit the subs. Mystic is right next to it.'

'You mean we're going to a motel that's worse than a Howard Johnson's?'

'The Mystic Motor Inn is so bad it's been known to make submariners beg for sea duty. You're going to love it. After you've had a couple of drinks.'

Nick had exaggerated, but not by much. Inside the room there was a lot of plastic, some of it broken, great expanses of dirt-camouflaging green and orange, both solid and patterned, and a lot of paper wrappers that assured you the glasses and toilet seat and God knows what else were sterile.

Nick went down the hall and came back with a cardboard bucket full of ice. They were on the ground floor, and in the room above them the Children's Crusade seemed to be on the march.

'I wonder how many people have committed suicide in this room,' she said.

He took the wrappers off the glasses and filled

them with lots of scotch and very little water. 'I told you you'd love it.'

'Now I understand why you didn't want to take the time to stop at a restaurant on the way. If I'd known what it was like, I'd have been impatient, too.'

Nick picked up the telephone and held a brief conversation with the man who'd checked them in. 'Now I want you to make this choice carefully,' he said when he got off the phone. 'There's a disco over in Groton that serves hamburgers till eleven-thirty – we just might make it if we rush – and there's a McDonald's down the road.'

'That's not a choice. It's a sentence.'

Nick went out and came back twenty minutes later, carrying a bag with grease stains and golden arches. They decided not to risk eating on unsterilized stomachs, so Katherine put the Big Macs and french fries on the radiator grating and turned the thermostat up to high while they each drank another tumbler of scotch.

There were two double beds in the room, and when they finished eating, they moved to the other one. 'That's one thing you can say for the Mystic Motor Inn. No crumbs.'

'Didn't I tell you you were going to love it.'

In the middle of the night Katherine heard a noise and opened her eyes, but since no light filtered in through the heavy draperies, it took her some time to get her bearings. The noise sounded like a man shouting, then a woman screaming. Stamps and a heavy thud shook the ceiling, and kids sobbed against a flood of obscenities. Slowly she remembered the ugly motel room and the Children's Crusade above them. The ceiling shook again. More screams made

Katherine open her eyes wider in the black room. She turned over, but it was too dark to tell whether Nick was awake. 'I know,' he said.

The noise couldn't have gone on for more than a few minutes, though it seemed longer. At one scream she flinched.

'Someone ought to stop it.' Nick turned over on one elbow.

'Not you.'

'I could call the desk.'

They heard the sounds of someone banging on the door upstairs. The noise continued for a while; but there were no more screams, and they both fell back to sleep.

Nick was up a little after eight the next morning. 'You can sleep for a while,' he whispered. 'The sub base isn't open yet.' But she could tell from the alarms he was raising at various points along her body that he had no intention of letting her sleep. She turned over, and her nose hit his chest. There was something downright subversive to the Advertising Council of America about people who drove five hours, drank too much scotch, ate Big Macs, and still had skin that smelled that good. She rubbed her nose against his chest. He mumbled something about submarines.

'Is this going to be a crash dive?' she asked.

He moved his hands down her stomach. 'A practice dive. And we'll keep at it until we get it right.'

At nine o'clock he began calling the sub base. By nine-thirty he was showered, dressed, and standing at the door with his camera and telephoto lens. Presumably his Swiss army knife was in the pocket of the old herringbone jacket.

191

Erica would have laughed. Beth would have turned over and gone back to sleep. Paige would have refused to leave the room with a tourist in baggy khakis. Cynthia never would have come in the first place.

'I don't suppose this grand tour includes coffee,' Katherine said.

Nick said if she wanted coffee, she'd have coffee. He left the room and returned three minutes later with two cardboard cups containing some murky liquid that had no aroma and very little taste and a package of tan crumbs that claimed kinship, according to the wrapper, with coffee cake.

'Torture me as much as you want,' Katherine said. 'I still won't give more than my name, rank, and serial number.'

She drank half the murky liquid while Nick threw the clothes they'd taken off the night before and his shaving kit into the suitcase. His method of packing did not demand the niceties of tissue paper. He asked her if she could manage the briefcase with the scotch, guides, and odds and ends and started for the car without waiting for an answer. Katherine put down the cardboard cup, put on her coat, and followed.

She flung the briefcase in the back of the car, and it bounced off the seat onto the floor. 'Easy,' he said.

'Aye, aye, sir.'

The United States Navy did not charge money for touring one of its fleet subs, only blood. They had to sit through an indoctrination film. An officer led their group, which was long on middle-aged men with crew cuts and preadolescent boys with shrill voices, into a large rectangular room with bridge chairs and a screen at one end. The linoleum reminded Katherine of a school cafeteria. There were several flags on either side of the screen.

192

The film began with an actor in a walrus mustache and derby – the navy's idea of turn-of-the-century props – paddling around in a small bathtublike vessel. A few seconds later the submarine was born. Toward the end a great mushroom-shaped cloud appeared on the screen, and the voice-over quivered with emotion at America's power.

'I don't believe it.' Katherine did not whisper, and a man with a crew cut in front of her turned and looked at her as if she'd better believe it.

Nick reached an arm around her and leaned over to whisper. 'I warn you, Katie, if you get us thrown out before the sub tour, I'll never forgive you.'

But she had no such luck, and Nick was the first off the bus that took them from the visitors' center to the sub pens. They stood at the head of the line, waiting for the other preadolescents to queue up behind them. The wind off the Thames River was cold and brackish. From this vantage point the sub was nothing but a small deck with a conning tower. The black water slurped at its sides. It didn't look inviting. It didn't even look safe. Katherine mentioned the fact to Nick. He was standing behind her and merely hugged her and kissed her ear. This from the man who looked abashed when she forgot herself and kissed him good-bye in front of the doorman.

The officer led them over the narrow plank onto the sub. Her boots slipped on the wooden slats that covered the metal deck, and Nick caught her arm. 'You shouldn't have worn your good boots,' he said good-naturedly.

'You didn't tell me we were going to see action.' Her tone did not match his.

'We're going to enter through the forward torpedo loading hatch,' the officer announced to the group at large. Nick looked as if he thought this was terrific news. 'Just hold onto the railing and swing your legs forward and down,' the officer explained.

Nick, ever the gentleman, stepped aside for Katherine to go first. She gripped the railing as instructed. It was cold and greasy. She took the step down preparatory to whatever leg swinging she was supposed to do and caught the low heel of her boot. As she bent to smooth the gash in the leather, she noticed the streak of black grease on her camel's hair coat. She looked up at Nick, who was beaming down at her. 'You fucking son of a bitch,' she said quietly.

'Didn't I tell you you were going to love it?'

When the officer, who looked like every other middle-aged man in the group – only Nick was out of place – had assembled them in the forward torpedo room, he began his act. 'Okay,' he said, and Katherine wanted to snap to attention. 'How many of you were in WW Two?' That was the way he pronounced it, double-u double-u two. Nick looked regretful.

The tour leader finished his introductory remarks and told them to stay together in the boat, but Nick had never had a sufficient regard for authority. He lagged behind in every compartment. First there was the fascination of the torpedoes, then the officers' head, the captain's cabin, the wardroom, where presumably he and Duke would sit over coffee in a silent bond of understanding of war and honor and the woman back home they both loved. The companionways were barely wide enough for one person, the doors between compartments were scaled to five-year-olds or dwarfs, and every inch was filled with equipment. Katherine kept bumping her head and hitting her shins and backing into grease-covered instruments. When they reached the maneuvering room, Nick's eyes took on a feverish glaze. His hands opened and closed as he looked at the wheels of the diving planes and the buttons on something called the Christmas tree and other assorted equipment he felt obliged to explain to Katherine. They were the last to leave the boat, and Nick kept trying to con the officer into taking them into the conning tower.

'I'd give anything to get into that tower,' he said as they headed back to the bus.

'I had my heart set on it,' Katherine answered.

She thought they were finished, but she hadn't counted on the museum. Nick said they had to see the museum. She saw it, case after case of battle flags and weapons and model ships.

'Nick.' Katherine called him over to a display. 'Now this is something. You didn't tell me they had anything like this. Forget the Whitney and the Modern. I'm giving up my Met membership. I mean, this is really something. A Japanese occupation dollar. Do you think it's genuine? With something like that there's always the problem of forgeries and reproductions.'

Nick agreed it was time to start for Boston. Boston was a definite improvement. Katherine said it couldn't have been anything else. They had a room overlooking the Public Garden and dinner in an elegant old house on Beacon Hill and breakfast in bed the next morning. The coffee was strong, the croissants fresh, and the Knott's Farms preserves right-wing, as Katherine pointed out, but sweet. 'And speaking of right-wing, I had no idea I'd gotten mixed up with a warmonger. I thought you were an old-fashioned knee-jerk liberal.'

'The ability to hold two opposing ideas at the same time and still function. Fitzgerald says that's

195

the test of a first-rate mind.'

'I saw you on that sub, ace. What makes you think you were functioning?'

They walked the Freedom Trail and went to the Fogg and wandered around Cambridge, but that depressed Nick because it had changed so much in the last fifteen years. 'I'm getting old,' he said when they got back in the car.

'I'll give you a copy of *Crisis* as soon as it comes out.'

Erica was pleased they'd gone away for the weekend and appalled at where they'd gone. 'New London. Why not Hoboken? Or Jersey City?'

'Because there are no sub bases in Hoboken and Jersey City.'

'You know, Kat, I like Nick. I really do. And I'm sure all those bizarre tastes are very endearing, but don't you think he's just a little selfish?'

'We went to Boston.'

'You went to Boston so he could take you to Cambridge and show you the scenes of his youth.'

'We had a nice weekend, Erica.'

'I'm glad, but I still think he's selfish.'

The following week things went back to normal and Nick drove out to get his kids on Friday night.

'I wish *you'd* married Michael,' Erica said when she called and heard the noise in the background. 'I'd pay to have someone take my kids every weekend. Not that I don't adore the dimpled darlings. I'd just like a little time off now and then.'

Katherine wasn't sure where Nick had gotten the idea of an aquarium. Perhaps he was still thinking underwater thoughts from New London. Perhaps he was inspired by the sight of Mark chasing

Franklin around the apartment. Nick decided the boys would feel more at home if they had some pets of their own there.

'I guess I ought to be glad you didn't decide on a guinea pig or gerbil,' Katherine said.

Nick's face lit up. 'I never thought of that.'

'The hell you didn't. I draw the line somewhere.'

Katherine worried about the cats, but the man in the fish store assured them he had both a fish tank and a cat, and one never interfered with the other. After a great deal of debate Nick and the boys decided on the aquarium, the color gravel, and the plants. They couldn't buy the fish until they had the tank in working order, but Nick bought a handful of paperbacks on the subject of freshwater tanks and tropical fish. He was nothing if not thorough. Katherine and Mark spent the afternoon washing gravel in the bathtub while Nick and David wrestled with the filter system. According to Nick, it bore no resemblance to the diagram and directions. Franklin and Eleanor raced back and forth between the two operations, and when the tank was finally set up on a table in the hall, the two cats sat on the floor gazing up at it raptly.

'They think it's television,' David said.

'Wait till we get them some actors.' Nick looked as excited as the kids.

'I give those fish a life expectancy of ten minutes,' Katherine said. 'Eleanor and Franklin know a good meal when they see one.' She was sure of three things. The cats were going to eat the fish. The loss of the fish was going to traumatize the boys. And she was going to be somehow responsible.

'Father fishes eat their own babies,' Mark said. The small imp's face seemed delighted at the prospect.

'Terrific. If their natural enemies don't get them, their friends will. A life expectancy of two minutes.'

'What's a life expectancy?' Mark asked.

'How long they're going to live. How old they can expect to get,' Katherine heard Nick explaining as she went into the kitchen for paper towels to mop up the floor around the tank. When she returned, they'd moved from the life expectancy of tropical fish to the equivalencies of human and feline ages.

'One cat year means six people years,' David announced. 'How old are Eleanor and Franklin?'

Katherine had to think for a minute. She was never good at keeping track of years, but Eleanor, looking like one of those adopt-a-kitten subway ads, had sidled up to her on Eighty-fourth Street when she was working on Altruist's first book, and she'd gotten Franklin a year later to keep Eleanor company. 'Eleanor's five, and Franklin's four.'

'That still makes you the oldest one in the house, Daddy.'

Nick took the paper towels from her and began to mop up the floor. 'You're forgetting Katie. You wouldn't believe she's sixty-seven, would you?'

'Don't listen to your father. I'm twenty-one. I have been twenty-one for the past fifteen years, and I plan to remain twenty-one for the next fifteen.'

'That's what Mommy told Grandma,' Mark said. 'That you were twenty-one.'

Down on all fours, mopping up the floor, Nick didn't look up, but Katherine could tell from the way his shoulders were shaking that he was laughing.

'I was teasing about being twenty-one,' she told the boys. 'I'm thirty-six.'

Nick took a last swipe at the floor and stood.

'Older than your mother.'

'Only by a year,' Katherine said.

'That's quite an image you have in Connecticut,' Nick said that night after the boys had gone to sleep. 'Twenty-one!'

'With bleached blond hair and melon breasts.'

'No, Gwen doesn't watch old movies. She probably thinks you wear T-shirts that say "Why Don't We Do It in the Road" and are heavily into drugs. She's going to be mad as hell when she finds out you're older than she is.'

Paige returned from Little Dix with a complexion that had been as carefully bronzed as if it had been Timmy's baby shoes. She no longer looked like an amateur hockey player. Now she had the aura of an Olympic athlete.

'I hate people who are tan in the middle of winter,' Katherine said when she returned from the basement laundry room one afternoon and found Paige in the hall in front of her door. Paige had telephoned before she'd come over because that was the rule by which they all lived. In the suburbs women dropped in. In town they called first. 'I think it shows a lack of social conscience. You look wonderful.'

'And you look very domestic.' Paige indicated the woven plastic basket full of clean laundry. 'It suits you.'

Katherine opened the door and let Paige go into the apartment ahead of her. 'Maybe we could get a picture for the book jacket. Everybody poses with cats. I could try a laundry basket. The author with her undies.'

Paige stopped in front of the fish tank. 'Where did this come from?'

'Nick bought it for the kids. I have cats. They

have tropical fish. And Nick has me. You can have instant coffee or real tea.'

'Tea with milk and without self-disparaging jokes.'

Katherine made a fresh pot, and they went back into the living room. She put the tea on the coffee table in front of Paige and sat on the floor beside the laundry basket. Paige sipped her tea and watched Katherine sort clothes.

'Don't you match Nick's socks?'

Katherine looked at the nest of tangled black and gray and navy and white she'd thrown onto one of the chairs and remembered that first Saturday morning when she'd opened his drawer and seen them all so perfectly mated. These days they were stuffed in the drawer in disarray. 'Devotion has to stop somewhere.'

'I always sort Stanley's.' Unlike Beth, Paige had never learned to control her face for her public. The set of her mouth said that men didn't marry girls who were too lazy to sort their socks.

Paige opened her handbag and fished around until she came up with a newspaper clipping. 'I brought this in case you hadn't seen it. Or rather in case Nick hadn't seen it.' She handed the article to Katherine. WORKSHOPS TO IMPROVE FATHERING SKILLS the headline ran.

Katherine put the clipping aside and went back to the laundry. 'Just what the world needs. Another workshop. I'm thinking of starting my own. The ultimate workshop. It sharpens your skills for taking workshops.'

'I just thought Nick might be interested. You said he was having trouble with his kids.'

'He's having trouble with himself about his kids.' Katherine picked up the article again. 'Listen to this. From a "media executive". "I pick up insights from other fathers. I watch them interact, relate, and I get a kind of biofeedback. A couple of months ago I would have watched Jennifer color. Now I get down on the floor and share the experience with her."' Katherine put the clipping aside and went back to the laundry. 'I told you Nick doesn't need a workshop. He's already shared the experience of coloring, model building, and game playing. Nick "relates" and "interacts" beautifully with his kids. He just feels guilty about not doing more of it.'

'But that's the point. Maybe if he had a peer group of other guilty fathers . . .'

'Nick's peerless.'

'You're so damn stubborn. You wouldn't even look at that book on stepparenting.'

'Because it was probably written by someone like Ego or Altruist – and ghosted by someone like me. Besides, the kids and I get along well enough. They can't help it if they wish I'd disappear and life would go back to normal with Mommy and Daddy in the same house.'

'It'll be easier when you and Nick are married.'

Katherine said nothing, and Paige's dark brows came together in a straight line as they did when she was worried. 'Does that ominous silence mean you and Nick aren't planning to get married?'

'Poor Paige. For two years you worried whether Nick would leave his wife. Now when you finally think you're home free, you have to start worrying all over again about whether he'll marry me.'

'Don't you want to get married?'

'Sure I want to get married. I want to get married so you can stop losing sleep over me. I want to get married so my mother can stop being embarrassed when her friends ask about me. I want to get married

201

so I have a name for Nick because I'm too old for "boyfriend" and too shy for "lover". How about "unhusband", like "uncola"? Then I wouldn't have to get married after all. Or do you think that's copyrighted?'

'In other words you're afraid to make a commitment.'

Katherine hugged her knees to her chest. 'I've made a commitment. You don't think I'd do just anyone's laundry.'

'The pendulum is swinging back, Kate. To marriage and children. The me generation has had it.'

'What about the me-too generation? Do you think I can get in on that?'

'Very funny, but I didn't marry Stanley or have Tim because it was the thing to do. Seven years ago it wasn't. Seven years ago you were supposed to have a career, not a baby. Ask our friends. Better yet, ask them about their hallowed careers. Beth writes books about middle-class housewives who talk dirty and screw around, Erica sells them for more than they're worth, and Cynthia peddles ladies' lingerie. And they sneer at me.'

'They don't sneer.'

'They do, but I don't care. I'm making a good home for a man who deals in life and death. Every day. I'm raising a wonderful, sensitive, intelligent child. That's another thing. Take a look at their kids. For ten years Cynthia lived through hers. Just the way she did through Doug. Now she's forgotten they exist. Erica vacillates between relying on her girls as crutches because she's so lonely and hating them because they remind her of Michael. And Beth has raised two precocious street urchins. She took Jessica straight from diapers to a diaphragm, and now she's working on getting Jonathan "initiated" by an older woman. I just hope it isn't her.' Paige stopped suddenly and tightened her lips as if she were reprimanding herself. 'I'm sorry, I didn't mean to be bitchy. Not about them or their kids.'

Katherine shrugged. 'Most people who have kids are at least a little bitchy about other people's. So, for that matter, are most people who don't.'

'But I'm not, Kate. I really do like other people's kids, and I think I'm objective about Tim. It's just that I get so tired of their condescending to me. I have a good marriage and a terrific son. I'm well read, and I spend more time in museums and galleries, to say nothing of auctions, than all three of them put together. I play the piano and can hold my own at dinner parties, and I don't have to go out and get a job to have an identity.'

Katherine held up a hand. 'I agree.'

Paige looked at her skeptically. 'Every time you say you agree I hear a "but" in your voice.'

'Well, don't you ever feel a little nervous about being so totally dependent on Stanley?'

'Of course not. I trust Stanley. Besides, he couldn't afford to leave me. Especially with the new equitable distribution divorce laws.' Paige shook the curtain of dark hair back from her face and laughed. 'Don't look so appalled, Kate. I was only joking.'

Katherine hadn't meant financial dependence, or at least she hadn't meant only that, but she knew it would be too dangerous to explain what she had meant.

'I'm not nervous,' Paige went on. 'I'm content. Remember that day we went Christmas shopping? You said they envied me because I was content and they weren't. Well, I realized you were right. I am content. And I've stopped apologizing to them and every other woman who condescends to me because she runs a boutique or pushes papers around a desk for eight hours a day just to make enough to pay someone to take care of her kids. I accept myself, Kate, and I think you'd be happier if you stopped trying to be a second Beth Sarmie and accepted yourself.'

'I'm not trying to be a second-rate Beth Sarmie.'

'I said "second", not "second-rate". Don't you ever wonder what it would be like to have a child? You must. After all, it's the most important thing a woman can do. Next to motherhood, the careers and the success and even the money are just . . . well, trivial.'

'Sometimes I agree with you. And sometimes I look at the people who have children and go back to my typewriter.'

Paige stared at her cup and saucer as if she were debating whether to make a bid on them. 'Is it possible – now don't get angry at me – that you really want children but are afraid to admit it because you think Nick doesn't?'

'Possible, but unlikely. I seem to lack the maternal instinct. Anyway, I'd make a terrible mother.'

'Who says so?'

'Nick, for one. According to him, I can't even discipline the cats.' Katherine had been half-joking, but she knew as soon as the words were out that Paige was going to take them entirely seriously.

'I'm not sure he's one to talk.'

Paige had spaced her words and their implications as if she were placing cakes on a tray. Nick wasn't one to talk because he'd left his children or because he was having difficulties with them now that he had or because he refused to take workshops in raising them. Take your choice; only Katherine wasn't going to. 'All the more reason for us not to have kids.'

Paige sighed exactly as she did when Timmy wheedled her into another cookie or an extra five minutes before bedtime. 'Okay, we'll table the kids, but I still think Katherine Larries has a nice ring to it.'

'If I did marry Nick, I wouldn't change my name.'

Now Paige looked surprised and a little annoyed. 'Not you, too?'

'It just wouldn't feel right. I've been Katherine Walden for thirty-six years, except those three when I was Katherine Hoffman, and that never felt right either. I can be married and still be Katherine Walden.'

'You can. I just can't imagine why you'd want to.' Paige stood. 'I have to get moving if I'm going to pick up Tim.' She walked to the hall closet and took out her coat. 'Speaking of being Katherine Hoffman, did I tell you we ran into Stephen in the airport the day we left?'

Katherine leaned her shoulder against the door. Paige knew she hadn't told her. 'How is Stephen?'

'He was on his way to China. For some high level wheeling-dealing. Stanley says he's going to be president of that company someday. Probably chairman of the board.'

'You're talking about the man who gave me my first subscription to *The New Republic*.'

'You can't sneer at success.'

'Some people can, but I'm not.'

'He asked about you. At length this time since Jill wasn't there.'

'What did you tell him?'

'That you were living with someone and would probably get married as soon as his divorce came through. I told him Nick was terribly nice and terribly successful and that you were blissfully happy.' Paige spoke as if she were pledging allegiance to the flag.

XI

Stephen took three days to call, more than that if you counted the time since he'd seen Paige, but then there was no telling how long he'd been in China. It was eleven in the morning, and Katherine was struggling through a long scene that she couldn't get right because no matter what Sydney Hellerman said, and despite the fact that she was opposed to sexual stereotyping and had always been careful about the toys she'd given her friends' children, she just didn't think the doll her parents had bought her for her fifth Christmas had ruined her life. She picked up the phone on the first ring.

'Kate?'

'Yes.'

'Don't you know who this is?' A forty-year-old man and he still made telephone calls like a teenager. If she guessed correctly, would he ask her to the sock hop?

'Stephen?'

'I didn't know if you'd recognize my voice.'

'It hasn't changed.'

They went through a few minutes of polite inquiries about each other's health and the welfare of his wife and children. He did not ask about Nick.

'I thought I could buy you lunch.'

Katherine ran a hand through her hair. 'Don't

you think that would be awkward?'

'Awkward?' he said as if it were a foreign word he didn't understand.

Comment dit-on? How you say? Dangerous. Titillating. Pointless. 'I'm living with someone, Stephen.'

'I'm only asking you to lunch.'

One point for the visiting team.

'Are you going to tell your wife' – she did not add, 'your wife who does not permit my name to be mentioned in her presence' – 'that you asked me to lunch?'

One point for the home team.

'Look, Kate, we were married for three years. At one time in our lives we meant a lot to each other.'

'Why else would it bother your wife or my' – she thought of trying 'unhusband' but didn't have the nerve – 'the man I live with?'

'Paige said you'd changed, but I didn't think anyone could do an about-face like this. Does he keep you barefoot and pregnant, too?'

She made a lunch date for the following week.

There was no reason to tell Nick she was having lunch with Stephen, but she must have felt there was some reason not to because she waited till the night before to mention it.

'And you said yes?' Nick asked. They were sitting in bed, eating supper off a tray. They used the dining table only when the boys or guests were there. Nick said it was one of the advantages of not having children. Paige hinted that the practice was irresponsible, immoral, and tacky. Beth said that when she and Topper were alone, they never left the bedroom.

'It's only lunch. Besides, it's not like Erica and

Michael or you and Gwen. I don't hate Stephen.
He's nice.'

'If he's such a great guy, why didn't you stay
married to him?'

'Because I was too young and couldn't stand being
married. And because he was too nice. Erica says
I'm a masochist.'

'That's why you need someone like me.'

Someday, Katherine swore, she would learn to
cultivate the virtue of reticence.

'When is this romantic reunion with this terrific
guy coming off?'

'If it bothers you that much, I won't go.'

Nick said nothing, but the way he was spearing
the underdone steak on his plate was sufficiently
eloquent.

The virtue of reticence, Katherine reminded
herself, then went straight ahead. 'You see Gwen
every weekend.'

'I see her every weekend when I pick up and
drop off the kids.'

'Those two hallowed words. The kids. Anything
is all right if it's done in the name of the kids.'

'All right,' he said, and his voice was very calm,
but the irises of his eyes were black, 'what crime
have I committed against you in the name of the
kids?'

'No crime. You just stopped talking to me every
time you saw them. I wasn't even allowed to meet
them for two or three months. Mustn't have them
know Daddy's screwing around.'

'I didn't know you were that hot to meet them.
You certainly aren't that eager to see them now that
you have.'

'Maybe that's because it took you so damn long
to decide I was fit to meet them.'

'So damn long by whose timetable? Your loyal protective friend Erica? That mother of the year Beth Sarmie? Or Paige and that horse's ass of a husband of hers. Is Dr Stanley an expert in child psychology, too?'

'You forgot Cynthia.'

'How could I forget Cynthia? The woman who's done as much for feminism as Idi Amin did for Africa.'

Katherine got up and took the tray into the kitchen. When she came back into the bedroom, Nick had turned on the television. There was, miraculously, a John Wayne movie on the Atlanta channel.

'I'm sorry for what I said about the kids.' Nick didn't say he was sorry for what he'd said about her friends. 'If you don't want me to go to lunch with Stephen, I won't.'

'Go ahead if it's that important to you,' he said without taking his eyes from the screen.

'It's not that important to me.'

This time Nick didn't answer. Like the Duke, he was a man of few words.

The next morning Nick did not ask if she was going to lunch, and she didn't offer to tell him. When she asked if he was angry, he said he was late.

Beth telephoned at ten-thirty to insist Katherine and Nick come to dinner the following week. Katherine said she'd check with Nick. If he's still around, she added to herself. 'Paige told me about your lunch. What are you going to wear?' Katherine said she hadn't decided. 'You're lying, Kitty. When a woman is having lunch with her ex-husband, the first thing she decides is what she's going to wear. Correction, the second thing. The first is whether she's going to sleep with him. Ted and I had some earth-moving lunches after we split up. Somebody ought to tell Masters and Johnson what divorce does for impotence.'

'I'm just having lunch with Stephen.'

'There's no such thing as *just lunch* with an ex-husband.'

Stephen had said he'd meet her at a small French restaurant with a big reputation. The room was long and narrow, and as soon as she entered, she saw him sitting on a red velvet banquette two-thirds of the way down the room. His face was fuller, more solid, but otherwise, he looked the same. The headwaiter led her between the tables. She felt as if she were crossing a minefield. Stephen stood as she approached. She'd forgotten how big he was. The pinstriped suit was too well tailored for her to tell whether the bigness was muscle or middle-aged flab. She thought of Nick's spare frame and the nice hard stomach.

The headwaiter pulled out the table, and as she moved around it to the banquette, she caught a glimpse of herself in the mirror behind. In place of that self-assured look she'd perfected in the bedroom mirror she saw an expression straight off the face of the victim in a horror movie ad. She found it grotesque, but apparently Stephen didn't because he leaned over and kissed her on the cheek. They were going to be civilized. They were going to forget that the last time they'd seen each other they'd fought about a print which she'd said was little enough to claim since she wasn't asking for a penny in settlement or alimony and which he'd said she didn't deserve any more than a settlement or alimony because she'd been such an un-adulterated bitch for three years. Besides, he'd added, and by that time they were both screaming, the only reason she wasn't asking for money was that she wanted to feel morally superior. He'd been wrong there. She simply hadn't wanted to feel more guilty.

He turned to face her on the banquette. His hairline hadn't given an inch in the battle against time. The hair and complexion were as dark as Nick's. Only the eyes were lighter. Maybe dark men were her type. Except that Matthew, the psychiatrist, had had auburn hair only a little darker than her own.

He asked her what she wanted to drink. She watched him while he gave the waiter her order and told him they weren't ready for the menus yet. Smoothly done, Stephen. Ego would call him a take-command person. Altruist would admire his self-enhancing behaviors. She missed the old shy streak that had run like a rich mineral vein through the rugged bluff of his confidence.

She asked about China. He took her on a brief guided tour but admitted he was getting a little tired of it. 'I've seen the Great Wall in summer and winter, fall and spring, rain and shine, heat and cold. I wouldn't mind if I never saw the Great Wall again, but they insist on entertaining. Not me, of course, just what I represent.'

'What's that?'

'I meant my firm.'

The headwaiter returned with the menus. Was Mr Hoffman ready to look at them? Mr Hoffman was.

'Okay, Stephen, I'm impressed. How much did you bribe the headwaiter to remember your name?'

He laughed quietly. It wasn't a hearty laugh, but it wasn't patronizing either. 'You bitch.'

'Now I feel comfortable.' She looked at the menu. 'Do you remember that clambake we gave at your parents' summer house?' He didn't. 'But you must. It was enormous. The police came because someone rigged a loudspeaker system to blast the Peter, Paul, and Mary records, and Stanley passed out in the bushes, and no one found him until the next morning, and those two friends of yours from the business school showed up with two girls they'd just picked up and disappeared into the attic and didn't come down until breakfast, and Larry somebody or other fell out of a tree and broke his arm. It was right after you passed your orals.' He said he remembered it. He also said he'd had the shad roe last week and recommended it.

'Well, what have you been doing for the past nine years?' Stephen asked after they'd ordered. Maybe he learned to keep his conversation simple out of deference to all those Chinese interpreters.

Katherine debated the answers. Should she tell him about the first few years after the divorce? Going back to school. Dropping out of school. Going to too many demonstrations and handing out too many leaflets. Moving to a new apartment every year. Screwing around. Or should she tell him about the recent years when her political conscience had shrunk and her leases grown longer, when she'd found ghosting and finally Nick? 'Writing other people's books.'

'Paige mentioned that. Can't be much of a career. Writing books for other people.'

'Fewer than three percent of the writers in this country make their living at writing, Stephen. I do.'

He smiled. This time it was patronizing. Obviously her idea of a living wasn't his idea of a living, but he'd let it pass.

'Anyway, I'm working on a book of my own now.'

'Nice.' He was looking at the wine list and managed to sound like a preoccupied father hearing his ten-year-old has just won the spelling bee. He'd always liked kids.

Stephen and his good friend the headwaiter discussed wines for a moment. When he finally ordered one, he sounded like Charles Aznavour singing in English.

Stephen handed the headwaiter the wine list and turned toward her on the banquette. His features were strong and regular. Over the years many people had told her they were very good features. She supposed they were.

'Do you remember that French professor when you were trying to pass the language requirements in graduate school? "It's all in the tongue," he used to scream, and wag his tongue back and forth with his fingers. God, he was repulsive.'

Stephen gave another small smile that admitted the memory without celebrating it.

'You never finished graduate school, did you?' he asked.

'I barely started graduate school. It was just one more thing I thought I ought to be doing while I was finding out what I could do.' His eyes slid away from hers for a moment as if he were embarrassed by her failure to get a graduate degree. Or maybe he really was working up to a pass and was uncomfortable about it.

'Tell me about your children.'

He managed to sound proud without being obnoxious. She'd been right. He was nice.

The waiter brought the wine and Stephen tasted and approved it, and the waiter brought their lunch and they ate and drank and talked about food. He'd had an excellent lunch aboard the president of Guatemala's yacht the previous week. The chef had once worked on the QE2. They talked about wine. He sounded a lot like Matthew. And they talked more about his work and hers. Books, he informed her, were on the way out. Silicon microchips were in. She wondered if she'd ever write a critically acclaimed, best-selling silicon microchip.

The waiter took their plates away, and she waited for Stephen to light a cigarette; but apparently he'd given them up.

'Paige said you're going to get married again.'

'Do you want to warn him off?' She'd expected him to laugh at that, but he just stirred his espresso thoughtfully.

'What does he do?'

Well, he worries about his kids a lot and he fences and he drinks a little too much – we both do – and he screws - we both do. 'He's an attorney.'

'What firm?'

She was pretty sure he'd already got all this from Paige, but she told him the name of Nick's firm.

'I don't think I've heard of it.'

'They don't do much business in China,' she said, but Stephen's expression didn't change. 'It's a small firm he started with a few other lawyers.' She dropped the name of the firm Nick had left to start his own, and Stephen picked it up like an old forty-niner spotting a gold nugget.

'What kind of law?'

'Corporate, but he specializes in heading off corporate take-overs.'

'Isn't much of a future in that these days.'

'I'd better get to a phone quickly. Before he wastes any more time.'

'Where'd he go to school?'

'City College.' Stephen's broad face seemed to swell with satisfaction. 'And Harvard Law.' It didn't deflate entirely, only shrank a little.

'He must be a bright guy.' Stephen gave credit where credit was due.

'No, he *mustn't* be just because he went to Harvard and worked for a good firm, but he is.'

They didn't leave the restaurant till after three. There was an awkward moment when they stood on the corner of Park Avenue and Fifty-fourth Street and Stephen took her hand and the bold features looked suddenly vulnerable and she thought, Oh, God, Beth was right – all this was only an elaborate mating dance – but then he kissed her on the cheek without touching any other part of her body and said good-bye and turned and walked away briskly like the busy man he was.

The day was cold with that profound late-winter dampness that neither heavy clothing nor heavy French lunches can cut. Overhead, dirty-looking clouds scudded rapidly across a metallic sky. It was one of those March days that thumbs its nose at the premature flowers in the planters and window boxes of the hotels and says you're getting exactly what you deserve for living on an island forty degrees north and seventy degrees west with no trade winds or gulf streams to recommend it. It was not a day for walking, but Katherine decided to walk.

Can't be much of a career, writing books for other people.

You never finished graduate school, did you?

I don't think I ever heard of his firm.

She understood now why Stephen had asked her to lunch.

Katherine heard the shriek of a horn and jumped out of the way of a taxi turning the corner. 'Go back to Jersey, lady,' the cabby shouted. Katherine pushed her hair out of her face. She was obviously losing her street smarts, though Nick said she had none. He was always amazed that she could do as much walking around the city as she did without getting run over.

By the time she hit Sixty-first Street she was smiling. By Sixty-second she was laughing. A delivery boy said something that was probably obscene in Spanish. She turned her face away but couldn't stop smiling. The score was even. She didn't have to feel guilty anymore. Stephen had listed his own accomplishments and her failures. He'd established his success and Nick's lack of it. And with the exception of one or two tepid comments, she'd let him. She couldn't say she felt free because she'd never felt especially haunted by the memories of her marriage, but she did feel better.

She started looking for an empty phone booth. Katherine was always amazed at the number of people who conducted their business and lives on the street phones of New York. She finally found one in the low Seventies. The receptionist put her through right away, but Nick's secretary kept her on hold for a minute. Katherine was sure the secretary had never put Gwen on hold. Nick said Katherine was paranoid.

'What's up?' he asked. He didn't sound angry, but he did sound businesslike. Of course, that could be the office.

She held her finger against her free ear to shut out the sound of the traffic. 'I thought I'd come down and pick you up. We could go to a movie. Or out for a drink or something.'

'Sure,' he said, 'but I won't be able to get out of here until after six.'

'I can kill time until then.'

As she hung up the phone, she wondered if he hadn't asked about lunch because he was still annoyed or because he assumed she hadn't gone. When she reached the Society Library on Seventy-ninth Street, she was still wondering, but after a few minutes in the stacks she'd forgotten about Nick and lunch. The library was in a converted town house. Each floor must have been divided into two and the small elevator that seemed suited to the fragile little old ladies clutching their Agatha Christies and Dorothy Sayers rose past level after level of low-ceilinged airless rooms, mile after mile of history and biography, science and travel, fiction and belles lettres. Katherine loved to wander through the stacks inhaling the dry, musty aroma, pulling down dusty books at random. She glanced at first sentences and dipped into paragraphs. Occasionally she flipped to the card in the back. One book had enjoyed a rush from '63 through '65, tapered off in '66, and been taken out only once since 1972. Another had won a steady stream of admirers all through the forties and been checked out five times in the succeeding four decades. Sometimes the name on the spine was familiar; more often it was not. The prolific writers were the worst. Katherine wandered past shelves of five, ten, or even fifteen books by unknown names. So much for immortality.

On the main floor on the shelves next to the desk the younger books, those still in their prime as well as in their dust jackets under protective plastic covers, looked pristine and confident, as if they expected to be on the current shelf forever. She thought of herself when she'd married Stephen. She thought of Erica and Michael and Michael's new wife. She tried not to think of her unfinished book and went up to the reading room, where she browsed through *Punch* and *Town & Country* and *The New York Review of Books* until it was late enough to start walking downtown again.

The receptionist had left, and Nick's secretary's desk was empty; but Katherine could hear voices in several of the offices. Nick was leaning back in his swivel chair with his feet on his desk. His tie was loosened, and his vest open. One of the young men she'd met at the Park Avenue party was sitting on the brown leather sofa. There was a small tear in one of the cushions that hadn't been there last time.

The man stood and said hello and that he'd better get back to work. Katherine told him not to let her drive him away, but he said she wasn't and left quickly.

Nick locked his hands behind his head and leaned back farther in the chair. He seemed very agile and compact after Stephen. She unbuttoned her coat and sat on the couch. It still smelled of cigarette smoke.

'How was your lunch?'

'How do you know I went?'

He looked at her without saying anything, and she remembered the silk blouse she was wearing and the Hermès scarf Nick had given her for Christmas. Stephen had commented on the scarf when he'd helped her on with her coat.

'He liked my scarf.'

'Like you say, he's a terrific guy.'

'It was a very boring lunch. He talked a lot about China and how well he was doing. He wanted to know all about you.'

Nick took his feet from the desk and came forward in the chair. 'If it's all the same to you, I don't want to know all about him.'

'Don't you want to know why he asked me to lunch?'

'I have a fairly good idea.'

'Just because you think with your libido doesn't mean everyone does.'

'Okay, he wanted to discuss Sino-American relations with you.'

'He wanted to even the score. Show me how successful he was – and what a failure I was.'

'What makes him think you're a failure?'

'I'm not married. I don't have children. I write books for other people.'

'Imaginative son of a bitch, isn't he?'

'He's not too impressed with you either. He never heard of the firm. Says you're in the wrong kind of law. You got one point each for Harvard and the old firm, and that was it.'

'Look, Katie, if you want to lunch with him . . .'

'I don't. Anyway, he won't call me again.'

'Why not?'

'Because he got what he wanted. I told you, he evened the score.'

'Why did he wait till now to do it?'

'The dramatic moment. He thinks we're getting married.'

Nick leaned back in his chair again, but this time he didn't put his feet up. 'Paige?'

'Paige. Anyway, he settled the score and he won't call again. If he does, I won't have lunch with him. I have enough lunching friends.'

'I can hear the girls now. Excuse me, the women. They'll blame me.'

'I'm not doing it for you. At least not just for you. It isn't worth it to me to worry you.'

'I wasn't worried.'

She crossed the room to his desk and sat on the

edge of it. 'You were worried. You were angry as hell, and you were worried.'

He put his hand on her knee. 'You're right. What do you want to see?'

'There's nothing decent playing that we haven't seen.'

'Do you want to go out to dinner?'

She felt as if she'd just finished lunch and shook her head.

'A drink?'

She shook her head again.

'What do you want to do?'

'Hang around here until everyone goes home. I have a thing about your couch.'

He looked surprised, then started to laugh. 'Christ, do you want to get me run out of here?'

She slipped off his desk and started to button her coat. 'Living in sin is making you stodgy. Just remember one thing, Larries. I'm your mistress, not your wife.'

Nick said he'd keep it in mind.

Beth put another log on the fire and jabbed at it with the brass poker until it sat on the andirons exactly as she wanted it to. She gave the log a final poke and returned to the couch. Katherine was curled up at the other end of it.

'Now I know why you and Nick agreed to come to dinner. He's as bad as the kids.' After dinner Nick had disappeared into what used to be Ted Sullivan's study with Jon and the child genius who was going to break into the Pentagon's computer.

'All I had to tell Nick was that you had Midway *and* the Battle of the Bulge.'

'And that I didn't have Topper.'

'That's one of the nice things about Topper. You

barely notice his absence.'

'*I* notice his absence, Kitty. I wish to hell he'd break his ankle again and get back from Vermont. It's the only thing that will save that whiz kid's' – she nodded toward the study – 'virtue.'

'All right, now that Nick's in the middle of Bastogne, tell me about Stephen.'

'Nothing to tell.'

Beth's small, pointed chin drooped a little in disappointment. 'Not even the tiniest pass? A casual suggestion of one for old times' sake?'

'Not even one to remember me by.'

'What a waste. I always thought Stephen was kind of sexy, too. Like one of those heroes on the covers of bodice rippers. The ones with riding crops and no shirts.'

'You've written too many best sellers.'

'Nobody has ever written too many best sellers.'

'Anyway, Stephen's too straight for you.'

'Straighter than Nick?'

'Nick's not straight.'

Beth's face crinkled in pleasure, and Katherine knew she'd been outmaneuvered. 'I'm glad to hear it, Kitty, but you could have fooled me. He always looks so buttoned up in those damn three-piece suits of his. He even looks buttoned up in that shetland. Then what did Stephen want?'

'To redress old wrongs. Show me how successful he's become and what a failure I am.'

Beth said she could understand that. 'Not that you're a failure, but that he wanted to get some of his own back.'

'He got it back all right. And all these years I've been thinking Stephen was still crazy about me. He could marry Jill and have kids and all that, but I'd always be the great love of his life. I've never admitted that to anyone, but I really did think it. Was I ever wrong! I should have listened to Nick and skipped lunch. Then I wouldn't have been disillusioned.'

Something happened to Beth's face then that reminded Katherine of the cats when they pricked up their ears. 'Nick didn't want you to go?'

Outflanked again. Katherine hoped Nick was doing better in Bastogne. 'He didn't make a fuss, if that's what you mean, but I think it bothered him.'

'In that case you were smart to go. To show Nick that you still have your independence.'

'Tell me one thing, Beth. When did "compromise" become a dirty word? We throw all the others around, all the four-letter ones, but the dirtiest word in the modern woman's vocabulary is "compromise".'

'Nick's into sexual possession.' Beth made it sound like a particularly nasty entry in Krafft-Ebing. 'He wants to keep you from growing. From discovering yourself and other people. Look at it in an historical context, Kitty. Originally sex was for procreation. Enter birth control, and it became a form of pleasure, a leisure-time activity, like reading books or going to the movies or watching television. Sex is a means of communication. And it's even more important for you than for most people because you're a writer. A creative person.'

'Oh, God, anything but that.'

'And Nick wants to corner the market on your creativity. It's as if you'd published your book and he bought up all the copies so no one else could read it.'

'Nick,' Katherine asked when they got home that night, 'do you want my book to sell?'

223

'Like hotcakes. I told you, when I left Stamford, I had to choose between you and a thirty-footer. The least you can do is make it up to me by buying a nice little – well, maybe not so little – sailboat with your ill-gotten gains.'

'Beth says you want to corner the market on me.'

Nick started to laugh. 'The only thing that amazes me more than your friend Beth is the fact that anyone takes her seriously.'

'She was talking about sex.'

'She always is.'

'You have to admit she's an expert on the subject.'

'That's like saying the Collyer brothers were experts on journalism. Beth is as misguided about sex as she is about everything else.' He took off his watch and propped it up on the night table so the face was toward him. 'Except about this. I do want to corner the market on you. Not your book, sweetheart, you.'

XII

Paige Richmond believed in role models. She'd had her mother. Her son, Tim, had his father. And now all three Richmonds would serve as models for Katherine and Nick and Nick's two children. She invited them for dinner on a Saturday night in late March.

'Not a dinner party,' she told Katherine. 'Just bring the kids for supper.'

'I've already been to Dr Stanley's this year,' Nick pointed out when Katherine relayed the invitation.

'Maybe the kids will like it. At least they'll get a good meal.'

'They love the way you make SpaghettiOs.'

Paige didn't make SpaghettiOs. Stanley made fresh pasta on his imported machine as they all watched in the long ground-floor kitchen. The adults drank martinis, the children apple juice, which David and Mark polished off quickly at the big oak table and which Tim spilled as he screeched up and down the ceramic tile floor. 'I know how to make pasta,' he screamed as he made a kamikaze run on the machine.

'Back up, Mr Galloper,' Stanley said. 'The pasta machine and Cuisinart are off limits. Remember?'

'Right, Mr Beard,' Timmy yelled.

'Stanley's James Beard, Tim's the Galloping Gourmet, and I'm Julia Child,' Paige explained.

'Cute,' Katherine said.

'Sweet.' Nick looked as if he'd just discovered a particularly painful cavity.

'Do you know how to make pasta?' the Galloping Gourmet demanded. Tim directed all questions to Mark, who was only a year older. David's two-year seniority intimidated him, a fact Katherine found encouraging. She hadn't thought anything intimidated Tim.

Mark shook his head. David contemplated his empty glass from under his long, thick lashes and looked as if he'd like to be somewhere else. Katherine thought he'd never resembled Nick more.

'It's okay, Mark,' Katherine said, 'as long as you know how to eat pasta. That's the important part.'

Mark watched Stanley stretch the first batch from the machine. 'That's spaghetti.'

'It's pasta,' Timmy insisted. 'He doesn't even know what pasta is.'

'Tim,' Paige said, but she didn't say anything else.

'Pasta, pasta.' Tim sang it now. He stopped in front of the oak chair where Katherine was sitting. 'Pasta's the food of the eighties.'

Paige was peeling an onion, but the tears in her eyes might have been from joy at her son's precocity. 'He picks up everything we say.'

'Kids always do.' Nick finished his martini. 'That's why you've got to be careful what you say in front of them.' He gave Katherine a look that she swore she'd make him pay for when they got home.

Paige pulled the Cuisinart forward on the counter. 'I keep telling Kate she ought to have one of these,' she said to Nick. 'I couldn't live without it.' She did some sleight of hand with blades and onions that produced a fearsome noise for a few seconds and produced enough minced vegetables for the hungry of New Delhi.

'You're better than the commercials on late-night television. Cuts, slices, minces, dices,' Katherine imitated the spiel.

'It does everything,' Paige said. 'You really ought to get her one, Nick. But make sure you get a Cuisinart. The American ones are cheaper, but they aren't nearly as good.'

'I don't want a Cuisinart,' Katherine said. 'Or even the less expensive brand. I'm still learning to use my salad spinner.'

'Don't listen to her, Nick. She'll love it.'

Stanley took off his chef's apron and pushed his glasses back up to the bridge of his nose. 'I relinquish the floor to Ms Child. Paige makes excellent white clam sauce. Excellent.' He turned to Nick. 'Would you like to look at a film before dinner? Kate says you're a buff, and I've taped some of the silents Thirteen has shown. I've got an excellent print of *Potemkin*. Tim loves the Odessa steps sequence. It's amazing how even a child can sense the power of that.' Tim raced to the end of the kitchen and began running up and down the stairs with his mouth open in a silent scream of agony.

'I'm not a film buff,' Nick said, and poured himself another drink from the pitcher Stanley had left on the table. Katherine wondered how many he was planning to have. 'I just like old movies. You don't happen to have *The Searchers* or maybe *Stagecoach*, do you?'

'The Larries men are John Wayne fans,' Katherine explained.

Paige and Stanley looked at her as if she'd said something dirty in front of the children, but Stanley recovered quickly. 'Well, there's a lot to be said for Ford's technique in *The Searchers*. The use of light and shadow in that shot from inside the house . . .'

Tim began running up and down the stairs again. The Russian peasants were getting restless.

'Tim, why don't you take Mark and Daniel—'

'David,' Nick corrected.

'David,' Paige repeated, 'upstairs to your playroom.'

Mark and David did not look happy, but they followed young Eisenstein up the stairs. 'Your kids are so well behaved,' Paige said to Nick.

'At other people's houses.'

Paige looked up from the Cuisinart and smiled. 'I know what you mean. I'm sure my friends think Tim is much better behaved than I do.' Katherine, the present friend, thought she wouldn't take any bets on that point.

Stanley refilled his own glass and topped off Nick's. 'I don't have *The Searchers*, but come take a look at my film library anyway. One of my patients, a well-known director – I can't tell you his name, of course, but you'd recognize it in a minute – said it was excellent. Really excellent.'

Nick stood and picked up his glass. Then he picked up the pitcher and followed Stanley up the stairs.

'They're nice kids,' Paige said as she took the pot of clams from the stove. 'A little quiet, but Tim will fix that. He's very gregarious.'

Katherine offered to do something, and Paige set her to making the salad. 'Maybe I should have warned you,' Katherine said as she tore four different kinds of lettuce, 'I don't know if the kids eat white clam sauce. Their palates are not what you'd call sophisticated.'

Paige was feeding clams to the Cuisinart. 'Kids will eat anything they see other kids eat, and Tim loves white clam sauce. Don't worry about it, Kate.'

As it turned out, Mark would not eat anything other kids ate, and he especially would not eat anything Tim ate. He tasted the pasta in white clam sauce, then ate a great deal of Paige's homemade bread with butter. David, on the other hand, would eat anything his father ate – at least in front of other people. He got halfway through dinner before he turned whiter than the natural wheat pasta. He was just outside the bathroom when it all came up.

'I'm sorry.' Katherine was almost crying.

'Don't be silly. It happens to kids.' Paige was using the same voice she'd used on New Year's Day to the woman who'd broken the Lalique ashtray. She ran down to the kitchen for paper towels.

Katherine looked at David. Tears were streaming down his face, and now there was a green tinge to his complexion. He looked miserable and horribly ashamed. Katherine told him everything was all right and fought the awful gagging feeling in her throat. Nick pushed past her to the bathroom with Timmy hard on his heels.

'He vo-mit-ed! He vo-mit-ed!'

Nick slammed the door in Tim's face, and the song turned into a wail. Paige fell to her knees to comfort him. Katherine followed and began cleaning up.

'Thank God you have hard wood floors and not carpeting.' If she worked quickly and kept talking, she would not be sick. There were little pieces of clam in the mess.

'Mr Larries didn't mean to slam the door on you,' Paige was crooning. 'Come on, Timmy. He didn't hurt you.'

The crying stopped. 'He did!'

'Show Mommy where he hurt you.'

'He hurt my feelings.'

Paige's face lit up like the city at twilight. She looked over Tim's head at Katherine. 'Sensitive,' she mouthed.

Katherine and Nick left the Richmonds early. When they got back to the apartment, David and Mark got into their pajamas, Katherine changed into a demure flannel bathrobe, and Nick stayed dressed. They all sat on the bed and watched an old movie until Mark fell asleep with his head on Nick's lap and David, half asleep on his father's shoulder, looked as if he'd almost forgotten his humiliation.

'You shouldn't have slammed the door in Timmy's face,' Katherine said after they'd opened the couch and put the boys to sleep on it.

'The kid's lucky I didn't slam my fist in his face.'

'I just hate to be rude to people. Especially when I'm a guest.'

'So I noticed when Cynthia asked who paid for what.' Nick turned out the overhead light and got into bed. 'Listen, Katie, David was sick. I wasn't insulting their kid. I was just trying to keep him away from mine.' He took off his watch and propped it up on the night table. 'From now on can we stay home with the kids and eat hamburgers?'

'There was nothing wrong with the food.'

'The food was terrific. But there's something wrong with a six-year-old kid who tells you pasta is the food of the eighties.'

'Don't forget the Eisenstein imitations. Anyone can do Bogie, but the entire Odessa steps sequence, now that's something.'

Nick started to turn off the lamp, then apparently thought better of it. 'But I can do *Birth of a Nation*.

You know the scene where the big darkie chases the flower of southern womanhood across the field?'

She thought of the kids, decided she was tired of thinking of the kids, and moved toward the center of the bed. 'Do I have to throw myself off the cliff?'

'Only if you want to, sweetheart.'

'Christ,' Nick said later. Katherine was just drifting off, and she'd thought Nick was asleep. 'Why do people like that have children?'

'Same reason you did. To reproduce themselves – only better.'

'Don't sound so superior. Didn't you ever want to reproduce yourself – only better?'

Katherine turned on her back and opened her eyes. The light from the street filtered through the curtains and made a Rorschach test of the ceiling. She remembered how sick she'd felt when she'd cleaned up the floor – physically sick, sick of herself, and sick of David. 'I'm still working on perfecting this model.'

'I'm serious. Didn't you ever want kids?'

'At one point I assumed I'd have them. Now it's too late.'

'Not really.'

'You sound like Paige – and Altruist. They're big on mid-life childbearing. But I'm not. I suppose you think I'm selfish.'

'Smart is more like it.'

'It's too dark to see. Is that really Nicholas D. Larries, father of the year, speaking?'

'I think if you have them, you owe them something, but that doesn't mean I think you ought to have them.'

Katherine turned on her side, and Nick wound himself around her. 'It's nice to know we're in agreement on one thing,' she said.

'We're in agreement on a lot of things. Your friends just don't happen to be among them.'

XIII

On the first Tuesday in April Katherine met Nick at the door with a pitcher of martinis. He still didn't kiss her when he came home at night, but he generally found a way to touch her. 'Seven chapters. Eighty thousand words. Two-thirds, roughly, of the great American novel.'

'That's a lot of words.'

'You always say I'm verbose.'

'Only during war movies. Are you going to let me read it right away this time or do I have to wait for Erica again?'

'You can read it tonight if you want to.'

It was raining out, and he took his umbrella and briefcase into the bathroom while Katherine went to the kitchen for glasses. By the time she'd poured drinks and carried one of them and the manuscript into the bedroom he'd taken off his suit, tie, and shoes and was stretched out on the bed with Franklin on his stomach.

'You can hit the bed faster than anyone I know.'

'Find me a good reason to stay vertical, and I'll manage it.'

She gave him the drink and the manuscript and went back into the kitchen. Eleanor followed with the slow, majestic gait of the queen of the jungle. She sat regally before the empty bowl, waiting for food to appear. Now there was patience, Katherine thought, and calm animal grace. The sound of the electric can opener brought Franklin into the kitchen on the double.

Katherine took the vegetable bin from the refrigerator and started to make a salad. At one point she turned off the water and called into Nick, 'What did you say?'

'I didn't say anything.'

The salad spinner made even more noise. She walked into the bedroom, still churning it. 'I didn't hear you.'

'That's because I didn't say anything.' He kept his eyes on the manuscript.

She went into the kitchen and began to tear the lettuce. Eleanor jumped up on the counter. 'Never cut the lettuce, Eleanor. Tear it.' Eleanor showed no interest in the niceties of salad making. Her fat red tongue darted out and wiped the invisible remnants of Little Friskies first from one side of her mouth, then the other. Katherine finished the salad and walked back into the bedroom with her drink. 'You hate it.'

'I haven't read it yet.'

'That's just the point. If you loved it, you'd be zipping along.'

He looked up from the manuscript. 'Why don't you watch television, Katie, or read a good book, or call Erica?'

'You're trying to get rid of me.'

'You guessed it.'

She walked around to her side of the bed and picked up *The New Yorker*. 'Do you mind if I read in here?'

'Not if you're quiet.'

She read through the listings of the revival houses.

'Why are all the best movies always in the Village or on the West Side?' Nick did not answer. She tried to read 'The Talk of the Town', but the perfection of the prose made her hands sweat and stick to the paper. 'Are you breathing like that because you don't like it?'

'I'm breathing like that because I'm trying to stay alive.'

'You sound asthmatic.'

Nick looked up again. 'Katherine, do you want me to read it or not?'

'I want you to read it.'

She went into the living room and managed to stay there with a book for forty-five minutes. Then she came back into the bedroom with the pitcher and refilled his glass. He thanked her, but she kept standing beside the bed. 'It's fine, Katie.'

'Fine! You're a pantywaist, Larries. If you hate it, say you hate it.'

'I don't hate it, and I want to finish it.'

'You didn't start from the beginning again, did you? You've already read the beginning.'

'No, I didn't start from the beginning.'

She went back inside for another hour, but her ears were as attuned to Nick as the cats' were to the can opener. He coughed twice. He shifted position on the bed several times. Then he gave the telltale sign. He tapped the pages against the manuscript box to align them. She was in the bedroom as quickly as Franklin could make it from there to the kitchen.

'Well?'

'I liked it.'

She took the box from him. 'You don't have to lie to me.'

He pushed himself up on the pillows. 'I'm not lying. I liked it. I think the kid's terrific.'

'Does that mean you hate the adults?'

She was standing beside him, clutching the manuscript box to her chest, and he took her hand and pulled her down so she was sitting on the side of the bed. 'And I swore to them at the hospital that the paranoia was gone. That's the only reason they released you in my care. Look, Katie, I'm not saying it's a masterpiece. I'm not saying it's going to make a million dollars in paper or be made into a movie. That's Erica's department. I'm not even saying it's the best book of its kind because I keep telling you I don't normally read books like this—'

'Women's books.'

He shrugged. 'All I'm saying is that I like it and I think you did a good job.'

Erica didn't agree. 'The heroine still isn't sympathetic enough.'

'If she becomes any more sympathetic, I'll have to canonize her.'

'The husband's a stick figure.'

'But a mean stick figure, you've got to admit that.'

'It isn't fun.'

'I thought you wanted a book about women's anger.'

'I do, but I want it to be done with humor, parody, and irony.'

'Weren't they a vaudeville act on the old Keith circuit? I'm sorry. I guess I don't take criticism well.'

'Who does? Listen, I'm completely tied up for the rest of this week, but why don't I come over Saturday and we can work on it? That is, if Nick will give his *au pair* the day off.'

On Saturday Nick joined several thousand other fathers dragging their children around the museum-planetarium-movie circuit like stage mothers hauling their kids from audition to audition, and Erica arrived with the manuscript. 'I hope you realize,' she said as they sat down to work at the dining table, 'that I don't do this for all my clients.'

'Who typed your Chaucer paper junior year?'

'That's what I mean.'

A long-standing admirer of Erica's efficiency, Katherine had expected to drive through the manuscript at top speed, but they kept slowing for the potholes of their shared lives.

'Now this scene where they discuss divorce' – Erica lit another small cigar – 'it ought to be explosive. We ought to feel the rage she's been suppressing over the years bubbling beneath the surface. Maybe if you dug down into yourself more, Kat, and tried to remember the way things were with Stephen.'

'I never suppressed my anger at Stephen. Anyway, in those days I was less angry at him than at myself. Maybe that's the trouble. I've never been treated really badly by a man.'

'What about Nick?'

Katherine's eyes slid from the pad on which she was making aimless circles to Erica. 'You think Nick treats me badly?'

'I think he makes a lot of demands on you. Like having your life revolve around his kids. You can't even go away for the weekend.'

'We went away for the weekend.'

Eleanor described a perfect arc from floor to table, and Erica blew a small cloud of smoke in her face. 'You went away for the weekend only because the kids were going away for the weekend. Or did you forget you told me that?'

'You'd think he was worse if he never saw his kids.'

'Have you ever heard of moderation, Kat? Look, I don't want to argue about Nick. I just want you to dig down in yourself and find some anger.'

'Dig for anger,' Katherine scrawled on the yellow legal pad. Eleanor blinked in perfect impassivity.

Erica put out the small cigar. 'Now don't jump on me about this. I'd just like you to give it some thought. What about physical violence?'

'I'm not writing a shoot-'em-up.'

'Let me finish. Wife abuse is a hot topic. I don't mean we have to make the husband a chronic wife beater, but what if he takes a few swipes at her during one of the arguments?'

'Erica, have you ever been hit by a man?'

'I hit Michael a few times. I was so damn frustrated.'

Katherine rubbed Eleanor's head with the eraser end of the pencil. 'I know wife beating exists. And rape. And lots of other abuses and injustices. I've sent donations to the organizations and marched in the streets, but I'll be damned if I'm going to write about that in this book. It doesn't belong.'

'You think only working-class men beat up their wives?'

'Of course not. I just don't happen to think this particular character would.'

Erica leaned back in her chair. Her smile wasn't exactly cunning, just a little sly. 'I'm trying to get you to strengthen that particular character. Just because something never happened to you or me, Kat, doesn't mean it isn't happening all around us. And I think it's something you could make a significant statement about. Just think of the terror and the helplessness.'

The pencil that was still making circles on Eleanor's head stopped. 'The motel in Mystic. There was a family above us. The father must have gotten drunk because in the middle of the night there was a lot of screaming and crying, and from the sound of it he was beating up everyone in sight. It was horrible.'

Erica's long chin jutted toward Katherine triumphantly. When Erica was excited, she always led with her chin. 'Exactly!'

'Wife beating in Mystic,' Katherine scribbled on the pad.

A little before five Katherine removed the teapot and chocolate chips and brought out the ice bucket. 'Just a short one,' Erica said. 'I'm going to clear out before Nick gets home.'

'There's no need to.'

'Thanks all the same, but I've lived through enough silent treatments in my life. Michael used to pull them every time he lost a job to another architect. Damned men. They guard their personal problems as if they were the Manhattan Project. I had to live with Michael's withdrawals, but I don't have to live with Nick's.'

'We're past the withdrawal stage. Now that the kids spend most weekends here, we're just one big happy family.'

'Do I detect a note of sarcasm? Still, it could be worse. They could be teenage girls. I don't envy Michael's child bride when my two dimpled darlings hit puberty. I think I might even develop an affection for the little bitch if she draws some of the fire. Why should Mommy get all the hostility?'

'Nick's kids aren't hostile. If anything, they're too polite. But then so am I. Nobody's comfortable.'

Erica slid her glasses down from her short hair to the bridge of her nose and looked at Katherine. 'What about Nick? I trust he's comfortable. Surrounded by his loved ones.'

Katherine stirred her drink with her finger and said nothing.

'Christ! What does he want?'

'Not to feel pulled apart.' Katherine drew her legs up on the sofa and wound her arms around her knees. 'He says when we're all together, the kids and I wage a tug-of-war over him.'

Erica sipped her drink. 'Do you?'

'I just wish he wouldn't act as if he didn't know me in front of the kids. If I ask him something, he answers in monosyllables. And he seems to think touching my hand would be tantamount to taking them to an X-rated movie.'

'He's wrong.'

'I'll tell him you said so.'

Erica drained her glass and stood. 'Look, I'm not saying, "Throw Nick out". I like him. I really do. I couldn't live with him, but you seem to want to. I just think you ought to give some thought to whether it's worth all the compromises.' Erica went to the front closet and took out her down coat. It was so thick Katherine had had to push her and Nick's things to the side to fit it in. Now she pushed the hangers back along the rod as Erica put on the coat. 'Only you know whether it's worth it, Kat, but I'm here to listen. Anytime you want. After all the bitching I did during the divorce, I owe you a couple of thousand hours.'

Katherine stood at the door of the apartment until the elevator came for Erica. Then she went back inside and put the cups and glasses in the dishwasher. She was standing at the table staring at the yellow pad – 'dig for anger; wife beating in Mystic' – when she heard Nick's key in the lock. He hung his duffle coat on the hanger Erica had vacated and came into the living room without looking at Katherine.

'How were the kids?'

'Fine.'

'What did you do?'

'Nothing much.'

And she'd told Erica they'd gone beyond the silent, brooding stage. Katherine expected him to keep walking into the bedroom, but he just stood there in the middle of the room. He was looking at her now, and his eyes were like charcoal smudges in his face.

'I ran into Erica in the lobby. She said she left you making codfish cakes.'

Katherine pretended to be arranging the manuscript, pad, and pencils she'd carried back to her desk. 'She was joking.'

'Terrific sense of humor. Is there something you want to tell me?'

'Of course not.'

'You must have been complaining to Erica about something.'

'I wasn't complaining. We were talking about men and women and anger. In the book.' She held out the yellow legal pad to him. 'Here, you can see the notes.'

He ignored the pad. 'And that was Erica's idea of a joke?'

'Maybe she was a little high. She had a drink before she left.'

'How the hell did she know about the codfish cakes?'

Katherine tried for a deprecating smile, but she knew without a mirror that she hadn't made it. 'I guess I must have told her.'

'I just want to know one thing. Is there anything you don't tell Erica?'

'There's a lot I don't tell her, and you know it, but there's a lot I do tell her, too. Not everyone can be the strong, silent type. Not everyone thinks the best way to deal with a problem is by going into a catatonic state. Some of us actually communicate.'

'Communicate! Are you quoting Ego or Altruist?' His mouth had assumed that thin, ungenerous line again.

'Excuse me, we talk.'

'Apparently. You tell Erica everything I say. And Paige that I worry about the kids, so she sends me articles about workshops on *fathering*. Tell me, do you report to Beth every time we fuck?'

'Don't flatter yourself. She wouldn't be interested.'

'I'm not flattering myself, and she would be interested.'

They went on that way for a while – neither of them had a talent for what Altruist called creative arguing – then Nick went into the bedroom, took off his shoes and sweater, and assumed Position A on his side of the bed. Franklin was on his stomach, WW II was on television, though without John Wayne, and a mean look was on Nick's face. The look was still there when Katherine turned her back and went to sleep.

The next morning she awakened to the cold war. Nick got up, padded to the front door, and came back with the Sunday *Times*. He dropped it between them on the bed as if it were the Berlin Wall. He took out the magazine section and turned to the puzzle. She reached for 'Arts and Leisure'. After she'd read the same paragraph three times, she glanced over at Nick. He'd already filled in a corner. The bastard.

'Look, Nick.'

He looked. His eyes reminded her of a discussion he'd had with the kids about black holes.

'I'm sorry. You're right. I talk too much.'

'Forget it.'

They both pretended to for a while. She made coffee and brought it back to bed on a tray with croissants and butter and jam. He finished the puzzle, and they traded sections.

She began to page through the magazine. Most people, including Nick, flipped through it from the back. She went through it methodically from the front. That used to bother Stephen. That and the fact that she read the front page of the paper in its entirety from the right-hand column to the left but rarely turned the page to finish an article. She was systematic, he'd complained, but not thorough.

She skimmed her way to the last three departments: design, style, and food. They were her favorites despite the fact that the apartment had arrived at its present state entirely by accident, her wardrobe was limited and had changed little since college, and she was incapable of following a recipe without taking shortcuts that were sometimes inspired and more often disastrous.

LOFTS, the headline read, THE URBAN AMERICAN DREAM OF THE EIGHTIES. Katherine looked at the pictures. They weren't kidding about the American dream. The bathtub raised on a platform and angled between windowed walls provided a view of spacious skies; miles of bleached hardwood floors looked like amber waves of grain; and a bizarre sculpture in the middle of everything did indeed resemble a purple mountain, though it had little majesty. The man responsible for this testimony to the American spirit and contemporary design was Michael Kenyon.

'Poor Erica.' Katherine regretted the words as soon as they were out; but Nick looked up, and she had to go on. 'Her ex-husband made the *Times* again. Or rather one of his lofts did. Erica's apartment was in it years ago.'

'Then why should she care? She got the apartment.'

'Come on, Nick. It's only natural to resent something like that.'

'Would you?'

'I don't resent Stephen's success, but then he didn't walk out and leave me with two kids. Erica has reason to be bitter.'

'At least we agree she's bitter.'

'Only about Michael.'

Nick didn't say anything.

They dismantled the Berlin Wall, but Katherine had the feeling the détente was fragile. Monday night she found out why.

'I'm going to call the kids,' Nick said when he got home. He said it casually as he always did, but the act was not a casual one for him. He telephoned from the bedroom, and Katherine, still at her typewriter, could hear most of the conversation. At least she could hear it if she didn't type.

Phone conversations with seven and eight-year-olds tend to be stilted, and no matter how hard Nick tried he never sounded natural. He would ask what they'd done at school. He would ask what they'd done after school. There were long silences, punctuated by 'No kidding' and 'That's terrific'. Only tonight Nick's answers sounded neither rote nor meaningless. 'I know it's frightening, Davey, but you can't stop going to school.' There was a brief silence.

'They're not tougher. They just want you to think they're tougher.' Then after another pause; 'You need some bigger friends.' Nick laughed; but it didn't sound convincing to Katherine, and she was willing to bet David wasn't taken in either. 'Stand-up guys.' The conversation went on for some time. She heard Nick say good night to both boys but didn't hear the sound of the receiver being replaced in the cradle, and she knew from the change in his voice that the lovely Gwen had gotten on. 'He can't just stop going to school.' There was a short silence. 'I didn't say I wouldn't consider private school. We'll talk about it, but I don't think we ought to pull him out of school and throw him into a private one just because of this.' The silence was longer this time, and when he finally spoke, his voice was so controlled that Katherine could picture the rigid line of his mouth. 'I know you're the one who's there, Gwen. What the hell do you think it's like for me not being there at a time like this?' That was a question Katherine wouldn't mind the answer to herself. 'All right, Gwen, it's my fault. I chose the neighborhood and the school. And I still think David ought to go back to it.' Apparently Gwen didn't agree. 'For Christ's sake, I'm not being macho. I'm trying to be sensible. You think I want him hurt?' Gwen's answer was brief, but it must have been to the point. 'I'm not going into that now, Gwen. Everybody hurt everybody. All right?' Whether or not it was all right, Nick repeated what he'd said about David's going back to school and hung up. Katherine waited for him to come into the living room, but after a few minutes she knew he wasn't going to. She went into the bedroom. He was not lying on his back staring at the ceiling. He was sitting on the edge of the bed staring at the floor. He looked up as she entered.

His eyes were neither hard nor flat. They simply weren't there.

'What was that all about?'

'David got beaten up by a bunch of kids.'

'Is he all right?'

'He's all right. It happened last Friday. I found out about it Saturday.' Last Saturday they'd fought about Erica and everything else, but not about David. Katherine listened for the undercurrent of reproach, but it wasn't there, any more than Nick's eyes or Nick himself.

She leaned against the doorjamb. 'Why is it your fault?'

'One of the reasons I wanted to move there was that there were blacks in the school. Gwen refused to live in town with kids, and I didn't want to bring them up in some lily-white suburban enclave. So we found a house that was big enough and old enough to suit her and a town that was real enough to suit me.'

'I take it the kids who beat up David were black.'

'More roughed up than beat up. The funny thing is that he was walking home with two other black kids, and the gang chased them away first. Then they pushed David around and took his money.'

'Sounds like New York.'

'That's what Gwen said.'

'I'm sorry. You realize it would have happened if you were still living at home.'

'I know that.'

'Then why are you acting as if it's your fault?'

'Because Gwen's blowing it up into a major crisis. David was fine Saturday. He told me what happened and showed me his black and blue marks – Christ, by the end of the day he was proud of them – and we talked about it, and I was sure he wasn't afraid.

But she's convinced him that he ought to be. And she's convinced herself that she's got to get both of them out of that school. She says if I won't send them to private school, she'll get her father to. That's how worked up she is. Gwen hates to ask Daddy for money.'

'There's nothing wrong with private school, you know. Given suburban schools, they'll probably get a better education.'

Nick had been staring at the floor, and now he looked up at her sharply. Katherine rarely felt an affinity with the lovely Gwen, but she did at that moment. 'I'm sorry. They're not my kids, and I don't know anything about children – as you've often pointed out. Do you want a drink?' He did.

Gwen did not ask her father for money, and David went back to school but the issue was not closed. Katherine knew that from what Nick said and what he didn't say. However, the kids were not hers, as she'd pointed out, and the book was. She had her own problems that spring, and they seemed to be blossoming at the same speed as the season. One week the trees were bare, the next the magnolia spread soft umbrellas of pink and white and the forsythia lay a yellow carpet throughout the park. Katherine wondered if the city always bloomed so quickly or if the phenomenon only struck her because she was walking more than ever. She walked on Park Avenue, where the yellow tulips standing like slim blond ingenues and the trees wearing an array of lipstick colors opened to rave reviews. She walked on Madison and looked in the shops and windows displaying cotton dresses and Easter candy and books on gardening. She walked on Fifth and noticed that the fur and down coats had disappeared and faces that had been tensed against the cold were now merely closed against fellow New Yorkers. After a while she began to walk on the west side of the street because she wanted to be closer to the park, where the lake glistened in the late-afternoon sun, reminding her of childhood summer vacations. Often she walked to Nick's office to pick him up. Then they'd go for a drink or to a movie or just walk home together. If Katherine was walking more than ever, she was also working less.

'That's because you're finally digging down into yourself,' Erica said. 'It's easy to write glibly. It's something else to get at the truth.'

'I can't do it,' Katherine said to Nick one evening when she arrived at his office a little after six. She threw herself into a corner of the brown leather couch. The smell of cigarettes was as pervasive as ever, but it aroused no memory. Proust was dead. 'I can't dig down into myself and I can't find enough anger and I can't write this goddamn book.'

Nick was leaning back in his chair with his feet on his desk. There was the beginning of a hole in the sole of one shoe. 'You and Stevenson,' she said. 'You'll never be President. And I'll never write this book. I'm not even sure I want to write it anymore.'

He looked at her over the tops of his shoes. 'Then don't.'

'Thanks.'

'What do you want me to say?'

'If I knew what I wanted you to say, I'd say it to myself. Maybe I ought to just have a baby.'

'Anyone who says "just have a baby" shouldn't have a baby. Besides, I thought we agreed on that.'

'What if I wanted to have children?'

Nick took his feet off the desk. 'Do you?'

'No.'

'You had lunch with Paige today.'

'We went to an auction.'

'Did you buy anything? Besides her line, I mean.'

'Okay, forget the baby.'

'Why don't you forget the book? Just for a few hours.'

When Nick got home the following evening, he found a new note stuck to the refrigerator door. 'Remember Flaubert.'

'Why do you want to remember Flaubert?'

'It took him seven years to write *Madame Bovary*. Or five, depending on your source. I stand a good chance of breaking his record. Without his final result.'

'Maybe you're working too hard at it. Maybe you ought to take some time off.'

She told him she was taking off too much time as it was and began haunting the museums. It wasn't a waste of time, she told herself, it was a renewing of perspective. Each night she came home with bits of information for Nick.

'Did you know that Wednesday afternoon is doctors' afternoon at museums? They were swarming all over the Met, and their wives were buying out the gift shops. Talk about rape and pillage.'

'I didn't know that,' Nick said.

'Did you know that the Frick has an admission charge now?'

'I didn't know that,' Nick said.

'Did you know that Robert Capa wasn't really Robert Capa?' she asked one night when she'd returned from the old Audubon house that had been turned into a photography museum. 'He made up the name. When he was starting out, back in the twenties and thirties, papers and magazines wouldn't buy pictures from an obscure Hungarian photographer, so he and his mistress – at least I assume she was his mistress – made up a rich American named Robert Capa who took pictures.'

'I knew that.'

'You know everything.'

'I didn't know Wednesday was doctors' day at the Met.'

'No, you didn't know that or about the difference between the hot dogs in front of the Met and the ones in front of the Whitney, but you know all the important things. You knew about Capa and you knew about the difference between Cézanne's peaches and Renoir's and you knew all about the ocean liners at the Cooper-Hewitt. How come you're so smart and I'm so stupid?'

'You aren't stupid, just uneducated. It comes from going to that classy school where they taught you to learn about things but never to question them.'

'Is that why you won't send the boys to private school?'

They'd been joking, and she should have stopped while they were still joking. He didn't say anything to Katherine, but when Gwen called the following night for another round in the private versus public school debate, Nick was more sarcastic than usual.

Then, just when Katherine was running out of museums, she discovered the charm of old movies in the afternoon. She refused to go to first-run movies during the day. It wasn't only that she was saving most of them to see with Nick. There was something furtive and disreputable about going into one of those glossy theaters in the middle of a weekday afternoon. It would be like lying on a park bench drinking cheap wine from a bottle camouflaged in a paper bag. But revivals had a different ambiance. Though the theaters were seedier, the pastime seemed to Katherine more respectable. Revivals were for buffs. Katherine was shocked at how many buffs there were in New York City. There were elderly buffs whose faces were as tight and distorted from lack of conversation as a starving child's stomach was from lack of food, unemployed buffs with attaché cases and eyes that read like résumés of despair, lone women buffs who wore meticulous clothes and full makeup to sit in a dark theater and take solace from the fact that Bette Davis had renounced Paul Henreid and faced blindness and been bested by a young Anne Baxter; there were illicit lover buffs with cheeks flushed from each other and the titillation of a public appearance, gay buffs who came in twos and threes and tried to beat each other to Joan Crawford's lines, buffs who brought their lunches, buffs who slept noisily through the movies, and one afternoon the classic buff in a trench coat who did obscene things to himself beneath it until Katherine changed her seat; there were would-be actor buffs, struggling artist buffs, and blocked writer buffs. There might be a broken heart for every light on Broadway, but there was a buff for every film Hollywood had ever made, enough buffs to half fill the theater for obscure movies that Katherine wanted to see for the slimmest reed of a reason – it was based on a novel by Marquand, contained some old Cole Porter tunes, featured Walter Huston in any role at all – and to pack the house for old classics that appeared on television regularly. And all this on a weekday afternoon, when the normal world was at work.

She told Nick about the buffs. He put his arm around her and said maybe she ought to go back to the book. She returned to self-discipline and later-afternoon walks, but the results were not impressive.

'It's one step forward and two back,' she told Erica.

In May bound books of *How to Be a Winner* arrived. If she ever finished her own book, she'd receive the customary author's ten copies. Now she received five. Ego had gotten to them before the publisher had sent them out. Inside each one he'd written 'Hope you enjoy it. Best wishes, Dr Leo Robbins.' He'd learned the old trick of autographing books in stores because signed copies could not be returned to the publisher for credit. Did he think she was so down-and-out she'd try to turn a quick profit on her own five?

A few days later Altruist called to complain about the sluggishness of his publisher. He wouldn't have bound books for another ten weeks, though he was hounding his editor to hurry the publication date. Katherine did not tell him hounding would do no good, but she did tell him not to bother.

'The most you'll save is a week or two, and that won't do any good. August is a terrible time to bring out a book. Too late for vacation reading, too early for review attention.'

Altruist made sounds of agreement, and she heard the machinery of assimilation creaking. Next time she spoke to him he'd probably give her a lecture on the importance of timing in publishing a book.

He launched into a report on his extraordinary popularity with the female population of the Midwest, as witnessed by a fan letter he'd received that morning, and Katherine looked at her watch. She hoped his next patient hadn't canceled. If he had, she was in for a long conversation. She heard the change in Altruist's voice and knew he was coming to the point. 'I'm having a little trouble with the jacket copy for this one. I hated what they did so I told them I'd write it myself, but I've been kind of busy . . .' When his voice trailed off, Katherine did not come to the rescue. 'I've got the bio down pat, but I can't seem to get the part about the book right.'

'What about Alison? If she used to do publicity, she ought to be able to handle a little flap copy.' When he'd first married his second wife, Altruist had hinted darkly to Katherine about a God-given gift to turn press releases into poetry.

'She took a crack at it, but she couldn't get it either. I was wondering if you'd take a look at it.'

Katherine started to say she was too busy, but she wasn't. 'Sure, why not?'

'I'll pay you, of course.'

Katherine told him she wouldn't think of taking money. He did not ask her how her book was coming, but then she didn't ask him how the novel that was going to show how he'd grown as a writer was progressing.

'Why did you say you'd do it?' Erica demanded when Katherine told her about the call. 'You ought to be working on your own book.'

'That's why I'm doing it. It'll be nice to be writing something again. Even if it's only flap copy.'

A few days later she got a brochure in the mail from Beth. The New School was offering a workshop for blocked writers. Among the noted authors on the panel was Beth Sarmie.

Katherine called Beth to thank her for the brochure. 'I can't imagine what you're doing on that panel, though. You've never been blocked in your life. In fact, you remind me of a writer in a Hollywood movie. You don't agonize. You don't even seem to spend much time writing. You just keep turning out best sellers.'

'I agonize all right, but I'm fast. Facile, my editor says. Are you going to take the workshop?'

'In place of, or along with, group therapy?'

'If you'd been in Paris in the twenties, Kitty, would you have called those sessions at the Dome group therapy?'

'Unfortunately I'm not Hemingway, and with all due respect, you're not Fitzgerald, and you may find a lot of crazies at the New School; but I doubt any of them is going to be Ezra Pound. Anyway, if I can't write, I certainly can't sit around talking to strangers about why I can't write.'

'I'm not a stranger.'

'You'll be one of many.'

'Okay, then let me read the manuscript, and we'll talk about it.'

'That's an imposition. You'll probably have more than enough blocked manuscripts to read from this workshop.'

'Kitty, you are the only person in the whole world who knows that I was the one who broke the new doll in Miss Geckler's kindergarten class, and you never told. The least I can do is look at your manuscript.'

Beth read the manuscript in a single sitting. When she finished, she called Katherine and told her to come right over.

'You mean you want me to get it out of your house immediately?'

'I want to talk about it while it's fresh in my mind. Besides, my masseuse is coming, and I can't stand listening to her. She sounds like Hermann Göring.'

'How do you know what Göring sounded like?'

'What I imagine he sounded like. She looks like him, too. Only he didn't have a mustache.'

Beth's masseuse did look like Hermann Göring, and smelled like the basement of Katherine's building after the exterminator had been there. Just as she'd always wondered what it would be like to ride in a limousine until Beth had taken her to the cemetery, so Katherine had always been curious how it would feel to have a professional massage. Nick's didn't count because Nick always had something else in mind. She'd wondered, but she wouldn't have let this big, musty-smelling woman with the black mustache and the huge, brutal hands touch her. Frau Göring was working over Beth's fragile body as if it were a piece of recalcitrant dough that refused to rise.

'I figured out what's wrong with the book.' Beth's voice came in little gasps as if someone were cutting off her air supply. 'You're too tight-assed.'

'Oh, you wordsmith, you.'

'I mean it. You're holding back.'

'That's what Erica says. She wants me to dig down inside myself for more anger.'

Frau Göring's hands moved farther up Beth's rib cage. 'Forget—gasp—anger—gasp—you've got—gasp—plenty of anger. You need more realism.' The last words came out in a rush.

'I don't know what you mean.'

The masseuse had moved to Beth's neck, and she put her head down on one side and closed her eyes. The gasps stopped, and her voice took on a dreamy quality. 'You've got a woman at the center of the book, right? But what kind of a woman? She never gets her period. She never pees. She never masturbates. I knew she was getting laid because the earth was moving in her head, but as far as I could tell, nothing else was moving. You've created a tight-assed heroine, not a flesh-and-blood woman who' – Frau Göring's big hands moved down from Beth's neck to her upper back, and the dreamy voice became uneven again – 'fucks . . . and farts . . . and bleeds.'

Katherine leaned back in the velvet chair. 'But I hate those books. The stains-on-the-sheet and the jelly-slathering-over-the-diaphragm school of literature. That's one of the things wrong with women writing today. They're so damn hung up on their own bodily functions.'

'You're looking at it too narrowly, Kitty. It isn't just women writing today. It's the whole trend of literature in the twentieth century. Look at Bloom and Stephen Dedalus peeing in the backyard. You can't fight *Ulysses*.'

Katherine wasn't even going to try.

'Think about it, Kitty.' Frau Göring was rubbing lotion into Beth's skin now, and her voice had turned dreamy again. 'Put your reader in touch with your heroine's body. It'll save the book.'

After the masseuse left, Beth put on a robe and had the housekeeper bring them herbal tea. Katherine missed her Earl Grey. Sitting cross-legged in the center of the big bed with the frilly canopy, Beth looked all of twelve years old.

'Now that we've solved your problem, Kitty, I wish we could do something about mine. How do you tell a fifteen-year-old the facts of life?'

'I think Jonathan knows them.'

'I'm not talking about Jonathan. Or those particular facts of life. You remember the computer whiz kid? Peter.'

'Why don't you let Peter's parents tell him?'

'Because they don't know. Peter doesn't know. Though he ought to have noticed by now. Poor little Peter has crabs.'

Drinking the herbal tea was like licking sugar off a metallic surface. Katherine put the cup on the table next to her. 'You gave Peter crabs?'

'Don't sound so shocked, Kitty. Everyone who's sexually active has them at one time or another.'

'But everyone who's sexually active doesn't pass them on to a fifteen-year-old. Why did you have to seduce the kid, Beth?'

'I resent that. Even from my oldest and dearest friend. I didn't seduce him. Jon went off the other night – he's working on a film with some kids in his class – and left Peter here with the computer. After a while he drifted in to talk to me.'

'It's nice to know some areas are still safe from automation. Still, you could have just talked. He's a baby, Beth.'

'Alfred Eaton was even younger.'

'Who's Alfred Eaton? I know the name, but I can't place it.'

'John O'Hara. *From the Terrace.* That scene with the maid when he was twelve or thirteen.'

'You've got the damnedest view of life following art.'

Beth straightened her thin shoulders. 'I don't know why I'm trying to justify myself. I'm not sorry about the kid, only about the crabs. I could kill Topper.'

'The plot sickens.'

'Topper didn't tell me until it was too late, and now I really ought to tell the kid. It's the moral thing to do. But how? I never see him without Jonathan. I can't very well take him out for a drink.'

'The moral of the story is don't mess around with kids on the dry side of the drinking age.'

'I can't even write to him in case his mother opens his mail. I guess I'll just have to let him figure it out for himself.'

'Have you thought of programing it into the computer?'

'I'm glad you're getting such a kick out of this. Do me one favor, though, Kitty.'

'I won't be the one to tell him.'

'Don't tell anyone.'

Katherine took her manuscript from Beth's night table. 'I've carried the secret of the broken doll for thirty years. You can trust me. But I don't know about a fifteen-year-old kid.'

'How's the hand that rocks the cradle?' Nick asked when he heard Katherine had been to Beth's that afternoon. 'Or do I mean robs?'

'Fine,' she answered without a moment's hesitation.

XIV

New York moved hesitantly into summer. Katherine walked downtown in the soft May afternoons as the sun slanted over the skyline of Central Park South. She wore dark glasses and espadrilles. Her stride was longer in espadrilles. At least she felt as if it were. She and Nick walked home through the shadowy canyon of Madison Avenue or the fading sun of Fifth. Sometimes they bought ice-cream cones that ran in pale fruit colors over white napkins. Occasionally they stopped at the outdoor café across from the Metropolitan Museum and sipped gin and tonics while the last rays of sun disappeared behind the mellow old building and the muted tones of French and German, Japanese and Arabic rose and fell around them in the golden dusk.

Summer brought unexpected showers from faulty window air conditioners and weekends in the country that were still pleasant escapes rather than the desperate flights they would become later in the season. It also brought the city's crazies out in force. Some of them were familiar figures to Katherine. She recognized the husbands' rights advocate who wore a sandwich board and signs in his hat that quoted the Bible, bemoaned the plight of men in the modern world, and simultaneously berated women for their sloth and ambition. The husbands' rights advocate was one of midtown's most celebrated crazies. He'd even made *The New York Times*.

One day early in June Katherine spotted the parader again. He was a tall, thin man with slicked black hair and a mustache like an English army officer's. A regulation trench coat that was filthy enough to have seen action in the Great War reinforced the military aura. He wore a scarf, gloves, and backpack even during the dog days of July and August and marched the streets of New York with a long, arm-swinging stride. Unlike the husbands' rights advocate, who seemed to be enjoying himself, the walker had a tortured look, as if he knew that war was hell and peace was no better. Katherine felt about him the way she did about the scary parts of movies. She didn't want to look at him, yet she couldn't help but stare.

Several new personalities made an appearance. Some were regulars, like the small evil pixie in a filthy jacket and check pants who carried his belongings in a piece of brown cheesecloth and occupied various benches along upper Fifth Avenue on the park side of the street. Katherine usually spotted him enjoying the warm weather and a quart bottle of beer in a paper bag on the bench across from the Guggenheim. 'My theory is that he's an ex-architect,' she said as she pointed him out to Nick on their way home one evening.

'Are you kidding? That's the president of the Former Attorneys of America Club. Anticorporate division – as your ex-husband pointed out.'

Katherine thought of eccentric watching as the city dweller's version of bird watching. Any serious student knew that certain areas of town, like certain marshes, were better than others, but sometimes the rarest specimens alighted in the most unexpected places. One afternoon when Katherine was standing in front of Scribner's window, a small woman with the rapid, darting movements of a sparrow turned to speak to her. 'I can tell you love books.' Her voice was a quiet chirp, and Katherine had to lean over to hear her. 'I love books,' the woman went on. 'I'm a writer. A poetess. I write a poem a minute.' The poetess was happy, and in a peculiar way she made Katherine happy; but some of the others frightened her. Walking down Fifth Avenue, she kept her distance and her eyes from the man storming past Saks, chanting, 'Nazi, fag, Jew, bastards', over and over. But the one who upset Katherine most profoundly was the man in front of the lingerie store window with the mannequin in bikini panties and a skimpy bra. The man was facing the mannequin, his head on a level with its crotch, and while his body thrust back and forth in an absurd parody of ecstasy, his tongue licked furiously at the dirty glass. He was oblivious to the people hurrying past him, and the people were, if not oblivious, then indifferent to him. They looked out of curiosity, nothing more. They were New Yorkers, quick and wary and street-smart. Katherine prided herself on all of those qualities, though she displayed none of them the day the quick, wary, street-smart kid crashed into her, tearing a gold chain and locket from her neck and disappearing into the crowd while she stood there, clutching her throat and staring after him dumbly. 'I didn't even scream,' she told Erica later.

'Typical. Some kid rips you off, and you're afraid of making a scene.'

'Are you all right?' Nick asked when she called him from a phone booth right after the incident. There was no logical reason for telephoning him, but she did it anyway.

'Unhurt but still shaking. So much for your theory that there's no more crime in New York than anyplace else.'

'He was probably some kid from the suburbs in for the day.'

'I'm standing in a phone booth shaking, and you're giving me one-liners.'

'I was trying to get you to stop shaking.' He asked her if she was all right again and told her to call the police. 'They won't do anything, but you have to report it to them if you're going to report it to the insurance company.'

'They asked me if I could identify the kid,' she told Nick that night.

'Could you?'

'He was small and skinny and had a mean little face. I told the cops he was Spanish-speaking. Then I realized how idiotic I sounded. I didn't speak to him, but I thought "Puerto Rican" sounded prejudiced. Anyway, I figure there are about half a million kids who look just like him in the city. Maybe more if you count all the boroughs. So I told them I couldn't. I kept thinking of that last scene in *White Heat*.'

Nick laughed and rubbed her neck because there was a small red mark from the chains. 'You've got to stop going to those revivals.'

'Look who's talking.'

'Do you mean old movies or knee-jerk liberal sentiments?'

'Both.'

Early in July Katherine gave Nick what she swore was the final draft of the first two-thirds of the manuscript. She hadn't sent it to the typist yet, and the untidy pile of yellow and pink and green paper looked less like a manuscript than a spring catalogue. 'Pastels are in this year,' she said.

'I liked it better before,' he said when he'd finished.

'That's encouraging, considering everyone else hated it before.'

'Why did you turn him into a wife beater?'

'Erica thought it was a good idea.'

'Why does she spend so much time worrying about her bodily functions?'

'Beth's idea of realism.'

'I rest my case.'

'The typists loved it,' she told him a week later. 'They said they can't wait to read the end. Of course, the fact that they get paid a dollar twenty-five a page for reading the end might have something to do with it.'

'Give it to Erica, and forget about it for a while.'

She couldn't forget about it for a while, any more than he could forget about his kids. Even when he didn't talk about them, she knew he was thinking about them, and he talked about them a great deal. One night he came home from the office and handed her a piece of plain white stationery that was covered on both sides with the most perfect example of penmanship she'd seen since grammar school.

'What's this?'

'A letter.'

She looked at both sides of the paper. 'There's no salutation.'

'Gwen can't stand to use my name anymore, and she sure isn't going to write "dear."'

'Are you sure it's to you?'

'I'm sure. Read it.'

I have several points to make and I don't want to

call the apartment because I'm tired of talking to your mistress and your sarcasm.

'Faulty parallel construction,' Katherine said.
'I didn't ask you to edit it; I asked you to read it.'

1. It has come to my attention that you told David and Mark they can bring friends for the weekend. I will not be responsible for allowing other people's children to spend the weekend in an apartment with a man and woman who are living in sin.

'Living in sin! What were you two doing in that apartment in the Village before you were married?'
'I told you. That was her rebellious period.'

2. From now on the children's medical expenses should be paid to me and I will pay the bills. If the checks go directly to the doctors, I have no way of knowing what has been paid. Especially in view of your attitude toward budgets and bookkeeping.

'What's your attitude toward budgets and bookkeeping?'
'Somewhat to the left of an eighteenth-century English gentleman's.'

3. I have taken David and Mark for interviews at two private schools in the area. I will notify you if and when they are accepted. Daddy says that it's your legal obligation to pay tuition, but if you refuse he'll find the money somehow.

'Is Daddy a lawyer?'
'Daddy's God. Also worth a couple of million.

He'll find the money somehow. Jesus.'

'What are you going to do?'

'Send her the checks for the doctors' bills.'

'I meant about private school.'

'What can I do? If I fight her, she'll turn the kids against me. If I go along with her on everything, I'll lose them anyway.'

Erica called the day after Katherine delivered the manuscript. 'You hate it,' Katherine said when she heard the familiar voice.

'It's fine.'

'You're trying to spare my feelings.'

'No, I'm not. It's okay.'

'Just okay?'

'Christ, Kat, you are sick. If I say it's fine, I'm lying. If I say it's okay, I'm damning with faint praise. Anyway, it's Sydney's opinion that counts. I'm sending it right over, but don't expect a quick response. She's going into sales conference.'

'Maybe with luck it will get lost in the mail.'

'It goes by messenger, and I have another copy.'

'So do I.'

In the middle of July the Greers invited Katherine and Nick sailing on a boat they'd chartered for the weekend. 'We have a Pearson thirty, and we don't have the kids. Do you want to come on Sunday?' Cynthia asked. 'Assuming Nick can leave his beloved offspring for a day.'

'Don't you want to be alone?'

'With Marty I want to be alone. With Doug I can stand to have friends along.' The cadences, Katherine noticed, were new, and she was willing to bet they belonged to Marty.

The alarm went off at seven that Sunday morning.

Katherine turned over and pretended she hadn't heard it.

Nick put a hand on her hip and shook her with more zest than anyone ought to have at seven o'clock of a Sunday morning. 'Come on, Katie, down to the sea in ships.'

She opened her eyes. 'It's still dark out.'

'Only overcast.'

'Forget it. If I can't get a tan, I won't go sailing.'

'You always say you don't tan.'

She sat up. 'I hate you when you're logical.'

Nick made her wear one sweater and take another. Katherine found that an ominous sign. She also took a thermos of coffee in the car and drank two cups on the ride out to Long Island. Nick didn't have any. He was functioning on his own adrenaline. He found the yacht club without any trouble and parked the car in a half-empty parking lot. The water looked as gray as the sky except where the wind whipped it into whitecaps.

'Feel that wind!' Nick said.

She felt it through the heavy sweater.

'You practically never get whitecaps in a protected harbor like this.' His voice had a grating, gleeful edge to it.

'I guess I'm just lucky.'

The dockmaster brought a breath of fetid, whiskey-soaked air to the cool morning. He directed them to a boat at the end of the dock. Cynthia and Doug were sitting in the cockpit.

'The good news is that we have extra foul-weather gear for you,' Cynthia said. 'The bad is that you'll probably need it.'

'Do you think it will rain?' Katherine asked.

'With this wind we'll be taking on so much spray you won't notice if it does.'

Doug had already started the engine, and Nick was running around the dock, uncleating lines. Cynthia looked from one of them to the other. 'Oh, that silent macho rapport. They don't even have to give each other orders.' She handed Katherine a yellow oilskin jacket. 'Foul-weather gear for foul weather. I should have stayed home and worked. They yanked one of my pages from the Christmas catalogue, and I'm left with three thousand units.'

'Christmas. I just got over July Fourth.'

'The world of fashion is always six months ahead of the rest of us,' Doug said.

'As opposed to philosophy professors, who are about three centuries behind.'

Katherine looked down as she fastened the snaps of her foul-weather gear. Nick looked out to sea.

'I want to wait until we get into the outer harbor before I decide which jib to put up,' Doug said.

'How many sails does she carry?' Nick asked.

Cynthia made a face at Katherine. 'Notice the feminine pronoun. Possessions are feminine, and women are possessions. Thank God you came. At least I'll have someone to talk to.'

'The captain would have been perfectly happy to talk yesterday,' Doug said. 'The crew was too busy working.' He looked at Katherine. 'She actually brought paperwork along.'

'I know you don't talk when you're sailing. Unless you're giving orders.'

This time both Nick and Katherine looked out to sea.

Cynthia lit a cigarette, though she'd just tossed a half-smoked one overboard. 'The bastard's on my back again. They move my department all the way to the back of the store in Bala-Cynwyd, and he wants to know why sales are down.'

Doug pushed the Greek captain's cap back off his forehead and looked up at the wind indicator at the top of the mast. 'Can't we forget the store for a couple of hours, Cyn?'

'You can forget it. You're not the one who's going to be fired.'

'First of all, they're not going to fire you. And if they do, there are other stores.'

'God!' She turned to Katherine. 'I wish I'd said that the year he was going crazy worrying about tenure. "Don't worry, Doug. There are other universities."'

Katherine concentrated on tying her sneaker; Nick, on the other boats in the channel.

'The irony of it,' Cynthia went on, 'is that my department isn't doing badly. I'm actually up eight point three percent over last year. But you think that bastard will give me credit? You know what he said when I gave him the figures? "Why not twelve point three?"'

Doug looked at the wind indicator again. 'You're not back at Smith, Cynthia. You don't get pats on the head for being a good girl.'

When they rounded the dogleg in the channel and came into the outer harbor, Nick went forward to raise the mainsail. He looked very nice standing with his legs apart, braced against the pitching motion of the boat, and his hair blowing forward over his forehead. Katherine, feeling like an ungrateful guest, wished that Cynthia and Doug were not aboard.

'Give me the winch handle, Katie,' Nick called back. Cynthia had gone below, and Doug was busy with some lines. Katherine looked around the cockpit for some object that might qualify as a winch handle. 'It's right in front of you. In that plastic case on the bulkhead.' Now all she had to do was figure out what a bulkhead was. 'Right in front of you, for God's sake!'

She took the long metal handle from the plastic holder and maneuvered toward the mast with it. 'Listen, Bligh, you aren't even captain, so watch it.'

'It was right in front of you.'

'Except I didn't know what *it* was. I've been a guest on boats exactly three times in my life. Try to keep that in mind. And try not to catch what's going around this boat.'

'Sorry,' Nick said to the sail he was watching with rapt attention as it went up the mast. Katherine knew that look. She'd even inspired it on occasion when she walked around with nothing on.

Cynthia returned to the cockpit with several cans of beer. 'Get used to it, Kay. There's something about salt spray that softens their brains. It's even worse when they race. We crewed for a couple once, and by the end of the day the wife and I were talking, and the husband and Doug; but there were no other lines of communication.'

Nick had come back from raising the jib, and he was pulling on some lines with his back to Katherine. She reached out and put her sneaker on the seat of his faded red sailing pants. 'Say something to me, Nick.'

'Give me the winch handle.'

Cynthia lifted her eyebrows until they disappeared under the fringe of blond bangs. Nick cleated the line and gave Katherine back the winch handle. 'See. A few minutes ago you didn't know what a winch handle was.'

'My idea of heaven,' Cynthia said, 'is a world where no one knows what a winch handle is.'

Sometime around eleven the blanket of gray

overhead began to break up into clouds that scudded rapidly across the sky. By noon the sun was filtering through, and Doug and Nick had peeled off their sweaters. Nick was wearing a polo shirt, and Katherine felt as if she could watch him working the sheets all afternoon. The shirt pulled against his shoulders, and the veins on the inside of his forearms stood out like deep blue cords. His long fingers moved quickly at the lines and cleats. When he sat beside her, she put her hand on his back. There was a pool of dampness between his shoulder blades.

By one o'clock the sun had burned off the last of the clouds and the wind had died so much that the men were beginning to complain about the lack of it. Cynthia peeled down to her T-shirt and laughed when she saw the expression on Katherine's face. 'The ultimate diet. I'm too busy staying one step ahead of that prick to eat.'

'You look terrific,' Katherine lied. She looked skinny but not terrific.

Cynthia went below to get lunch, and Katherine followed. 'Actually it's work and sex. Beats diet pills.' Cynthia took a plastic container from the ice chest and a loaf of bread from a shelf behind the stove. The boat was wallowing so much that Katherine had to hold onto the handrail, but Cynthia was almost as efficient in the cramped, unsteady galley as she was in her own kitchen.

'I'm assuming from the climate in the cockpit that you mean Marty, not Doug.'

'You assume correctly. They're driving me crazy at work, and Doug's no help at all; but Marty is totally supportive. I can't tell you how good that relationship is. For both of us. He says he's had affairs before, but never anything like this.'

Watching Cynthia put the top piece of bread on

each sandwich and slice it neatly in half, Katherine said nothing. It was not the kind of comment she wanted to answer.

They handed the sandwiches and more beer into the cockpit and climbed back up themselves. Cynthia passed the food around, then pulled the tab off her own can of beer. 'The worst part of it is that the bastard doesn't let up for a minute. The other day he called and started giving me a hard time about some terrycloth robes that hadn't moved, even on sale. I told him if I were a goddamn seer, I'd be on the *Today* show making big money instead of buying bikinis and bras for him. I swear, I'm not going to take it much longer. One of these days he's going to start riding me and I'll walk right out. I just hope it's before Christmas or inventory. That'll serve the prick right.'

Katherine took a bite of her sandwich and told Cynthia the chicken salad was good. She also told her if she quit, she wouldn't get unemployment.

'The hell with unemployment,' Doug boomed. 'We'll take the kids and go to England for my sabbatical.'

Cynthia put down the half of a sandwich she'd just picked up. 'Haven't you forgotten something, darling?' She drawled the last word as if she were savoring the bitter flavor. 'This is a two-career marriage. I can't pick up and go to England just because you have a sabbatical.' Katherine recognized the knowing smile and knew more was coming. 'But you can go without me. Think of all the fun you'd have – a single man with a vasectomy.'

Doug tossed the last piece of his sandwich overboard and went forward, where he pretended to adjust the shape of the jib.

'Never again,' Nick said when they were in the car.

'I thought you loved sailing.'

'I do. I just don't love your friend Cynthia.' He pulled the gearshift around into reverse. His arms were a deep terracotta color now. 'She doesn't let up for a minute.'

'She's worried about her job.'

'Now she knows what equality is. And she's still got less to worry about. What Doug didn't say when she made that crack about his getting tenure was that he had a wife and three kids to worry about at the time.'

'There are women who support families.'

'There are, but Cynthia doesn't happen to be one of them. If she were, she'd worry about unemployment, as you pointed out.'

'I feel sorry for her. She's too thin, and she's chain-smoking.'

'I feel sorry for Doug.'

'He holds his own. Besides, that comment about the sabbatical was insensitive.'

'As opposed to her sensitive comment about his going to England alone. If Doug's such a bastard, such an unfeeling, demanding, male chauvinist pig, why did he have a vasectomy? Christ, Katherine, I'm not saying there aren't injustices, I'm just tired of Cynthia's pretending they're all happening to her. And trying to convince you they're happening to you. It's like the wife-beating scene in the book.'

'Let's keep the book out of this.'

He looked at her. 'I'm sorry, but you know what I mean.'

He turned back to the road, and she twisted around until she was facing out the window.

'Are you going to sulk?' he asked after a while.

When she turned back to him, her sunglasses were spotted and her cheeks wet. 'I'm not sulking. I'm crying. All right?'

They were in traffic, but he took his hand from the gearshift for a moment and put it on her thigh. 'Why are you crying?'

'Because of Cynthia and because I spent the whole day lusting after you and you didn't even know I was there . . . and because of my goddamn book.'

'I knew you were there.'

'When you needed a winch handle or someone to tail for you.'

'I knew you were scared when we were heeling this morning.'

She reached under her dark glasses and rubbed her eyes with her fingers. 'How?'

'Because you were chewing your lip to beat the band. And I knew you'd beaten the fear when you finally agreed to take the wheel. And I knew you were cold when we were coming back into the harbor.'

'I didn't complain.'

'You didn't have to. In that T-shirt your nipples are a dead giveaway.'

'Don't you ever think about anything except sex?'

'You're the one who said you were lusting. And I was thinking, before we started to refight Doug and Cynthia's battle, that it would be nice to charter a boat for two weeks this summer.' He took his hand from her thigh and put it back on the gearshift. 'David and Mark would love it.'

'You mean that's going to be your vacation?' Erica asked when Katherine called to find out if Sydney had read the manuscript. She hadn't. 'Two weeks on a sailboat with two kids.'

273

'And Nick.'

'I keep saying it, but it's true. I wish Michael had married you. He takes the girls for one weekend a month and thinks he's doing me a favor.'

'Then why criticize Nick?'

'Because I'm not interested in Mrs Larries's freedom. Only my own. Why are you and I always on the wrong end of the stick?

'Have you spoken to Beth yet? I got a hundred and twenty-five thou from the movies for her last book. That or three percent of the producer's budget – whichever's higher.'

'Terrific.'

'An excellent reading, Kat. I couldn't even detect the envy. Be patient. This is her fourth or fifth and the first to go to the movies. I'll make you rich and famous one day, too.'

'If Sydney ever reads the book.'

'Stop sounding like an author.'

'God knows I have no right to.'

Katherine called Beth to congratulate her. 'It came just in the nick of time,' Beth said.

'Don't tell me they were going to foreclose the mortgage.'

'Worse than that. Jon found out about Peter. Apparently a case of crabs is a real achievement at that damn progressive school I send him to. Funny, I could have sworn those kids were more sophisticated. Anyway, Jon found out and went into an adolescent snit. Wouldn't speak to me. Started making noises about going to live with Jimmy. Then this movie deal came through. Jon's jaded. Best sellers weren't enough for him anymore, but movies are something else. I don't know why I'm surprised. If Tinsel Town could seduce Faulkner and West and Huxley, why should it have any trouble with my son? Jon has forgiven me. Though I have to admit that business with Peter wreaked a little oedipal havoc. Maybe I ought to find him an understanding older woman of his own. You aren't interested by any chance, are you?'

'If it's all the same to you, Beth, I'd rather take him to a baseball game. Lord knows I've got the time.'

Katherine had plenty of time that summer. While she sat in the apartment and waited for Sydney Hellerman to read her manuscript, she had time for everything and the inclination for nothing.

'Why didn't you get away for the summer?' Erica asked. 'You and Nick could have rented a house in the Hamptons. It might have kept you sane.'

'Because Nick has to be in town and because I don't want to go out there alone and because we can't afford it. I'm waiting for the second third of an advance, and he already has a house in Connecticut – or at least the bills on it.'

As July progressed, the city began to fester. Weather forecasters talked of low air quality and high humidity as if they were predicting Armageddon. The streets smelled from too many people walking too many dogs and producing too much garbage. Women and children fled. Men emerged gasping from the thick, fetid air of the subways and talked, some salaciously, some sadly, of 'baching it'. Nick returned home one night and said it seemed to him women were wearing less than ever this summer. Katherine was not. She sat in front of the air conditioner in shorts and a shirt and tried to think about the end of the book and not about Sydney's reaction to its middle.

One morning toward the end of July a woman

telephoned and said Sydney Hellerman had suggested she call. Despite the air conditioner, Katherine began to sweat. The news must be bad if Sydney didn't have the nerve to call herself. The woman introduced herself and said she was a writer. Katherine ran a hand through her hair. Did they think she needed a ghost? 'I'm doing a book on postfeminism,' the woman said, 'and Sydney gave me your name. I'd like to interview you.' Katherine said she'd love to help, but she was behind on her own book and couldn't spare the time. She thought of saying she'd gone beyond postfeminism to some new heightened consciousness but decided she'd learned her lesson.

The following morning she was in front of the air conditioner again, drinking iced coffee and reading the paper at her desk because the desk made her feel more respectable, when Paige called. She and Stanley had a house in Sag Harbor, but she was in and out of town all summer. She didn't like to leave Stanley alone in the hot city for too long at a time.

'I was just thinking of you,' Katherine said. 'I've found the ultimate workshop. It puts that one you found on fathering to shame. This one is on shyness. Some professor of speech communication teaches the art of small talk at simulated cocktail parties. And that's at an accredited university.'

Paige did not laugh. She didn't even sound as if she were smiling when she asked if she could come over.

If Katherine had not known her friend as well as she did, she would have been reassured by Paige's appearance. The khaki skirt looked crisp despite the steamy drizzle playing on the windows, the dark hair had a glossy just-washed-and-brushed look, and the small amounts of lipstick, eye shadow, and mascara had been discreetly applied. Paige's eyes, however, had a raw, red cast to them. Katherine offered her iced coffee.

'No more coffee. I've been up half the night drinking coffee. We both were. I wouldn't want to have Stanley operating on me this morning.'

They went into the living room and sat on opposite sides of the sofa. 'What's wrong?' Katherine asked, though she had a feeling she knew the answer.

'Everything. My marriage, my life, my whole goddamn world.'

'Could you be a little more specific?'

'Stanley's having an affair.'

'I don't believe it,' Katherine said, although she did.

'He admitted it. Last night. We were sitting around after dinner, watching television. He'd taken off his shoes and had his feet up on that hassock thing, and I noticed one of his socks was on inside out. I always roll his socks in pairs with the right side out. He gets up too early in the morning to have to scrounge around for socks that match or turn them right side out.'

'You could have made a mistake sorting.'

'Not with these. He was wearing the cashmere ones I bought him at Bergdorf's. Seventy dollars for a pair of socks, and he wears them for someone else.'

'I still think you're jumping to conclusions.'

'He admitted it, Kate. When I saw the sock, I just assumed he'd gone to his club to play squash yesterday, but he never does on Thursdays. Grand rounds. So I said, "You didn't tell me you played squash today," and he said he hadn't. Then we sat there for another half hour, Stanley staring at the ten o'clock news and me staring at his feet. Finally, during the weather forecast, I asked him why he'd gotten undressed. He could have lied. He could have said he'd taken a shower after surgery or something, but he didn't. He just took off his glasses and rubbed his eyes and looked at me the way I've seen him look at patients before he gives them a bad prognosis. It's such a damn impersonal look, and they all have it. I think they teach it in first-year med school. "I'm seeing someone," he said. Talk about euphemisms. She's an internist. They were in on the same tax shelter. He's always hated internists. Calls them fleas. All the surgeons do. Because they're the last to leave the body. She's younger, too. Thirty-one. Not a baby, but young enough to make him feel young again. That's what he said. So while Timmy and I are off in Sag Harbor, he and his internist have been romping in the nursery.'

'I'm sorry, Paige.'

Paige started to cry, and a thin ribbon of mascara trickled down one cheek. Katherine went into the bedroom and came back with a box of tissue. 'I never thought I'd become a statistic.'

'If you're talking about divorce statistics, don't jump to conclusions. Just because he sleeps with her doesn't mean he's going to leave you.'

'He doesn't know what he's going to do. That's what he said.'

'What do you want to do?'

'Kill the internist.'

'What are you going to do? Short of killing her, I mean.'

'I don't know what to do. I asked Stanley if he loved her. He said he doesn't know. I asked him if he loves me. He said he thinks so, but he's ambivalent about marriage. He thinks it may not be a feasible life-style for him. He's setting up a whole bunch of appointments.'

'For you all to meet?'

'With therapists. He wants to go into analysis, and he feels I could use some crisis counseling, and then there's family therapy to consider. He wants us to talk it all out before we decide anything.'

'At least you're not seeing divorce lawyers. That's a good sign.'

Another ribbon of black ran down Paige's cheek. She blotted it, then looked at the tissue. 'Women whose husbands are in love with internists shouldn't wear mascara.'

'He's not in love with her. He's sleeping with her.'

'He says he won't promise not to see her anymore. He says he has to be free to work out his own life.'

'Stanley's a forty-year-old man whose wife and son went to the country and who had a fling with a girl in the hospital. He'll get tired of her.'

'Nick didn't get tired of you.'

Katherine had been wondering how long it would take Paige to get around to that. 'Nick said his marriage was in bad shape before he met me. You and Stanley have a good marriage.'

'I thought we did.'

They went in circles for the rest of the morning. At one o'clock Katherine made some tuna fish, which Paige pushed around her plate with a sick look that made Katherine ashamed of her own appetite. At one-thirty Paige called Stanley's office. He'd managed to get them an appointment with a family therapist at three that afternoon and another the next morning for Paige with a crisis counselor. 'They're squeezing us in out of professional courtesy,' she explained.

'Are you going to stay here or go back to the

country?' Katherine asked when they were standing at the door.

'I've got to stay over to see the crisis counselor. Then I'll go back to the country. I left Timmy with the girl.'

Katherine offered to drive out to keep her company and take the train back, but Paige said she'd be all right. She'd made Stanley promise to come out for the weekend. 'You can do me one favor, though. Don't tell anyone. I know they'll sound sympathetic, but they'll really be thinking, I told you so.'

When Paige left, Katherine tried to work, but it was no good. She looked out the window. Across the way a relief doorman – the regular one was probably on vacation – kept mopping his face with a red bandanna. It was not a day for walking.

Sensing that the typewriter was not going and that Katherine was at loose ends, the cats wandered in from the bedroom. They paced and circled, squaring off with each other and her; then Eleanor settled on her lap, and Franklin curled up on the desk with his head hooked over her arm. Katherine sat there scratching their heads and thinking of the renovated town house. 'I've finally got it the way I want it,' Paige had pronounced several months ago, and she'd sounded as if the Landmark Commission had given her historical status. But New York did not bestow historical status so easily, and in the meantime, Stanley had gone out and hired a bulldozer.

XV

The following afternoon Katherine called Erica on the outside chance that Sydney had taken time out from lunches, publication parties, and screenings to read the manuscript. She hadn't.

'Why didn't you tell me about Paige?' Erica asked.

'She said she didn't want anyone to know.'

'Well, she's changed her mind. I can't say I'm surprised. I hope she takes him for every penny. And his heart, lungs, and both kidneys. I got her the name of a good lawyer. A good woman lawyer.'

'That was fast work.'

'She has to protect herself. If I know Stanley, there's a lot of property involved.'

'To say nothing of a heart, lungs, and both kidneys.'

'Okay, Kat, I admit it. I'm a bitch. My first reaction was another recruit for the army of abandoned wives. But I'm not all bitch. Every divorce starts out amiably. Have you ever seen one end up that way? Once people start talking money – especially those two – things get ugly. So I think Paige ought to protect herself. And a woman lawyer is more likely to help her do that. She's coming back to town Monday. I'm going to take her to the lawyer, then lunch. She needs all the support she can get. That's one thing I remember from my own divorce.'

'Maybe there isn't going to be a divorce.'

'Maybe the sun isn't going to rise tomorrow morning. There'll be a lot of talk and some attempts at reconciliation, but there'll be a divorce. What else do you think Stanley means when he says he has to be free to work out his own life? He won't even agree to stop seeing the popsie.'

Katherine didn't think 'popsie' was an accurate description of a thirty-one-year-old internist, but she'd heard the edge in Erica's voice growing sharper and decided not to try to split hairs against it.

A few days later Cynthia called and asked Katherine to take Paige to lunch. 'I was supposed to, but I've got a major crisis here. Twelve hundred quilted robes disappeared somewhere between Hong Kong and New York. When I called Paige to tell her I couldn't make it, she sounded . . . hold on a minute.' Cynthia must not have put her hand over the mouthpiece because Katherine could hear her telling her assistant that she'd call someone back. 'Sorry, Kay, I told you it was a madhouse. Anyway, maybe you can talk to Paige. She says I don't understand. I understand that Stanley's . . . hold on, will you?' This time Katherine heard the assistant's voice in the background. 'Listen, Kay, I've got to take this call. Talk to Paige. If she goes on this way, she's going to end up in a funny farm.'

'You don't sound too sane yourself,' Katherine said, but the phone had already gone dead. As she hung up the receiver, she realized she was perspiring just from listening to Cynthia.

The heat made walking uncomfortable and the idea of taking a bus impossible, so Katherine walked the two dozen blocks to the restaurant where Paige had suggested they meet after her appointment with the crisis counselor. The restaurant was new and terrifyingly chic. The few people who spoke English pretended not to. Despite the fact that both the temperature and the humidity were in the nineties, people stood waiting in a subwaylike crush at the bar for the half dozen highly visible outdoor tables.

Katherine and Paige settled for one in the back that had been placed to catch the crosswind between two vicious air-conditioning outlets. While Katherine ate, Paige pushed her fruit salad around the plate and recounted her visits to the lawyer, the crisis counselor, and the family therapist. The lawyer had told her to empty all joint accounts, which she'd promptly done. The crisis counselor had encouraged her to express her hostility. The family therapist had said that emptying bank accounts without making a joint decision was a hostile gesture.

'Maybe you ought to stop talking to all those professionals and try talking to Stanley.'

'We have been talking. With the family therapist. Alone. Over the phone when I'm in the country or when I'm in town and he stays at his office.' Paige looked up from her lunch, and her eyes were dangerously wet. 'At least that's where he says he stays, when he doesn't come home for the night. When he does, all we do is talk – about his child internist, trial separation, reconciliation, divorce, Tim, custody, everything.' Paige opened the straw handbag in her lap and took out a photocopied article. 'My attorney gave me this. It's about joint custody. I thought Nick might be interested.'

That was exactly what Katherine was afraid of, but she took the article and put it in her handbag.

'Everything, that is, but money. All Stanley says is "Don't worry," but I can tell he's worried. One wife we know actually turned her husband in to the

IRS during the divorce. He had three safe-deposit boxes stuffed with cash. And they weren't small boxes either. Of course, being a surgeon, Stanley never got much cash.' Paige's handsome features turned wistful for a moment. 'We talk more than we ever did when things were going well, but nothing's getting any better.'

After lunch they walked down to Christie's because even though Paige wasn't buying these days, she couldn't resist keeping her hand in. By the time Katherine got home it was a little after five, and Nick was already there. He'd left the office early to go up to Connecticut for a meeting with the headmaster of the school Gwen had chosen. Katherine could guess how the interview had gone from Nick's position on the bed and the four o'clock movie on the television, but she asked anyway.

'We didn't even get the real headmaster. He's in Europe for the summer. This is his assistant who runs the summer school. A pompous, tweedy, uptight son of a bitch.'

'You look like a tweedy, uptight son of a bitch.'

'I may look like one, but he is one. He said he understood David was having trouble adjusting in school because of our separation.'

Katherine turned off the sound and stood in front of the television screen. The least he could do was pay attention to her when he said he was leaving.

'I told him getting the shit kicked out of him—'

'You didn't say that.'

'No, I said getting beaten up by a group of kids didn't mean he was having trouble adjusting. I was pissed at him. Gwen was pissed at me, and he just sat there flexing his fingers together. You know, that church and steeple crap.' Nick put his long fingers together and demonstrated for her. 'It was even worse after we left. The kids just sat in the back of the car and sulked. I don't know if they're angry at me because they don't want to go and think I'm making them, or because they want to go and she told them I'm opposed. Or maybe they're just angry because I left. All I know is they're angry.'

'So you're going back.'

He was stretched out on the bed with his shoulders propped against the headboard and his eyes on his feet, and now he looked up at her as if he were the one who was angry. 'Christ, Katherine, I'm not going anywhere. I'm just trying to straighten things out with the kids.'

Cut, print, no retakes. She was perfectly willing to go with the scene as they'd played it.

'What are you going to do?'

'I told you, I don't know. She's got my hands tied. They live with her. She could turn them against me in a minute.'

Katherine took the article Paige had given her from her handbag and gave it to Nick, though she was fairly sure she'd be sorry she had. She watched his eyes move over the first page rapidly. He was a fast reader. When he looked up, his eyes were opaque.

'You can tell your friends I've heard of joint custody. You can also tell them I plan to fight for legal joint custody, but I'm not about to start shuffling the kids from one house to another every couple of days. There was a kid in Mark's class in nursery school who hadn't gotten the days of the week straight yet. Every day he had to ask the teacher, "Do I go to Mommy's or Daddy's today?" Great life for a kid. And that's assuming we move to Connecticut. Do you want to live in the suburbs?'

She'd lived in New Jersey for one of her three

years with Stephen. None of the years had been anything to write home about, but that one had been the worst.

'Neither do I.' He slid farther down the headboard. 'I've had it with leaving the house before it's light and getting home after dark and sitting on trains with guys who talk endlessly about their grass and going to someone's house every Saturday night because it's Saturday night and we live in the same neighborhood. We moved there because Gwen insisted it was better for the kids, but it's not. I've seen city kids on buses. They're ten times better off.'

'Then what are you going to do?'

'I'm thinking about it. Is it all right with you and your friends if I just try to think things over for a while?'

She turned the sound back up and moved away from the set. 'Excuse me,' she said, and knew she was pulling her upper lip down in that self-righteous way, making what Erica called her Katherine the Great face.

'I'm just trying to work things out, Katherine.'

He went on trying to work them out for several days. There wasn't a single John Wayne movie on television, but he made do with *Shane* and an army of old World War II films. Katherine was not as fast a reader as Nick, but she began to average almost a novel a night. On the fifth morning after the fifth night of silence he rolled over and pressed himself against her for the fifth time.

'Well, I suppose it beats Valium,' she said.

Nick got up without a word and went into the bathroom. He didn't slam the door; but he stayed in the shower for a long time, and when he came out, he didn't say anything to her, not even good-bye when he left for the office.

Paige was in town for a meeting with one of her professional advisers, and they started out for a walk and ended up in a late-afternoon movie.

'Why are we doing this?' Katherine asked. Neither of them was particularly eager to see the movie.

'Because for ninety minutes we'll feel only half as bad as we normally feel these days.'

'It's weak. Nick's in his office. Stanley's probably at the hospital.'

'With his internist.' Paige slipped a five-dollar bill through the metal opening in the cashier's cage. 'I am weak, Kate.'

Nick had already assumed Position A by the time Katherine got home. 'I didn't know you were going out,' he said over the evening news.

'I'm surprised you noticed I had.'

He turned up the sound. 'Do you want a drink?' she asked over it.

'Sure.'

She came back with two gin and tonics and sat on the end of the bed. 'I don't think I can go on this way.'

His face when he turned from the television to her was impatient. She felt like a commercial break. 'Are you telling me to leave?'

'You know damn well I'm not telling you to leave.'

'Then what do you want?'

'I want you to stop.'

'Stop what? Worrying about the kids?'

'Ruining our lives over the kids. I don't think you've said more than ten words to me since that damn meeting. I'd like to talk occasionally. Is that so terrible?'

'About your book?'

'What about my book? Did Erica call?'

He smiled that damn tight-lipped smile. 'I would have told you if Erica had called. When you say "talk", you mean, worry aloud about your book.'

'I don't talk about my book that much.'

'Not as much as you think about it, if that's what you mean.'

'Thanks for being so supportive.'

'Okay, which one were you with just now? Whenever you come home talking about being supportive, I know you've been with one of your friends. And by the way, telling you everything is going to be all right isn't supportive; it's just plain stupid. I can't tell you your book's going to be a best seller. I can't even tell you whether that bitch of an editor is going to like it.'

'Just because she's a woman, you don't have to call her a bitch.'

'Christ! Cynthia calls every man she comes into contact with a prick, but if I call your editor a bitch – and just for the record, sweetheart, you're the one who said she was a bitch – I'm a sexist.' His eyes swiveled back to the television, but she caught the disgust in them.

'That's right, go back to the idiot box. It's almost time for the eight o'clock movie. Maybe you'll get big John tonight. A double feature. First he kills the Indians; then he kills the Japs.'

He switched off the set and turned to her. 'Okay, what do you want to talk about?'

'We could try discussing what's bothering you.'

'You know what's bothering me.'

'End of discussion.'

'How many times do we have to go over it?'

'We don't go over anything. You complain; then you turn off. I mentioned joint custody, and I got an announcement that it was the worst thing in the world for kids. That's not discussion; that's pontification.'

His mouth got tight and sarcastic again. 'You want joint custody, sweetheart? You can barely handle weekends.'

'And what about you? Are you really so torn up about your kids, or do you just want to salve your conscience by making everyone think you're torn up? Or maybe you just want to beat Gwen. Prove something to her and her goddamn rich father.'

He stood and walked into the living room.

'It's nice to know you're still ambulatory. I was beginning to wonder.'

He came back and stood in the doorway. 'Your editor isn't the only one who's a bitch.'

'Because I want to talk? If only I'd be seen and not heard. Keep my mouth shut – except for sexual purposes, that is. Then you'd be a happy man.'

He went into the living room and this time didn't return.

She sat staring at the wall until she finished her drink, then went into the kitchen. Nick didn't look up from his book as she passed through the living room. She washed out the cat bowl and dumped another can of cat food into it. On her way back to the bedroom she knew without looking that Nick did not raise his eyes. He'd stay there reading all night, and when he was tired enough to sleep, or drunk enough if he had several more drinks, he'd get into bed with his back to her, pull the silence over his shoulders like a quilt, and go to sleep. Nick had told her once that he and Gwen had gone for two months without speaking a single word. When it came to torture by silence, Nick was a latter-day Torquemada, and the lovely Gwen must have been his match. But Katherine wasn't. She could endure being bent on the rack of sarcasm or even verbal vivisection, but she broke easily under silence. Nick did not look up when she walked through the living room a third time. She wondered if he had when he heard the front door open and close.

As Katherine walked down Madison Avenue looking through the grilles into the windows of the closed shops, New York turned from twilight gray to black. After what seemed like an hour she looked at her watch. The recalcitrant face said quarter to nine. She'd been walking for twenty minutes. She could go to the movies, but she'd just come from a movie. She knew she couldn't go into a bar alone, or rather she could go into one alone, but she couldn't sit there alone. She went into a coffee shop and ordered iced tea. Her watch reported another fifteen minutes tortured to death. There was a pay telephone next to the door, and telling herself it was a mistake, Katherine dialed Erica's number. 'I know this is an imposition, and if you're doing something, please tell me honestly; but would you like some company?'

'What's wrong?' Erica asked when she opened the door.

'What makes you think something's wrong?'

'I think I showed remarkable restraint by not saying, "What did Nick do?"'

The girls came out of their rooms and said hello, and Katherine managed to joke with them for a few minutes until they drifted back. A glass of wine stood on the coffee table, and a manuscript box lay open on the couch. 'Do you want wine? Or something harder? Or something softer?'

'Do you have any gin and tonic?'

'Do birds have wings?' Erica polished off her wine and made two drinks. 'Okay, what did he do?' she asked when she'd settled herself back on the sofa.

'We had a fight. God knows about what. The kids. My book.' Katherine stopped and looked over the rim of her glass at Erica.

'If I had any news, I would have told you.' Erica put her drink down and lit a small cigar. 'I have a definite sense of *déjà vu* about this. If I call Nick "Stephen" when he comes to get you, don't blame me.'

'Nick's not coming to get me. I won't call him, and he wouldn't come. The bastard probably doesn't even know I'm gone.'

Erica raised her eyebrows. 'You said it, I didn't.'

Katherine said she didn't want to talk about it. Then they pinned Nick to the table as they had frogs to the dissecting boards so many years ago in Biology 101 and went to work.

Two hours later, when Erica invited her to stay the night, Katherine said she'd rather go home, but as she got into the cab, she felt a nauseous churning in her stomach that had nothing to do with too much gin and too little food.

In the apartment all the lights were on, but Nick wasn't in the living room. The door to the bedroom was open, and Katherine entered it hesitantly. He wasn't in there either. She didn't have to look any farther. Two of his drawers were open and empty. The door to his closet was ajar, and his clothes were not in it. He'd left both keys on top of his dresser.

She slammed the door and the drawers closed. Pig! He couldn't even close things or turn out lights. She combed the apartment, but there were no notes. As she passed the fish tank, she made a mental note to ask the night elevator man if he wanted it. Ever since they'd bought it, he and Nick had discussed nothing but tropical fish.

Nick had left a glass on the coffee table without a

coaster under it. She took it into the kitchen and came back and mopped up the table; then she made herself another gin and tonic and took it with a collection of Irwin Shaw short stories she'd already read into the bedroom. She undressed and got into bed, and Eleanor and Franklin settled themselves around her. She opened the book. Halfway through the first page of 'Mixed Doubles' she realized she wasn't concentrating, but that was all right. She felt fine. She felt better than fine. She felt terrific. Free.

Katherine awakened at five the next morning with that sharp completeness that meant she wasn't going back to sleep. She opened her eyes and saw that Eleanor was curled on Nick's pillow. Everything fell into place, or rather apart, and she didn't feel fine or terrific or free. She felt hung-over and depressed and absolutely awful.

XVI

Katherine was grateful for her friends those first days. They filled her hours. They strengthened her resolve.

'I didn't want to say anything while he was still around,' Beth said, 'but I never did understand what you saw in him. He was just another middle-aged lawyer. I mean, he wasn't supergoodlooking or superrich or superpowerful. You can do better, Kitty.'

'I didn't for thirty-six years.'

'I'm not so sure about that. Stephen's richer. He's got a lot more power. He's even better-looking.'

'It wasn't my place to say anything,' Erica said, 'but I never thought it would last. He just couldn't hack leaving his kids. I always knew he'd go back to his wife.'

'What makes you so sure he's gone back to his wife?'

'Because that's where his kids are. And because Nick's the kind of man who likes being taken care of – as you've pointed out. He'd leave one woman only if he knew another was waiting.'

'At least you won't have to spend two weeks with two kids on a Pearson three-sixty-five,' Cynthia said, and put Katherine on hold.

'What's this about a Pearson three-sixty-five?'

Katherine asked when Cynthia came back on the line.

'He chartered the boat through a friend of Doug's. Doug said it's a lousy boat – doesn't sail at all – but it's the only thing he could get that would be comfortable enough for four for two weeks. Oh, hell, Kay, hang on again.'

'How do you know it had to be big enough for four?' Katherine asked as soon as Cynthia returned.

'That's what he told Doug originally when he was going to take you, but he didn't say he'd settle for anything smaller now.' Cynthia told her to hold on for a third time, but Katherine said she didn't have time and hung up. She was lying, of course. She had no Nick and no work, but she had plenty of time.

Paige begged her to spend some of it with her and Tim in Sag Harbor. 'I'm desperately – or is it pathologically? – in need of company.' Paige and Tim had an appointment with the family counselor, so they couldn't leave until three. Neither apparently could several million other New Yorkers.

As they inched along the FDR Drive, the temperature in the car inched down the thermometer. 'I have to keep the air conditioner way up or it doesn't cool the back,' Paige explained. Tim had established residence on the rear seat with several hand-held games, a bag of cookies, and a thermos. He was playing electronic football and singing along with a rock group that blared from the car radio. 'I'm sorry about that' – Paige nodded toward the radio – 'but it keeps Tim happy. It's a long ride.' Katherine thought it was going to be.

'The family therapist says he's dealing with his feelings beautifully,' Paige whispered. 'We've been completely open with him about what's happening and what might happen, and he's letting his hostility out.' Katherine was afraid it might be a long weekend as well as a long ride.

She glanced around at the other cars. The traffic was stop and go, and they kept passing and being passed by the same vehicles. There was another air-conditioned Mercedes with a man in a seersucker suit at the wheel and an air-conditioned Cadillac with two men in shirt sleeves who looked tired and a sleek-looking couple in an MG and a woman in an old Pinto station wagon with two kids in the back and a sheep dog on the seat next to her who stared at Katherine's closed window with an expression of pure hatred. The lines at the toll booths were long, and Paige bought Tim a Popsicle from one of the men hawking them while Katherine paid for a *Post*.

'Are you ready for your horoscope?'

'I've given up on my horoscope. And my future.'

'This ought to be a terrific weekend.'

'At least we have Tim,' Paige said.

Katherine turned around. Tim had stopped singing and was banging an electronic game in frustration.

They passed through the toll booth, and Paige veered to the right. Katherine watched the sports car with the young couple head left toward Connecticut. She wondered where Nick would take David and Mark this weekend. Then she realized he wouldn't have to take them anywhere. They could all stay home together. She opened the newspaper and found her horoscope. 'A business undertaking will finally bear fruit. Domestic affairs are better than ever,' she read aloud.

Saturday started out gray and stayed that way. The sky was overcast; the air, damp and sticky. Tim was sullen because the friend with whom he was supposed to play had a cold. They went to a flea market and three antique shops.

Paige, who had declared an end to the moratorium on new acquisitions, bought a mirror and a bench for the house in the country and a cachepot for the house in town. She also paid for a bowl that Timmy had broken while running down the narrow aisle of one store. Katherine bought nothing.

'I still haven't received the second third of my advance, and there isn't anyone around to help with the rent anymore.'

'Maybe Cynthia was right about contracts,' Paige said.

'Nick doesn't owe me anything.'

'Well, Stanley owes me.' Paige dropped her voice so Timmy couldn't hear. 'The lawyer figures my various services were worth about forty thousand a year, and we've been married for ten years. I don't want to sound mercenary, but I have to be practical. And I have to think of Tim. If Stanley decides to leave for good, he'll have to take care of us. Properly.'

They drove to the Bridgehampton shopping center because Paige wanted to pick up some gardening supplies at Woolco. On their way through the paperback section Katherine noticed that Ego's last book was still on the display racks. She tried to think of her share of the royalties and not of how dispensable everyone had found her.

On Saturday night Katherine wanted to take Paige out to dinner, but she refused. 'With the girl on vacation Tim would have to come, and eating out with him is like going to a four-star restaurant after you've had a Novocain injection. Pointless.' Paige had never meant the jokes she'd made about Timmy's behavior, but these days her reading of them was flatter than ever. 'Besides, I don't want to be mistaken for part of the singles scene.'

They bought steamers and lobsters and corn on the cob. Timmy made a scene over the steamers and refused to eat the small lobster they'd bought for him – apparently when James Beard departed, the Galloping Gourmet turned into Ronald McDonald – so Paige made him a hot dog. When they'd finished their own dinner, they picked at Tim's uneaten one. Paige's inability to eat had passed after the first few weeks. She leaned back in her chair and put a hand on her stomach. She'd always been sinewy rather than thin, but tonight there was an unmistakable bulge under the khaki shorts. 'Cynthia has a husband and a lover and she's thin as a rail, and you and I sit here stuffing our faces. I feel as if I'm back at school. Only I usually had a date on Saturday night.' Paige took a piece of store-bought Italian bread and dunked it in the bowl of melted butter. Some of it trickled down her chin, and she mopped it up with her napkin; but her chin was still damp and shiny, and so were her eyes. 'I wasn't brought up to be on my own. I was brought up to be married and taken care of.'

'Who wasn't?' Katherine said, and then, because she'd sounded harsh, added, 'You're not on your own, and you're not going to be. People don't throw away ten years that easily.'

'I hope you're right.'

'I know I am. Nick had his tenth anniversary last summer.'

On Sunday the sun came out, but the air was still sticky. They took Tim, a friend, and the *Times* to Long Beach.

'I'm going to renounce the magazine section for life,' Katherine said as she tossed it aside. The sun was unrelenting, and her eyes burned from trying to read in it. 'There are always at least two articles I feel morally obliged to read, and when I finish them, all they've told me is what I already knew. In fact, I've decided to give up on all self-improvement and sink into sloth.'

Paige was leaning back on her elbows, watching Tim and his friend at the edge of the water. 'I'd probably try suicide if it weren't for Tim. People say divorce is easier without children, but they're wrong. I couldn't stand it if I didn't have him. Even if Stanley leaves for good, even if I spend the rest of my life alone, I'll always know I've done that.' She raised her chin in Timmy's direction.

'And all I've done is a lot of ghosting and one unfinished, unpublished, and probably unpublishable novel.'

'You could call him, you know.'

Katherine did not mention that she had called Nick at his office. His secretary had said Mr Larries was on vacation. She hadn't recognized Katherine's voice or had pretended not to, and Katherine had left no message.

'He's probably gone back to his wife. At least that's what Erica says.'

'Do you think so?' Paige turned to Katherine, and the hope in her face was unmistakable even with the oversized dark glasses.

Katherine took the train back to town alone on Sunday night. Paige didn't have an appointment until Wednesday. Her family therapist had gone on vacation, and her crisis counseling was winding down. Shuffling off the train with the crowd of hot, depressed weekenders in varying states of undress, Katherine saw the back of a man's head that looked exactly like the back of Nick's head. The day before, she'd seen a man on the beach with Nick's wiry

body and slightly overbroad shoulders. When she'd
had lunch with Cynthia the previous week, she'd
followed a man down Fifth Avenue just because he
walked with Nick's long, loping stride. Outside Penn
Station Katherine beat the man who had the back of
Nick's head to a cab. It just showed what a little
anger could do.

When she got home that night, both the doorman
and the elevator man welcomed her back. They
didn't ask if Mr Larries was away on business, but
she could tell by the way they looked at her that
they were wondering.

The air in the apartment was heavy and stale and
reminded her of the basement of her grandmother's
house. As a child she'd always been afraid of that
basement. Eleanor and Franklin must have heard
her key in the lock because they were sitting in the
hall, but they turned tail and sauntered off as soon
as she entered. They'd make her pay for her
defection for at least three minutes. She turned the
air conditioner to high and went straight to the
answering machine. The white flag was up. There
was no reason to think it was Nick and no chance of
not hoping it was. She rewound the tape. There had
been only one call, but then one could be enough.
She turned the dial to 'playback calls'. Her mother's
voice sounded annoyed at having phoned long
distance to talk to a machine.

As she dialed her mother's number, Katherine
decided not to tell her about Nick. Her mother would
ask how he was and Katherine would say fine. Telling
her mother would only confuse matters if he
returned.

'How's Nick?' her mother asked three minutes
into the conversation.

'Gone. We had a fight and he left. Or rather I left

the apartment, and when I got back, he was gone. With his things.'

'I gather from your voice you're sorry.'

'Shouldn't I be?'

'I don't know. You weren't with Stephen. And you did leave first. Have you called him?'

'His office said he was on vacation.' Katherine told her about the weekend in Sag Harbor. 'They're all taking good care of me.'

'We'd take good care of you down here.'

'I can't leave now.'

Her mother did not ask why, and changed the subject. 'About your friends,' she said when they'd started what was always the long process of getting off the phone. 'Don't let them take too good care of you. Or rather don't let them give you too much advice.'

'I don't pay attention to it.'

'You think you don't, Katherine, but some of it sinks in. Your generation says men don't talk enough, but sometimes I think women talk too much.' Katherine could hear another voice in the background. 'Jack says I'm giving you advice on not taking advice.'

After she got off the phone, Katherine went into the kitchen to make herself a drink. There were no limes in the refrigerator. She remembered the rituals of being sick as a child. When she'd had a fever, her mother had made hourly trips up and down the stairs with freshly squeezed juice and glasses of Coke and ginger ale to settle her stomach. As the fever had subsided, her mother had brought her baked potatoes and chicken that had been taken off the bone and homemade rice pudding. At three o'clock she'd move Katherine's bed so she could look out the window and see her friends coming home from school. Each night her mother would give her an alcohol rub. Katherine remembered the cold, bracing sensation of the liquid on her skin, the smooth, soft dusting of talcum powder that followed, and finally the immaculate-smelling flannel pajamas with the pink roses on them.

There would be nothing wrong with going to Florida for a week or two, except that she was neither sick nor a child, and if she went, she wouldn't be here if Nick called or if Sydney Hellerman finally got around to reading her manuscript.

Katherine spent Labor Day weekend at Beth's house in East Hampton. The best-selling author was back from the Coast, where negotiations were under way for her to write the screenplay for her book or at least the first treatment. She had not returned empty-handed. 'You'll be proud of me, Kitty. He's a contemporary. Only four years younger than we are.'

He could have fooled Katherine. Clark – Beth said that was his real name, not one made up to break into the movies – looked as if he had barely six months on Topper, and that he'd spent them chasing the perfect wave. Either that or applying Ajax cleanser to his hair, baby oil to his body, and a variety of hallucinogens to his mind. His smile was as beatific and as vacant as Topper's, his conversation as sparse, his sexual appetite, according to Beth, as insatiable. Katherine found it hard to believe he'd actually walked this earth for thirty-two years, married, and had children, though Beth assured her he'd done all those things. The experience seemed to have left less of a mark on him than Beth's nails.

'Okay, Kitty, so he's not the smartest thing to come down the pike in the last decade. He has other attributes. That's something else men have always known and women are just beginning to learn. If the dumb blonde hadn't existed, men would have invented her. Because she, or in this case he, is so nice to have around. You know what Clark said when he walked into my bedroom and saw that shelf with all my foreign-language editions on it?'

'What?' Katherine really wanted to know.

'Wow.'

'He has a real flair for the English language.'

'You can joke, but he was absolutely floored. The Japanese ones blew his mind. Ted made fun of everything I ever wrote – in the guise of constructive criticism, of course. And Jimmy was sure I'd never write anything more than my signature on a charge slip. So maybe Clark isn't as smart as Ted or as successful as Jimmy; but he's blond and beautiful, and he makes me feel good in more ways than one.'

Katherine said she was glad and envious and wasn't lying.

On Sunday night Beth gave an A-list party, but Katherine had a C-minus time. On Monday evening she took the train back to town. The summer was officially over, but the weather, like the streets, remained filthy.

Katherine didn't think she should call Nick again and knew she wasn't supposed to call Sydney, so she kept calling Erica.

'I just spoke to Sydney. She said she meant to look at it this past weekend, but she had some really important reading.'

'As opposed to my manuscript.'

'Keep calm, Kat. She swears she'll get to it this week. Anyway, you'll see her Thursday night. She'll probably be at Altruist's party.'

Katherine said that Sydney might be there but that she wouldn't. 'No one will miss the ghost.'

Erica didn't agree. 'This is no time to let down the flag, Kat. In this business the minute people think you're in trouble, you are.'

'Then you're finally admitting I'm in trouble. Professionally, that is. I don't have to ask about personally.'

'I didn't say you were in trouble, but I don't want people to think you are. A few years ago I asked an editor if the rumors I'd heard about one of his colleagues being fired were true. A week later someone asked me the same thing. A month later the man I'd asked about was fired. Maybe he'd been marked already, but I always had the feeling the gossip did it more than anything else.' Katherine agreed to go to the party.

Altruist was not important enough to warrant the expensive elegance of the River Club or the overpriced ostentation of the Tavern-on-the-Green, but he was too profitable to be dismissed with a small party at his editor's or agent's apartment. This was his third novel, and he was, as the saying went, building nicely. His party was held at the Metropolitan Club. At least the room was large and, Katherine hoped, well air-conditioned.

In ten years she'd learned to go to parties alone. In less than one she'd forgotten how. Entering the room was the easy part. The first ten minutes were harder. She followed custom and headed straight for the bar. When she heard one woman asking another, 'Are you a novelist, too?' she knew where she was and that she'd been here before.

Erica had not yet arrived. Sydney Hellerman, her squat body angled forward like a cannon aimed for firing, was talking to another woman. Ego and his agent, Frank Reidy, were huddled in conference near the second bar at the far end of the room. At first glance there were no men in the room with heads or walks or mannerisms like Nick's.

Altruist was holding court in front of a long table spread with the reds of publishing party hors d'oeuvres – pink ham and coral smoked salmon, rust caviar and garnishes of scarlet pimentos. When he saw Katherine coming toward him, he looked the way she imagined John Dillinger had when he'd discovered the federal agents in front of the movie theater. He ran a thick hand over the bald head that had been sunburned to a shade somewhere between the ham and the smoked salmon.

Katherine congratulated him, and he thanked her and said she'd done a nice job on the flap copy. One of the men in the group asked Katherine if she worked for Altruist's publisher. Katherine saw the chains on Altruist's chest stop moving and knew he was holding his breath.

'Free-lancer,' she answered, and Altruist's respiratory system began to function again.

'Everyone thinks the book is dynamite.' Altruist had a rare trait for a grown man who was also a psychologist. He was absolutely gullible. 'It's the lead book for fall.' If you didn't count a new novel by a Nobel Prizewinner and a biography by the dean of American historians, Katherine thought. She'd seen the publisher's catalogue. 'I really think I broke new ground with this one.' He rocked back and forth from heel to toe, and Katherine knew he wasn't afraid of her anymore. Why should he be? He was the successful novelist they'd all come to honor. She was . . . oh, hell, she saw Sydney Hellerman across the room and decided if she were going to abase herself, she might as well do it to some purpose. She started off in that direction, but Frank Reidy stopped her with a damp hand on her arm. His face had already assumed the mean edge, and he smelled of gin.

'Hi, sexy, meet your successor.' Reidy indicated the young man at his side. 'I told you ghosts were a dime a dozen.' The boy was small and slim with thick blond hair and wire-rimmed glasses that were as delicate as his features. He reminded Katherine of the old movie line 'Why, Miss So-and-So, you're beautiful without your glasses.' Only, like Miss So-and-So, the boy was beautiful with them.

Erica turned up, and Katherine pointed out Ego's and Altruist's new ghost. 'I can't stand it,' Erica said. 'First they take all the best men; now they're taking all the jobs.'

'You can't accuse him of getting it on his back. Or should I say knees? Reidy and Ego are too macho, and Altruist's too busy understanding women.'

'You're forgetting Ego's editor. I got the whole story the other day at lunch. The editor left his wife about the same time your successor left the guy who was keeping him in California. The way the ghost tells it, he was a housewife for eight years. Then the liberation – I'm not sure if he means women's or gay – movement hit him, and he decided he wanted to be a writer. Now he's living with Ego's editor and ghosting Ego's and Altruist's books.'

'I find that story demoralizing.'

'I was hoping you'd find it instructive.'

Erica took Katherine in tow and began to work the room. They talked to a moderately successful writer who didn't mean to be condescending but couldn't help himself. He suggested they might get together over a drink to talk about her work one of these days.

Katherine looked up at him. He was tall, much taller than Nick. She didn't have the energy for his invitation, or the heart, or the stomach.

Erica indicated a glass in need of a refill and, taking Katherine with her, slid away from the writer. Katherine had never learned the art of perpetual motion. Once she'd spent seventy minutes at a party with a small, wheezing man who, Erica said, was the oldest living copy editor in captivity. The next day Katherine had felt guilty about boring him.

They made a side trip to the bar; then Erica zeroed in on a man whose name even Katherine recognized when she was introduced. He was very successful, for the moment, and very powerful, for the moment, and said 'bottom line' to Erica and 'Henry James' to Katherine, and had perfect breath. Katherine was more fascinated by his breath than his conversation. At cocktail parties most people smelled of whiskey or overgarlicked hors d'oeuvres or a quick shot of breath spray taken surreptitiously in the cab on the way over. This man smelled of nothing. He had zero-level breath. Over his shoulder Katherine noticed Sydney. She'd been watching them but dropped her eyes immediately.

They moved on. Erica discussed a book she had on submission with an editor while Katherine talked about equal-pay-for-equal-work with a woman who read for one of the book clubs. The woman had an intelligent face and a sharp wit, and though Katherine found her a little strident, she enjoyed talking to her.

'I like her. Who is she?' Katherine asked Erica as they made another pass by the bar.

Erica handed her glass to the bartender and laughed. 'I really do have to take care of you, don't I? She's interested in your body, not your mind, Kat. You just had the make put on you.'

Katherine handed her own glass over to the

bartender. She remembered a discussion she'd had with Nick. She'd told him it would hurt her more if he left her for a man than a woman. He'd said the same about her.

They turned back to the party. Sydney Hellerman was standing in the middle of the room with the condescending writer. She came only to his chest; but she was leaning forward and he was leaning back, and Katherine felt almost sorry for him.

'I'm going to introduce you to the art director at Sydney's house,' Erica said. 'Be nice. Oil the wheels. Do yourself some good.'

'What makes you think I'll ever have a book to put a jacket on?'

The woman had a small, pretty face and wore a soft silk dress on her beautiful iron-hard body. Erica had introduced the woman as the art director, but there was nothing aesthetic about her.

Katherine let Erica go on alone and drifted toward the sidelines. Through the tall windows she saw it had begun to drizzle. Ego was standing a few feet away, talking to a reviewer. He'd always been furious that reviewers didn't even pan his books. They simply ignored them – as he was ignoring her now.

Erica had said Katherine ought to come tonight to hold up the flag, but all she'd been doing was dragging it around the room, letting people trample over it. One more conversation, the only one she'd come for; then she'd leave. Katherine made her way across the room to Sydney. Sydney turned a little as if she hadn't seen Katherine approaching and went on talking. Sydney was skillful, but Katherine was desperate. She moved into Sydney's line of vision again. Sydney mumbled something about it's being nice to see her and how she'd been meaning to call and how she'd be sure to give her a call tomorrow because they had lots to talk over. Surely something would happen to Sydney – her nose would grow longer or lightning strike her – but there was no retribution, divine or otherwise. Sydney just stood there, looking up at Katherine with her calculating eyes.

'Does that mean you've read it?'

'Of course, I've read it.' The squat body rocked back on the birdlike legs in indignation.

'And?'

'There are some problems.' Sydney was already beginning to move away. 'I'll give you a call tomorrow.'

'Sydney says there are problems,' Katherine reported when she found Erica.

'There always are.'

'I get the feeling these are not your run-of-the-mill problems. I get the feeling I'm being stalled. In fact, I get the feeling she read it longer ago than she'll admit and doesn't know what to do about it.'

'Don't panic, Kat. Sydney's a good editor. She can fix anything.'

'If she wants to fix it. Are we going to dinner? I don't think I can hold up the flag much longer.'

Erica's long face assumed a hangdog expression, and Katherine knew she was going to apologize. 'It's okay,' Katherine said. 'I'm not hungry anyway.'

'I should have told you before. The call came just as I was leaving the office. Someone from the West Coast agency. If this thing comes off, Kat, I'm going to be bicoastal.'

'Does that involve a sex-change operation or only a second wardrobe?'

Erica smiled. Katherine knew it was meant in reassurance, but it was actually in relief. 'They haven't got you yet, Kat. Not as long as you can still joke.'

Erica was wrong. They did have her. She passed the condescending writer, who looked at her with an expectancy that might or might not be an invitation to stop. She smiled and kept walking. Near the door the book club reader said she'd enjoyed their talk and they ought to have lunch sometime. Katherine agreed and kept going.

Outside the air-conditioned building the night came at her as a hot rush of damp air. She started across the curved driveway, caught her heel in the uneven cobblestones, and cursed quietly and inordinately all the way to Madison Avenue. Rush hour had passed, and yellow cabs swarmed up the street with their lights on. She hailed one with windows closed on the assumption it was air-conditioned. For once appearances didn't lie. Inside, the leather seat was cold against her bare arms. It smelled of cigarette smoke and reminded her of the couch in Nick's office.

Sydney did not call Katherine the next day. She called Erica.

'No guts,' Katherine said.

'Correct procedure,' Erica explained.

Sydney was going to wash out the book. 'She said the heroine isn't strong enough. In fact, she thinks she's something of a simp.'

'Is that short for sympathetic?'

'And the husband's too much of a brute.'

'Men who go around beating up women generally are.'

'But mostly she felt it was too derivative.'

'Of what?'

'A decade of feminist novels. She said if she'd

309

seen it ten years ago, she would have snapped it up, but the market's been saturated. Don't panic, Kat. This is just the beginning. There are plenty of other houses in town. We'll sell it somewhere.'

'If you say so. How did the bicoastal dinner go?'

'Promising. Very promising. If this thing goes through, you're going to have an agent with real clout.'

XVII

Now that Katherine had been doubly wounded, her friends rallied round with redoubled force. Erica said she was sending the manuscript out to another editor that morning.

'You're only wasting postage.'

'Postage. This is a hot property. It goes by Indian foot runner.'

At one of Beth's high-level parties, she'd met a great lady of the American screen who wanted to write her autobiography. 'Of course, she can't write her name, so I suggested an as-told-to. At least it's a step up from ghosting.'

'One small step for Katherine Walden, one giant step for literature.'

Paige suggested crisis therapy. 'You've got to understand your feelings about this.'

'I understand my feelings. It's Sydney Hellerman's I can't understand.'

Cynthia offered advice gleaned from her own battles in the world of American business. 'Networking, Kay. You've got to learn to use the old girls' network!'

'The old girls' network! My agent was my college roommate. I had the editorial advice of a best-selling author who just happens to be a childhood friend. And Erica sent it to an editor who is, supposedly, a friend of hers and just brought out a book on the old girls' network.'

During the following days Katherine realized that her friends, like Nick, were capable of concentrating on more than one thing at a time. In their rush to offer support for her professional setback, they did not forget her personal disaster.

'You're better off without him,' Erica said for perhaps the tenth time.

'Why do women always say that when a man walks out?'

'In this case it's true. He was selfish. Demanding. Opinionated.'

'I knew you liked Nick, but I never realized how much.'

'He was obsessed with his kids, and he slowed down your work.'

'Not nearly so much as Sydney Hellerman.'

'It's the best thing that ever happened to you,' Cynthia pronounced.

'Easy for you to say. You've got a husband, a lover, and a flourishing career. I've got two cats and two-thirds of a manuscript I can't give away.'

'My career isn't so flourishing. In fact, if I have one more morning like this one, I'm going to walk out.'

'I thought you just got a raise.'

'I did. And that bastard was on the floor this morning telling me now that I was making more, I'd better bring in more, and why weren't those Dior nightgowns moving faster?'

'You're probably better off,' Paige decided. 'My mother used to say, "Never get involved with a married man because if he cheats on his wife, he'll cheat on you." And I ought to know.'

'What's the current status report?'

'Stanley says he needs space.'

'So did Hitler, only he called it *Lebensraum.*'
Katherine caught herself. 'I'm sorry. I shouldn't make
jokes.'

'His analyst says I shouldn't pressure him to come
back on a permanent basis, but the family therapist
believes in commitment.'

'What do the crisis counselor and the lawyer
say?'

'I was graduated from the crisis counselor. The
lawyer says, "Give him enough rope to hang
himself." If this does end in divorce, it isn't going to
be no-fault. I'll charge adultery and fight for every
penny. I've got to think of Tim.'

'You had an old-fashioned wedding. You might
as well have an old-fashioned divorce.'

Beth didn't even waste time telling Katherine she
was better off without Nick. 'Do you know what a
man would do in your position?'

'At the risk of sounding naïve, I think it would
depend on the man.'

'Go out and get laid.'

'Drown my sorrows in some ripe young body.'

'Listen, Kitty, even over the phone I can hear the
ice tinkling in the background. A ripe young body
would be less fattening than booze, healthier than
pills, and not as lonely as masturbation.'

'I wouldn't bet on the last.'

Katherine hung up and finished the drink Beth
had heard in the background, but she didn't pour
herself another. Beth made her feel one step away
from a blowsy old boozer, two from a bag lady. She
looked at her watch. It was ten o'clock, but she still

hadn't had dinner. Left to her own devices, Katherine didn't give up meals, she just put them off. The previous night she'd made herself an omelet at eleven-thirty. Ten o'clock was practically the shank of the evening. 'If you're in Madrid,' she said to Eleanor. On her way to the kitchen the fish tank caught her attention. She kept forgetting to ask the elevator man if he wanted it.

She took a can of tuna from the cabinet and turned on the radio. She recognized the halting, whispery voice of a woman disc jockey who took a long time to say little to the host of megalomaniacal celebrities she interviewed.

This is not just a book for . . . well, it won't appeal to just . . . let's see, how can I put it? . . . this is a book for, like, everyone . . . not just for women. Wouldn't you agree?

Katherine interpreted the sales pitch. This was obviously a woman's book. As she opened the can of tuna and drained the oil into the sink, she pictured the millions of women just like her in the city – to say nothing of the millions more divorced, widowed, and abandoned in the suburbs – listening eagerly for word of this book that was going to give them solace.

Oh, I'd definitely agree with that. This is a book for everyone.

Katherine stopped flaking the tuna in the bowl. She'd know that voice anywhere. Hadn't she listened to it making salacious comments on her tape for five years?

After all, it was . . . uh . . . written by a man. By this man we're talking to now. I'm speaking to . . . uh . . . Dr Barry Greene. A noted psychologist and the author of . . . uh . . . Crisis.

'Truth in advertising,' Katherine said to the radio.

'Haven't you ever heard of truth in advertising?'

How do you feel, Barry, about the fact that you . . . well, how can I put it? You, like, appeal so widely to an audience of . . . uh . . . women. I mean, so many of your readers are . . . uh . . . women.

'I understand women,' Katherine said.

Well, you see, I feel I really understand women.

'Some of his best patients are women.'

Of course, as a practicing therapist, I have to.

Let's talk about . . . well, let's talk about that for a while, Barry. About what it's like to . . . like, to wear two hats. I mean, you're a practicing therapist and a novelist. Now as a novelist . . . uh . . . wearing that hat, I mean . . . do you, like, have trouble writing?

As a matter of fact, I love to write.

The jar of mayonnaise was new, and Katherine banged it against the counter to open it. She used more force than necessary, and Eleanor and Franklin ran from the kitchen.

You might say writing is my therapy. Therapy from therapy. Ego guffawed, and the disc jockey giggled. After a long day of helping patients, writing provides an outlet for the creative juices.

Do you . . . now how can I ask this without . . . well, without embarrassing you or your patients? Do you, like, base your characters on . . . like, on your patients?

Well, my office is my laboratory. My subject matter is the human mind. Human emotions. But I find – speaking as a writer now rather than a therapist – that the best characters are the ones that get up off the page and take off on their own. Sometimes I don't know what my characters are going to do on the next page.

Katherine slammed an English muffin into the toaster. 'Bet your ass.'

Tell me, Barry, if you had to . . . uh . . . to choose between . . . I mean, between writing and . . . uh . . .

being a therapist, which is, well, which is, like, most important to you? I know that's a tough one.

Katherine took the muffin from the toaster. 'Helping people.'

Helping people. Through therapy. And through my books. I wouldn't write another word if—

Katherine switched off the radio and picked up her sandwich. Then she put it down again, opened the freezer, and took out an ice tray. She carried the fresh drink and the sandwich to the dining table and sat at one end. Eleanor jumped to the chair at the side.

Tell me, Katherine, as a . . . like, a writer and a . . . like, a woman, how do you feel about your . . . uh . . . self?

'Indecisive,' Erica would say.

'Misguided,' Paige would add.

'She's naïve,' Beth would point out.

'She's never understood the way the world works,' Cynthia would pronounce.

But what about . . . uh . . . you . . . I mean, like, what do you think yourself?

'I agree with all of them.'

The second week in September Erica called to say the second editor had rejected Katherine's manuscript.

'That was fast.'

'I sent it to her because she never sits on things.'

'Unlike our friend Sydney.'

'Listen, Kat, I have clients who have gotten fifteen and twenty rejections.'

'But did they sell the book in the end?'

Erica came back immediately with plenty of conviction. 'Sometimes.'

The mail brought another article from Paige, this

one from Stanley's alumni bulletin. A recent study showed that a surprising number of women graduates were choosing careers as wives and mothers.

'Part of me feels vindicated,' Paige said when she called later that day. 'But part of me is worried because I keep thinking they want to be a wife to my husband and a stepmother to my son. Still, I was surprised.'

'Big surprise. Maybe somebody should have told them work isn't all fun and games.'

'You're getting awfully cynical.'

'I'm digging down and discovering my anger.'

In the country autumn brought death, or so Katherine had learned from books because, as she'd pointed out to Nick, she'd never spent much time in the country. According to all the bucolic writers, the fields, after the harvest, lay fallow and finally frozen, and the trees stood bare and unforgiving. The city was another story. In the city fall meant rebirth. Except this year in the city fall refused to arrive. The usual outward signs were there. Store windows displayed furs and woolens, newspapers reviewed new plays and art openings, kids swarmed through the neighborhood in flannel and gabardine uniforms that made them look like an army of small Anglophiles; but the air each September morning was tired, and each afternoon heat shimmered up from the pavement in thick waves. Descending into a subway was like returning to the worst days of August. Summer had a stranglehold on the city, and aware of the convenient lie, Katherine blamed the weather for her lassitude and defeat. She was not alone. Paige was depressed. Erica was short-tempered. Beth was absent. Cynthia was frantic. She called one morning and insisted Katherine meet her for lunch. 'I've got to talk to someone.' She sounded as desperate as Paige had the morning she'd learned about Stanley's affair, and a lot angrier.

Katherine turned off her typewriter, which had been humming in disuse rather than clattering in activity, took her second shower of the morning, and dressed to go downtown. By the time she reached the restaurant her hair was sticking to the nape of her neck and her blouse to her back. Her face, she noticed in the mirror near the door, looked both uncomfortably red and unappetizingly pale.

When Cynthia arrived ten minutes late, her mouth was a tight slash across her round, flushed face, and her eyes darted nervously about the room. As soon as she sat down, she lit a cigarette, her hands fluttering at the cloud of smoke between them. Her fingernails were chewed ragged. At school the joke had always been that you could tell exams were coming by the state of Cynthia's nails. Her cuticles used to bleed all over the blue books.

'I have had it with that prick.'

'Your boss?'

'Who else?'

'Sometimes it's hard to tell. You use "prick" and "bastard" alternately about him, but then you use them alternately about Doug, too.'

'I don't need a wise ass today, Kay. I need support.'

Katherine said she was sorry. 'Are we drinking?' she asked when a waitress approached the table, but Cynthia didn't have time, so they looked at the menus and ordered.

'I got my own back this morning, though. He must have known he'd gone too far yesterday afternoon because he came up to me on the floor

318

this morning and actually tried to be nice. I walked away.'

'Was that smart? I mean, it may have been personally gratifying, but it isn't going to make working with the bastard' – now she was doing it – 'any easier.'

Cynthia lit another cigarette and fanned the smoke impatiently. 'You sound like my mother. "You get more flies with honey than with vinegar." Typical feminine acquiescence.'

The waitress dropped their salads on the table as if the plates had been too heavy for her. When Katherine asked for more dressing, the girl gave her a sullen look. Cynthia stubbed out her cigarette. 'I won't stoop to his level.'

'Come on, Cynthia, a few civil words to the man in the morning isn't exactly a compromise of moral principles.'

Cynthia speared a piece of chicken. 'You just don't understand.'

'I understand working isn't as glamorous and fulfilling as the movement promised you it would be.'

'Now you sound like Doug.'

'I can remember a time when you meant that as a compliment.'

'If it weren't for Doug, I wouldn't be in this predicament. If I'd gotten a job right out of school or, better still, gone to graduate school the way I wanted, I wouldn't be a lousy buyer of ladies' lingerie working for that cretin.'

Katherine had no memory of Cynthia's desire to go to graduate school. 'A year ago you thought the job was great.'

Cynthia looked up from her salad. 'I never said it was great. It was the only thing I could do. Thanks to Doug. I still get furious when I think of it. One week I was all set to go to grad school; the next I was pregnant. I told Doug I wanted to have an abortion. I mean, I love the kids and all, but I didn't want them then. I didn't even want to get married, but he kept saying it would be all right. Sure it was all right. For him. It was terrific for him.'

'That's not fair. I can still remember the string of jobs Doug held all through graduate school. His parents didn't support you entirely.'

'You can say that again.' Cynthia pushed her half-full plate away and lit another cigarette. 'It's easy for you to talk, Kay. The summer after we were graduated, while you and Erica were running around Europe, writing me witty postcards, I was sitting in a stifling apartment in Cambridge – Doug's father said we didn't need an air conditioner – gestating the Greer son and heir. And while you two were working at glamour jobs—'

'We were secretaries.'

'—I was working at getting a baby from a three- to a four-hour feeding schedule. So don't tell me about fair, Kay, because you were never the good little grad student wife who learned how to make tuna fish fifteen different ways and you never had three kids in diapers at the same time because the idea then was to get your kids over with quickly and the high point of your life was never a goddamn wine and cheese party where the men talked department gossip in the living room and the women talked pediatricians in the kitchen.'

'You're right, Cynthia. I was never the good grad student wife or the supermother, so now I don't have to be the great militant. I also don't have to blame everything that happened in my life on someone else.'

320

'I'm not blaming everything in my life on someone else. I'm blaming a sequence of events on Doug.'

Katherine told herself to keep silent, and she might have if she weren't so dissatisfied with her own life; but she'd made a mess of the book and of things with Nick, and she had as little patience with the rest of the world as she did with herself. 'Don't you remember what happened spring of our senior year?'

'A lot of things happened spring of our senior year. Doug got me pregnant for one. That's what I've been talking about.'

'I mean the terry-cloth robe.'

Cynthia rattled the ice in her glass with her straw. 'Now you sound like that bastard my boss. What about terry-cloth robes?'

'You had a terry-cloth robe, and you washed it with your diaphragm in the pocket. And ran it through the dryer. Then you went off to Cambridge for the weekend.'

Cynthia looked surprised. Maybe she really hadn't remembered. Or maybe she was simply shocked that Katherine had the bad taste to bring it up. 'I'd forgotten it was in the pocket. I didn't put it through the washer and dryer on purpose.'

'I'm not saying you did, but after you had, the sensible thing to do would have been to get a new one. We all told you that.'

Cynthia's mouth was a sullen line now. 'I was on scholarship, Kay. Remember?'

'How much would it have cost, Cyn? A couple of dollars? And Doug would have paid for it. You knew that. But you never even mentioned it to Doug. You told me that afterward.'

'Are you saying I was trying to get pregnant?'

'I'm saying you must have known it was a possibility. You'd read the little booklet that came with the diaphragm. And you were graduated cum laude.'

'Pregnant and cum laude. And a week later I was pregnant and married, and the cum laude didn't make a damn bit of difference.'

And a week later the scholarship you'd gone through school on didn't make a damn bit of difference because you were married to a boy whose family had a lot of money and whose Yale/Harvard-graduate-school/future-philosophy-professor credentials had a lot of cachet, and that was exactly what you had in mind when you went to Cambridge with a diaphragm that had been laundered, bleached, and run through a heavy-duty dryer, Katherine thought but did not say.

'And that's why I'm a lousy underpaid, overharassed buyer now. I could have been something important.'

'I could have been a contender,' Katherine said in a bad Marlon Brando voice. She was already regretting her outburst, and the waitress seemed to be taking forever to bring the check.

Outside the restaurant the heat lay in wait for them. It rose from the pavement and settled on their bodies heavily. On the corner of Forty-ninth Street and Madison Avenue Cynthia stepped on the cigarette she'd carried out of the restaurant and turned to Katherine. Cynthia was several inches shorter and had to look up, and maybe that was why her eyes seemed hooded.

'You don't know, Kay. You've always had it easy.'

It was not the sort of comment anyone ought to make while saying good-bye on a street corner at lunch hour, and especially not the sort of comment anyone ought to try to answer under those circumstances, so Katherine said she supposed she had and told Cynthia to take care of herself and started up Madison Avenue. By the time she got home and dialed Erica's number she was not feeling as if she'd had it easy.

'You don't by any chance know anyone who's looking for a ghost. Beth's great lady of the American screen said she'd prefer a male ghost. Actually she said she'd prefer a man. I'm assuming she meant ghost.'

'Take it easy, Kat. There's still a chance of selling your book.'

Katherine noticed that the language was deteriorating rapidly. A week ago Erica had been sure they'd sell it. 'Maybe, but in the meantime, I need some work.'

'You're compulsive.'

'How else would I have ground out trash for Ego and Altruist at that rate?'

'Why don't you get out of the apartment and do something constructive instead of sitting around waiting for Nick to call?'

'I'm not. I've got a machine for that.'

'After three weeks? Face it, Kat, he's gone back to the little woman. Don't you think it's time you went back to a normal life?'

'What do you consider a normal life?'

'No more kids every weekend, no more silent treatments, no more romantic trysts to New London, Connecticut.'

'I've got a normal life.'

'Stop feeling sorry for yourself. You're well out of it.'

'Stop lecturing me and find me some work and I'll stop feeling sorry for myself.'

'I'll keep my ears open for someone who needs a ghost, but don't expect anything right away. I'm pretty busy with movie people these days.'

The next morning Katherine decided to get out of the apartment and do something constructive. She would spend the morning at the Whitney. She looked down at her ratty robe and ugly bare feet. No, not the Whitney. She felt too much like one of those Duane Hanson figures of unkempt women and slovenly men drinking beer. She didn't want to be mistaken for the art. She'd go down to the Frick and look at the Sargents instead. Maybe she'd even go to a movie afterward.

She went into the bathroom, but as she reached over to turn on the shower, she caught her reflection in the mirror. Which buff are you? One of the lonely ones, hungry for conversation? Not likely. It seemed that since Nick had left, she'd spent half her life on the phone. One of the carefully groomed ones, taking solace from Bette Davis's hardships? Not in that ratty robe. Katherine went back into the bedroom, sat on Nick's side of the bed, and turned on the television. Why go out when there might be a perfectly good movie on television? She began to switch channels aimlessly until she was brought to a stop by Ego, alias Dr Leo Robbins, telling an audience composed mainly of women How to Be a Winner When Everyone Around You Is Losing at the Game of Life. The thick lips were pulled back in the requisite sincere but sexy smile, revealing the large, perfectly capped fangs that were supposed to spell success. Katherine had heard that television added pounds, but she'd never known it diminished an already dangerously narrow forehead. The camera did not love Leo Robbins.

The host loped down the aisle toward one of several women with raised hands and stuck his microphone in front of her face. The woman, who was of indeterminate age and had two wattles swinging from either side of her broad, fleshy chin, licked her lips nervously. 'When you talk about the self-actualized person – is that right? – you say we should get rid of shoulds, but how are we supposed to bring up our children without some rules?'

The camera swung back to Ego, and Ego swung into action. 'When I say in my book' – Katherine noticed that he held it up to the camera and had to admit he was a pro – 'there should be no shoulds, I don't mean there are no moral, religious, or philosophical rights and wrongs. What I do mean is that a self-actualized person is a shouldless person. A person who feels free to be free.'

'Please not the prophylactic-on-the-nose example,' Katherine said to the screen, but the host and the camera had already moved on to another woman. She couldn't have been older than thirty, though the tight lips and severe eyes looked as if she'd witnessed several lifetimes of wrongdoing. 'What about God? What about His shoulds?' A murmur of approval, like a light breeze in a field of wheat, ran through the studio audience.

Ego screwed up his face, presumably to give the impression he was pondering the question, and his forehead disappeared into his hairline. 'As I said, I'm not speaking about religious truths, but I will say that each of us is somewhat unique—'

'You can't modify "unique", Ego,' Kath... ...id.

'—and surely it's our religious dut... that individual uniqueness.'

'Do you understand a wor... Katherine asked Franklin, who ... lap.

The woman did not look... moved on. Katherine ...

woman spoke that she was a convert. Perhaps it was the clothes that looked as if they'd come from a sixties peace march by way of an Indian reservation. Perhaps it was the way she beamed at Ego. She'd gotten the macho message of his smile. 'I for one want to thank you. You changed my life.' Another murmur, stronger than the light breeze, ran through the audience. 'In your book you talk about one of your patients – Gwen was her name – and I had the feeling you were talking directly to me.' The camera cut to Ego, and Katherine noticed the forehead disappear again. That would teach him to skip the case histories when he read the galleys. 'But my question,' the woman went on, 'is about the no-sickness person.'

'I swear,' Katherine said to Franklin, 'that's his term. I wanted to use "healthy."'

'Do you really think,' the woman asked, 'that you can actualize yourself out of a sickness?'

'Absolutely, and I'll give you an example from my own personal life.' He flashed the sincere, sexy smile as if he expected the audience to swoon. The camera panned to the woman who'd asked the question, and she looked as if she might. 'When I started out on this tour a few days ago, I felt a cold coming on. Aches and pains. A runny nose.' Ego smiled again over the intimacies he was sharing with his public. 'Now I could have canceled the tour, but then a lot of people would have been disappointed. I could have dragged myself around the country, sniffling and apologizing, but the self-actualized person, the person who wins at life, doesn't apologize. So what did I do? I said to myself, "Leo, those germs aren't making you sick. You're giving permission to make you sick." And' – he threw ~s as if he were God presenting His work on the last day of creation – 'here I am!'

The camera panned to the applauding audience, and the host loped across the studio and thrust his microphone in front of a young woman with a face like a piece of linen that had been laundered too often. Her eyes were desperate and she spoke haltingly. 'I read your book, and I understand about not expecting other people to help you and having to make it happen for yourself—'

'Excuse me.' The camera swung back to Ego. 'I didn't say others couldn't help you. I'm in a helping profession. I said only you can actualize your own happiness.'

The woman looked as if she were going to cry, though she nodded dutifully. 'But what about the problems that aren't your fault? I mean, sometimes there are real problems. Like your husband drinks or something.'

The host swung and dipped as if he were dancing and came up facing the camera with the microphone in front of his face. 'She has a point, Leo. There are people who accuse you of oversimplifying.' No patsy, this host. He was there to fan the fires of controversy or at least breathe on the embers occasionally.

Ego beamed into the camera as if the smile alone would enlighten. 'I don't oversimplify, but I do cut through the self-defeating mechanisms that we all use to keep ourselves from being our own best selves. You used the word "fault". There's no such thing for the no-blame person. A no-blame person doesn't say, "My husband is making me miserable." She says, "I'm giving my husband permission to make me miserable."'

'But it's not that easy. Like, if there are kids.'

'Excuses!' Ego held up one finger as if he were

delivering an old-fashioned jeremiad. 'The self-actualized person doesn't waste time on excuses.'

The host and camera moved on, and Katherine turned off the television. She hoped the woman had taken the book out of the library and not wasted her money on it. Then she got angry at the woman for trying to solve her problems on a talk show and at herself for sitting here in her bathrobe watching it and at Ego for being such an ass, but such a successful ass.

She'd put on a skirt and a decent blouse and even some makeup and go down to the Whitney. She was looking for a belt when the phone rang. One of the nicest things about those months with Nick right after she'd sold the book had been her new relationship with the telephone. It had become a casual friend she'd neither feared nor loved. She'd even gone for days without thinking about it, though not without using it.

'Kay?' a man's voice asked. It wasn't Nick's voice. 'It's Doug.' The only times Doug had ever called in the past were to report the births of the three kids. Katherine wound the belt she was holding around her arm as if it were a tourniquet and told herself Doug and Nick had gotten along, but not that well. Doug would not have heard from Nick. The call had nothing to do with Nick.

'I'm sorry to bother you, but Cynthia wanted me to tell you. She's in hospital. She took half a bottle of Valium last night.' He was talking very quickly, as if he had to get rid of it all at once. 'She's okay now. Apparently you can't kill yourself with Valium. Luckily she didn't know that. They took her to Bellevue – what a nightmare that was – and pumped her stomach. They wanted to keep her there, but I said no way. We finally got her into St. Jude's. She wanted to go to Payne Whitney, but they didn't have any beds free.'

'You put her in a mental hospital?'

'That's what the doctor advised.'

'The doctor was probably some medical student in the emergency room.'

'Christ, Kay, what did you expect me to do? Take her home so the kids could see what their mother looks like fresh from a suicide attempt? After they pumped her stomach, she went on one of her abusive tirades. This didn't start last night, you know. It's been going on for months. Longer. She was really losing touch. You talk to her all the time. You must have noticed.'

'I know she was worried about the store.'

'Worried about the store! She was pathological about it. Convinced everyone there had it in for her.'

'She said something about personality conflicts.'

'She must have been watching herself with you. At home she talked about personal vendettas. Even the kids were beginning to pick up on it.'

'How are the kids? Can they manage by themselves?' The youngest was twelve, but Katherine wasn't sure how resourceful a twelve-year-old might be.

'They have been for some time now.'

'Should I call her?'

'You can't, but she'll probably call you. There's a pay phone, and she made me leave her a lot of change. In fact, she said this morning she wanted to talk to you. To explain something. She wasn't making much sense.'

Katherine took the belt off her arm and wound it through her fingers. She had a pretty good idea what Cynthia wanted to explain. 'Why last night, Doug? I mean, if you don't want to tell me, I understand, but did something set her off?'

'Hell, why should I keep anything from you?' Doug said, and Katherine realized she'd never heard his voice sound mean. 'From you and the other girls. Excuse me, women. You were all in on the Marty thing, weren't you?'

Katherine made an apologetic sound.

'She quit yesterday afternoon. Apparently this time of year the store panics because it's overbought, and when she got back from lunch, there was a memo on her desk telling her to cancel some orders. All the buyers got one. Anyway, she marched right into the boss's office and said she stood on her word – and her orders. She'd quit before she'd cancel. You can imagine what he said. Unfortunately I made the mistake of saying the wrong thing, too. When she got home and told me, I said I didn't care if she wanted to quit, but I thought she should have given them notice. I also told her I didn't think it was the melodrama she was making it out to be. All the other buyers got the same order. She even admitted it happens every year but she didn't see any contradiction between those facts and her theory that they were out to get her. And I was dumb enough to try to show her. And pretty soon we'd gotten from how I'd ruined her life to how someone else was helping her salvage it.'

'Marty?'

'She wanted to tell me all about him, but I didn't have the stomach to listen, so I walked out. I guess it was a dumb thing to do. She's tried to commit suicide before.'

'I didn't know that.'

'No, she didn't want to tell you. Maybe she didn't think the attempt was impressive enough. Only half a bottle of aspirin. The doctor joked that next time she ought to try Bufferin. It wouldn't upset her stomach as much. She has a lot of pride when it comes to your little group. Anyway, I stayed out for a couple of hours – walked around a little; hell, I got drunk – and by the time I got home she was asleep. At least I though she was asleep. Then I found the empty bottle. She'd left it on my dresser.'

'After I went out, she called Marty. It seems she expected him to back her up. Refuse to deliver his orders, which, as I understand it, were not among the canceled. Needless to say, he wouldn't. She told me this morning that was the final betrayal.'

Katherine remembered the way Cynthia's hands had beat at the clouds of smoke yesterday. 'What do you mean the final betrayal?'

'First me, then the store, finally Marty.'

'Can I do something. For the kids or for you?'

'You can do me one favor. Call the others. Erica and Beth and Paige. This time she wants everyone to know where she is, but I don't want to go through the whole explanation again. Besides, I just don't feel like talking to them.'

XVIII

'I knew something was wrong,' Paige said when Katherine had repeated Doug's story. 'After I saw her last week, I told Stanley what she was like – he was over for dinner – and he said she was heading for a breakdown.'

'Did Doug sign her in?' Erica asked. Katherine said she didn't know but assumed so. 'What a rotten thing to do.'

'At least she's safe there. She can't make another try.'

'I suppose you're right, but it still makes me nervous. I sure as hell wouldn't have wanted Michael to have that kind of control over me.'

Katherine called Beth next, though she doubted she'd be back from California. As soon as she returned from a trip, Beth usually checked in 'as if I were a baggage desk,' Katherine had joked once. She'd regretted the words as soon as they were out because Beth's face had assumed the same just-slapped look it had worn that time she'd gotten the devastating review in *Newsweek*.

'I was just about to call you, Kitty. Give you a full report on the land of sun and cellulose. They are not dying to have me as a screenwriter, but they're going to start production next month. I can see it on the silver screen now. "Based on the book by Beth

333

Sarmie." I've got to talk to Erica about the credit.'

'Beth . . .'

'Have you had any word from her? About your book, I mean.'

'No, but—'

'Listen, not to worry. Someone will buy it. Maybe she'll sell it to original paper. Speaking of paper, you should see what was waiting for me in the mail when I got back. The cover for the paperback of my last book. Those people must be crazy. The heroine has cellulite. Her face is okay – if you don't mind that blond Barbie doll look – and of course, they gave her enormous tits, but she's got cellulite. I called the editor and told him he ought to send her to La Costa. He asked if I meant the heroine or the artist. I said both if they needed it. I also said—'

'Beth!'

'What?'

Katherine told her about Cynthia. She went through all the details except their lunch the day of the suicide attempt.

'I thought she seemed depressed. What now?'

'Doug says she'll probably be there for a while. She can have visitors after the first week. He thinks she'd like to see us.'

'God, no, Kitty. Hospitals are bad enough, but funny farms! I wouldn't know what to say to her.'

'She's still Cynthia.'

'I don't want to go.'

'I think we ought to.'

'Well, I won't visit alone.'

'You won't have to. Hell, we probably wouldn't let you.'

Cynthia's friends went to visit her in a group, as Katherine had predicted they would. Cynthia had called Katherine a few days after she'd been admitted and asked her to come. 'If you're not afraid, that is.' Katherine told her not to be silly.

'You'll love it, Kay. I'll show you my belts. I've been making belts. Occupational therapy. Maybe I'll sell them to the store when I get out. When that prick Doug lets me out.'

'Did he sign you in, or did you sign yourself in?' Katherine asked the question on which they'd all been speculating.

'I did it – at his suggestion. And that damn doctor's at Bellevue. I must have been crazy.' Her laughter sounded brittle. 'That's why they locked me up. Come Wednesday night. That's my first anniversary here. We'll go out to dinner.'

'Can you do that?'

'I'll talk to the nurses.'

Katherine called Doug. 'She wants to go out to dinner. Should we take her?'

Doug's laugh sounded as brittle as Cynthia's. 'They won't let her off the floor.'

Visiting hours were from four to eight. They met at Erica's office at five. A hot, sticky drizzle had been starting and stopping all day. Erica's dress was damp and wrinkled because she hadn't been able to get a cab on the way back from lunch. Paige was wearing boots, though it was still too hot for them. Beth's dark hair was a frizzy mop. Katherine knew her own hung lankly.

'I thought of renting a limo,' Beth said, 'but not to go down to St. Jude's.'

'Doug should have put her in Payne Whitney,' Paige said.

'He couldn't get a bed there,' Katherine explained.

'Stanley says he wouldn't put his worst enemy in St. Jude's.'

'He could have taken her home,' Erica said. 'I

can't believe she'd try it again.'

In the Checker cab going downtown conversation ricocheted around the back seat nervously.

'It looks like the jacket of a gothic novel,' Beth said as they got out of the cab in front of the bleak gray-stone building. She clutched Katherine's arm. *'She pursued a dream of passion – and plunged into a nightmare of peril.'*

'She dared a moment of love – and was doomed to a life of madness,' Erica added.

'Would you two stop it?' Paige snapped. She was not accustomed to disciplining, and her voice had come out sharp and impatient. Chastened, Beth and Erica followed her into the building like children returning to class from recess.

The grim corridors were muggy and reeked of a nauseating amalgam of illness, medication, and institutional cooking.

'Catholic hospitals always make me nervous,' Paige said. 'I keep thinking about their saving the baby and letting the mother die.'

'Cynthia's not in the maternity ward,' Erica observed.

'All hospitals make me nervous,' Beth said. 'Every time I walk past one I remember my mother. She was in and out of them for a year at the end.'

'I remember that,' Katherine said. 'You visited her practically every day.'

'Every day except the last. She'd been in a coma for a week, and the doctor said she'd probably hang on for another, so I went to Philadelphia for an autographing party. I signed eighty-three books the afternoon my mother died.' Beth's voice was so unrelentingly bright that she might have been talking to Johnny or Merv or thirty million viewers.

They got off the elevator at the fifth floor. Through

the iron mesh-reinforced window of the door opposite, they could see a long corridor with a few people milling around. Erica, her long chin stuck out in determination, crossed to the door, but the knob didn't turn in her hand. An orderly let them in from the other side. When the door slammed closed, Paige turned and stared, startled by the noise. 'I didn't expect a locked door.'

The ward was even more stifling and rancid than the rest of the hospital, and the few windows left open onto wire gratings and fetid streets provided no relief. Paint flaked off the walls in large chips of a discouraging avocado green that someone must have thought soothing.

'If you weren't suicidal to begin with, this place would do it,' Beth said.

Erica pushed a few tendrils of hair back from her damp forehead. 'Remember that scandal last summer when some mental patients died from the combination of medication and heat?'

'I think that was a state hospital.' Paige looked around warily as if she'd strayed farther from home than she'd intended. 'Though this doesn't look much better. Stanley was right.'

Patients and staff wandered about with varying degrees of aimlessness, taking no notice of the visitors. A girl in a nurse's uniform sauntered by. Another girl, about the same age, in blue jeans and T-shirt, stood staring at the wall six inches in front of her. A big man advanced on them. His sweat-stained unbuttoned shirt hanging outside baggy pants gave him an unfinished appearance. The skin of his face looked like a bowl of mayonnaise that had yellowed and hardened on a lunch counter. Angry red blotches glowed on both temples. The women scattered before him like a flock of startled pigeons, then clustered again after he'd crashed through. When he reached the door, he turned and started back up the hall.

Halfway down the corridor they found the nurses' station. Two attendants stood smoking in front of a long mirror. A nurse had a phone tucked between her shoulder and ear to free her hands for the emery board she was working back and forth along her nails. When Katherine asked where they could find Cynthia Greer, they didn't look hostile, only bored. One of the attendants directed them farther down the hall.

There were six beds in the room, each with a small table beside it, but that was all Katherine noticed because on a bed in the far corner a woman was sitting cross-legged. Her hands were moving rapidly over a shoe box in her lap. She looked up when they entered and waved. Katherine knew the woman was Cynthia but didn't believe it could be. No one could have changed that much in a single week. She was worse than unkempt. She looked dirty. It wasn't simply the blond hair that hung in greasy strands around her face or the same yellowed-mayonnaise appearance of her complexion. The uncleanliness was more pervasive than that, and more profound, as if she were decaying from within.

'My God!' Erica whispered.

'I don't believe it,' Beth murmured.

They all stopped in the doorway until Cynthia's wave turned into a gesture hurrying them forward. 'Come along, children. Not to be afraid. There's nothing wrong with me that a couple of hours at Monsieur Marc wouldn't fix. I meant to wash my hair for you, but I didn't have time.' As they drew closer, Katherine noticed that Cynthia's T-shirt had coffee stains on the front and white circles, like water marks, around both armholes.

They told her she looked fine and bent in turn to kiss her cheek. Katherine came last. She watched the mayonnaise skin come closer, touched it with her own cheek, and pulled back quickly. She hoped Cynthia hadn't noticed.

'These are my friends,' Cynthia said to a woman sitting in a chair near the bed. She was short and, beneath the smock that covered her blouse and half of her slacks, solid-looking with a flat, incurious face. 'My best friends. We all went to school together.' Cynthia gave the woman their names and erratically selective biographies. Beth was a famous author of whom the woman must have heard. Cynthia had stayed at Erica's house during every Thanksgiving vacation from school. Paige didn't have a job, but Cynthia was working on her, trying to raise her consciousness. She and Kay had been inseparable. Cynthia stared at Katherine for a moment from under the dirty bangs, her eyes cloudy. The woman, whom Cynthia introduced as Bridget, smiled with her mouth, but her eyes remained dull.

Cynthia put the chain of small leather pieces she was holding in the shoe box. It was covered with red smudges from her chewed cuticles. Several of the marks were so clear that someone might have been taking her fingerprints. 'I guess Doug told you what happened.'

The air grew hotter and thicker as they shuffled and mumbled embarrassed assent.

'This time I almost pulled it off.'

Katherine glanced from the discolored tile floor to Cynthia's mottled face. It looked old or at least worn, but her voice was tinged with youth and astonished pride. *We're going to do it. We're going to get married,* she'd announced when she'd come back from the phone that night.

'The doctor said I came damn close,' Cynthia went on. She might have been back in that happier institutional room that smelled of cigarettes and coffee and the cool Massachusetts spring rather than in this one that reeked of sweat and sickness. 'He said it was a miracle I was still alive with all the shit I'd taken.'

Katherine heard the enthusiasm simmering beneath the words and was relieved that behind this cracked and soiled façade the old Cynthia, infuriating as she could sometimes be, survived. The other women must have felt the same way because they stood in a tight semicircle around the bed, smiling like overaged cheerleaders.

'They tried to keep me for observation, but I said no way. Not at Bellevue. I wanted to go to Payne Whitney. After all, I wasn't sure you'd stoop to visit me here, Paige.' The women laughed too hard and too long, even Paige, who had a light film of perspiration on her upper lip.

'Doug said he couldn't get a bed at Payne Whitney. He probably didn't even try. Too cheap, just like his daddy. The old bastard wouldn't pay for a private room when I had the kids either. Remember Mass. General? It was almost as bad as this.' Cynthia peered up at Katherine with the grin of a precocious child. It sat pathetically on the puffy, jaundiced face. 'You remember that room, don't you, Kay? When I had Gary.'

Katherine smiled as if her mouth were made of crystal.

Cynthia put the box aside and got up suddenly. Bridget stood, too, startling Erica, who was closest to them. 'I have to call Marty before his place closes. I haven't seen him for more than a week. He says he's going crazy without me. Wait here.' She took a handful of change from the pocket of her jeans and started for the door. Bridget followed. Halfway across the room Cynthia turned and came back to pick up the shoe box. 'Put that on my chart, Bridget. "Takes her belt box everywhere."' She turned to her friends and threw them a wicked smile that invited their complicity while it dared their pity.

'Well?' Paige whispered as soon as Cynthia was out of the room.

'She's overwrought,' Erica said, 'but who wouldn't be, locked up here? She seems all right otherwise.'

'She seems like vintage Cynthia. And I'm not being bitchy,' Beth added quickly.

'Maybe,' Paige said, 'but I don't think we should have let her call Marty.' The film of perspiration had spread from her upper lip to her entire face.

'Look,' Beth began, sounding bitchy after all, 'I know you believe in closed marriage, but Cynthia's sanity is a little more important than a minor matter of fidelity.'

'I was thinking of Cynthia's sanity. I got the impression Marty had dropped her that night.' Paige turned to Katherine for confirmation.

'That was the way Doug made it sound.'

'Doug!' Erica's intonation implied he was responsible for the steamy, foul-smelling room and their as well as Cynthia's presence in it, but she must have heard her own voice because she went on quickly. 'All I meant was that Doug isn't exactly a disinterested observer when it comes to Cynthia and Marty.'

'Exactly,' Beth said. 'There's no reason to assume Marty's going to drop her because of this.' But her face looked stiff and uncomfortable.

Cynthia came pounding back into the room, with

Bridget a few steps behind her. 'What a bitch! The receptionist says he's gone for the day. I know she's lying. He never leaves this early. She was always jealous of me. I bet she doesn't even give him my messages.'

There was a moment of silence during which none of the women dared look at the others because their flushed faces would attest to more than the heat. But if her friends were embarrassed, Cynthia was not. She'd returned to the hothouse world of the closed ward, sinking into it like a seedling spreading its roots, and her visitors, like Marty, were only shadowy and momentary presences.

She sat on the bed again and took a chain of leather scraps from the box. They stuck to her sweaty fingers. 'Stunning, isn't it? I'm thinking of starting a new career as an accessories designer.' She turned to Bridget. 'Why did you tell me there were no more pieces this morning? You gave Stephanie more pieces. Does that mean you like Stephanie better than me?' Paige caught Katherine's eye, and they managed to look away just as Cynthia whipped her head around and gave them a triumphant grin. 'Don't forget to put that on my chart, Bridget. "Persecution complex."' The smile disappeared with as little warning as it had arrived, and Cynthia stood up. 'Come on, I'll give you the grand tour. You can stay here, Bridget.'

'Perhaps we could be alone for a while.' Erica had spoken in her best executive tone, and Cynthia started to laugh.

'I was teasing her. I'm on constant. Paige, explain what "constant" is to Erica, or does Stanley only talk about surgery? Constant observation. They're afraid I'm going to try to kill myself again, so Bridget has to go everywhere with me. Even to the bathroom.

She stands outside the door. Talk about glamour jobs. Bridget spends her life standing around listening to other people pee.'

Again they chuckled, and again the sound was as synthetic as a laugh track.

Cynthia threw her arm around Bridget's shoulders. 'I'm sorry, Bridgie. I was only teasing.'

Cynthia led the way out of the room, and the four of them followed, with Bridget bringing up the rear. The girl was still standing and staring at the wall and a woman was hugging it as she made her way down the corridor. The man was still pacing. They prepared to scatter, but he stopped in front of them and stared down at Katherine. 'Where's the subway?' His voice seemed to come from some distance, like a ventriloquist's dummy. He grabbed her arm. 'You have to come with me to the subway.'

Bridget stepped in quickly and pried his hand off Katherine's arm, and the man began pacing again.

'They shock him,' Cynthia said quietly. She might have been explaining one guest's impoliteness to another. Then her head swiveled to Paige, and her tone changed. 'So much for the wonder of modern medicine and the infinite wisdom of doctors.' She chanted the words like an evil incantation. Paige's face turned as white and fragile as tissue paper.

'I didn't know they still used shock therapy,' Erica said. Her tone was one of informed interest, but Katherine recognized the little half-moons playing around the corners of her mouth.

'Not on me they don't. I'll kill Doug if he ever lets them shock me. That pair of scissors was a joke, but it wouldn't be if he ever let them do that to me.'

Cynthia started walking again, and they fell into step, each of them careful not to look at the others, each of them thinking of that line about the scissors and trying to pretend she wasn't thinking of it. No matter what happened, Katherine knew, they'd always remember that comment, but Cynthia, caught up in her role as tour leader, had already forgotten it.

'That's the quiet room,' she said with the same touch of pride she'd displayed years ago as an undergraduate when she'd shown prospective students around the campus. 'That's the libe,' she'd said with a smug air, 'that's Paradise Pond.' They were standing in front of the open door to a narrow room with padded walls and mattresses on the floor.

'Talk about euphemisms. You haven't lived until you've gotten up in a padded cell. A locked padded cell. It happened the second night I was here. They wanted me to go to sleep, but I didn't feel like going to sleep, so I made a fuss. Acted out, right, Bridget?' Bridget said nothing, and Cynthia went on. 'I put up one hell of a fight. It took three of them to give me a shot, and the next thing I knew I was coming to in my little padded cell. Four walls, no windows, and a locked door. I've been trying to figure out which is worse – the quiet room or a straitjacket. I think a straitjacket. Imagine not being able to scratch your nose or anything. Either that or hydrotherapy. That would be the worst. Trapped in a tub with one of those rubber sheets. Only a tiny hole for your head. Water racing all around you and no control. But maybe they don't really do that. Maybe I only saw it in a movie. Not *The Snake Pit*. I think it was some grade B thing. I remember the actress's head sticking through the hole in the sheet. And the steam rising all around her. You wouldn't think they'd use hot water.'

Cynthia's face was damp, and her voice was gathering momentum with each word like a juggler on some crazed amateur hour who begins slowly but picks up speed as she goes, tossing objects faster and faster as the applause grows louder and louder, adding more and more oranges or apples, driving the audience, driven by it, in a frantic attempt to push the needle on one of those electronic meters to the breaking point.

'Bridget was in there with me. I'm not sure if that makes it better or worse. I was afraid she was a dyke. But she's not. Put that in my chart, Bridget. Sexual fantasies. Homosexual fantasies. I'd love to read that chart. You ought to show it to my friends, Bridget. They're writers. Or at least Beth is. Kay, too, but Kay hasn't published yet.' She gave Katherine a broad smile. 'I have very successful friends. We're all achievers.'

Cynthia was still racing along, her words coming faster and faster, the beads of perspiration standing out on her face. Erica put her arm around Cynthia's shoulders and leaned her cheek close to the lank hair. 'Take it easy, Cyn.'

For a moment Cynthia reacted as if she'd finally pushed the needle to the top. The sweaty cheeks swelled with success; the eyes flashed with triumph. Then the face collapsed, and the eyes clouded over. She shrugged off Erica's hand and started the tour again. Erica dropped a few steps behind, walking with her hands plunged into the pockets of her dress, her head pulled down into her shoulders, and her eyes on the floor. She was walking, Katherine thought, the way she used to before some force of will or improved self-image or maybe only Michael's criticism had taught her to walk. And Cynthia, leading the tour once again, seemed willing to leave her behind.

'You see that mirror?' Cynthia pointed to the

glassed-in nursing station. 'It's a one-way window. They watch us. I'm not supposed to know that. See how the aides hang around it? Pimply-faced little boys from Fordham. That's how they get their rocks off. The little pricks. The other night I got undressed facing the mirror. Just to shock the horny little bastards. I bet that will go on my chart. Hell, Bridget, if you want material, you ought to talk to Beth. I'm just into a little harmless exhibitionism. Beth screws babies. The younger, the better. Says she likes young bodies. I think there's more to it than that. Must be more. Maybe she's afraid of someone her own age. Her equal. Pick on someone your own size. Pick on her. If you're going to lock someone up, why not Beth? Or one of the others. Why me?' Cynthia's eyes caught each of the women's in turn, but theirs proved too slippery to hold. 'Beth even gave her son's friend crabs. Oops, I wasn't supposed to tell, was I?' Cynthia threw her arm around Beth's shoulder. Beth shrugged and tried to smile but only succeeded in rearranging her features in such a tight, asymmetrical grimace that her face looked less like a valentine than a broken heart. Cynthia let go of her shoulders but didn't move away. 'I'm sorry, Beth. You're not angry with me, are you?' Beth said she wasn't. 'Promise me you'll forget I mentioned it.' Beth promised, but it wasn't enough. 'Swear it,' Cynthia insisted. There was an urgency to her voice that reminded Katherine of the sacred childhood rituals. Cross your heart and hope to die. Step on a crack, break your mother's back. Nothing crossed counts. Beth swore it, and Cynthia took her arm and started walking again. She was still holding it when they stopped in the doorway to a large room with card tables, chairs, and couches scattered around it. In one corner stood bookcases half-filled with books and games, and on the other side of the room a television droned. Three women sat on a couch opposite, tears streaming steadily down their cheeks as they watched. 'This is the dayroom,' Cynthia said.

She'd left childhood behind and arrived at college again. Her voice had assumed the faint superiority she'd reserved for those eager touring applicants. Katherine heard the echo in the voice, so at variance with the glazed eyes and sallow skin. Cynthia was no longer a model student and this was not an idyllic campus and her pride was nothing more than a hollow memory that left a dull ache.

Two elderly men, one in a bathrobe and slippers, were playing checkers at a table. Nearby a young man sat staring at a chessboard. 'The poor kid,' Cynthia said. 'He just sits there all day. Never moves anything. He says he can't remember the moves. They shock him, too.' Cynthia was still holding Beth's arm, but she might as well have forgotten all of them. She'd moved beyond past and present to some imminent and threatening future. Fear turned her mouth slack and settled in her eyes. The eyes reminded Katherine of the cats' when they looked out of the plastic carrying case she used to transport them to the vet's.

Patients shuffled in and out as the women stood there waiting for Cynthia to return. Some stared; some hung their heads in shyness; some didn't even notice them. An aide was standing behind a young man who was cutting something out of a newspaper. Cynthia's head swiveled from the boy they shocked to the young man with the scissors, and her mouth snapped back into its tight, sardonic shape. 'Kindergarten,' she explained. 'If you want to use a sharp instrument, you have to have supervision. They keep everything locked in that closet. The way they keep us locked on this floor.'

She led them across the room to a girl leaning over another shoe box filled with leather scraps. 'This is Stephanie. These are my friends.' Cynthia ran through her litany of introductions again. The words were almost exactly the same, as if she'd memorized them. 'I'm going to find Stephanie a job when she leaves here. She had a full scholarship to Vassar, but she dropped out. Her parents keep hassling her to go back. They're blue-collar and think a diploma means something. I set her straight on that.' Cynthia turned to Stephanie. 'Fuck diplomas and fuck scholarships. You know what I learned in four years? Nothing. Not a fucking thing that ever helped me in life.'

If Cynthia had dumped the hundreds of books she and Doug had accumulated over the years in the center of the dayroom and set fire to them, the other women could not have been more stunned, but they stood there smiling the small, tight smiles that were meant to reassure her. Or, Katherine wondered, were the smiles intended merely to absolve themselves? Their friendship was not so indestructible that it couldn't be severed by a pair of scissors drawn in violence or consumed on a pyre of burning books. In contrast, Stephanie's mouth was a straight line and her eyes were hooded with fear. There was no telling whether she thought Cynthia was preaching the Gospel or speaking in tongues.

But Cynthia's mind had already careened off in another direction, and her unkempt body followed as she led them back to the nurses' station. 'These are my friends,' she said to the nurse and ran the same litany in the same words. 'They're going to take me to dinner, so you can sign me out to them.'

Now she was a friendly but slightly condescending guest at an expensive spa. Over the years, as Cynthia's weight had fluctuated in reverse proportion to her spirits, she'd dreamed of going to one of those spas. Katherine had always told her that anyone who paid a few thousand dollars to have some quack dole out a handful of calories and a penny's worth of pop psychology was crazy.

'You've already had dinner, Cynthia.' The nurse's voice wasn't patronizing, only bored.

'But I didn't.' Her tone was suddenly reasonable, and she moved closer to the nurse's desk. This was the Cynthia who knew how to manage and manipulate people and situations and worlds, not cruelly, but practically, to her own ends. 'I didn't eat it because I knew I was going out.'

'You know you can't.'

'But I promised them. We made plans.'

'It's okay,' Katherine said. 'We don't have to go to dinner. We just came to see you.'

'But I want to go out. I planned to go out.'

'Come on, Cyn, we'll go back to the dayroom,' Erica said. 'We can all sit there.'

Katherine had expected Cynthia to continue arguing, but she turned and started back.

'We can play bridge. It'll be just like school. They used to lock the dorm, too. Do you remember those marathon games? Till two or three in the morning. On and on. One weekend – junior year, I think. Yes, I'm sure. Junior year. That blizzard when no one could get out of Northampton. Hell, no one could get out of the dorm. We must have played for three days straight.' Her voice was racing again, and Katherine felt a hot rush of fear and defeat that left her suddenly exhausted. She thought longingly of her cool, orderly apartment and the fresh sheets she'd put on the bed that morning.

But Cynthia, for the moment at least, did not appear to want to be anywhere else. She was organizing, and she'd always been happy organizing. 'You be my partner, Erica. And Paige and Beth. Kay can watch. All right, Kay? You're the worst player anyway. Paige is better than Erica, so that will even everything out. I'll get the cards.'

'I don't think we have that much time,' Paige said.

There was another silence, almost as thick and uneasy as the one that had followed Cynthia's return from calling Marty. It was out. They were abandoning her, leaving her alone in this sweltering hell and returning to the outside world, where people went to the bathroom in privacy and to dinner freely and to bed when they chose.

Cynthia opened her mouth, and Katherine waited for the word 'traitors' to come howling from the gaping wound. Instead, Cynthia's voice emerged wheedling and childish. 'You can't leave. You just got here. Maybe we can go for a drink. Come on, Bridget, sign me out. Just for a drink. We'll even buy you one. Beth will treat. Beth has lots of money.'

'The nurse told you you can't go out,' Bridget said.

Cynthia turned from her constant companion to her friends and screwed up her face in a grotesque parody of a baby about to cry. 'Just five minutes. Please.' The words carried Katherine back to her own childhood, not to the inevitable plea for a reprieve before bedtime but to the old radio personality of Baby Snooks. When she'd discovered that the voice did not belong to an infant but to a grown woman, she'd been disappointed, then angry, and finally heartbroken. She felt the same way now.

'Only five minutes,' Cynthia repeated in the small, synthetic voice, and, taking Beth's hand, led them to a couch and chairs in one corner. Katherine sat on the end of the sofa, and an old woman in a cotton dress and bedroom slippers squeezed in beside her, reeking of stale perfume and cabbage. 'You can't sit with us now, Mrs Downey,' Cynthia said. Hers was the voice of authority and discipline again. The woman stood and shuffled off.

'You're the mayor of the floor, Cyn,' Erica said.

'Mrs Downey wants a divorce, but her husband won't let her go. He locked her up. I promised to help her when I get out.'

'When do you think that will be?' Paige was whispering as one does in a sickroom.

'My doctor thinks I'm terrific. She says she's never had such a quick patient.' Mrs Downey came and stood beside the sofa, and Cynthia shooed her away again. 'She said it's no wonder I tried to kill myself with all I had to put up with. You'd think Doug would feel guilty, but he doesn't.' Cynthia tilted her head to one side and smiled at Katherine. 'What about you, Kay? Do you feel guilty?'

Katherine shifted her position on the hot plastic cushions. Ever since they'd arrived, she'd watched Cynthia veering from manipulation to helplessness and back, but now she couldn't tell which held sway. Cynthia's voice was earnest, but her off-center smile gave her a dazed air.

'I'm relieved you're okay.'

'Then you think I'm okay? You don't think I'm crazy?' The smile was frozen now, and the alert face that had rarely missed anything looked slightly stupid.

'Of course I don't think you're crazy.'

'Just overwrought?'

'I'm not a doctor, Cyn.'

'No, but you know all the answers. At least you knew them last week at lunch.'

'I didn't mean anything at lunch,' Katherine said.

Cynthia's eyes slid from Katherine to the faces of the other three, but her smile remained fixed. 'Kay thinks I got pregnant on purpose.'

They were all staring at Katherine now, but when she turned, they dropped their eyes as quickly as they did when Cynthia looked at them. Only Bridget's eyes remained steady, although the tiny spark of curiosity died without igniting a flame and her face remained as dull and dusty as ashes.

'All I meant . . .'

'You're not supposed to argue with me, Kay,' Cynthia said in a singsong voice. 'I'm in the hospital.' She leaned over and hugged Katherine. 'Anyway, I'm only teasing.'

Again the women fell silent. For almost twenty years they'd talked, seriously and mindlessly, intimately and warily, 'for your own good' and 'because I've got to tell someone.' They'd talked in twos and threes and fours and all together, in dormitories and on telephones, in stores and theaters, in maternity wards and each other's bedrooms. They'd talked about boyfriends and husbands, lovers and parents, each other and themselves. But now, as they sat in the airless locked ward of a mental hospital, they found they could no longer talk. Perhaps there was nothing left to say, or perhaps there was too much and they didn't want to say it in front of Cynthia. And me, Katherine thought, remembering how they'd been unable to meet her eyes a moment ago.

The women were pretending preoccupation, with their perspiring hands, the unswept floor, the faded pictures on the wall, but Cynthia didn't have to pretend. Her eyes were riveted to the amnesiac chess player just as his were to the board.

'You're right, Kay,' she said quietly, almost in a whisper. 'I fucked up everything. I got pregnant on purpose, and I made Doug marry me, and then I fucked it all up. Marriage, the kids, my whole damn life.' She was crying now, talking and crying and ineffectually dabbling at the tears with her hands. They left greasy black smudges on her cheeks. Katherine produced a tissue, and Paige a handkerchief, but Beth smoothed away the dirt with her thumb.

'You're not a disaster,' Katherine said.

'Nobody who has three terrific kids and a good career is a fuck-up,' Beth added.

'You're even married.' Paige managed a smile.

'That's more than I can say for the rest of us,' Erica chimed in.

Cynthia shook her head slowly with an infantile stubbornness. 'No, Kay was right. I fucked up.'

'I never said that,' Katherine insisted, but Cynthia would not be stopped. 'Fucked up. Got pregnant on purpose. Knocked up, Doug's roommate said. The diaphragm.' She was chanting now like a priestess worshiping at the altar of her own despair. 'The superclean diaphragm. Sterilized it. Should have sterilized Doug instead. Or me. Knew I'd get pregnant. Smart. You said I was smart, Kay. Read the little booklet. Beware. Tiny little rips and tears. Not visible to naked eye. No match for naked bodies. Knew it would work. It wouldn't, and I would. Ten days to two weeks. Perfect timing. Everyone knows that. Doug would marry me then. Wouldn't otherwise. Mommy and Daddy said no. I had no money. Truth was they just didn't like me. Not good enough for their little boy. I showed them. A boy, too. And then another boy and a girl. Perfect family. Perfect wife. Only she fucked up. And fucks around. And keeps taking these pills. Doug didn't tell, though. No one knew. Not even you. Any of you. See, I didn't tell you everything. Kept a secret. But fucked up. Even the pills. Aspirin. Doctor said next time try Bufferin. Arrogant prick. Valium no good either. Failure. See, you were right, Kay. Absolutely. Fucked up everything.'

'I never said you fucked up everything,' Katherine repeated, but she knew the reassurances were as futile as her attempt to distinguish the manipulations from the helplessness. They were the warp and woof of Cynthia, and if you tried to separate them, you'd only unravel the fragile fabric that barely held her together. She sat there mopping at her face with Paige's handkerchief and muttering about her failure and soaking up their consolation with a heartbreaking thirst. After a while she stopped crying and began smiling her little-girl smile again. When Mrs Downey returned, bringing her rancid aroma and Doug, Cynthia gave Paige back her handkerchief and made a pathetic pantomime of fixing her hair.

Katherine felt, if not the wave, then the ripple of relief that ran through the group. They'd rather have Cynthia hiding behind a series of façades, no matter how grotesque, than naked and defeated.

'Look who's here,' Cynthia said. 'The prodigal husband.' Doug kissed her on the cheek with no sign of being repulsed.

'How do you feel?' he asked after he'd greeted the rest of them. He'd grown his beard again, and while the thick, curly hair covered the sharpness of his chin, it couldn't soften the anxiety of his eyes.

They were alert and nervous and seemed to be begging for help.

'Fine – for a crazy woman. Did you speak to the doctor about when I can leave?' Her voice dared Doug to answer. She was as sure of herself now as she had been of her failure a moment ago.

'I spoke to her, but she wants to talk to you tomorrow.'

Cynthia turned back to her friends. 'Doug pretends he's in a hurry for me to get out, but I think he's having the time of his life. After he leaves me every night, he goes straight to singles' bars and picks up popsies. Tell me, Doug, how many times have you gotten laid since I've been here?'

Behind the beard Doug's thin mouth curved in a weak smile. 'Not once.'

'You ought to, you know.' He was standing beside her, and she reached up and patted his stomach. 'You still have a nice body. Not nice enough for Beth – right, Beth? – but pretty good for a middle-aged man. I'm sure you could find some sweet young thing. Think how impressed she'd be when you told her about Descartes. I fuck, therefore I am.'

Doug sat on the arm of Cynthia's chair. 'I'll think about it, Cyn.'

Cynthia turned back to her friends. 'Shouldn't Doug get laid while I'm in here? You must think so, Kay. You always defended him.' The eyes in the smudged face taunted Katherine. They were the eyes of a naughty child peeking out from the defeated wreck of a woman Cynthia had been only moments ago, and Katherine realized that the playful girl was neither more nor less real than the abject failure. Cynthia believed in both of them just as she did in the superjuggler and the smart, successful manipulator, and as long as she went on believing in them, they'd keep her here, locked up with her constant companion, her varying truths, and her eternal fears.

'I think you ought to go home as soon as possible,' Katherine said as if it were an answer to Cynthia's question.

'I think' – Erica stood – 'that we'd better go.'

Cynthia stood, too. 'Don't go. Stay just a little longer. Please.'

'We can't really.'

'Tim . . .'

They all muttered half explanations, interrupting each other's words, reinforcing each other's excuses.

Doug stayed in the dayroom while Cynthia and Bridget and the four visitors walked down the long hall to the locked door. The girl was gone, but the man was still pacing.

'You'll come again, won't you?' Cynthia asked. 'I'll call you tonight, Erica. Paige, why don't you come back tomorrow? You don't have to work. You, too, Kay. You both come. Beth, call me when you get home. I want to talk to you. Stay just a little longer. I'll get the nurse to give me a pass. We'll go out for a drink. Just wait a minute.'

Finally an aide came and opened the door, and the four of them slipped through, leaving Cynthia behind. Though Doug was waiting for her in the dayroom, she continued to stand on the other side of the reinforced window. She waved. They waved back. She mouthed good-bye. They did the same. The indicator above the elevator door moved from one to two. She stuck her tongue out at Bridget, who had turned her back for a moment. They smiled. The dial inched up another floor. She pantomimed banging on the window. They laughed. The elevator climbed to four. She waved again. They waved again.

The dial passed five and kept going because they'd pressed the down button. She grabbed the doorknob and pretended to struggle with it. They pretended to laugh. The elevator reached the top floor and started down. She raised both hands so they were clearly visible in the window and began sawing away at the wrist of one with the fingers of the other. They shook their heads as if to say, Cynthia, you are too much. The elevator doors opened and they started to enter. Cynthia dropped her hands, and suddenly without warning, tears began to flow again. As the elevator door closed, Cynthia was still standing in the window, the iron reinforcements making a blank yellow graph of her face, the tears running down the decaying skin, the mouth contorted in the off-centered idiot's smile.

'My God!' Beth said finally.

No one else spoke. Four sets of eyes were riveted to the numbers above the door, willing them to hurry as they lit up in descending order.

'I need a drink,' Erica said when the doors opened on the main floor.

'I need more than one,' Beth announced. 'Let's go someplace really good. And well air-conditioned.' Katherine could tell from Beth's tone that she was slipping into her public self, hugging it around the raw skeleton of exposed feelings and fear as if it were her sable. 'We can try the Coach House as long as we're this far downtown, or I can get us into Elaine's.'

'Couldn't we go someplace a little less . . .' Katherine didn't finish the sentence.

'If you're worried about money,' Beth said, 'I'll treat.'

'I didn't mean less expensive. I mean less . . . in. Less chic.'

357

'We have to eat, Kitty. Cynthia isn't going to get better because we have dinner at McDonald's.' Katherine heard the tightness in Beth's voice, remembered the way she'd pulled the belt of her fur coat close when they'd reached the cemetery last winter, and knew she was girding herself.

'I know what Kate means,' Paige said. 'Let's go back to my house. There must be something in the fridge. Stanley came over for dinner last night.' She pushed through the door to the street as if she were in a hurry to get out of the building, and they passed from nauseating medicinal odors to fetid street smells.

'I never thought I'd be taking Stanley's leftovers instead of the Coach House,' Beth joked, and stepped into the street to hail a cab. When she reached for the door, Katherine noticed her hand was shaking.

'Do you think she was on medication?' Paige asked after she'd given the driver her address.

Katherine looked out the window at Fourteenth Street. Beneath the neon signs that created coronas of hazy light in the damp night air, shoppers and wanderers and hustlers went about their business. 'Doug said they've got her on tranquilizers. He mentioned a name, but I never remember things like that.'

Erica took a small black cigar from her handbag. Her fingers weren't much steadier than Beth's. 'In that case, I'd hate to see her *au naturel*. She's like a thirty-three record being played at seventy-eight. Did you notice the way she kept jumping from one thing to another? And she was the logical one.'

'Don't talk about her as if she's dead,' Paige said.

'She's our first casualty.' Beth's voice was flat, and they all turned to look at her. Her eyes held theirs steadily. 'You know it's true, but you're all too squeamish to admit it.'

'You can't just dismiss her that way,' Paige said.

'I'm not dismissing her. Christ, it practically broke my heart when we walked into that room and found her playing with those damn belts. But there's no point in pretending she's not sick.'

'I just don't understand how something like that happens,' Erica said. 'Is it genes or upbringing or what? I mean, why Cynthia?'

They were all remembering that Cynthia had asked the same question; only she'd added, 'Why not one of you?' When Beth spoke, her voice was suddenly hard, as if it had been forged from the meaner realities of life. 'Why not Cynthia?' They all looked at her again, and again she held their eyes.

Tim met them noisily at the door. He was doing his best to live up to his Superman pajamas, but his audience was less than receptive to his act. Paige told the girl to take him to bed and she'd be up in a minute to say good night.

They all trooped down to the kitchen, where Paige directed Erica to a liquor cabinet and began foraging in the refrigerator. Beth sat at the long oak table in the center of the kitchen. 'I don't suppose anyone has any grass.'

Paige looked up from the shards of cheese and pâté she was arranging on a board. 'Not with Tim in the house.'

'Sorry. It's just that I feel kind of rattled.'

'Who doesn't?' Erica poured three-quarters of a bottle of Beefeater over the ice in the pitcher.

Katherine put a basket of crackers on the table, took a lemon from the refrigerator, and began slicing small pieces of rind. 'I just didn't expect her to be that sick.'

Erica poured a few drops of vermouth into the pitcher. 'I still don't understand how something like that happens. Was she unstable all along or did something set her off or what?'

Beth turned to Erica. Beneath the smooth surface of her face, lines of fear were as clearly defined as the grain in a piece of fine wood. 'Christ! All of life is a fight against that. Cynthia just gave up.'

'Stanley said he'd seen a manic-depressive pattern for a long time. Cynthia was always either on top of the world or down in the depths.'

'I don't remember her being down in the depths that much,' Katherine said as she took glasses from a cabinet.

'She wasn't,' Beth agreed. 'Of all of us, Cynthia was the one who always knew what she wanted and how to get it.'

'I thought that was you,' Paige said.

Beth gave her a long, appraising look. 'I took forever to learn, but Cynthia was born knowing. Maybe that's why seeing her tonight was so awful. Like discovering feet of clay. Or' – Beth looked from one to the other – 'that your parents fuck.'

'It's not funny,' Paige said.

Beth uncrossed and recrossed her legs as if a television camera were focused on them. 'I was trying for a little comic relief.'

'My God!' Katherine said, and they all turned to look at her. She was standing at the counter staring at a line of glasses. A sliver of lemon peel curled in the bottom of each. 'I took out five glasses. I kept thinking we were all together, and after all these years it's a reflex to think in terms of five.'

'It's a normal mistake,' Erica said.

'It's an eerie feeling,' Katherine answered. She carried four of the glasses to the table.

Paige picked up the fifth, dumped the lemon peel into the sink, and put the glass in the dishwasher. When she turned back to the table they were all staring at her. 'I couldn't let it sit there like some ghost of gatherings past.' She crossed to the table and picked up one of the glasses Erica had filled. 'Everything's falling apart.'

'You'll never make it as a toastmaster, Paige. Toastmistress,' Beth corrected herself, and sipped her drink. 'Cynthia will pull out of it. As soon as she realizes there's no percentage in being sick.'

'I don't think it's that easy,' Paige said.

'I didn't say it was easy. I know what it's like to fight your way back. Depression is another country, and I've been there. The summer Ted and I split up,' Beth said. Paige put down her glass and focused her attention on Beth like a spotlight on a leading lady. 'I was in Chicago on a publicity tour. There I was an hour away from taping *Kup's Show*, and Ted called from New York to say he was giving up. And that was after a year of not being able to get it up. What timing! I went to pieces. The publicity girl and the Chicago salesman practically had to carry me to the studio. Afterward they took me out and got me schlossed. I think I slept with the salesman.'

Erica raised her glass in Beth's direction. The makeup under her eyes had worn off, leaving small pockets of soiled-looking flesh that made her appear tired and suddenly old. 'It beats going to the hospital.'

Beth raised her own glass in return. 'Whatever gets you through the night.'

'I know it's a terrible thing to admit,' Erica said after a moment, her eyes on her hands that were folding and refolding the wrapper from the box of small cigars, 'but I'm beginning to think my life isn't such an unholy mess after all. I mean, I may not have much, but I'm still together.'

'I wish I could say the same.' Paige's face had that fragile-tissue paper look again. 'At least, when Cynthia gets out, she'll still have Doug.'

'For how long?' Erica looked from one to the other of them and went on quickly. 'I'm not wishing for a split, but be realistic. That marriage was in trouble before. How long do you think Doug's going to put up with Cynthia now that she's sick?'

'According to him, she's been sick for a long time,' Katherine answered.

Erica plunged a knife into the brie. 'Which just means he's even closer to the walking-out point.'

'I feel sorry for Doug,' Katherine said. 'I know Cynthia's sick and can't help herself, but it was awful the way she was riding him tonight.'

'She was riding Doug' – Erica spread brie over a cracker with slow, deliberate motions – 'because it's the only way she can strike back at him. A classic case of women's impotence. Cynthia sent me an article from *Ms* on the subject a few weeks ago. Women belittle men verbally because they're powerless in every other area.'

'Maybe,' Katherine said, 'but I still feel sorry for Doug. And I think he handled himself well. It couldn't have been easy for him to be baited that way in front of all of us.'

Erica handed her a cracker covered with brie. 'Maybe Cynthia wasn't baiting him. Maybe he does go out and pick up sweet young things after he leaves her.'

Beth smeared pâté over a cracker. 'Why not? We were with her for an hour, and we're all falling apart. Doug goes through that every night. I wouldn't blame him if he went out and fucked anything that moved. Or everything that moved.'

'With his wife in the hospital!' Paige said.

'But he doesn't!' Katherine stopped abruptly and put her glass down. She was drinking too quickly. 'I mean, you could see he doesn't.'

'Whether he does or doesn't is beside the point.' Erica sipped her drink thoughtfully. Though the soiled pouches beneath her eyes were still noticeable, she looked suddenly less tired, as if she'd washed her face or as if she'd finally found an answer to the question that had been worrying her all night. 'Did it ever occur to any of you that Doug might be partially responsible for the shape Cynthia's in? Oh, sure, he's great at parties, but as Cynthia always said, that's the public Doug. I stayed with them on the Cape a couple of years ago. Cynthia didn't exaggerate. Doug can spend an entire day staring out the window. Living with someone like that would make anyone crazy.'

'You can't blame it all on Doug,' Katherine said without looking up from the overlapping rings of moisture she was making on the table with her glass. She knew the table was treated.

'I'm not blaming it all on Doug. I'm merely saying that if he'd done more for Cynthia, she might not be in the shape she's in now.'

'What more could he have done?' Katherine's gin had gone to war with Katherine's common sense, and Katherine knew that she was the one who was losing; but she went on anyway. 'Cynthia wanted to get married, and he married her. She wanted children, and they had children. Though not necessarily in that order. She even admitted it tonight.'

'For God's sake, Kat, you can't take anything

Cynthia said tonight seriously.'

'She's lost touch,' Beth agreed. Paige stared at her glass and said nothing.

'And while we're on the subject, luv,' Erica went on, 'I wasn't going to mention it, but now that you have, why on earth did you dredge up all that at lunch about getting pregnant intentionally? You must have known what kind of shape she was in.'

'I didn't. I knew she was overwrought, but I didn't expect anything like this. Besides, I thought it was time someone reminded her she wasn't the victim she imagined herself.'

'Don't ever go into psychiatric practice, Kitty,' Beth said. 'Not with your bedside manner.'

'I have to agree with them, Kate.' Paige's tone was apologetic, but she looked as if she were relieved that blame for something could finally be placed somewhere. 'Bringing up that diaphragm incident wasn't exactly therapeutic.'

'Besides, Kitty,' Beth added, 'only you could still be worrying about one meaningless fuck that happened years ago.'

'The point is, Kat, Cynthia needed to be reassured, not attacked.'

'I didn't mean to attack her, but agreeing with everything she says or reassuring her that everything is going to turn out the way she wants is just stupid.' Katherine stopped. She realized she was quoting Nick. 'Anyway, I'm sick to death of the woman as victim. You go to a dinner party and some woman tells you she would have been a brain surgeon if it weren't for her husband. What she doesn't tell you is that she dropped out of college after two years because getting married was more fun than writing papers – and easier. Or so we were told.'

'That's exactly the point.' Beth leaned forward

and rested her small, pointed chin in her hands. 'What we were told. If you're going to blame Cynthia's breakdown on anything, blame it on that. We were all sold a bill of goods.'

'We didn't have to buy it.' Katherine felt like a frustrated child insisting on the truth of some fairy tale while all the adults smile patronizingly. 'That's what I was trying to tell Cynthia – before I realized how sick she was. Somewhere along the way we have to stop blaming parents and society and men and everyone except ourselves. There must be some core of conviction or judgment or something, some center that says, "This is me and the choices I've made." Or is it like the health food slogan? We are what we read and hear and watch?'

'Let's hear it for Miss Solid Core of Conviction,' Erica said. 'Nick wants a two-night-a-week affair, and you set up your life so it revolves around those two nights. Nick decides to leave his wife, and you say, "Of course, move right in, take over my apartment, my life, my work." Nick leaves, and you go to pieces. And for what? A second-rate lawyer who thinks he has a direct line to revealed truth because he's headed off a couple of corporate mergers.'

'Erica's right,' Beth agreed. 'He didn't make that much money – at least as far as I could see – and he wasn't a power in one of the big firms. You didn't even get many perks with him.'

'He was a man, Beth, not a corporate policy.'

'Face it, Kat,' Erica went on. 'He may have thought he was a legend in his own time – and convinced you – but he was just a mediocre suburban lawyer who came to town to get laid.'

'If he was so mediocre, why did you—' Katherine stopped abruptly and took a long swallow of her drink. 'Forget it. We were talking about Cynthia, not Nick or me.'

Erica pushed her glasses to the top of her head. 'You mean Paige's New Year's Day party? I wondered if he'd ever mentioned that to you. I was drunk. And depressed. The way I felt that afternoon I would have gone to bed with Donald Duck.'

Beth lifted her face from her hands and sat up straight. 'You slept with Nick!'

'Sorry to disappoint you, luv. Nothing beyond an abortive drunken grope.'

Beth slumped against the back of her chair, and Paige got up and went to the refrigerator. 'Maybe we'd better eat something.' She returned to the table with a bowl of vegetables and a small roast, which she began to slice. Her cheeks were flushed with the excitement of what had gone on in her home at her party, but her voice was pitched to a soothing bedtime-story key. 'I admit Cynthia was hard on Doug, but I still think he should have gotten her into Payne Whitney.'

Katherine looked at the roast beef and wondered if it absorbed gin. She took a piece with her fingers and told herself not to talk with her mouth full or, more to the point, not to talk.

'I'm sure she'd be better off there. St. Jude's is so tacky. Stanley says—'

'For God's sake,' Katherine said, 'Doug was trying to get her a bed in a hospital, not a table at Lutèce or the Four Seasons.'

Paige tossed the smooth curtain of hair back from her face and straightened as if she were going to take this shot with dignity. 'All I meant is that the quality of treatment is better at Payne Whitney. Stanley says—'

'Stanley says,' Katherine repeated. 'The man left

you, and you're still quoting him like the goddamn Bible. When you're not talking about taking him for every penny he's worth and turning him in to the IRS for tax evasion.'

Erica smiled, and her long face became lupine. 'You're turning the big guns on everyone tonight, aren't you, Kat?'

Katherine turned to Paige. 'I'm sorry. I didn't mean that. I just wish everyone would stop carrying on about the fact that Cynthia's not in Payne Whitney.'

Paige looked at Katherine as if she were a stranger being introduced at a cocktail party, a badly dressed stranger. 'You don't understand. You never really had a husband. Or a child.'

'No, and I've never tried to live through them either.'

'I knew we should have gone to the Coach House or Elaine's,' Beth said. 'You can't be bitchy while people are watching you.'

'I can.' Katherine finished her drink, but no one offered to pass her the pitcher. 'Besides, no one watches me. I'm not a celebrity.'

'Stop feeling sorry for yourself, Kitty. It's just as I said. We never should have gone to visit Cynthia. Depression is contagious. So's failure. I wrote that line in one of my books. About someone's father during the Depression. After he lost his job, people used to cross the street rather than say hello to him because they were afraid his bad luck was contagious.'

Katherine reached for the pitcher. 'So much for compassion.'

'You know what compassion gets you in this world?' Beth's voice was light, as if she were telling one of her prepared anecdotes. 'Absolutely nothing.

367

Nada. Publishers don't sell your books out of compassion and producers don't make them into movies out of compassion and nobody ever got rich or famous or even laid out of compassion.'

Katherine picked up her glass, then put it down again. 'Beth, you're my oldest friend. And I love you dearly. But your values – to borrow a phrase from your daughter – suck.'

Beth's expression didn't change. The veteran of network talk shows was not so easily rattled. 'Because I'm not afraid to admit I enjoy money and power and nice young bodies? They beat sitting around pining for Mr Mid-Life Crisis. I may be a Humberta Humbert, Kitty, but I'm happy.'

'Happy? You're lovable and loyal and generous to a fault, but with your A-list parties and adolescent sex and misguided readings of Nabokov and Joyce and John O'Hara, you're funny. I just feel sorry for your kids.'

Beth was no longer the picture of prime-time composure. 'My kids are fine.'

'Your kids aren't kids. You took Jessica straight from diapers to a diaphragm and . . .' Katherine saw the way Paige was looking at her and closed her mouth.

'It's lucky we all love you, Kat,' Erica said.

'That's right, you all love me. In fact, you never loved me more than when Nick walked out. Why, someone might have thought you resented my being happy with him.'

'At least we were supportive.'

'You were supportive all right. You all rushed in to take my mind off Nick – by telling me what a bastard he was. First he insulted me by not letting me meet his kids, then he exploited me by bringing them in every weekend. He communicated too much about submarines and old movies and not enough about the way he felt and I felt and we felt and everybody was supposed to feel. He was a nobody, but you couldn't forgive him for not wanting to go to your parties with all your celebrities. He was a prick when he was still living with his wife and sleeping with me and a fool when he was living with me and didn't sleep with one of my best friends. Even when he tried to do something right, he was wrong. Like taking me to New London. Why wasn't it Europe or the Caribbean? Well, I had a good time in New London.'

'Sex in a seedy motel,' Erica said. 'I'll bet Kat saw the old colored lights in New London.'

'Maybe I saw things I'd never seen before and got a kick out of them.'

'I didn't know you were into submarines.'

'Maybe I'm into being with Nick. Christ, Erica, according to you, Nick was even responsible for what was wrong with my book.'

'Are you saying I was?'

Katherine stood. 'I'm saying I was. Just as I was stupid to talk to you all about Nick. And dumb to listen to you about him. Maybe if women talked less to each other, there'd be fewer divorces.'

They were looking up at her, their faces tilted at various angles like a cubist study of discomfort and disgust.

'The veteran of long-term relationships has spoken,' Erica said. 'Three years with Stephen and one with Nick. Or are you going home to call Nick now?'

'I'm going home to bed. I'm drunk, and I'm feeling sorry for myself, and for Cynthia, and maybe for all of us because something's over.'

'Stop being melodramatic,' Erica said. 'Just

because Cynthia couldn't hack it doesn't mean the rest of us can't.'

'Well, I can't.' Katherine heard the shrillness in her voice and fought it back into its corner like an animal tamer with an unruly lion. 'At least not the way you all want me to. So I'm going home.'

'We'll take you,' Beth said.

Katherine raised her palm toward them, then dropped it because she felt melodramatic and silly. 'Thanks, but I can take care of myself. For once.'

She clattered noisily up the stairs to the entrance hall, giving the lie to her statement and making one of the clumsiest exits in the carefully choreographed history of Paige's town house.

A new front had come through, as the weather forecasters had predicted, and the thin cool night air was exhilarating against her face.

Two cabs cruised down the cross street, but Katherine let them pass. She walked west to Fifth, then started uptown. The cars raced toward her, swerving in and out of lanes, their headlights illuminating her path, then veering off. Some bumped and rattled over the pavement; others glided past, their tires making long, low sounds like heavily running water. At intervals, when a red light stopped the traffic, she heard the softer sound of the new wind through the leaves in the park. The trees looked black, and above them the Art Deco towers of Central Park West pierced the dark gray sky. Illuminated windows made vertical and horizontal patterns like the blanks in an oversized crossword puzzle, and Katherine's imagination filled in the spaces with people quarreling and making love, walking crying babies and watching television, waiting for guests to leave and for mates to come home, with the entire vocabulary of human experience.

370

She passed a man with an ascot and two corgis on a leash, another with a briefcase and tomorrow's paper under his arm, a young couple wound around each other, a black woman in a white uniform with a white poodle in a black sweater. The woman and Katherine smiled at each other. The gesture was a tacit celebration of the change in the weather.

In front of the museum a single hot dog wagon out of the army that guarded the steps in the afternoon lingered. Katherine bought a frankfurter. Nick had said once that street hot dogs always tasted better when you ate them with someone else. That was true, though this one tasted pretty good.

'Nice night,' the doorman said when she reached her building.

'Looks like fall's on the way,' the elevator operator said. Katherine remembered the fish tank but didn't say anything.

Franklin and Eleanor were waiting for her in the front hall. They followed her across the living room to her desk. She picked up the phone and dialed information. A few months ago she and Nick had argued about calling information.

'You're lazy,' she'd said. 'And extravagant.'

'Extravagant,' he'd repeated. 'You just bought me – not you, who cares about these things, but me – a sweater for a hundred and fifty bucks, and you call making a ten-cent call to information extravagant.'

'It's the principle of the thing.'

She asked the information boy if he had a listing – a new listing – for Nicholas Larries. He did not.

Katherine went into the bedroom, took the Yellow Pages from under the bed, and sat cross-legged on the mattress with the book on her lap. Franklin jumped up on the bed and rubbed his head against her forearm. 'Okay, so it's hopeless, but I've got nothing better to do.'

She turned to *H*. Health, hobby, hotels. Nick had told her once that before he'd met her, he'd left Gwen for three days. He might have lasted longer, he'd said, if it hadn't been for the hotel he'd moved into. He'd chosen one of those midtown places that advertise on late-night television with pictures of sex-crazed couples admiring red and gold lobbies and cable television in every room. She tried to remember the name but drew a blank.

The hotel listings ran for fifteen pages, though a good deal of the space was taken up by oversized ads. There had to be a systematic way to do this. The systematic way, no, the smart way, she told herself, was to call Stamford and find out that Erica and Cynthia and Beth and Paige had been right. He'd gone back to the lovely Gwen. Or at least wait until morning and let him tell her himself from his office. Only she wasn't smart, so she tried to be systematic. Nothing below Thirty-fourth Street, above Seventy-second, or west of Sixth Avenue. In fact, the closer to his office, the better. She decided to skip the Plaza, St. Regis, and all the big expensive hotels, as well as the New York numbers for hotels in the Catskills, Las Vegas, and the Caribbean. She probably had it down to a mere ten pages now. What did 'tourist class' signify? Red and gold lobbies and cable television in every room or a wino on every bed? Maybe it was the martinis, but she was beginning to enjoy the search. There were still hotels for women. And there was an Amoeba Social Svcs., a hotel and country club that billed itself as Jerry Lewis's favorite, and another that promised she could slenderize while vacationing. She went back to the A's and dialed the first number. It had no Nicholas

Larries registered. After fifteen calls, she'd been honeyed and sweetied, yelled and barked at, and even hung up on, but she hadn't been put through to Nicholas Larries. After several more calls she decided she was getting too sober for the work at hand and made herself a gin and tonic. When she came back, Franklin was still sitting on the bed beside the phone. She tried to remember the name of the hotel in the commercials, but she'd always been too busy laughing at Nick's jokes to pay much attention. It had a foreign name, a foreign place-name. Katherine ran the list. Lancaster, Lombardy, New Normandie, Orleans. None of them sounded right. Riviera, St. Moritz, Toledo. That was it. 'Very Spanish,' Nick had said. 'If Goya had stayed at the Toledo he wouldn't have been horrified by the Napoleonic invasions.'

There was no reason to assume he'd return to a place like that. She told herself he wouldn't be there. She told Franklin and Eleanor he wouldn't be there. The tired voice at the other end of the wire said, 'One minute.' Did that mean one minute until he found out if Nicholas Larries was registered or one minute until he connected her with Mr Larries's room? Katherine didn't know, and it seemed like more than a minute until she found out.

His voice sounded angry when he said hello. When she said it was Katherine, he didn't say anything at all. She took a swallow of her drink and asked how he was.

'Fine.'

'You don't sound fine.'

'How do I sound?'

'Brave and true and very far away.' The line came from an old John Wayne movie, and the first time

373

she'd heard it she'd threatened to be sick all over the sheets.

'That was Donna Reed.'

He wasn't going to help. Maybe they were right. Maybe he wasn't worth it.

'I don't suppose you'd like to come home. I don't mean Stamford. I mean here.' She'd been rubbing her forehead with her thumb and fingers as she said it. Her watch was turned in on her wrist, and she could see the sweep hand move through five seconds. 'If you have to debate for that long, forget it.'

'I wasn't debating. I was surprised. I expected recriminations. Or at least discussion. I thought you'd want to talk it through. *Communicate.*'

'I said forget it.'

'Katherine, wait.'

She waited, but he didn't say anything.

'What?'

'Wait there. I'll be right up.'

He looked awful. He also looked wonderful. He'd lost a little weight, and his face was thin and very tense. His hair, slightly in need of a trim, grazed the back of his collar. He was wearing the shirt he must have worn to the office; but the sleeves were rolled up, and his arms were tan against the white. They looked hard and beautiful with the network of prominent veins like the road map of an exotic country. No longer familiar with the lay of the land, she looked back at his face. There were shadows beneath his eyes despite the tan, and the pupils were black and guarded.

They went into the living room and sat on the couch.

'What now?' he asked.

'I don't know.'

'I didn't mean to be sarcastic on the phone. I

suppose you want to discuss things.'

'Not now,' she said, and they sat for a few minutes while Franklin came over and nested in Nick's lap and Eleanor sniffed around his legs and finally Nick took her hand.

'Maybe there's something on *The Late Show*,' she said. 'I haven't seen a John Wayne movie in three and a half weeks.'

Nick stood and Franklin tumbled to the floor. 'I've seen three hundred and forty-seven John Wayne movies in the last three and a half weeks.' He started to unbutton his shirt. 'But I haven't communicated once.'

'There is one thing I want to discuss,' Katherine said the next morning. 'Why didn't you call me?'

'Sweetheart, did you ever try to communicate with an answering machine?'

'Which one were you, the heavy breather or the hanger up?'

'Both.'

Nick took that day, Friday, off, and they went away for the weekend. He'd actually called his kids and told them he couldn't make it this Saturday, but he'd pick them up the following Friday night and they should plan on staying the whole weekend. Katherine suggested New London, but Nick said Battleship Cove in Rhode Island would be better because there they could see a cruiser and a destroyer as well as a sub. In Boston he wanted to take a suite at the Ritz-Carlton, but Katherine said that would be extravagant, especially since they weren't likely to use the second room.

'How would you feel about looking for a new apartment?' Nick asked on the drive back from Boston.

'It'll be more expensive.'

'It'll be a lot more expensive. But there'll be a room for the kids on weekends. And it'll be ours rather than yours.'

That Monday Katherine received a letter from Erica. She said she was going to the Coast for two weeks and that she didn't have much hope of selling Katherine's book, but she'd found an editor who liked the way Katherine wrote and wondered if she wanted to try an outline and several chapters for her. The editor, Erica wrote, did a lot of women's books. 'She's just published a novel about a middle-aged woman who shoots her lover after he leaves her for someone younger, another about a woman who picks up men in bars and murders them, and a third about a woman who strikes back at her analyst after months of sexual degradation. There's a lot of interest in violence against men,' Erica wrote.

Katherine showed Nick the letter when he got home that night. 'Are you going to try it?'

'Are you out of your mind?'

'What are you going to do?'

'Write a book. Not the book Sydney wanted or Erica or Beth. Maybe not even one you want to read, but it will be one I want to write.'

'Sounds good to me. Now all you need is a plot, a few characters, and a couple of hundred pages.'

'I've already got the first paragraph. Want to hear it?'

Nick said he did.

'"Amanda Russell was not unaware of the alienation of modern life in general or the impersonal indifference of New York City in particular. When she read of the stabbing of a woman while neighbors watched from behind locked windows ..."'

A selection of bestsellers
from Headline

LONDON'S CHILD	Philip Boast	£5.99 □
THE GIRL FROM COTTON LANE	Harry Bowling	£5.99 □
THE HERRON HERITAGE	Janice Young Brooks	£4.99 □
DANGEROUS LADY	Martina Cole	£4.99 □
VAGABONDS	Josephine Cox	£4.99 □
STAR QUALITY	Pamela Evans	£4.99 □
MARY MADDISON	Sheila Jansen	£4.99 □
CANNONBERRY CHASE	Roberta Latow	£5.99 □
THERE IS A SEASON	Elizabeth Murphy	£4.99 □
THE PALACE AFFAIR	Una-Mary Parker	£4.99 □
BLESSINGS AND SORROWS	Christine Thomas	£4.99 □
WYCHWOOD	E V Thompson	£4.99 □
HALLMARK	Elizabeth Walker	£5.99 □
AN IMPOSSIBLE DREAM	Elizabeth Warne	£5.99 □
POLLY OF PENN'S PLACE	Dee Williams	£4.99 □

All Headline books are available at your local bookshop or newsagent, or can be ordered direct from the publisher. Just tick the titles you want and fill in the form below. Prices and availability subject to change without notice.

Headline Book Publishing PLC, Cash Sales Department, Bookpoint, 39 Milton Park, Abingdon, OXON, OX14 4TD, UK. If you have a credit card you may order by telephone — 0235 831700.

Please enclose a cheque or postal order made payable to Bookpoint Ltd to the value of the cover price and allow the following for postage and packing:
UK & BFPO: £1.00 for the first book, 50p for the second book and 30p for each additional book ordered up to a maximum charge of £3.00.
OVERSEAS & EIRE: £2.00 for the first book, £1.00 for the second book and 50p for each additional book.

Name ....

Address ....

....

....

If you would prefer to pay by credit card, please complete:
Please debit my Visa/Access/Diner's Card/American Express (delete a applicable) card no:

Signature ....Expiry Date ......